The Long Way Home

(James K Burk writing as)
Rob Jackson

WolfSinger Publications Security Colorado

Dedicated to
the memories of Brad Beeson and Jim Hooper

Chapter 1

Reynaud walked across the tarmac with Bill Taylor. It felt good being in his flight suit again, even if he had an angry mob of butterflies in his stomach and still felt a little weak from his bout with the plague.

Of eighteen pilots in the squadron, only he and Bill remained alive and duty-ready. Half had been lost in combat and the rest had either died of the plague or were still recovering. Reynaud's memories suffered some fuzzy spots and he couldn't remember the exact day in early May when the war broke out. He was already bed-ridden with the plague at the time. After the outbreak of the plague, the war sputtered along like a damp fuse. Both sides had launched some missiles, almost on a one-for-one trade-off, and within the first four days both sides had destroyed most of the oil refinery capacity of their enemies and almost everyone else. Most major military bases had been hit, with varying degrees of accuracy and damage, and some major cities had been devastated.

It was a measure of the Air Force's desperation that he and Bill had an escort mission for a lone B-1B to wipe out a major staging area. The bomber was still sometimes derisively called "the Groundhog" or "the Hangar Queen," although they'd finally worked out most of the kinks in the system.

Bill grinned at him. "Break a leg, Lieutenant Dechaine," and walked to his boarding ladder. Reynaud smiled at Bill's quirky way of wishing his wingman luck. He continued to his own machine, an F-22 Raptor, a deadly, shapely bird that looked as predatory as its namesake.

Most of the groundcrew had also been killed or incapacitated by the plague and as Reynaud climbed the ladder to his "office" he saw the remains of the old Russian Frogfoot that attacked the base and destroyed several hangars and aircraft before it had been shot down.

Reynaud still felt more than a trace of admiration for the gutsy Russian pilot. Too bad he'd augered in with his plane.

Bill and Reynaud had chosen the best of the surviving aircraft. Bill, as the senior officer, had first choice of aircraft, and he was to lead the mission. He settled himself, pulled on his flight helmet, and ran through the pre-flight checks before closing the canopy.

Bill led the way to the strip and into the air, then to the rendezvous point with the bomber. They stayed low and formed up with the bomber at an altitude of less than two hundred feet and sped eastward, keeping to one of the alleys cleared through the SAM screen. They crossed the safer German airspace and flew over the Polish border within less than a quarter of an hour. After they'd cleared most of the population centers, they opened their formation. The bomber stayed on the deck, seeming almost to touch its own shadow while the fighters climbed above and half a mile away in the two and ten o'clock slots.

He was never sure of what happened next, although he guessed Bill's electronic countermeasures system had suffered an attack of gremlins and, instead of being invisible to Russian radar, drew it like a magnet.

The first warning was a flash of motion then Bill's plane blew up. Almost simultaneously, a pair of MiG29s flashed past in a shallow dive. No time for thought, only reaction. With no time to turn before the MiGs would be out of range, he dropped his external tanks and kicked the rudder, throwing his Raptor into a spin. The missiles his ship carried were the new Rocs, which supposedly needed no lock-on time but were armed when launched and locked onto the target within half a second. As his plane lurched around in a wickedly fast spin, Reynaud saw a flash and launched.

The missiles leapt out from under his fuselage then Reynaud had to give all his attention to snapping out of the spin. He was losing altitude rapidly, the ground rushing up to meet him while he tried to stave off an attack of vertigo that would leave him helpless. On one of the sweeps around he saw the red and black petals of an explosion blossom then he fought the fighter out of the spin.

As soon as the fighter was again under control, he scanned the air and ground below him. He noticed a broad river he took to be the Vistula and, just east of it, he discerned a black arrowhead that had to be the bomber and, behind it and closing rapidly, the other MiG.

"Big Friend, bandit at six o'clock," Reynaud chanted then opened the throttle and put his plane's nose down. He'd begun to close the distance when two missiles streaked away from the Russian fighter. One of them hit a ridge the bomber had just cleared, putting up a cloud of rock fragments while the other went off almost inside the port engine nacelle. The MiG sprang upward to avoid the airborne debris and almost centered itself in Reynaud's sight.

Reynaud guessed either the Russian's warning system had also failed or he was so fixed on killing the bomber he was ignoring it. The Cajun couldn't launch another missile—the bomber was too close to the MiG for him to count on the electronic brain of a numbskull missile. Reynaud continued to close. Still apparently totally absorbed in stalking his prey, the Russian never saw Reynaud slip into the kill-slot.

He checked his own tail. Clear. He chopped the throttle to avoid overshooting, centered the exhaust of the MiG in his sights and, as soon as he could see the national markings on the upper sides of the wings, touched off a burst with his cannon. The gun growled for an instant and the Russian fighter simply came apart in the air. Pieces of plastic and metal flew along the slipstream then the jet exploded.

Reynaud had reflexively closed his eyes as wreckage streamed back toward his own bird, but he heard and felt the hammering of metal against his own plane. Something gashed the canopy above his left shoulder and he knew the vacuum cleaner of his engines were sucking in everything from a fifty-foot radius, and the sweeper was rushing forward at almost the speed of sound. He hit the speed brakes and the plane yawed sharply. Some of the hydraulics had been damaged and only one of the brakes had opened. He tried to close the open brake but the machine continued to yaw, while warning lights flickered like lights on a Christmas tree and the engines began to emit a grinding sound as they started to come apart. He tried to chop the throttle again but the grinding sound became louder and the engine began to howl like a banshee warning of death.

The engine was building up to an explosion. Reynaud jettisoned the canopy then jerked the ejector ring.

It felt like being flung, face-first, into a brick wall while being shot out of a cannon. Black seeped around the edges of his vision as the shell exploded and he was hurled into winds of over four hundred miles an hour. Somehow, he remained conscious and as he reached the top of the arc he kicked free of the ejection seat. He started to fall, then the opening shock slammed him against his parachute harness with bruising force as the chute billowed out above him.

Hanging from his chute lines, he looked around and saw three black smudges still staining the sky and saw his own plane spin into the ground. Immediately it exploded and a geyser of flame shot upward. More smudges in the east, where the damaged bomber, one of its engines leaving a black trail, was already nearly out of sight. Four planes and three men gone, another plane damaged, all in fifteen seconds or less.

He was captured within hours by local militia, and was glad to see regular troops, convinced the locals were ready to lynch him—or worse. After he was sent to the prison camp, he decided he'd merely traded an ugly death that might last for hours for a death just as ugly, but lasting for months.

~ * ~

Reynaud shivered, partly from the cold, partly from suppressed horror, rage, and shame. The POW uniforms provided him and the airmen around him were too thin for the early winter in these mountains on the Russian-Polish-Czech border. More chilling than the cold was the reason the airmen had been assembled on the parade ground.

Reynaud's eyes scanned the compound, taking in the chain-link fence and the guard towers with their machine gun posts. Inside the fence stood the prisoners' huts and just outside it the ugly, blocky administration building and the guards' barracks. To the north, beyond the patch of cleared ground, a pair of guards led out a prisoner who moved as though drugged.

Another guard held up a sheet of paper and, in Russian, bellowed, "This prisoner is being executed for insufficient diligence in carrying out his assigned duties." This meant the supposed reason for his execution would be "malingering." The actual reason was always the same; Colonel Chernikov and Lieutenant Oshevsky were vicious sons of bitches who liked to feel a prisoner's bones break or tissues tear under their hands. He wondered which of them would carry out this murder.

Both the colonel and the lieutenant strode out to the guards and the prisoner. Halting, the colonel stripped off his bearskin coat. As usual, when he carried out an execution, he wore battle-dress rather than his dress uniform, though even his battledress was always immaculate and neatly pressed, with creases like razors. Chernikov was known almost as much for his fastidiousness as much as for his cruelty, and he'd beaten one prisoner to death for a couple of drops of wine spilled on the colonel's tablecloth.

The colonel neatly folded his coat and handed it to the lieutenant then drew on a pair of white cloth gloves.

Guards prowled among the ranks of prisoners. Closing one's eyes or looking away would be punished by the guards beating the offending prisoner to a pulp, with the colonel or the lieutenant finishing the job on the following day.

The prisoner, although he could hardly stand, brought his arms up like a boxer as the colonel advanced toward him. He tried a feint with his right and a jab with his left but he was too slow. Chernikov was as fast as a cat. He blocked the jab with his left arm then his right hand shot up as he pivoted beside the prisoner, then behind him.

They all heard the crack of bone and the scream of the prisoner, who doubled over, his left arm bending the wrong way, then he fell to his knees.

"Get up," Chernikov commanded in his perfect English.

Somehow, the prisoner managed to struggle to his feet and face the Russian, his left arm dangling, useless, his right fist close to his body to protect or, if he got the chance, lash out.

Chernikov swung a leg in a sweep that took the prisoner's legs out from under him and, as the man fell, the colonel kicked him in the face.

The man spat blood and broken teeth into the dirt then he surprised everyone. He came up from the ground in a tigerish leap and, after driving home a short jab into the colonel's body just under the ribs, he tried to grapple. Before he was thrown off, he was able to spit a mouthful of blood into the colonel's face and onto the front of his tunic.

"You filthy spine," the colonel howled. "You'll pay for that." He caught the man's right wrist in his left hand and slammed the man in the armpit with his right elbow. Still holding the prisoner's wrist, he ducked under the man's arm so he was behind the prisoner with the man's arm bent upward behind his back. He wrenched upward and the POW screamed again as ligaments and tendons were ripped apart.

Chernikov flung the crippled man face-down onto the frozen ground then stepped around him and, with a kick, shattered the man's lower jaw. He sprang onto the man, his knee pressed against the lower spine. His white-gloved hand caught the man's upper jaw and pulled the man's head up and back, even as he was driving his knee into the small of the man's back.

The noise made by the dying man was more a wail than a scream, and they all heard bones snapping. The colonel got to his feet and kicked the shuddering body several times then stalked to his quarters, almost certainly to put on a fresh uniform.

Reynaud imagined himself firing belt after belt of machine gun fire into the Russian, thought of a thousand ways to butcher the monster with a dull knife, visualized the colonel's thick neck being cut with a garroting wire. The lieutenant turned to the corporal of the guard and, in Russian, told him to select two prisoners to haul the body to the shed. The corporal pointed at Reynaud and the man at the head of the next column of prisoners.

Reynaud and the other prisoner approached the body with a certain trepidation. Diseases were rare for plague survivors but, if contracted, were more debilitating. Reynaud immediately felt ashamed of himself. This man had been possibly sick and probably drugged but he'd tried to fight. He hadn't simply given himself over to his murderer and, as a fighter, he deserved respect.

"You take his legs," Reynaud said, then he reached under the man's body and wrapped his arms around the man's chest. Together they lifted the body and carried it to the shed just inside the western fence of the prison compound and laid it atop the stack of corpses. In these mountains, in early December, the temperature never rose above freezing. Reynaud saluted the body and, after a moment, so did the other prisoner.

He strode past the guard, back to the compound and his own barracks shack. Even outside the hut he could hear the "band" had warmed up. The harmonica wailed and even the homemade flute sounded mournful. He'd grown to hate harmonica and flute music, although he knew the other prisoners used the sounds to cover conversations from the bugs planted in the building.

He never joined the conversations. As conditions at the camp deteriorated he'd become silent and reclusive. A few prisoners were certainly spying for the FSB, the replacement for the KGB, and almost none of the prisoners were totally sane. Most of them had developed some quirk into a retreat from the hideous reality.

As he entered the hut, Paulson gestured at him. He suspected Paulson might be a spy. He seemed to cooperate with the Russians, helping do clerical work and maintaining the camp's computer, which helped him avoid the worst of the menial labor the other prisoners shared. He'd also noticed, though, that Paulson seemed to share any extra food with the other prisoners in the hut. At least he was no bully like Madison, who'd taken a man's tin plate, so the prisoner had been forced to hold out his bare hands for the scalding slop the guards served for meals. It was that or starve.

And it was Paulson who'd organized the group that had engineered the "accident" that left Madison with a broken back.

Reluctantly, Reynaud approached Paulson, making his way through knots of men involved in loud, pointless arguments. As soon as he was near enough to hear, Paulson murmured, "Congratulations. You won the lottery."

Not sure what sort of joke Paulson was making, Reynaud managed a crooked grin. "What did I win? A new Cadillac and a weekend in Paris?"

"Better than that; you won a chance to get out of here."

Despite himself, Reynaud's heart leaped, then he dampened the hope. Just another prisoner headed around the bend, talking nonsense.

"The committee chose one prisoner from each barracks. You're the lucky man in this crowd."

Reynaud stared at Paulson. "I hate to seem ungrateful but, why me?"

"You're as healthy as anybody, considering the deprivation,

and we know you're not a rat or a plant."

"Who else is going?"

"You'll see them tomorrow. Now, shut up. I don't have much time to talk. You'll be ordered out as part of a wood-cutting detail in the morning. Everybody on the detail is set for the escape, just like you. Do what you can, do what you must, but get away. After you're gone we're going to kill as many of the bastards guarding us as we can."

Reynaud tried to guess whether Paulson was really sane. If it were a trap—well, he'd die here before too long anyway. "Do you want us to come back and try to help you?"

"Hell no! Don't think we're so stupid we think we can survive a revolt. You'll be sent to get wood for the pyres. They figure to kill everyone in the camp, load as many bodies as they can into the shed, and set it afire. The rest of the bodies will be heaped in one of the huts. The extra wood you're being sent to gather is to make sure the fire lasts until all the bodies are burned."

Reynaud felt like ants with cold feet were marching up his spine. "How do you know all this?"

"You think I work in the office because I like playing 'Captain Video?' on computers? That's the only way to learn anything, and I make out the rosters for the prisoners' jobs." He handed Reynaud what looked like a handkerchief and a spoon. "Be careful with that spoon. The handle's been sharpened. Sorry, but that's the best weapon we could come up with. The map's pretty rough, and all we could get on it were some generalizations. We don't know the lay of the land, roads, nothing, but we can figure Krakow is northwest of here."

"What good will getting there do? It'll still be a damned long walk back to the states."

"Remember, Poland was in NATO before the shake-up, and I gather Russians aren't very popular there. From the messages I've seen and been able to decipher, there are independence movements in Ukraine, in Georgia, even in Russia itself. As for Poland, it's not your last shot, it's probably your only shot."

Reynaud ran his fingers through his beard. In the six months he'd been imprisoned, he and the others had come to look like wild men. "But what about Chernikov? I hate to think of getting away and leaving that rotten son of a bitch still breathing the same air as human beings."

"I've got a feeling you'll get him sooner or later—or he'll get you. He's been reassigned. His superiors want him to go to the U. S of A. I'm not sure what sort of project he's being sent to take care of, but I'm willing to bet it's something rotten. The codename for the project is Operation Alpha or Operation A.

"I'm not sure where he's going in the states but from the hints being dropped, it might be Texas or the Southwest. Now, stay quiet until dinner and try to get a good night's sleep. You'll be getting plenty of exercise tomorrow.

~ * ~

Reynaud lay on the bunk, wishing there were room to stretch out on it without hanging off one end or the other. The slop that evening had been neither better nor worse than usual—a sort of soup of beets, turnips, and potatoes, and something green and slimy. He stretched for a moment then drew himself into the fetal position. Not only were the bunks too small but the cold and the two thin blankets he'd been issued made him sleep as huddled as possible.

He wished he had a cigarette, then snorted, bitterly amused. He might as well wish for a cup of coffee to drink with it, or a bottle of wine. He might as well wish for a bath, a shave, and clean clothes.

Major Fergusson should be here to see this. Major Fergusson should be here, period. He was the swivel-chair pilot who'd ordered the last mission.

Originally, they'd all been told the plague was a Russian biological warfare attack, and he didn't find out until later, after he'd become a prisoner, that the Russians' manpower had been, proportionately, as depleted as that of the NATO troops. If they'd planned a bio-war attack, they'd have inoculated at least their elite troops, but almost everyone on both sides had contracted the plague, and over half those infected had died.

He found a new perspective on the war in the camp. The most common guesses among his fellow prisoners were that the plague was an accident, a recombinant DNA experiment that had gotten out of control, or it had been started, deliberately, by the FSB, the CIA, or both organizations. It'd obviously worked to no one's profit.

The prison camp was another pointless agony. All the prisoners were pilots or aircrew, all with some experience with computers. Paulson had suggested originally the Russians might've intended to keep the prisoners to use in rebuilding after the war but in the apparent breakdown in central authority, the p-camp seemed to have devolved into a playground for sadists.

~ * ~

Reynaud learned to hate the prison camp. He'd come to hate the sounds of flutes and harmonicas. He'd always hated bullies but in the camp it became a steady fire in his guts. One of the things he'd learned in the camp was that he really hadn't known hatred before he was caged like an animal, that his deepest hatred before he'd been hauled into this circle of Hell paled into a sort of peevishness compared to the degree of hatred he could lavish on even trivial things in the camp. He'd especially come to hate the metal-on-metal cacophony with which they wakened in the gray dawn and, lately, in the dark.

He pulled on the rough shoes he'd been issued, picked up his plate and spoon and, with the others in his barracks, stumbled into the frigid morning.

The lieutenant prowled along the edge of the parade ground as the prisoners in each barracks fell into their ranks in the first head-count of the day. After the count, the sergeant looked at a sheet of paper and bellowed, "After breakfast, the following prisoners will report here for wood-cutting detail; Juho Tartakainnen, Logan Reid, Franz Schiller, Reynaud Dechaine, William McCluskey, Richard Smyth-Davis, Steve Villareal, and Michael Teller."

Reynaud paid no attention while the Russian called out prisoners for other work details. On the way to the mess shed he reviewed the list of men on the work detail with him. For a moment, he had trouble placing the name William McCluskey, then realized it was Billy Joe McCluskey. He'd almost forgotten the man's given name because most of the prisoners simply called him "the Deacon." McCluskey's insanity had taken a different form. In the camp he'd turned to a paperback Bible like a drowning man clutching anything that would float. Reynaud wondered if the other prisoners had chosen the Deacon to go so they could die in some measure of peace.

The prisoners filed into the mess shack and Reynaud held out his plate for the morning slop, then found a place on the cold floor where he could sit cross-legged and eat. Juno Tartakainnen would be the one they called Juho the Finn. Juho's English was limited but the little man seemed as hard and silent as a rock, with a face of stone, carved with a hatchet. His bearing made him seem much bigger. He'd be valuable, both in the attack on the guards and in the long trek to escape.

Reynaud spooned the garbage into his mouth and chewed, biting down on something that cracked between his teeth, and he guessed he'd gotten a cockroach in his soup. He chewed and swallowed the mouthful, feeling like the punchline in an old joke. "Waiter, there's a fly in my soup!" "Well, keep it quiet or everyone will want one." He'd been the lucky one to get a bit of protein.

As he ate, his gaze flicked from face to face. He located Logan Reid just as the man glanced at him. Reid winked.

Reid was a strange one. He was three inches shorter than Reynaud's own five feet ten and probably at least ten pounds heavier. Even with the meager food of the prison camp, he was a blocky, gnarly little man, well able to take care of himself in a hand-to-hand fight. He laughed a lot and he always had a joke but Reynaud had the feeling the jokes and laughs were like the small eruptions of a volcano, bleeding off pressure which, if not allowed release, would result in a violent explosion.

Schiller, a large, blond man was easy to spot. Like Logan, even the prison diet seemed not to have weakened him. He was a German who, with his shaggy blond hair and beard, looked like a Viking on his day off.

Steve Villareal wasn't much taller than Reid and more slender than Reynaud but what was left of him was whipcord-tough and quick. A Hispanic-American from Colorado, he was a graduate of the Air Force Academy at Colorado Springs but he seemed a thorough fighter, nothing like a ring-knocker.

Smyth-Davis was an unknown quality. He was quiet and reserved, even for a Brit. He and Teller were both hard men to find in a crowd, since neither was outstanding in any way. This could be a survival trait in a prison camp, since they attracted less

11

attention from the guards and were probably beaten less.

Reynaud grinned at himself. If the others were also assessing strengths and weaknesses, he could hardly guess at what they were thinking of him. He was a copper-colored Cajun, almost half French but with more than a trace of African-American and American Indian, and he'd had a great-grandfather named Vazquez. He treated the Russians with polite contempt but had avoided any contact other than the purely necessary with his fellow prisoners.

The prisoners finished their meals and returned to their barracks where Reynaud stowed his plate under his trunk, slipping his spoon, along with the spoon with the sharpened handle, into his waistband. He glanced at Paulson and snapped him a salute, which Paulson returned, along with the old fighter pilot's "thumbs up."

Reynaud had to remember to let his shoulders droop in the manner most of the prisoners, too long without hope, had fallen into. When he reported for work detail, everyone but Teller was already waiting. Teller rushed out of the barracks at the end of the row of shacks and hurried, so he reached his place only a few paces behind Reynaud. After cuffing Teller, the sergeant glared at the prisoners then snapped, "Get in the truck."

Together, the prisoners trudged to the back of the truck and, one by one, clambered into the back. Three guards followed them into the bed of the truck and took seats near the back. All the guards wore Russian winter army uniforms with fur collars and all wore fur-lined hats instead of helmets. One of them wore a greatcoat over his uniform and he carried the SVD sniper rifle while the others carried AK74s, but none of them seemed to carry any extra magazines.

That worried Reynaud. If the escape attempt failed, it'd all be over so quickly the guards would have no need to change magazines but if some or all of the prisoners got away, they'd need all the ammunition they could carry.

Reynaud spent most of the brief trip studying the grain of the wooden truck bed, trying to hide the attack of nerves afflicting him.

The truck bounded along a rough road then slowed to a stop and the guards piled out. They gestured at the prisoners with their rifles. One at a time, the prisoners strode to the rear of the truck and jumped out. The driver and corporal climbed out of the truck cab to join the other guards, both of them wearing great-coats over their uniforms. The corporal carried an AKR, the shortened AK with the side-folding stock and a conical flash hider at the end of the short barrel, more a submachine gun than an assault rifle, and at his belt he wore a long, wicked-looking knife that lacked a crossguard. The driver's weapon was another AK74.

The corporal detached six axes and a two-man saw from the outside of the truck and threw them to the prisoners. Unlike the colonel or the lieutenant, the corporal was part of the original gar-rison of the camp and, also unlike them, he spoke no English. In Russian, he shouted, "Start work," and waved his hand at the edge of the forest.

The trees cut off the worst of the wind, although it was still bitterly cold. The POWs started to work, with caution. Chopping frozen trees was dangerous work, as the frozen wood could easily turn an ax blade and men had lost legs cutting wood. Usually, the guard simply shot them where they fell.

In a short time they'd felled two trees, and Teller and Smyth-Davis used the saw to cut the logs to manageable length. Reynaud realized the prisoners must make their attempt soon. The guards, who stood huddled, shoulders drawn up almost to their ears, were stiff with cold, while the prisoners had been working long enough to limber up stiff muscles but not so long they were exhausted. That might prove a crucial advantage.

Pausing a moment, Reynaud glanced around the party, hop-ing the prisoners were poised to strike at the first thing that might distract the guards. He observed Juho had managed to work with-in a dozen feet of the man with the sniper rifle.

Deciding it was time to provide the diversion, Reynaud, as he swung again at the tree, twisted the ax handle so the flat of the blade rang against the trunk. Immediately he screamed and crum-pled, doubled over, both arms wrapped around his right leg.

As soon as Reynaud went down, Juho rushed two steps forward and swung his axe, catching the guard with the Dragunov in the back of the neck. Blood shot upward from severed arteries and the body pitched forward onto its face then the Finn scram-bled after the rifle the corpse had dropped.

Logan Reid, anticipating any sort of diversion, also reacted instantly, swinging his axe at the corporal and releasing it. The top of the axe struck the Russian in the belly and, as the man doubled over, Logan sprang at him. His knee swept up into the Russian's crotch and his fist smashed into the corporal's face, pulverizing his nose. With his left hand, Logan grabbed the AKR's forestock while his right clutched the hilt of the big knife.

Logan slammed his body into the guard and the two of them went down together. He snatched the knife out of its scabbard and thrust upward, driving the blade into the underside of the corporal's jaw, ramming the point up into the brain.

Franz Schiller had also thrown his axe at one of the guards but the Russian stumbled backward to avoid the blade. By the time the guard was able to bring his weapon into play, the German had seized the gun. In a panic, the Russian pulled the trigger and both men winced at the muzzle blast in their faces, but both clung desperately to the weapon.

Steve Villareal and the Deacon had both flung their axes at the man nearest the truck and, when he fell, Villareal was atop him. The Russian had a bayonet hanging from his belt and Steve tore it loose then slashed at the guard's throat. Blood shot from the carotid artery, splashing Steve until it was almost impossible to tell who was wounded. As the Russian died Villareal grabbed at his rifle and rolled under the truck, raising the weapon to fire.

Teller and Smyth-Davis were the furthest from the guard they had to attack, and without weapons to hand. Teller snatched up a double handful of sawdust and flung them at the guard's face but the Russian fired off a burst at the two prisoners. One of the bullets creased Smyth-Davis' head, dumping him, and Teller's legs folded under him as a round tore through his upper chest.

The Russian spun and saw Schiller and his guard fighting for the guard's AK and he fired another short burst.

Schiller felt the impact of the bullets and knew he'd been mortally wounded but he only clung more doggedly to the weapon. The last thing he saw was the look of astonishment on the face of the guard with whom he struggled, as the bullets that hit Schiller tore into him, too, then the Russian's eyes rolled up in his head and he went limp.

Juho had caught up the sniper rifle and snapped off a shot at the man firing at Schiller, a shot that spun the Russian around, then a burst from Villareal made the guard jerk and dance before he was thrown to the ground.

Schiller turned, slowly, like a great bear, holding the captured Russian rifle over his head like a trophy. His eyes were already glazing and he took a single awkward step forward. His mouth opened, as though to speak, then a gout of blood rushed over his chin and he fell.

Reynaud had struggled to his feet at the first sound of gunfire and he rushed at the guard firing, just as Juho and Steve shot the man. The Cajun saw the back of the Russian's head explode at Juho's shot, and ragged holes and a spray of blood appeared at the man's chest and back. By the time he'd reached the body, the guard was dead, his lower jaw smashed, the back of his head blown away, and four holes in his chest.

Catching the guard by the arms, Reynaud dragged the corpse to the back of the truck. "Get everything in the truck," he shouted, and dashed back to where Teller and the Englisman lay. Teller mumbled incoherently and his eyes were unfocussed. The bullet had taken him in the right upper chest and he was bleeding badly. "Give me some help over here," Reynaud screamed, then he became conscious of the sound of gunfire from the camp, a little over a mile away.

Suddenly, the Finn was beside him, the sniper rifle slung over his shoulder. He tore Teller's shirt open and glanced at the wound, then, as Logan ran toward them, gestured at Teller then at the back of the truck. The two of them carried Teller to the truck while Reynaud checked Smyth-Davis. The Briton's wound was ugly and there was too much blood to see how badly he'd been hit. Reynaud found a thread pulse and he could see the man's breath in the cold air. At least he was alive.

Juho and Logan returned and carried Smyth-Davis to the truck then Reynaud looked around. The Deacon was bent over Schiller, while Villareal collected guns and axes. As Reynaud approached the Deacon he heard, "...and I will dwell in the house of the Lord forever."

McCluskey stared up at him. "He's gone."

"Help me get him into the truck," Reynaud snapped. "He deserves better than to be left here."

The Deacon's long face showed no expression; he only

nodded, and the two of them half-dragged, half-carried the body to the truck and wrestled it up into the bed.

The gunshots in the camp became more scattered and Reynaud was eager to be as far away as possible but they took another minute or two to load all the guards' bodies into the truck.

After a quick final check to be sure they'd missed nothing, Reynaud dashed to the cab and clambered up behind the steering wheel. He found the ignition switch and turned it but nothing happened, then realized this machine was like the ancient farm trucks he'd driven when he was a boy. He pulled out a knob he hoped was the choke and pressed his foot down on the gas pedal with the starter switch under it.

The truck snarled at him before starting with a roar and, after a grinding of gears, lurched forward. The can was warm, after the icy breeze outside, and he felt almost comfortable. For the first time in months, he felt the thrill of hope. The road led deeper into the woods, running northeast. Their destination lay northwest but, for the moment, the desperately needed to put all the miles behind them they could.

The road would never have appeared on any map worthy of the name, Reynaud decided. It had no border, except that trees were somewhat thicker off the road, and it veered for only the most hazardous of obstacles. The truck bounced and swayed as the trail followed the edge of a ridge then swept down a steep slope that curved at the bottom. Riding the brake, Reynaud kept to the trail.

Judging time was difficult and judging distance was all but impossible. In what Reynaud guessed to be about forty-five minutes, the truck had covered perhaps fifteen miles. Reynaud was trying to coax the machine up another slope when the engine sputtered and died. He used the brake and let the truck roll back to a stop then tried to start it again but the engine couldn't be revived. He cursed then realized the truck had probably been only partially fueled, not much more than what was needed to bring back a couple of loads of wood.

Cursing again, he shoved open the cab door and strode to the rear of the bed. "Free ride's over, boys. We're going to have to get out and hoof it from here. How're Teller and Smyth-Davis?"

The Deacon, wearing a guard's hat and greatcoat over his

prison uniform, waved at the wounded men. Both had their wounds bound with scraps of prison uniforms. "Teller's been hit really bad," Billy Joe murmured. "I don't think he's going to make it. Looks like maybe the bullet clipped the top of his lung. They've both lost a lot of blood. Smyth-Davis is beginning to come out of it, but he says he can't feel anything but a headache. I don't know how bad a concussion he's got, but the wound didn't seem to penetrate the skull."

"Here you go, Caje," Logan said, as he handed over a Russian uniform and boots. "The Deak's big feet won't fit these. Well, any ideas where to go from here?"

Reynaud looked up the slope. "Those look like birch up there. You suppose you and a man or two might be able to cut some young trees and rig stretchers?"

Logan grinned. "Well, I'll be a son of a birch. How about a couple of travois?"

"If you can set them up to be used as stretchers, too. Some of this country is too rough for anything like that."

"Forget it," Teller said in a weak voice. "You guys stay here too long, and none of us will escape. Maybe you can take the Brit, but I'm probably dying anyway. Leave me. Just try to let my family know. They're at Lackland."

"That's punishment enough," Logan said. "They don't need to lose someone."

"We all go," Reynaud snapped. "Deacon, about fifty yards back along the trail you'll find a rock bank that's collapsed. Bury Schiller there." As he dressed in the Russian uniform he turned to look at Teller. "Forget the dime-novel heroics, Teller. I wouldn't want to die alone of exposure and you don't either. As long as you're alive, you're with us."

Teller sighed and relaxed. "I guess I really didn't want to die here but John Wayne always made speeches like that sound so ballsy."

Reynaud forced a grin. "Yeah, well, you'll have to make it back to get your Oscar."

Logan and Juho had taken axes and climbed the slope, and Billy Joe and Steve were digging out a depression in the rocks for Schiller. Reynaud checked the wounded men to be sure they were as warm and comfortable as possible then decided to look over the truck's cab for usable supplies.

In the open glove compartment he found a map and a small box of matches. The floor and dashboard were bare but when he went around and opened the passenger's door he discovered a latch which, when pressed, allowed the seatback to fold down, exposing a storage space.

In the depression he found a coil of rope, a couple of folded blankets, and a paper bag. The bag contained what looked like half a loaf of dark bread and a sausage. When he picked up the blanket he felt something slip and heard the clink of glass tapping against glass. When he laid the blankets on the seat and unfolded them he discovered two small bottles of vodka one of the guards must've hidden.

He hauled the food and blankets back to the bed of the truck and covered the wounded men with the blankets then returned to the cab for the rope. Besides the map and matches, now in his pocket, there seemed nothing else useful in the truck then realized the seat covers could be put to several uses. With the sharpened spoon handle he cut the covers away and took some of the foam padding, too.

By the time he'd finished plundering the truck the other men returned, Juho and Logan dragging poles of birch saplings. Within minutes the two of them had assembled two travois, using the seat covers as slings for the wounded men to lie on.

"It's funny the Russians haven't caught up with us before this," Steve said.

"I think other prisoners put things in the Russian fuel tanks," Juho replied.

"They've bought us a little time." Reynaud finished by pulling on his new boots. "They paid a lot for it. Let's make sure we don't waste it." He unfolded the map and pressed it flat against the side of the truck. It was, of course, in Russian but it seemed to show an area of the Russo-Polish-Czech border. From pencil marks on the map they guessed at the location of the camp and the road they'd followed.

The region appeared to be bare of roads or settlements. The road ahead seemed to take a turn to the north, within thirty kilometers or so, and ran into a highway that looped around the point of what they guessed was the Polish border. The highway seemed to run only ten or fifteen kilometers from the border.

Reynaud frowned. "I don't see Krakow on this map. That means a long trip."

"Then we'd better get started," Logan said. They moved the wounded men as gently as possible to the travois and set out, moving in the direction the Finn pointed out as west.

They took turns pulling the travois or carrying them as stretchers in the rougher places. In many areas, the forest through which they traveled gave way to bare, stony slopes. By late afternoon they'd covered perhaps another ten kilometers and were exhausted, and had begun to search a place to spend the night.

Suddenly Juho pointed to the base of an overhang where fallen rocks gave some shelter from the wind. He motioned for the rest to stay where they were while he prowled up a slight incline to a jumble of rocks. He ducked in under the overhang, the sniper rifle ready, then reappeared moments later, waving the party forward.

As the climbed in over the rocks, Reynaud caught a strong odor. "What's that smell?"

"A big animal. It is not here," Juho said, and patted the stock of his rifle.

"A bear?" Reynaud demanded.

"Right," the Finn said with a grin. "I forgot the word. It is out—eating. Maybe it will come back here to sleep. Then we will have meat."

"Or maybe he will." As Reynaud's eyes adjusted to the dimness he realized the place under the overhang was actually a shallow cave. Juho gestured to Logan and they wrestled a few of the slabs of rock around so any warmth from the fire would be reflected back into the cave. The rest of those who could move gathered what dry wood they could find. Using some dry grass and an old bird's nest, Juho built up a small mound of tinder and started a fire.

Almost the only things the guards had been carrying, besides their weapons, were canteens. The escaped prisoners passed them around and Reynaud gave Teller a mouthful of water. He coughed, but he kept the water down.

Using a bayonet, Reynaud divided the bread and sausage as equitably as he could. The taste of meat seemed an almost alien sensation but a very welcome one. Between the food and the unaccustomed warmth, Reynaud began to doze. He shook his head to clear it, then began to study the AK74 he'd been carrying. Pressing the magazine release lever, he rocked the magazine out then counted the cartridges. He'd been given the weapon the guard had used to fire at the group, or perhaps it was the one Steve had used, and thirteen rounds had been fired.

Each man checked the weapon he carried. Steve's rifle had seven rounds gone. The other AK74 and the AKR, carried by Logan, had their full thirty rounds apiece, and the Dragunov had nine of its larger, rimmed cartridges in the magazine.

Seven men, two of them wounded, with no food, little water, only five guns and less than a hundred ten rounds of ammunition, facing a trek through rough country in enemy territory; the situation did not look promising.

"We'd better keep at least one guard alert through the night. The Russians aren't going to be too far behind us," Reynaud said.

Logan grinned. "Those clowns couldn't catch a cold. I think maybe they're afraid to come after us. Most of those assholes have never pointed a gun at anybody who might shoot back. They're garrison bullies."

"Mostly true," Steve agreed, "but Chernikov and Oshevsky are a different breed. If they don't have anything to keep them busy they'll have the troops after us. I think it's a matter of fear, and those guards are more afraid of those two than anything else. It probably helped that we left the road. They probably expected us to follow it."

The Deacon stirred. "We are in the hands of the Lord of Hosts, Who has confounded the Godless."

Logan caught up the submachine gun and crawled to a place he could watch down the slope. "I'll take first watch."

Juho was instantly asleep and Reynaud and the others slipped into slumber, then they all woke to the sound of gunfire and a roar.

Chapter 2

Reynaud tried to see and think through the fog in his eyes and his mind then a blur that must've been Juho paused for only a second before he fired a single shot louder than the bursts. Crawling to the mouth of the cave, Reynaud looked outside. Darkness fell early here and he judged it to be late evening, but in the gloom he could just make out a massive shape jerking spasmodically.

"Wait until it is all dead," Juho said

"He's right," Steve agreed. "Even weakened, it could still take off an arm or a leg."

Reynaud finally found his voice. "What the hell happened?"

"I was just sitting here, keeping watch," Logan replied, "and the next think I know, this bear was about fifty yards away and coming like a freight train. I hit him with at least three bursts, and he just kept coming." His face was pale and his lips pressed into a straight line.

After a few minutes, when the bear had stopped thrashing about, Juho worked a crossbrace loose from one of the travois and slipped outside. He approached the bear carefully, prodded it with the pole then said, "It is okay."

All but the wounded men made their way outside to examine the carcass. In the moonlight, the bear's chest appeared to be a mass of blood, then Juho pointed to a ragged exit hole at the base of the skull and showed how the bullet must've gone in through the bear's open mouth. "Mine," he said, proudly.

Using the four bayonets and the knife Logan had taken from the corporal, they skinned the bear, and Reynaud felt a little queasy as he stared at the skinned body. With the fur gone, he discovered, a bear looked enough like a man to make him nervous.

They found more bullet holes in the bear, most of them in the chest and shoulders, then Juho began cutting meat away in strips. Steve impaled some of the meat on sticks for roasting and a large, flat rock at the edge of the fire served as a crude skillet.

They often had to stop their butchering to hone the blades of the knife and the bayonets on the rocks, and it was hard work, but they cooked up enough for everyone to eat.

Smyth-Davis woke again and Reynaud fed him and gave him more water to drink. That'd be the next problem; they were running out of water, and Reynaud knew drinking the vodka would cause them to lose body heat faster and die quickly of exposure.

The bear meat was greasy, thick with fat, which their bodies needed in this cold. Juho had sawed off the top of one of the empty canteens and cooked more bear meat in its own fat, then cooled it quickly so the fat congealed on the meat, sealing it. He repeated the operation several times, leaving the cooked meat out on the frigid rocks with strips of raw meat.

By the time night had fallen, perhaps five-thirty or so, they were tired again but well-fed, for the first time in months.

Reynaud took the next watch. He felt a deep satisfaction, partly from having a full belly and partly from feeling the odds against them weren't impossible. Captivity hadn't broken him but it'd made him deeply pessimistic; it hadn't made him fatalistic but had charged him with caution. He'd never surrender to the odds but he preferred knowing the odds, and he preferred to examine problems now with an eye for several solutions.

The night was still and the only movement he saw was the gentle swaying of branches in a faint breeze.

"Could I have some water?" Teller's voice was thick with pain and sleep.

Reynaud carefully poured a canteen cap of water and gave it to Teller, who drank and sighed then asked, "Do you really think we can make it back?"

Reynaud shrugged then realized the other man probably couldn't see the movement. "It looks better than it did this time last night, doesn't it?

"I don't know," Teller replied. "Last night I didn't have this hole in me." After several silent moments he said, "If you could, look up my family in San Antone."

"What're they doing there?"

"That's where I was stationed before I got rotated to Europe, and Rachel's still stationed there. We've got a little girl, Ginny. She'd be about six now."

Teller seemed lost in thought for a time, then he asked, "Are you married?"

"Never got around to it. I played around a little in college but I never found the right woman. I'm glad you did. It gives the rest of us hope."

"Yeah, Rachel's a winner all right. Biggest blue eyes you ever saw. Not to mention some other things." He started a chuckle that ended in a cough and a moan. When he'd caught his breath, he said, "She's one of those women who can do damned near everything but she never learned to fry an egg. Great cook, but her best fried eggs were best nailed over rat holes. Back in that prison camp, when they gave us our morning garbage, I'd remember those fried eggs. You know, I think I would've traded anything for one of her lousy fried eggs."

After another long silence he spoke again. "Ginny would've started school this fall. I remember her first-day jitters at kindergarten but she took it like a trooper. Real good kid." He paused. "I can't help worrying about them—scared, maybe hungry—we don't know how bad the plague hit the states. If I don't make it, try to find them and tell them I was thinking about them."

"Tell them yourself, when we get back."

"Yeah." The word was tossed out in a sardonic tone. "Don't try to bullshit me. What do you think my chances are?"

Reynaud answered as honestly as he could. "I really don't know, but I think your chances will be better if you can get some rest."

"I could rest easier, knowing if I didn't make it, you'll take word to them."

"All right," Reynaud said, "you have my word. If you don't make it, I'll see them for you, if I can. Good enough?"

"Good enough." Teller's voice broke.

A little later Reynaud heard a moan, then, "Who's there?"

"Dechaine."

"Ah." Reynaud thought he detected a clipped British accent. "I seem to be able to move my limbs a bit."

"How's the wound?"

"I've a bit of a headache."

"Just try to get some rest. We'll see if you're up to walking tomorrow."

When Reynaud found sleep impossible to fight off he woke Steve to take the next watch and almost immediately fell asleep.

~ * ~

Reynaud woke feeling better than he had in months. Someone was frying what smelled like bacon. Outside the cave it was still dark but he guessed dawn was less than an hour away. He rose slowly, favoring stiff muscles and found Smyth-Davis sitting by the fire beside Juho and Logan.

"How are you feeling this morning?" Reynaud asked.

"Better, thank you. The noggin still throbs a bit but I should be able to get out and about with you."

Reynaud knew the Brit's head must feel as though an avalanche had fallen on it but he said nothing. He accepted the "bacon" and ate. If Smyth-Davis could walk, they could use some of the seat cushions to carry some of the meat they'd frozen last night, and it freed a man or two for carrying supplies.

Juho handed him a piece of bearskin the Finn had rough-scraped. "Now we all have hats," the Finn said.

Reynaud took off the rags of prison uniform he'd wrapped around his head and put on the piece of fur then used the rags to bind it on. That could help a lot.

"How's Teller this morning?" Reynaud asked.

Logan frowned. "Not good. He's got spells of clarity but he's out of his head a lot of the time."

Using a scrap of rag on which he'd sprinkled some of the vodka, Reynaud cleaned the wound as best he could and splashed a little of the vodka directly into the wound.

Teller moaned and his breathing became more labored but he seemed to relax as Reynaud bound the wound. "Your turn," the Cajun informed Smyth-Davis.

"I suppose it'd do no good to tell you I'm a devout teetotaler?"

"It saves me buying you a drink when we get back," Reynaud said, "but, no. I'm sadistic enough to want to find out if you'll scream instead of getting an infection that will rot off the top of your head."

"Y'know," Smyth-Davis said, "you'd make someone a marvelous mother."

"That's what I've been telling him," Logan interjected, "that he's a real mother."

"You're just bitching because you aren't getting any vodka," Reynaud said around a grin. "Go ahead, we've got time for you to shoot yourself so you can get me to pour some of this into the hole."

"Maybe another time."

By then, the rest of the group were awake and Reynaud busied himself making a pack for the meat. When he'd put on the Russian uniform he'd removed his prison clothing, using the shirt as a sort of turban. Now, he shook out the pants, tied the legs shut, and put the cooked meat into one leg, the raw frozen strips into the other, then draped the pants over his neck. The Russian winter uniform was well enough insulated he'd be unlikely to warm the meat enough to let it spoil.

They left the cave at first light, Logan drawing the travois, Juho scouting ahead, and Reynaud staying at the tail of the group, watching their backtrail.

The Finn had apparently grown up in country like this, and he seemed as tireless as the rocks they traveled across, and almost as hard. He ranged well ahead, occasionally coming back to report a better way across the rock and the brush.

Reynaud stayed far to the rear. Occasional clumps of trees thrust their way up through country that seemed to hate all life, where even the spots of scrub looked tortured and stunted. The sky remained a clear blue, so at least snowfall wasn't an immediate threat.

What sort of problems might they encounter? Crossing any body of water larger than a puddle would be difficult and dangerous. The Russians might've mined some country around the camp but this was farther away than they'd expect prisoners to escape and, from the country he'd seen, he doubted there was enough topsoil in a square mile to cover a single mine. They might've dispersed butterfly mines, tiny anti-personnel mines that were almost colorless and could be dispersed by air. That was possible but unlikely, because aircraft and the fuel to get them airborne were scarce.

Suddenly Logan appeared ahead, his back to the ridge to conceal himself from whatever might be on the other side and waved Reynaud forward. Reynaud pushed himself into a trot until he was close enough for Logan to put a finger on his lips and motion for Reynaud to stay down.

Bending to a crouch, Reynaud followed Logan around the ridge and into a shallow cleft where, fifty yards further, the rest of the group waited for them.

"Soldiers," Juho said, pointing to the east. "It is ten men. They march close together, no more than twenty meters apart."

"What kind of soldiers are they?" Reynaud asked,

"Not good. They have parts of uniforms, old guns. Good soldiers would be apart more. They are not using cover, not using their eyes. Shall we kill them?"

Reynaud glanced at the other men. The Deacon's eyes were burning with an almost feral light. "The Godless communists have killed our friends. 'An eye for an eye.'"

Logan checked the chamber of his submachine gun. "How close can I get?"

"Maybe thirty meters. You will have to hide yourselves until you hear shooting."

Reynaud tried to balance advantages and disadvantages. These troops sounded like militia of some sort, not FSB or even regular army. He doubted they were searching for the escaped prisoners. More likely, they were simply patrolling the border. Patrolling this far inside the border probably meant the terrain north of the highway was even rougher.

Ambushing the patrol had its risks. These were obviously not elite troops but then, neither were the ex-prisoners, and the patrol had them outnumbered. Also, if this was a regular patrol, they might have a checkpoint near.

Against the risks were balanced need and hatred. These men might not be FSB or MVD but they were the Russians who allowed the FSB to take and keep power. Also, they almost certainly had supplies his group needed—guns, ammunition, food, water, and—maybe—medical supplies.

He nodded to Juho. "Where do you want me to take a position?"

"Good." Juho returned the nod then turned to Smyth-Davis, wounded and unarmed. "You stay here," he said gesturing at Teller, "and watch for him."

Leaving the wounded men in the cleft, out of the worst of the bitter breeze, Juho led Reynaud to a low bush in a cluster of boulders. "Get under bush and stay back so your gun does not make a shadow. You kill the last two men." He led the rest of the men away.

Reynaud crawled into the cover. Juho had chosen the site well, a place with good concealment—the branches would break up the fog of his breath—and hard cover, as well as an excellent field of fire that commanded the trail below as it followed the edge of a bluff. From this position, the trail offered no cover at all. The only drawback was, if he had to fall back, he had no cover to speak of for more than forty yards. He stretched out under the bush, moved the fire-selector lever on the AK to semi-automatic fire, and centered the sight on the trail below so he would hardly have to move his weapon at all when the Russians came into view.

The wait was a long one, and he was unable to see any of the rest of the group from where he lay. He'd almost decided Juho had made some mistake, that the Russians had taken some other route, when a man in a Russian army greatcoat and a steel Russian helmet worn over a fur hat, appeared on the trail below. The man peered about as he walked but seemed sure of himself.

Reynaud had heard it was dangerous to stare at a man's head or torso, that a man could feel the enemy staring at him. He fixed his attention on the man's boots, observing his steady pacing. Fifteen seconds later another figure stepped onto the path, pacing slowly. Perhaps twenty seconds later another man appeared and yet another almost immediately followed him. Reynaud began to count the pairs of feet. After the ninth man he had to wait forty-five seconds for the final man to reach the trail below.

His fingers grew numb with cold and he carefully flexed them then put them in his mouth for a moment. His mouth was dry and his nerves were on edge. He'd never killed a man before; not like this. In some ways, it was easier in air-to-air combat—you never saw the enemy pilot. The planes you'd shot down had only been enemy aircraft. A MiG 29 was a warbird, not a man. You saw it and you destroyed it, but now he was centering his rifle's sight on a man's back.

He'd never thought of Russian soldiers as people before. Maybe the man he was preparing to kill had a wife, or even a family, waiting for him. The Russian was obviously tired and cold and probably looking forward to his next warm meal.

There was no time for this, he told himself. He thought too much. He could be sure the Finn made no such mistake. If he thought at all at a time like this, he was only selecting his second the third targets. Reynaud again gave his attention to his target and the sights of his rifle. What if his shot missed, or only wounded the man? The Russian would probably go to ground and fire into everything he could see that looked like cover. Reynaud's finger began to take up the slack on the AK's trigger.

He heard a gunshot and squeezed the trigger. The soldier in his sights flew forward and Reynaud couldn't tell whether he'd missed and the man had sprung forward or whether the Russian had been knocked down by the bullet. He jerked the trigger for a second shot at the man, knew he'd jerked the shot too much and missed, concentrated on the man, who was still in the air, and cursed himself again. He'd forgotten to use the sights and fired too high. He forced himself to take more time, sight carefully, and squeeze the shot. This time he noticed how the man's coat jumped up where the bullet struck.

Immediately he swung his rifle to point at the next soldier in the line. The Russian was prone on the rocks, working the bolt of an old bolt-action rifle. Reynaud placed his sights on the patch of paler color under the edge of the man's dark fur hat and squeezed off a shot. The trooper slumped.

Then Reynaud realized all the Russians were dead or badly wounded. No one was still shooting back. He gave himself a moment to relax, to let the last of the excitement drain out of him, then he chuckled, only partly from relief. Before the first shot, he'd been unsure and afraid. He might've simply held his fire, hiding in his patch of cover, but the party had been committed. He'd known if he didn't kill the Russians, they'd kill his friends. He'd found no joy in the battle, but his grim determination not to let his friends down had paid off.

Now it was over.

Forcing himself to his feet, he had to fight stiffness in his muscles and joints, the result of lying motionless on the cold rock. He lurched forward, gun ready, then remembered, with a shock, that the only shot he'd heard in the firefight had been the single round Juho had fired at the scout, the signal to fire. He hadn't even heard his own gunshots.

He approached the nearest body warily until he could see the two bullet holes in the corpse's back. He noticed the Russian's rifle lying three or four feet from the body. He'd begun to stalk toward the next dead Russian when he heard a groan.

The Deacon had just pulled the pack off one of the soldiers when the man moaned and moved his arm. Covering the man with his rifle in one hand, Billy Joe used his left hand to tug the Russian's boots off then he unbuckled the man's belt and pulled off the gear at the man's waist.

The Russian groaned again and propped himself up on one elbow. The Deacon kicked the soldier in the side hard enough to fling him to within inches of the bluff's edge. The man cried out at the kick and when he hit the rock he lay stunned, breathing raggedly. Billy Joe glowered at the Russian with a hostile glare. "Mercy is to precious a quality to be wasted," he growled and kicked the man over the edge of the cliff.

The soldier's scream lasted only a second or two, then the body hit the slope, eighty feet below.

Of the two men Logan had been responsible for, one had been shot twice and had been finished off by Juho with a single shot to the base of the throat. The other corpse had eight bullet holes and one of the trooper's two canteens had been pierced.

"You sure leave a messy corpse," Steve observed. "The army has something called 'fire discipline.' Ever heard of it?"

"God, it was great," Logan enthused. "I love rock and roll. I damned near came. This is almost as good as sex."

Steve turned the body over and noticed the holes in the man's pack and blanket roll. "I wonder if it was good for him, too," he said dryly.

"Hey," Logan retorted, "I'm here to avenge, not to entertain,"

They gathered the weapons and supplies they found on the bodies. Only the men on point and tail-guard, and the officer, who'd been second in the file hadn't carried packs, and their equipment had apparently been distributed among the rest of the troops.

The group had no bread, only a few packages of crackers and a few hard biscuits, and only a few cans of food, but they'd carried a few cabbages, onions, beets, some dried meat, and hard cheese. Medical supplies consisted of a few pills and capsules, a couple of paper packets Logan thought might be sulfa, and a handful of dressings.

The clothing they wore was a mixture of Russian military, some of it apparently from three or four wars ago, and heavy woolen civilian clothes in drab colors, and only half of them wore military boots. Still, it was enough to help the party stay warm, and the extra footgear might help.

The arms and ammunition were a bewildering mixture. The officer had carried an old Tokarev pistol and one of the older AKs, chambered for the short thirty-caliber cartridge. Two of the men had carried light autoloading rifles Steve identified as SKS carbines. One of the carbines was well cared-for while the other was mottled with rust and some parts were still gummed up with heavy grease. That carbine was jammed, with a round half-chambered. Two more troops had carried the old submachine guns with wooden stocks, perforated barrel jackets, and drum magazines. The weapons were heavier than they looked and both were in poor shape. Most of the remaining weapons were bolt-action rifles, with two unusual weapons in the lot.

One of the odd weapons caught Reynaud's eye because it was similar to a gun one of his uncles had owned, although instead of the slender barrel and short, sporty stock, the barrel and forearm of this weapon resembled a musket, but it was definitely a Winchester 1895. His uncle's weapon had been chambered for the old .30-40 Krag. Reynaud picked the weapon up and examined it critically. The wood was dark with grease and dented here and there, while the bluing of the metal had turned brown, with some surface pitting, but the gun was clean and it seemed basically sound.

He swung its lever through its arc and ejected a spent cartridge case, leaving three rounds in the magazine. This rifle apparently took the old long Russian rimmed cartridges, the same round used by the sniper rifle Juho carried.

The Winchester was bulky but no more so than most of the rifles, and Reynaud was familiar with the action. If it was slower than a good autoloader it was still faster than the old turnbolt actions most of the Russians had been carrying.

They decided Smyth-Davis should carry the shortest and

lightest weapon, which was the AKR Logan had used. By adding all the remaining AK74 ammunition, the Brit would have a few rounds more than two full magazines. To replace the submachine gun, Logan appropriated the officer's AK, with its four loaded magazines and the pistol.

Steve chose the well-tended SKS carbine while the Deacon picked a long, slim autoloading rifle. The Finn identified it as a Tokarev and showed him how to load it with stripper clips of ammunition the soldiers had carried.

One backpack and a blanket were so shot-up as to be worthless, and it was obviously impossible for the ex-prisoners to carry away all their booty but the experiences of the camp, where everything that could be found or stolen was hoarded, caused them to regret anything would be left behind.

Juho found a fissure in the rocks and into it they dumped the bodies and everything else they couldn't haul away with them. They even tossed in the excess weapons, after Juho had pulled the bolts from them and thrown the bolts over the cliff.

Finally they returned to where they'd left the wounded men. Smyth-Davis stood as he saw them. "You lads had been at the party so long I'd begun to wonder."

Steve handed him the AKR and its magazines. "Next time there's a party, I'll see you're invited, too."

"Thanks awfully, but my tux is at the cleaner's. Hate to make a bad impression, y'know."

Logan grinned. "We made plenty of impressions on those Russkys, and they were all good ones."

Reynaud knelt over Teller. The man looked pale but his breathing was steady. Opening one of the packets Reynaud poured the powder Logan had identified as sulfa into the wound then used one of the Russian dressings to bandage it. "I hope you're right about this stuff being sulfa. With the luck we've been having, it could be talcum powder."

"Well," Logan replied, "he'll never have diaper rash again."

Logan treated Smyth-Davis' head wound and bound it up again with a clean dressing, then they gnawed at dried meat, ate most of the crackers the soldiers had packed, and washed them down with water from the canteens.

Juho pointed to the west. "I think the ridge slopes down to

the highway that way. We must get across the highway and into the mountains still today."

The Finn scouted ahead and, in the very early afternoon, found a narrow trail that snaked down to a highway, a harrowing route on which they almost lost Teller as they tried to maneuver the stretcher around a hairpin turn. They'd reached the road and dusk found them in the mountains, anxiously searching some cover from the night's cold.

The best cover Juho could find was a place where the trunk of a fallen tree formed a vee with the ridge. Using the poles from the travois and some of the extra blankets, they managed to provide themselves with some shelter.

Juho cut away the webbing from the two helmets they'd taken and used them as stewpots, filling them with snow then adding cabbage, onion, and, after frying it on a slab of rock, some of the bear meat.

Teller groaned and opened his eyes. Reynaud held a spoonful of the stew over Teller's mouth. "Chow call."

"Nothing for me. I'm not hungry."

"Look, Teller," Reynaud said, "If you want to have a chance to eat bad fried eggs again, you're going to have to eat this stew."

"You've convinced me," Teller said, with a weak attempt at a grin, and ate the stew Reynaud spooned into his mouth. For a short time he seemed stronger, as though the food had revitalized him but, by the time darkness had fallen he'd become lethargic and drifted into a troubled slumber.

"We've got to get him to some kind of medical help, soon." Reynaud said.

"We're in the wrong place to find doctors, much less any that make house calls," Logan observed. He looked around where the bare rock loomed up in the darkness. "This must be the border. You could use this place as the border for Hell."

"Not an original thought; somebody's already thought of it." Steve fed more wood into the fire. "If we can make it through the mountains it should be easier going."

Staring into the fire and taking his own turn at dinner, Reynaud said, "You get around in the mountains pretty well."

Steve ran a hand down his skimpy beard. "I grew up in Colorado; Colorado Springs."

"You didn't have far to travel to the academy, then. Practically commuting distance."

Steve spooned some of the soup into his mouth and, after chewing and swallowing, said, "Pretty close, in more ways than one. You don't meet many poor boys from the barrios or kids from the southwest who're still wringing the Rio Grande out of their pants at the academy. My given name is Esteban, but even my family called me Steve. They were fourth-generations Americans, and pretty well-off." He sounded as though he had some regrets about the lack of obstacles.

"Nothing wrong with that," Reynaud said, as he washed some stew down with a drink from a canteen. "Personally, I think poverty is much-overrated."

"Nothing wrong, but nothing great, either. You can't master a challenge you've never been issued."

"Look at it on the bright side," Reynaud replied. "If it wasn't you, it might've been some poor kid from the barrio in this fix."

Steve chuckled. "Thanks. I feel better already. I notice you've got a touch of a drawl. I thought Cajuns were all from Louisiana."

"Not all of them. There are a lot of Cajuns in southern Arkansas and eastern Texas. Originally, our family was from Louisiana. My dad worked on an off-shore drilling rig. Just when I was getting at home on the bayou, his company transferred him to Port Arthur, Texas. Then, to make things really complicated, I went to college at Creighton." He laughed. "You think you had it tough at Colorado Springs. Hell, you don't know what tough is. All you had to contend with were Air Force officers and noncoms. I got taught by Jebbies, high school and college."

"Jebbies?" Logan asked.

"Blackrobes. Jesuits. Hell, half my high school teachers could eat Marines for breakfast, and without even buttering them or pinning their ears back. We had one guy; a big gorilla by the name of Hartmann. He was the kinda guy who had to duck his head and turn sideways to get through a door. He was so big he was afraid to discipline anybody.

"You know how kids in public school talk about sitting outside the principal's office? It doesn't work that way in a Jeb school. They never bother the principal with little details like that. For real discipline problems they have a Prefect of Discipline, and he's the loneliest guy at the school because nobody gets sent to the Prefect for trivial things—nothing much less than murder or homosexual rape. Trivial things are cleared up right in the classroom; a quick punch-out and it's all over.

"Anyway, Hartmann was trying to teach English and things were getting out of hand. He was afraid to slug anybody because parents get upset when they're called to the school to identify the body. The class didn't know why Hartman was holding back but we all figured it was open season until bodies started flying. Finally, one day, Hartmann reached the end of his tether. He walked over to the corner and picked up the wastebasket.

"Catholic schools or public, they all use the same kind of wastebaskets—metal, usually painted olive drab or gray, and all of them made of old Sherman tank hulls. Hartman picks up the wastebasket, and he tears the damned thing—tears it like a piece of scratch paper. Man, it was so quiet in that room you could hear the participles dangling."

Steve laughed. "I won't try to one-up that yarn. How about you, Logan? Where did you grow up? Or did you spring, like Athena, full-grown from the brow of Zeus?"

"Pretty close. I was raised on a farm near Lawrence, Kansas, but I'm also the last surviving descendant of the Lone Ranger. And the Green Hornet."

The rest of them grinned at him, waiting for the punchline of the joke.

"Hey, you think I'm shittin' you? Look it up. The Lone Ranger's given name was John Reid, and the Green Hornet, Britt Reid, was the grandson of the Lone Ranger's nephew, Dan."

Reynaud wondered whether Logan was simply pulling their legs or whether he actually believed what he was saying. He decided to sidestep. "How about you, McCluskey, where are you from?"

"From God's country. Asheville, North Carolina, where the air is still pure and—"

"Who were you going to nominate, Deak?" Logan inquired, with massive and transparent innocence.

Billy Joe glared at him. "Like you, I turned away from the

birthright of my faith to become a mocker. I'd just returned to the fold when God called me to my country's service, and in that Hell of a camp I learned about heaven and God's message."

Reynaud turned to the Finn. "How about you? Where you from, Juho?"

"From Kuopio." The Finn seemed to feel what he'd said was sufficient answer, for which Reynaud was beginning to feel grateful. He'd begun to feel like a guest at a dinner party who's just learned that at least half the other guests were escaped lunatics. He enjoyed company and conversation but had learned the hard way that verbally bumping into someone else's beliefs could be dangerous. His own paranoia was beginning to seem very normal, by comparison.

"Any of you guys married?" Logan asked.

"No," Reynaud said, and all the others shook their heads. Reynaud felt he should elaborate. "Teller's married but I figured I had enough trouble already. How about you?"

"No, although I once tried to convince some bimbo a taxi driver who owns his own cab qualified as a captain and could perform marriages."

"How'd that work out?" Steve asked.

"Aw, the bimbo ran off with the cabdriver."

Steve laughed again, then pointed a thumb at Smyth-Davis. "Anybody know anything about the Brit?"

No one spoke. Finally, Reynaud said, "We can ask him when he's up. I'll take the first watch."

After the others had settled into their blankets, Reynaud stared up at the stars. Here in the mountains, under a cloudless sky, they were so brilliant they seemed near enough to reach out and grab. He sat with the Winchester across his knees and thought about the lies they'd shared. He hadn't married simply because he'd never met the woman he'd wanted to spend the rest of his life with. In a way, it left him more alone than Teller, who desperately missed his wife. Reynaud had no one to miss, and no one to miss him, which made his loneliness all the deeper.

He shook his head. Reflecting like that would do no good. He was going to need all the stamina he could muster to get across these mountains, and a grim mood would just be another weight to carry.

Waking Steve at the end of what Reynaud guessed to be his watch, he curled into the still-warm blankets.

~ * ~

During breakfast Juho nodded at Steve. "You lead today. I will carry Teller." Using some of the rope, he tied Teller to his back then picked up one of the poles from the travois to use as a walking stick.

During the night, clouds had rolled in, turning the sky the color of lead and sharpening the wind's bitter edge. Reynaud wore mittens over gloves, and his fingers still stiffened and lost their feeling. His feet had long since grown as numb and heavy as two logs, and he began to wonder how many of them would lose fingers or toes—or worse—to frostbite. After two hours of steady traveling, they halted for rest in a shelter of rocks.

Reynaud stared at the clouds, which looked far more threatening than they had in the morning. He noticed Juho and Steve were also on edge.

"We're going to have to find some place to hole up, and we're going to have to do it soon," Steve said. "If we get as much snow as those clouds look like they're ready to dump, it'll choke off the passes and we'll have to worry about avalances."

Logan pulled off his pack and handed it to Juho. "I'll carry Teller for awhile."

The next few miles were the hardest they'd traveled. Most of their hiking was diagonal on trails unworthy of the name, or even drawing themselves up or lowering themselves by rope down bare slopes.

The dim light faded as they made their descent into a valley thick with conifers and bare trees. Reynaud was exhausted. He'd taken his turn carrying Teller, although he'd had to quit after an hour, not having Juho's or Logan's strength. For the last mile he'd been moving like a robot, only dimly aware of the way ahead of him. He was ready to collapse under the next fir he saw when Juho stopped and pointed to a ridge ahead and to the right. "There is a house there," the Finn said.

Reynaud stared at the ridge but saw nothing. "Not in these mountains. Hell, why would anyone want to live in a place where you have to look down to see the birds flying?"

"There is a house," Juho insisted.

Reynaud gritted his teeth and plunged ahead. He knew he was in no worse shape than the rest of the group, and not as bad off as Teller or Smyth-Davis, who'd fallen twice. The Cajun stumbled then realized he'd been walking through the stubble of a field. When he looked the way Juho had pointed, he saw a wall of stone and wood, screened by a clump of firs.

Unslinging his rifle, he checked the chamber. They'd seen no signs of life but the grain in this field hadn't harvested itself. Another two hundred yards, and he could see the shape of the building among the trees. It seemed to be a small house, little more than a cabin, but something about it gave the impression this house, or one like it, had stood here before the first log cabins built by whites had been thrown up in America.

Juho set Teller down beside the trunk of a massive pine tree and signed for Smyth-Davis to stand guard over him, then he pointed at Reynaud and the Deacon and made a sweeping motion to the right, indicating for them to circle on that side and gestured for Steve and Logan to go around the other way. The Finn squatted on his heels and studied the place through narrowed eyes, his rifle across his knees.

Creeping through the trees, Reynaud suddenly felt exhilarated. His body was still exhausted but the surge of excitement gave him a second wind. Stopping for a moment, he pulled off his mittens and flexed his fingers. A chimney stood on the near side of the house but no smoke rose from it. A well-trodden path led from the front around to a patch of brown stems and vines that must've been a garden. At the head of the garden stood a stone well.

Reynaud signaled for the Deacon to take up a position where he was, concealed behind a naked oak tree with a good view of both the front and back of the house. Behind the house stood a barn and, between them, two outbuildings, both made of stones and logs, and a long, low mound that looked like a grave for a giant, twelve or fifteen feet long.

Reynaud had been watching for Logan or Steve and finally saw Villareal directly behind the house and seventy-five yards from the back door. The Cajun indicated for Steve to cover him and crept toward the back of the house. As he moved nearer he saw Logan pass on a signal to Juho and guessed the Finn was approaching the front of the house.

He started as something moved near his face then realized it had begun to snow, and the air was filling with great, moist flakes. He studied the back of the house again. Nothing moved but the falling snow; there were no signs of life.

Trying to avoid stems that might crackle and leave some sign of his passing, or patches of earth where he might leave a footprint, he stalked forward. One of the small outbuildings, he could tell by the odor, was an outhouse. Opening the door to the other, he found sickles and other farm implements, all of them hand tools.

The sheds stood only a dozen yards from the back of the house. At this range, he could see curtains in the windows, heavy and motionless, and drawn closed. He strode to the back door, put his hand on the simple latch, and opened the door. The daylight had dimmed to dusk and the inside of the building was too dark for him to see his way around.

He side-stepped to avoid being silhouetted in the doorway and bumped into a low table. Something clattered. Reaching down, he almost knocked over a lamp. He caught the lamp then bent to look at it. It resembled a hurricane lamp but was heavier, and had obviously seen much use. A snap of a match and he had the lamp burning. He carefully lowered the glass chimney just as Juho entered the front door.

The Finn had only opened the door enough to slip inside and instantly stood against the wall, his rifle pointed toward the light.

"Easy," Reynaud said, "it's just me." Raising the lantern he stared around the room. Ornately painted chests and cabinets stood against the walls and, near him, rested a table and chairs. Diagonally across the room from the table stood a bed, with wooden headboard and footboard painted in elaborate patterns with bright colors.

"No one home," Reynaud observed. He set the lamp on the table and waited for the others to come inside. "Do you need help moving Teller?" he asked the Finn.

Juho shook his head and strode outside. While the others approached the cabin, Reynaud made a rough examination of the place. Whoever lived here, he decided, was what many people would call a primitive. The furniture was embellished with patterns in vivid colors. Only a "primitive" would use such colors. "Civilized" people preferred their furniture built with fragile, flowing shapes and plain finishes, or they bought disposable plastic junk that wouldn't last as long as a good coat of paint.

The place was neat, which implied a woman's presence, and she or they hadn't been gone long. He swung the lamp gently, noticed it was almost full of kerosene or coal oil. Whoever lived here expected to return soon.

At first, he'd missed seeing the stove, which was also decorated with what looked like tiles of pale blue and yellow, arranged in patterns, with designs painted on or baked in. Wood lay stacked in a rack near the stove and he fueled the stove and lit it.

The Deacon entered and pointed to the crucifix over the bed. "At least these people aren't Godless atheists or heathens."

Steve entered and said, "Let's remember we're guests here. We do no damage and we use only what we need—wood and the fuel in the lamp."

Reynaud's weariness returned, hitting him like the blow of a fist, with the same stunning effect. He set his pack down by the floor and on it laid both gloves and mittens then held his hands out to the stove until he could bend his fingers without fearing they'd snap off. As the room became warmer he took off the Russian greatcoat and the coat under it, placing them on the floor where he intended to sleep.

Juho returned with Teller and Reynaud opened the man's coat and shirt. The wound looked about the same, with no sign Reynaud could see of infection but the man was obviously in bad shape. His face was as pale and gaunt as a skull, with deep hollows at the temples and under the cheekbones.

Teller opened his eyes. "How about a drink?" he managed to rasp out.

A bucket of water stood by the stove and Reynaud got a dipper of water for Teller but the wounded man shook his head. "I'd just as soon have some more of that vodka, but taken internally this time."

Outside, it would've been dangerous but in a warm house, the alcohol would at least relieve some of the man's pain. He dug through his pack until he found the half-empty bottle, took off the cap, and poured a little into Teller's mouth. Teller swallowed then coughed, his face twisted in pain and he coughed up pink foam. After he'd regained control of his breathing he sighed. "It's all right. Just remember your promise. You gave your word."

"I remember," Reynaud replied, "but we've gotten this far. Now we're warm, we've got plenty of food, and the worst of the trip is over."

Teller's lips twitched into an ironic smile. "Not for me. I'll be okay here. Get something to eat."

"How about you?"

"Maybe in the morning."

Reynaud was too tired to cook. The rest of the men lay sprawled on the floor, on their coats, gnawing at the trail rations. He cut off a piece of the cooked bear meat and chewed it until his jaws ached then washed it down with clear, sweet water from the bucket.

He knew they needed a guard, preferably two guards, in case someone returned to this place, but it was difficult to even sit up. He tugged off the boots and almost wept with relief, He hadn't taken those boots off since the escape—how many days ago? He couldn't remember, as the events of the last several days became lost in a sort of mental fog. He struggled to sit but it cost too much effort. He stared at the rest of the group with bleary eyes: they were already asleep. Something hit the back of his head then he realized it was the floor, and he slept.

Chapter 3

From far away, it seemed, Reynaud heard a voice—a woman's voice—speaking words he could almost understand then he realized the words were in a language like Russian, and the woman was screaming, "Get out!"

He opened his eyes and stared into the unblinking gaze of a double-barreled shotgun. His hands rose reflexively. The woman pointing the shotgun at them was a stolid, broad-faced peasant woman, who appeared to be middle-aged. The woman spat out a word that sounded like "Russky" and repeated the demand they get out.

The only way he could answer was in his bad Russian. "Not 'Russky.' 'Americansky."

"Americanski!" The woman's voice dripped disbelief.

Reynaud, moving slowly and carefully, unwound the part of the prison uniform he'd worn as a scarf and held it up for her to see. Logan got the idea and cautiously dug out his dog tags. "Americansky."

The woman stared at them and Reynaud could almost see her balancing on the edge of belief, then she said something he couldn't understand. Speaking slowly in his shaky Russian, he said "I do not know what you mean."

The woman repeated what she'd said, more slowly, and it sounded like, "Show me your teeth." She emphasized the demand with a gesture and a grimace that showed crooked teeth.

He grinned at her, showing his teeth. The woman leaned forward, staring intently at his mouth, so he opened his mouth and let her see his teeth. The woman grinned back. "Yes, Americanski. Only Americans have good teeth." At least, that's what it sounded like, but she'd apparently decided they were what they claimed to be. She strode over and set her shotgun in the corner with the rifles she must've taken while they were sleeping.

"Our friend is wounded," Steve said, pointing to where Teller lay.

Reynaud looked at Teller, then at Steve. "I'm afraid not." Teller lay staring upward, mouth agape, with dark lines of blood formed from his nostrils and the corners of his mouth onto the floor.

"We will bury our friend tomorrow," Reynaud said. He reached over and closed Teller's eyes but the jaw muscles were slack and the mouth wouldn't stay closed. They all pulled on boots and coats and Juho helped him carry Teller's body outside where the woman pointed to the tool shed. As they placed the body on the frozen ground the Deacon knelt beside the corpse and recited the twenty-third psalm as Reynaud crossed Teller's hand over his chest.

When they returned to the house the woman bustled about and began making a chicken soup. While the soup was cooking, she looked at Smyth-Davis' wound and prepared a poultice of herbs from crocks in a cupboard. After they'd eaten the soup and the bread she gave them, she put the poultice on the stove to warm and they appreciated her having waited until after they'd finished eating before heating the concoction, which emitted an odor that choked them and brought tears to their eyes.

"If you're going to wear that stuff," Logan informed Smyth-Davis, "I'd appreciate if you'd walk downwind of me."

Smyth-Davis stared at the greenish mess in the kettle with horrified fascination. "I'm just grateful she's going to put that on me instead of trying to put it inside me."

At last they were able to get back to sleep.

~ * ~

When Reynaud woke the next morning, it was to the smell of tea. The woman had risen earlier and was already changing the dressing on Smyth-Davis' head wound. She handed him a cup of tea.

"Thank you." Reynaud sipped the hot tea, which helped. "We have meat we can give you."

The woman shook her head. "'A guest in the house is God in the house.' Later I will go to—" Reynaud couldn't quite catch the name "—and bring back Father Wojcik and Adam. Adam is a man who can guide you to a place where you can get to Krakow."

Reynaud pointed at the woman. "Polski?"

The woman laughed and shook her head. "Goral." She swept her arm to mean all the people of the mountains. "We are

Gorale."

He nodded then became conscious of his appearance. "Do you have—?" The word escaped him but he made scissors of his fingers and pretended to cut his beard. She nodded and fished in a drawer then handed him a pair of scissors. The other prisoners had finally wakened and Juho decided to go to the village with the woman, using a sled to take Teller's body down for burial. While Juho and the woman were gone, Reynaud and the others cut each other's hair and trimmed their beards.

There seemed little they could do to help the woman beyond washing the floor and the few utensils they'd used for breakfast. The only other thing they could think of was to cut more wood for the stove. Using the axes they'd taken in the escape, they replenished the woodpile outside the house, then waited for Juho and the woman to return.

Late in the afternoon they saw three people approaching. They took cover until they could see it was Juho, the woman, and a man with a long, white beard but who strode like a young man. As they neared the house the old man gestured at the direction they'd be taking. "The road is shorter," he said, "if you start with a rest."

~ * ~

As they walked away the next morning, Reynaud looked back to where the cabin lay hidden among the trees. They'd left the remaining vodka, some bear meat, and three of the axes—all they had to give. Adam obviously knew his way through the mountains as though he were in his own backyard. Several times he led them away from apparent paths, saying, "Fresh snow hides many traps."

They spent the night in a makeshift shelter of evergreen boughs which was surprisingly snug, and continued on their way in the white dawn. "We want to reach Ustrzyki Gro soon, or the snow will trap us here."

Late in the afternoon, as they wended their way down a ledge overlooking a highway curving to the south, Adam pointed out a log barricade on the road. "Something is wrong." He crouched and, from the cover of a boulder, studied the road then pointed to a small tent among the trees, obscured by snow.

"Russki." Adam carried a hunting rifle converted from an old Mauser military rifle. He raised the gun, then lowered it. "They must also be in town."

"Can you talk to the people in the town?" Steve asked.

Adam nodded then led them down to a trail that gave the barricade and its guardians a wide berth. Taking advantage of all the cover the forested mountainside offered, he led them into the edge of town. He signed for them to hide themselves while he crept toward the nearest houses.

The wait was a long one. The Finn studied the church steeple through the scope of his rifle.

"See anything?" Reynaud asked.

"One Russian soldier in the top."

After nearly an hour of waiting, Reynaud was almost ready to suggest they fall back, set up a concealed camp, and bypass the village in the morning when Adam returned, two men with him.

"Bad trouble here," Adam said. "This is Jan and his uncle, Kasimir. They live here. Russians came in, took the mayor and his family as hostages, took all the guns."

"Where are they?" Steve asked.

"Many Russians are in the mayor's house. The rest are in the church across the street from the mayor's house. Two men watch the road to the north, and two more watch to the west."

Juho checked the chamber of the Dragunov. "How many Russians in all?"

"Twenty or twenty-one," Jan said. "They came in the morning in two vehicles."

"What kind of vehicles?" Logan asked.

"One of them is a BTR-70. The other is a UAZ-469."

"That tells us a hell of a lot," Logan snapped. "Do they have wheels or tracks?"

"The UAZ has wheels," Kasimir replied. "It is small—five, six men. The BTR has eight wheels. It carries fourteen soldiers and a driver and a gunner. It has a big machine gun and a smaller machine gun in a top." He mimicked a gunner in a turret.

"Are you guys all crazy?" Reynaud demanded. "This is a job for professionals—some kind of surgical strike team."

"They don't have any available," Logan replied, pointing at the villagers. "I think we can pull this off, but we've got to plan it out. Preferably somewhere where we won't freeze our asses off while we plot it out." He turned to Kasimir and, in Russian, asked, "Where can we find a warm place to sleep?"

"Follow me," Kasimir said, and led them to an abandoned cabin. Jan and Adam followed, obscuring the trail they left in the snow. A fire in the stove and a hot meal helped restore Reynaud's morale. "All right," he agreed, "but how do we go about this. If I'm going to get my head blown off doing something stupid, I want to at least pretend to have thought it out."

Steve turned to Jan. "How many good men do you have, and how many of them are armed?"

"Maybe twenty-four, twenty-five men. All the guns are in the mayor's house. When the Russians came, they took them all. Now they are all there."

Steve scratched at the beard that grew only sparsely on his cheeks. "Do they keep the vehicles between the mayor's house and the church?"

"No, they're parked to the west of the church."

"What the hell do the Russians want from you people?" Logan asked.

"Food and fuel. They also asked us if we had seen any Americans."

"They don't think we got out of the mountains, but they're covering all the bases," Reynaud said. "Do any of your people know how to drive the Russian vehicles or use the guns on them?"

Kasimir nodded. "Several of us. I, myself, was in an armored division when I was younger, and I used the gun on an OT-Sixty-Four. It is the same kind of gun."

"Would you make a drawing of the mayor's house and a map of the house, the church, and the buildings around them? We'd also like to know about the rooms in the mayor's house."

Jan grinned and laid out a floorplan of both floors of the mayor's house and a diagram of the area, even showing where the vehicles were parked. Reynaud, staring at the floorplan and map, scowled. With two targets, any raid was going to be dangerous and messy. "We'll have to divide into teams; one to go after the troops in the church and the vehicles, the other to spring the hostages and arm the locals. We'll need a sniper at the church—that'll be

Juho. I can cover him. We'll need at least one more man, and one or two locals to help us grab the vehicles. That leaves three men and most of the rest of the villagers to hit the mayor's house."

"Four," Logan said. "I can let one of these fellows use my rifle. We've got to get inside the house. If this back bedroom is still empty, we might be able to get in there. Once in, it'll be knife and pistol work anyway. We'll need to leave one man at the back of the house to give us cover if anything goes wrong."

"I'll go in with you," Smyth-Davis said. He touched the AKR. "This is almost as compact as a pistol, and is rather better for extended conversations."

"Where are the doors and windows on the church?" Reynaud asked.

Jan added some lines to his diagram of the church. "As you can see, the church makes an L with its leg on the wrong side. The leg of the L, at the northwest corner of the church, is the sacristy. There is a door at the west end of the sacristy and a door in the front of the church, which faces south. The windows are small and high. There are two of them on either side of the church and two in the front."

Reynaud nodded. "Okay, if we take up a position west of the church we should be able to cover the vehicles and bottle up the Russians in the church, but you guys hitting the house are going to have to watch the front door. That means you'll have to start the party, unless we're spotted moving into position. Juho, you take the sniper in the bell tower. If there's another man up there, the Deacon and I will both try to take him out—that way, we'll have a better chance of hitting him."

They went over their plans several times, then bundled themselves in their blankets and caught a few hours of sleep. Jan slipped away a little after midnight and returned two hours later with four more men and the information other villagers would be ready to go to the mayor's house as soon as firing broke out.

Reynaud sipped at a canteen but the thought of food nauseated him as his stomach fluttered like a homesick pigeon. The group wrapped themselves in some sheets Jan had brought back, and set out for town. Behind a fringe of trees, the groups split up, Kasimir leading Reynaud's team behind a row of houses until they took cover under shrubbery behind the church.

~ * ~

Logan followed Jan through the falling snow. The flakes had changed to lighter, dryer flakes, driven by a stiff breeze, and the locals behind them used brooms to hide the tracks. With the fresh snow and the light wind, their trail would be invisible within minutes.

The wan light was ghostly, with a lonely quality, reflected off the snow, and was so dim they didn't realize they'd reached the mayor's house until Jan put a hand on his shoulder to remind him of the need for silence. They crept past an outhouse and, ten yards later, stopped at the back of the house. The windows, at least those on the south end of the house, were dark, and they heard nothing. Logan handed his AK to Jan, who slipped the sling over his arm then crouched, fingers laced together, to give Logan a boost up to the roof.

Logan was sweating heavily by the time he lay on the slick, wood-shingled roof. He moved slowly, trying to keep his ascent silent until he'd crawled to where the roof jutted from the second-floor wall. He was aware Smyth-Davis had followed him, then he gave all his attention to the window, which was locked from the inside. He drew the long, thin knife he'd taken from the corporal and slipped it between the frames of the window then probed at the latch until he heard a faint click.

He glanced back at Smyth-Davis, who was now immediately behind him, and used the blade to pry the window open.

They had to move quickly. The house faced north but the draft from the open window would be quickly noticed. Logan slipped into the room, the pistol in his hand. The room appeared to be empty, although it was too dark to see more than a dim light at the bottom of the door. As soon as both men were inside, Smyth-Davis closed and locked the window. As their eyes adjusted to the darkness they saw several blankets on the floor, and several lengths of rope. At least some of the hostages had slept in this room but they'd already been wakened.

The two men removed their boots and coats then crept to the door. Logan slowly turned the knob, then drew the door open and peered down the hallway. Nothing moved.

Slipping out into the hall and keeping his back to the wall,

Logan moved toward the source of the light, a lamp on a small table, then he noticed a door standing slightly ajar and prowled toward it.

Smyth-Davis followed him out and they both, as much as possible, avoided the lamp. Besides the room they'd left, they saw two more doors on the outer side of the hallway, both closed. On the opposite side of the hallway stood the slightly open door, a stairway leading down, and a hook at the other side of the stairs that probably ended at a room directly facing the church.

Every nerve alert, Logan crept to the crack of the open door. The lamplight in the room was brighter than the dim corridor, and he risked a glance into the room. A Russian noncom stared into a mirror, brushing his hair.

Smyth-Davis soundlessly moved past Logan and took a position on the other side of the door, the AKR held ready. Logan guessed the Russian was alone and he motioned for the Brit to draw a knife. Very carefully, Smyth-Davis set the submachine gun down and drew a bayonet.

They heard footsteps in the room and the light dimmed. Logan pressed himself against the wall, wishing he could become a coat of paint, then the Russian pulled open the door and stepped into the hallway.

Logan swung his hand, stiff and flat, around in a vicious chop that caught the Russian in the throat and Logan felt the cartilage collapse. Instantly, Smyth-Davis struck with the bayonet, burying it to the guard in the Russian's lower chest, and blood gushed like water from a faucet.

The Russian made a hideous gurgling sound and started to fall but Logan caught the body and set it down gently, as quietly as possible. He snatched the Russian's pistol from its holster, handed the Tokarev to Smyth-Davis, then checked the chamber and the safety on the Makarov.

Only seconds were needed to check each of the upstairs rooms. All stood empty.

When they reached the stairs and started to descend, Logan kept to the right side, almost riding the bannister. Halfway down the stairs, Logan saw a man carrying a tray with a teapot and two cups. Intent on not spilling the tea, the Russian didn't see Logan until the American stepped in front of him, pistol pointed, a finger to his lips signing silence.

The Russian simply froze. Logan grinned and poured a cup of tea, then drank it. When Smyth-Davis appeared behind Logan, still bloody from killing the man upstairs, the Russian's eyes widened. Logan took the tray from him and set it on the floor, took the AK slung over the soldier's shoulder, leaned it against the doorway, then looked in the direction the soldier had been taking the tea. On the other side of the stairway stood a closed door.

Leaving the Brit to watch the prisoner, Logan crept to the door. He couldn't guess how the Russian soldier would've delivered the tea. Logan shrugged, tapped the door, said "tea" in Russian, and pushed the door open, pistol in hand.

Another Russian soldier, probably an officer, sat in the corner of the room, his feet resting on a desk. In the opposite corner sat a man in rumpled civilian clothing, tied to a chair. "Silence," Logan hissed in Russian, then, in English, muttered, "If you make a move or a sound, you'll be wearing the wall."

The Russian, if he didn't understand the words, certainly caught the meaning. "Take your pistol out," Logan whispered in Russian, "and put it on the desk."

The Russian swung his feet down then slowly opened the flap of his holster and, using only the tips of his fingers and thumb, drew his pistol. He'd almost placed the gun on the desk when it slipped from his fingers, then his right arm shot out and deflected Logan's gun hand.

In the closed space of the room the sharp crack of the shot hit the eardrums like a blow. Logan slammed his heel down on the Russian's instep, mentally cursing himself for having taken off his boots, then his left hand shot a jab into the Russian's short ribs.

The Russian grunted and drove his right fist at Logan's face while his left hand fumbled for the pistol he'd dropped on the desk. Logan's left hand punched upward into the Russian's elbow then he shoved his pistol under the man's chin and pulled the trigger, again and again.

As the Russian was flung backward, he collapsed into the chair and took it over with him as he sprawled to the floor, most of the top of his head now dripping from the ceiling. Logan whirled just as Smyth-Davis fired a short burst into the Russian who'd carried the tray, then the Englishman raced toward the back of the house, which echoed with gunfire and screams.

~ * ~

Steve had helped Smyth-Davis onto the roof and had taken a position at the back of the house where he could try to see into the kitchen window. A dim light appeared in the window then grew brighter but the glass was fogged and it was impossible to see anything but blurred shadows. He heard the clatter of wood being fed into the stove and, a few times, the grumble of sleepy male voices speaking Russian, although he couldn't make out the words.

Standing by the door, shivering, he wished he could lean or sit. As the room became warmer the mist on the window thickened then drops of water condensed, clearing lines in the fog. When he could finally look inside he saw three women and three Russian soldiers. The women were obviously making breakfast for their unwanted guests.

One of the soldiers picked up a tray with cups and a pot of tea and trod out of the kitchen, toward the front of the house. The other two soldiers sat at a small table, one with his back to the door, his rifle leaning against the wall, the other facing the door with his AK74 on the table. As one of the women, a girl in her early teens, walked past, the man grabbed at her skirt.

They all heard the sound of a pistol shot. Steve swung down with his carbine, smashing the glass of the window and fired two shots into the guard facing him, then snapped off two more shots at the back of the man who was reaching for his rifle.

Jan reached inside the broken window and twisted the latch then snatched open the door. As Jan and Steve almost fell into the kitchen the women stopped screaming and Steve heard Logan bellow, "Hold it!"

Steve screamed, "We're in!" then spun as a figure in a Russian uniform and carrying a gun dashed toward the kitchen from the front of the house. He swung the SKS around then dropped to the floor, shouting," Hold fire! It's us!" as he recognized the white bandage on Smyth-Davis' head.

Smyth-Davis stopped and lowered his submachine gun. "A bit hectic, isn't it lads?"

"Goddam disorganized—" Steve muttered, then noticed the

pile of guns and ammunition in the dining room. Already, four or five locals had rushed in through the open back door. Two of them had armed themselves with the AKs from the Russians in the kitchen and the rest dug through the mound of old Mauser and Moison rifles and double-barreled shotguns. Logan appeared for a moment in the dining room then stalked back to the front of the house. A few moments later a tall, sturdy man in rumpled clothing rushed from the front of the house to the kitchen.

Gunfire began from across the street. After the first few almost tentative shots the rattle of gunfire grew heavier and a fusillade of bullets slapped into the outside wall and shattered the front windows.

~ * ~

Reynaud glanced back as more Poles joined them, one wearing a heavy coat over a black cassock. Wonderful, he told himself. All he needed was a priest to add up penance while he shot at men hiding in a church. All they were waiting for was for Logan to open the ball.

The door to the sacristy was flung open and a Russian stepped outside. The man glanced around as he stamped his feet, then he turned and strode toward the vehicles. He was apparently headed for the BTR, an eight-wheeled metal monster topped with a small turret from which jutted a large gun barrel. The Russian opened a hatch and disappeared inside and, after a moment, the starter motor howled then the diesel engine roared to life, shooting black exhaust.

Reynaud glanced at the Deacon and the Finn. Juho seemed unconcerned, all his attention fixed on the bell tower, while the Deacon's lips moved, probably in prayer. Reynaud decided it was time to pray or curse and, since the Deacon was taking care of his end, the Cajun snarled an imprecation.

Adam pointed at Reynaud and the Finn, then at the steeple, then pointed to himself and the BTR. Reynaud considered it for a split-second then, reluctantly, nodded. Adam and Kasimir sprang to their feet and, staying in a crouch, rushed to the personnel carrier, taking cover beside the rear wheels.

Because of the noise of the diesel engine, Reynaud almost didn't hear the first shot fired in the mayor's house. He sighted in on the bell tower, just above the railing, and waited. A man appeared in the belfry then a second head bobbed up. As soon as the second man appeared, Juho fired, catching the first man in the neck. Reynaud and Billy Joe fired immediately after the shot, and the shots were so close together it sounded like one rifle. The second man went down, but the Deacon kept firing, his bullets slamming into the heavy wooden structure.

Working the lever of the Winchester, Reynaud glanced at the BTR. Both of the Poles had climbed into the carrier after Adam fired a shot into it. The machine abruptly lurched forward. The engine was only idling, but the carrier pulled across the lot to the church and was picking up speed when it struck the side of the building. For a moment he saw a contest between the wounded metal monster and the stout log wall, then the BTR's engine stalled.

Reynaud heard another shot nearby and realized he'd let himself be distracted. A Russian soldier had tumbled out the sacristy door, firing wildly, and Juho shot him through the chest. Another soldier appeared, carrying what looked like a LAW launcher. Reynaud shot the man just as he knelt beside the wall, then they heard the rattle of gunfire at the front of the church.

The gunshots were followed by the sound of glass shattering and the priest, shouting in Polish, dashed to the BTR, his cassock flapping. Suddenly, the heavy machine gun bellowed, a loud, thumping sound, and the wall of the church was obscured by a mist of frost and splinters as the gun pounded the building.

They heard more explosions at the front of the building and more Russians scrambled out the side door. Reynaud caught one of them in his sights and squeezed off a shot, swung the lever, and fired at another. The second shot kicked up a puff of snow fifty yards beyond the man he was aiming at. Reynaud worked the lever again, corrected, and the gun snapped on an empty chamber.

Frantically, Reynaud dug more ammunition out of his pocket, opened the action, and stuffed fresh rounds into the magazine.

By the time his weapon was loaded and charged, Juho had the magazine out of the SVD and was reloading it. Most of the Russians were down but two of them were still firing. One of them raised his rifle, which had a tube under the barrel, and fired the tube. Reynaud sighted on him and fired just as a puff of smoke shot from the tube. The Cajun saw the Russian slump, then had to duck, burying his face in the snow as the other soldier sprayed a burst of rifle fire at him.

Something exploded nearby and Reynaud felt something tug at his coat's back, then he was showered with snow.

In the momentary silence after the blast, Reynaud snapped to firing position and spotted the Russian rocking a fresh magazine into his rifle. Holding the sight just under the man's chest, Reynaud squeezed the trigger. Throwing up his arms and sending his rifle spinning into the show, the Russian dropped, face down, into the churned snow.

The Deacon had grunted and Reynaud turned to see him holding his left arm. Billy Joe took a single step forward then his left leg folded under him and he fell.

Juho stood like a rock, although Reynaud could see a hole in his coat.

Watching the Russians to be sure none were in any condition to shoot back, Reynaud dashed, crouched, to lean over the Deacon. "How bad are you hit?"

Billy Joe's long face showed no expression, although his voice was thick with pain. "Not too bad. I was hit in the arm and upper leg. I don't think either hit a bone or an artery. You'd better check the others."

Juho was bent over a Pole who was clutching his belly with both hands and kicking grooves in the snow. The man's face contorted into a mask of agony, with thick, dark blood running out of his mouth and into his beard. He coughed up more blood and made a horrible, gasping sound as he tried to draw in a breath. His eyes were wild with panic then they fixed on something a million miles past Reynaud's shoulder. The tormented face went slack and the Pole's body relaxed.

Another Pole lay in the snow, a ragged hole above his left eye. "Grenade," Juho said. "I was scratched."

"Let's move." Reynaud stared around at the damage. "The sooner we get this cleaned up, the sooner we can get the wounded into shelter." He joined the four or five Poles who'd dashed to the sacristy door. He realized then that the heavy machine gun on the vehicle had been silent for the last few minutes.

The BTR started again and backed away from the wall then

turned and rumbled out into the road, taking the northern route out of town.

Three of the Poles at the back of the church had already armed themselves with the Russians' weapons and the firing at the front of the building had stopped. Reynaud cranked the Winchester open and reloaded it then, staying close to the wall, side-stepped around to the sacristy and chanced a look inside. Seeing no movement, he slipped inside and crept to the door to look into the rest of the church.

His eyes hadn't had to adjust to the dimness to see daylight through the holes in the walls. Within the first few steps he almost tripped over the body of a soldier, and a glance assured him the man was dead, the whole left shoulder torn apart, the arm lying two or three feet away.

A figure appeared at the front door and Reynaud swung his rifle around then he heard Logan's voice say, "Jeez, they shot this place to kindling."

~ * ~

Logan had darted into the dining room, saw with relief Smyth-Davis hadn't gotten himself shot into doll rags by barging into the kitchen, then spun and snatched up the AK he'd taken from the Russian. In the office, the mayor seemed to be going mad and speaking Polish much too rapidly for Logan to understand. "The hostages are safe," Logan said, in Russian, then cut the man free. "Tell them to get out the back of the house and lie down." As the mayor rushed out of the room Logan swung up the rifle to knock out the small window in the office when the first burst of rifle fire slapped into the wall, then something heavy hit the wall near the window and exploded, blowing glass through the room.

Looking out the shattered window, Logan saw a Russian carrying a rifle with a tube under the barrel. He shoved the barrel of his own AK out the window and touched off a burst that slammed into the church wall and pounded the soldier, who'd been running for the corner of the building. The Russian was hit in mid-stride and fell, spinning, to wind up on his back.

As Logan fired, something smashed the window in the next room and exploded, the blast making his ears ring. Logan shifted his sights to cover the dark rectangle of the church door and fired another short burst. Another Russian stumbled out into the street, trying to hold his guts in. He stumbled three paces forward then half-turned. His knees folded, dumping him onto his back.

All hell seemed to break loose as a heavy machine gun made its rolling thunder and the whole church seemed to quiver. Another man stumbled through the door, a machine gun in his arms, firing wildly. A single shot from the next room answered and the Russian collapsed.

Almost immediately another Russian lurched into the church's doorway, pointing a rocket at the mayor's house. Logan held down the AK's trigger and the man jerked strangely, one leg kicking upward almost in a dancer's step, then the soldier fell back into the church.

Logan decided to spray into the church's windows but when he pulled the trigger, nothing happened. Yanking the bolt open, he saw the weapon was empty. Snarling wordlessly, he pressed the magazine release and ripped the magazine out of the weapon. He dashed into the dining room and saw four men down; three Poles and Smyth-Davis lay sprawled on the floor.

Logan bent over what was left of the Russian's body and found the magazine pouch, tore out two magazines, and loaded one into the AK.

The Pole in the far corner was obviously dead, almost decapitated by shrapnel. The man on the other side of the window was, unfortunately, still alive but only semi-conscious, just enough to scream. His right leg was gone from below the knee and his back was liberally peppered with shrapnel wounds. The man just beyond him had taken less steel from the grenade but his left arm bent at an unnatural angle. Smyth-Davis was trying to struggle to his feet although his eyes couldn't seem to focus, there was a hole in his left sleeve, and blood ran down his arm to drip from his fingers.

"Just stay down," Logan said. "If your head clears up enough to get up, just look after these guys." After charging the rifle, he shoved open the bullet-scarred front door.

Nothing moved in the street or in the door of the church. Holding the rifle at the ready, Logan darted across the street and slammed, back first, against the side of the building. Hearing nothing, he stepped into the doorway of the church.

The sight inside almost overwhelmed him; the place was a shambles. The ornate hand-carved wooden altar was holed and broken with chunks of painted wood torn away and the pews were shattered and thrown about. Something moved near the back of the church and Logan recognized the Cajun. "Jeez, they shot this place to kindling."

The two of them examined the corpses. Most of them had been shot down by the heavy machine gun or by secondary missiles. They collected the weapons, most of which were undamaged, and stepped outside. As they reached the door they heard small-arms fire to the west of town and, to the north, more light weapons laced with the deeper pounding of the heavy machine gun.

"Sounds like the Poles are cleaning up the Russian road guards," Reynaud observed. They stacked the captured weapons by the front door then Reynaud jerked a thumb in the direction of the back of the church. "We've got wounded out back. Give me a hand, will you?"

Stepping out the back door, they saw Juho supporting the Deacon, limping toward them.

"The building is clear," Logan said. "Go on across the street. We'll clean up here."

The priest knelt between two dead Poles, praying and anointing the bodies with oil. Another Pole had a wound in his hip and had broken his left arm when he fell. Logan and Reynaud helped him to the mayor's house, which had become a makeshift hospital—and morgue. Of the four men caught in the front room by the grenade, two were dead while another, besides a shattered elbow, had been only lightly wounded.

Smyth-Davis was up and moving again, although slowly. The wound on his forearm had already been dressed and he cocked an eyebrow at their approach. "It seems everyone in our merry little band has survived the recent excitement. Not bad for amateurs, eh?"

"Lucky amateurs," Reynaud replied. "How badly were you hit?"

"Just a nick in the arm. Oh, and the headache's back."

Juho had taken off his coat and the shirt under it and one of the women daubed at a long wound across his chest. A piece of shrapnel had nicked the bottom of his left arm then torn a long gash across his chest. The Deacon's wounds were painful but not serious; a shallow wound in his left thigh and another in his left upper arm.

After assuring himself he could do nothing to help the wounded men, Reynaud strode out behind the house to the Russian bodies, which had been dumped out onto the snow to make room for the Polish wounded. Besides basic military equipment, the first corpse he examined carried a small black book bound in leather or plastic. Reynaud opened the book, glanced at a photograph of the dead soldier and several lines of Russian writing. Not being able to read Russian, the book was of no use to him but, if he could get it back to someone in authority, it might be a valuable source of information for someone.

Searching the other bodies turned up more of the books but little else of use or interest. He'd begun to shiver at the cold. As he returned to the house he motioned Logan aside. "Have you seen Steve?"

"I think he hauled ass with some of the Poles to kill a few Russ road guards."

"Did you notice the soldiers were wearing undershirts with blue and white stripes?"

"Come to think of it, even the officer was wearing one."

"What do you think it means?"

"Lousy fashion coordinators?"

Reynaud shrugged. "I'd just like to know who I've been killing."

The priest entered the house and prayed over the dead Poles, then spoke quietly with each of the wounded, anointing them. By the time he'd finished his ministrations, Steve and the Poles who'd gone to assault the road guards returned. "One of the Russians almost got away," Steve said.

The priest approached them as Reynaud showed Steve the books the soldiers had been carrying and picked up one of the books. "It is a paybook," he said, in heavily accented English. "It is sort of a diary. It will tell you where he has been stationed and with what units he has served." He flipped through the pages. "According to this, he is of the Hundred and Third Guards Air

Assault Division of the VDV."

"What does that mean?"

"They are Russian paratroopers. I do not think you can find out from this book, though, whether they might be FSB or Spetznaz."

"Thank you, Father," Steve said. He introduced the rest of the group. "Do you think the villagers will let us take this vehicle? We're trying to reach Krakow."

"Not immediately," the priest replied. "I am Father Vadim Szymanski. First you will need to be fed and your wounds tended. We will have the funerals for our dead tonight, and there will be a wake afterward. If I know my flock, the wake will become a celebration that we are only holding funerals for six of our men. You may be able to leave in two or three days."

"Hot damn!" Logan exclaimed. "A party! After six months of rotten food and worse company, I can wait a few more days to get back, especially if it's for a party."

The former prisoners were well-fed and given rooms upstairs in which to sleep, and were roused only when it was time for the funeral Mass. After the Mass, the bodies of the six Poles were buried in graves dug in the rock-hard ground then everyone returned to the mayor's house. All the men of the village seemed to be crowded into the front room and dining room and the wake started with men standing and solemnly toasting the men who'd died.

Two hours later the vodka was being put away without the ceremony of a toast. Reynaud's ears burned as he understood part of the speech given by the mayor, which made the other ex-prisoners and himself sound a little like a cross between the Lone Ranger, Robin Hood, and the Second Coming.

Time and faces began to blur. He ate the food he was given and drank the vodka, which was served ice-cold and which went down as smoothly as water. He reached the point where he no longer winced when someone slapped him on the back. He vaguely remembered stumbling upstairs to fall across the bed and, on waking, stumbling back downstairs, where the eating and drinking continued. He could never remember how many times he made the trip up and down the stairs or outside, to the toilet.

He didn't know whether it was two or three days later when

he woke with a throbbing head, a mouth that tasted and felt as though the Chinese army had been holding mud maneuvers in it, and a stomach that was one large, angry knot. He forced himself out of bed and shambled to the nightstand, broke the film of ice on the water in the pitcher, poured it into the basin, then buried his face in the icewater. His screams came to the surface in a shower of bubbles.

At least the shock brought him back to full consciousness.

When he made his way downstairs he found the women in the kitchen. They'd made tea, something that looked like bacon, and, surprisingly, eggs. Large kettles at the back of the stove steamed and Reynaud asked the older woman what she was cooking.

"Not cooking. Is for bath."

Reynaud had started on breakfast but he looked up. "Oh, do you want me to leave?"

"Is for *your* bath."

Reynaud finished breakfast, then one of the women rolled in a large wooden tub, poured in water from melted snow, and added a kettle of water from the stove. The woman gestured for Reynaud to undress.

"With you in here?"

"I've seen men before."

"Not this one."

"*Bathe!*"

Reynaud reluctantly peeled off his clothes and tried to hide himself as much as possible until he realized the women were largely ignoring his nudity. He found himself a little disappointed the women found him so easy to ignore. After stepping into the tub he sat in the warm water with a sigh. His last few baths had been cold-water showers and they'd been irregular. He was handed a cake of hard soap and scrubbed himself vigorously while one of the women scrubbed his back with a brush. He even washed his hair and face with the lye soap and ducked under the water to rinse it away. When he felt he'd finally washed away the accumulated grime he stepped into another tub and a bucket of clean, warm water was dumped on him and he was handed a towel.

He was very pleased to see freshly cleaned clothes waiting for him; a Russian winter uniform with the holes carefully patched. When he finished dressing, Steve walked down the stairs, apparently none the worse for wear—until Reynaud noticed a faint trembling and eyes that looked like bicycle reflectors. "Eat breakfast first," Reynaud advised. "You want to give the ladies time to at least skim the scum off the top of the water."

Steve grunted a reply and dropped into a chair.

One by one, the other former prisoners descended the stairs, ate breakfast, and bathed. The only one who balked at bathing with the women in the room was McCluskey.

"You got a choice," Logan told him. "You can get rid of the stink, or you can run along behind the car."

"Remember," Steve added, "cleanliness is next to Godliness."

Still grumbling, the Deacon submitted to undressing in front of the women and having his back scrubbed. As the Deacon dried himself with a towel, Logan grinned at him. "I'd feel awful silly making such a big fuss over such a little thing."

They checked their equipment and, just before stepping outside, donned clean white Russian coveralls then walked out to the BTR. Kasimir, dressed as they were, was putting the finishing touches on paint applied to the vehicle. The Poles had painted a black rectangle on the front of the hull, with the Polish eagle in white. On the sides of the turret they'd painted the red and white Polish flag.

"I'll drive you to Komancza," Kasimir said, "where I have a cousin. You can refuel there and he will take you into Krakow."

They climbed into the carrier and Kasimir started the engines, Reynaud learned the BTR had two engines to drive its eight wheels and soon learned both motors were fuel hogs.

With the driving snow, which had deepened during the wake, he couldn't have found the road, and even Kasimir had to keep the speed to about twenty kilometers per hour, about the speed at which a man could run. Occasionally, they had to climb out to clear snow from some of the deeper drifts across the road.

Just after noon they pulled into what was left of a town Kasimir identified as Cisna. It'd been a fair-sized town before the war and the plague—they could tell that from the rubble. Now, it was a deserted ruin with only a single building still standing, its shattered windows like blind eyes watching the road, while some of the remains of the town were only indistinguishable lumps under a blanket of snow. They counted the hulks of eight armored vehicles, either burned out or blown up.

"What the hell do you think went down here?" Logan asked.

"Russians," Kasimir replied, and spat on the metal wall beside him. "They must have struck Cisna when they were falling back. This is what they left."

Reynaud and Billy Joe dismounted from the BTR, the Deacon carrying his new weapon; an AK74 with the tube of a grenade launcher mounted under the barrel. The fuel, for which they'd come in the first place, had either been taken or used.

"I hope Komancza is in a lot better shape," Reynaud said, "or it looks like we're going to have to get out and walk again."

In the early afternoon the snow started again and the wind howled and shook its fist at the vehicle and they had to slow to little more than a walk. By late afternoon, they'd begun to worry night would find them still on the road and out of fuel, then they began to see more armored hulks, like the discarded carapaces of monster insects.

"We're almost there!" Kasimir shouted.

"Any idea what we'll find there?" Steve asked.

Kasimir shrugged. "My cousin, I hope."

"Let's hope that's your cousin with the tankbuster, and he's just brimming over with family feeling." Logan pointed to where a man with a man with an assault rifle had stepped out of a snow-covered mound and they could see another man, to their left, with a rocket-propelled anti-tank weapon pointed at the personnel carrier.

Kasimir stopped the BTR and climbed outside, moving slowly, careful not to alarm the men. Steve had climbed into the turret and already sighted on the man with the rocket launcher. They watched as Kasimir and the man with the AK talked. Both men gestured broadly, Kasimir more violently. Within a few moments Kasimir led the other man back to the vehicle and both clambered inside. Kasimir introduced the other Pole to them then climbed back into the driver's seat and the BTR advanced.

The road led upward then dipped, and a town appeared. The street was almost blocked with more burned-out hulks and several houses had been reduced to rubble but the rest of the town, although battered, had apparently survived the assault.

They found Kasimir's cousin, Andrzej, who agreed to take them where they could contact the perimeter of the Krakow garrison. They learned the worst battles had been in Germany and northwestern Poland and, while some Russian units had fallen back in good order, many more had disintegrated into armed rabble and bandit gangs. Andrzej also found them a place to spend the night.

~ * ~

In the morning they traded their extra equipment and some of their rations for enough fuel to top off their tanks and left at dawn in the ghastly light and deathly stillness that follows a snowstorm. They passed through ruins of small towns, other towns battered but still standing, and eventually they reached a city where the ORMO, the militia, gave them passes.

The light faded as they reached the city of Nowy Sacz, which had once had a population of over thirty thousand. The city was now held by the militia and what appeared to be about a company of regular army troops. The group and their driver were given a place to sleep and, early in the morning, set out on the last leg of the trip to Krakow. A working telephone line still ran from Nowy Sacz to Krakow and the army troops sent three of their men along, as well as notified the Krakow garrison that escaped Allied prisoners were on their way to the city.

While they'd been allowed to keep their weapons, Reynaud worried. He hadn't expected a ticker-tape parade but their treatment was uncomfortably close to that accorded prisoners. When they arrived at the outskirts of Krakow they were given an escort to a complex of massive ancient buildings the guard identified as the Wawel.

A Polish officer approached the BTR. "Follow me, please," he said, in accented English. As the group climbed out of the personnel carrier, the officer turned and gestured. "You will leave your weapons with the vehicle, please." Despite the courtesy, it wasn't a request.

The officer led them to an ornate antechamber which, while it was far more impressive, reminded the Cajun of a dentist's waiting room. He began to look around for year-old magazines.

The Polish officer stared at each of them in turn then asked, "Who is your senior officer?"

They looked at each other in confusion. They'd forgotten rank. The officer scanned their faces then crooked a finger at Reynaud.

Reynaud stood and followed the Pole into an office.

Two men sat behind a desk in the office and one of them gestured at a chair. "Have a seat. I'm Frank Piotrowski," the man said, in perfect American English. The man's Polish army uniform was topped with a green beret bearing an American Special Forces badge.

Chapter 4

Reynaud sank into a chair, staring at Piotrowski, his mind working rapidly. His first feeling was it was some kind of trick; that a Pole who spoke American was going to interrogate him then he caught at another thought. There was no need to play games with prisoners who had no worthwhile military information. He nodded at the green beret. "I'm Reynaud Dechaine, first lieutenant, U. S. Air Force."

"Frank Piotrowski, formerly captain, U. S. Army."

Reynaud smiled. "Formerly? What are you now?"

"Now I'm a sort of liason with the Krakow ORMO. This gentleman with me is Captain Wyszynski, Polish army. I've got to admit the situation is a little confusing. I'll be happy to update you. How long have you been out of it?"

"I was shot down about six months ago." Reynaud studied the men behind the desk. Piotrowski appeared to be shorter, with a slim but powerful build and a baby face with brown eyes. The Pole was tall and so blond his hair was almost white. Both men impressed him as being direct.

Piotrowski leaned back in his chair. "I guess you went out close to the end of the first phase. The second phase was dominated by ground combat, as the air forces on both sides were depleted. Nobody knows what started it but the Russians stormed across Poland and into northeastern Germany and got thrown back.

"The Russians regrouped and counterattacked and shoved the line back into Germany. The Poles fought the Russians, even after the first assault then fought the Germans, who seem to have decided to go after some of the territory they lost after World War II. Most of the Russian reserves never made it to the Polish border. Those that hadn't deserted had too much to do at home. Some of the better Russian units made a fighting withdrawal, while some of the others circled the wagons and held fast.

"It looked like everyone was ready to call it a draw and go home, then Colonel Marcus found out a lot of allied pilots were being held in a Russian camp near the Polish border. The Polish government had collapsed so Marcus contacted the Polish military and cut a deal with them to let him run a rescue column through the country. The colonel grabbed whatever NATO units were available and took volunteers.

"We were about ninety clicks from Krakow when we were hit by the remnants of two Russian divisions. They creamed us—really chopped us to pieces. We'd hurt them on the way down, though, and the Polish army moved in and mopped up the Russians.

"I was Colonel Marcus' liason officer. I'm first-generation Polish-American—grew up in Motor City. I decided to stay here, where I could help rebuild Poland. Now that you know about me, it's your turn. Where were you kept?"

"I don't know the name of the place. It was near the Czech and Polish borders."

"Sounds like Zheltyye Vody. They used to have a Spetznaz training center near there. Major Phillips made it back from there about a week ago."

"What? That's bullshit!" Reynaud leaned forward in his chair, almost springing to his feet. "I saw Carl Phillips die, I knew Carl; he was in our barracks. He was beaten to death by a walking pile of shit named Chernikov."

The other two men stared at each other. "You're certain?" Piotrowski demanded. "No possible mistake?"

"Not a chance. What did the guy calling himself Phillips look like?"

Piotrowski frowned, an expression of intense concentration. "Big man, about six-one, close to two hundred pounds. Had his hair cropped close. Brownish hair and gunmetal blue eyes. And he was very fastidious; the first things he asked for after a bath and a shave was a fresh uniform."

Reynaud leaped to his feet. "That's Chernikov, the Russian commandant! Where's the bastard now?"

Piotrowski and Wyszynski both looked at the floor and Piotrowski's face reddened with embarrassment. "We repatriated him," he said in a low voice. "We sent him back to Belgium on the last C-5 to go back. Excuse me for a moment." He stood and strode from the room.

Reynaud prowled around the room, trying to pace off some

of his anger, barely able to keep from pounding or kicking the furniture in his rage.

"What about the man with him?" the Polish officer asked.

Reynaud spun to face him. "What man?"

"He identified himself as Lieutenant Carter. About four centimeters shorter than the other man. Perhaps ten kilos heavier. Blond, with gray eyes."

"That was Lieutenant Oshevsky, Chernikov's second-in-command at the camp. Did he get away, too?"

"No, he's here—in Krakow." He looked down at his hands. "We will have our men bring him in."

Frank strode back into the room. "They're going to try to pick the man up in Belgium." He sat as Wyszynski rounded the desk to sit on the edge. "Your guards, what color shoulder boards did they wear, and what were the markings?"

Reynaud had to stop and remember. "Dark red boards with yellow lettering. The letters looked like two capital Bs."

"MVD." Wyszynski snapped. "Interior army. They're known for political reliability, stupidity, and brutality."

"As far as I can tell, their record is intact," Reynaud said.

"What about this Chernikov and the lieutenant—Oshevsky? Did they have the same shoulder boards?"

"No," Reynaud replied. "They came to the camp about two months after I got there and replaced the original commandant and his aide. They didn't seem to get along with the regular guards. They both wore blue shoulder boards—looked like about a royal blue. The letters looked like a circle with a vertical line through it, a capital C and what looked like the number six."

The Pole frowned and turned to Piotrowski. "FSB Special Units. It looks as though this operation was planned some time ago." He faced Reynaud. "We think the plague was started by the CIA, the FSB, or both together. We think they were trying to beat each other in bacteriological warfare, and everyone lost."

Frank nodded. "Everybody lost, all right. After the president and vice-president died of plague the Secretary of State took over. He was securely in the pocket of the CIA before he ever took the oath of office."

Reynaud stared at Frank as though he'd changed into a *loup garou*. "And he's running the country?"

"No, he was assassinated within two months. The plague hit the states with a vengeance and, in the riots and general madness, the presidency became a relic. The only people he had any power over were his immediate circle and whoever they could point a gun at. There hasn't been any real national government in the states since."

"God!" Reynaud tried to grasp the notion his country was no longer a country.

"The Russians didn't do any better," Frank continued, "Three quarters of the *Politburo* died of the plague or were assassinated. The head of the FSB took over for a while but a lot of army units refused to obey their orders. A few of the smaller units actually defected to Poland. About two months ago, about the same time as the collapse in the states, several Russian army units, spear-headed by Spetznaz troops, took out the FSB government that had been set up in Petrograd after Moscow was flattened."

"Isn't Spetznaz part of the old KGB or the FSB?"

"No, Spetznaz is the action arm of the GRU, the Russian military intelligence branch. They and a bunch of paratroopers—*desantniki*, the Russians call them—toppled the FSB regime, which most Russians thoroughly detested."

"So who's running the show there now?"

Piotrowski spread his hands "It's a mess. If it's Tuesday, the army is probably back in."

Lieutenant Wyszynski returned to questions about the camp, the number of prisoners and guards, and any Russian units they'd encountered on their way to Krakow. Reynaud handed over the two Russian paybooks he'd kept and told them the rest of the books were in the BTR.

Finally, Wyszynski returned to his chair behind the desk. "Lieutenant Dechaine, we'll try to get you out of Poland and back to your own country as soon as we can. Until then, I will give you a pass. You may stay in the barracks and take your meals at our mess."

Frank spoke up quickly. "I'll be responsible for the lieutenant and his friends." Frank and the Polish officer stared at each other for several moments, as though holding a silent conversation.

At last, Wyszynski nodded. "Very well. I will give you chits for the mess hall and you can meet him there later." He smiled at Reynaud. "Your friends will join you there as soon as we have spoken with them."

Frank opened the door and said something in Polish to the guard outside, who gestured to Reynaud and led him to the mess hall.

While the food was plain, there was enough of it. The tea was awful. After eating, Reynaud made himself as comfortable as possible and tried to digest both the meal and the information he'd acquired. He'd just found a comfortable position in which to doze when Logan strode into the mess hall.

Before Logan had finished his meal, they were joined by Smyth-Davis. One by one. The rest of the escapees drifted into the hall and gathered around the table Reynaud had chosen.

Smyth-Davis smiled slightly as the Americans compared notes on the information Frank had given them. "What's so amusing?" Reynaud finally asked.

"I was just thinking of how I shall have to adjust to being a subject of a monarchy. I rather wonder if King William has revoked the Magna Carta."

"Sounds like England is as crazy as the states," Steve said.

Reynaud rubbed the back of his neck. He felt awkward asking the Englishman any sort of personal question. "Do you have family waiting for you?"

"None." Smyth-Davis paused a moment. "I'm divorced and there are no children."

At that moment, Frank appeared at the door, located the group, and approached. "Thanks for waiting. I wanted to see you guys to discuss 'matters of importance.' There's a bar not too far from here. You up for it?"

"Any time," Reynaud said as he got to his feet.

Frank led them outside. For a moment, Reynaud stared back at the Wawel, squinting through eyes narrowed against the snow, which had begun to fall again, and the wind, which was driving the tumbling flakes diagonally. The complex of buildings, with their pillars and Romanesque arches gave the impression that they were ancient when New Amsterdam was a village with a log palisade.

"Hey," Logan announced, to most of Krakow, "somebody's

stolen the BTR."

"Don't worry," Frank said. "The army's got it. If you need to leave the city, it'll be returned to you."

"That's damned small consolation," Logan roared. "Everything we had, including our rifles, were in that car."

"Don't get bent," Frank said, "this is Krakow. You don't need all that hardware now. You gotta have a positive mental attitude."

"Bullshit!" Logan said, very positively. "I'm not leaving myself naked in a city like this and leave my safety in the hands of a bunch of third-stringers."

"Take it easy, man," Frank said, with a pumping gesture with his hands as though he were trying to physically lower the volume of Logan's outrage. "You've still got your sidearms, and I'll get your rifles released to you as soon as I can get you formally enlisted in the ORMO, and I think I can take care of that tomorrow. Besides, there's no open warfare in the city."

"What kind of warfare is there?" Reynaud asked.

"Very sharp. We'll discuss that at the bar. This street," he pointed to the cross street they'd just released, "is *Paulinska.*" He pointed to a building near the end of the street. "Just past the trees is the Vistula, which the Poles call *Wisla.* The bar is at the end of that last building."

A sign at the front of the section he'd indicated proclaimed *Zyc, Nie Umierac!*

"The best translation for that," Frank said, "is 'this is the life!'"

"You sure that's a bar?" Logan demanded. "I don't see a 'Coors on tap' sign."

"Take my word for it. A couple of friends of mine should be waiting for us."

The twilight dimness of the bar seemed even darker because of the group's snow blindness. The group stood just inside the bar until they could see the three steps leading down to the sunken floor. The weak light was provided by alcohol lamps. The bar ran almost the length of the far wall and a dozen tables were scattered throughout the open room. Most of the tables were occupied by soldiers in uniform, and some of the others by men in rough work clothes, but a single table was surrounded by four men in ill-fitting civilian suits.

Following Frank, they threaded their way between the tables and chairs to a table just far enough from the bar to permit discreet conversation. Two men sat at the table, one wearing olive-drab battledress and the other in the greenish Polish raindrop camouflage. As Reynaud sat, he scrutinized them. The man in the Polish uniform was older, perhaps forty, with a rugged face, marred only by what looked like pockmarks, and a very military handlebar moustache. He wore a black beret with a Polish eagle on the side. The other man was younger, although Reynaud couldn't have guessed his age within five years with any confidence. His refined features were set off with deepset eyes and a neatly trimmed black moustache and chin beard, and his red beret was canted to the left, opposite the fashion of all the other berets in the bar. On the side of the beret he wore a large circular badge with a winged fist holding a dagger or short sword.

Frank drew an empty chair from another table and sat, waiting for the others in the group to find chairs, then introduced the two men as Tadeusz Woydziak and Jean-Marie St. Jacques. The Pole gave the impression of iron competence, while the Frenchman lounged with a sort of feline grace.

When Reynaud's name was mentioned, St. Jacques' lips twitched and he looked more closely at the Cajun. When the introductions were complete, he asked, *"Etes vous francais?"*

"Non," Reynaud replied. *"Je suis un acadian."*

"I was thinking of extending our hospitality to these guys," Frank said.

"Is that wise?" The Frenchman's English was slow and precise, with an emphasis on the th sound, as though he had to stress it to remember to say it at all. He leaned toward the group. "I do not wish to suggest you are not welcome, but we have attracted some…untoward attention."

"They're the ones who brought word our last 'escapees' were FSB agents," Frank said. "I think they've already made the hit list on their own."

A stocky young blond woman strolled to the table and Jean Marie leaned toward Reynaud. "They have a fine dry wine from the Georgia that used to be a Soviet republic."

Reynaud ordered the wine; Logan, Smyth-Davis, and Steve

had whiskey with a beer chaser, the Finn had vodka; while Billy Joe firmly refused to drink anything but water. "'Wine is a mocker, strong drink is raging,'" he quoted.

"I'm raging just a little myself, right now," Logan grumbled. "First, I get left naked except for a little bitty pistol—"

"Two little bitty pistols," Frank pointed out.

"Then I get drafted into the Polish army, now I'm a sitting target and I'm being put into harness with a crowd with possible bizarre personal habits…" He stared at the Frenchman as he finished.

Brown eyes generally seemed warm and soft, Reynaud thought, but Jean-Marie's eyes were cold and hard; as if they were peering through a gunsight. After looking back and forth between the two men, Reynaud realized the source of their apparent mutual dislike. They were both predators but St. Jacques was a cat, while Logan was more like a wolverine.

"Drink up, Shriners," Frank said. "I think this discussion should be finished more privately."

Reynaud, who'd been sipping the surprisingly good wine, drained the glass in a swallow as the rest of the group bolted down their drinks. Taking out a bundle of what looked like military script, Frank left most of it on the table and they made their way into the street, buttoning their coats. Frank and the Pole led them east along *Paulinska*, then south.

Jean-Marie, who'd been at the rear of the group, paced rapidly to the front, leaned toward Frank, and murmured, "It seems we have two gentlemen following us. I enjoy good conversation, and they look as though we might have interests in common. The two men have each gone to opposite sides of the street, so I will require assistance in striking up an acquaintanceship. You might have one or two people wait somewhere discreet on this side of the street to offer one of them directions to our apartment."

Logan heard St. Jacques' remarks. "If you can handle one of them, I'll take the other. If you're still alive when it's over, you can lead us to the rest of the crowd."

For a moment the Frenchman stared coldly at him then said, "We should not wish to disturb any neighbors with unnecessary noise."

"Fine by me." Logan slammed his right fist into his left

hand and ground it against the palm.

Within a score of paces they'd reached a narrow alley on their left and, directly across the street, a dark arch of doorway. The Frenchman whipped off his coat and strode across the street, dragging his coat to obscure his tracks, leaving only faint marks quickly hidden by the drifting snow. Logan slipped into the alley, wiping out his own tracks as he went.

~ * ~

From where he stood against the wall, Logan was unable to see the Frenchman in the shallow cave of the doorway. He considered putting his coat back on then decided he could bear the cold and he wanted his arms free. If whoever followed them was bright enough to be bundled up, it would be a waste of time to use body blows, which would be cushioned by a heavy coat.

He began to shiver with the cold and to wonder whether the Frenchman hadn't just been paranoid when he heard the faint crunching of footsteps in the dry snow.

A man across the street, walking as rapidly as he could safely move, was already past the doorway and another man, in bulky work clothes, reached the alley. The Frenchman struck. He appeared behind the man across the street and kicked at the backs of his knees. As the man went down, St. Jacques kicked again, with a move that looked a little like a martial art, a little like ballet.

Logan heard the crack as the man's head snapped to the side and he collapsed into the snow.

The man at the mouth of the alley spun to stare across the street and Logan caught the shoulder of his coat, spun him around, and drove his right fist into the man's face. The man gave a muffled cry as his nose was smashed level with his cheekbones. Moving his hands to the man's coat collar, Logan jerked the man into the alley, lowering his head. He butted the man in the face, followed it by slamming his knee into the man's crotch.

The man's legs wobbled but his right hand reached into his coat. Logan trapped the hand with his left while he thrust his right at the enemy's face, thumb stabbing.

He felt the thumb drive into the man's eye and he closed his fingers around the opposite temple, so he was holding the man's head almost like a bowling ball. Swinging him around, he drove the back of the man's head into the brick wall, again and again. At each impact the head made a more liquid sound.

"Shit!" Logan said, as he let the body fall. "This is messy work." He bent over the corpse and wiped his hand on the man's coat.

"If you were trying to determine whether the wall or his head was the harder, I could have told you." The Frenchman stood in the mouth of the alley. "I misjudged my kick. The other one is too dead for conversation, and I suspect this one has succumbed to an excess of your enthusiasm. You should learn economy of force."

"Hey, John, a good fight is like good sex. You wouldn't hurry that, would you?"

"*Touché.* Take his weapon and any papers you find on the body. A street patrol will probably be by here soon, and I would rather be absent then."

Logan quickly pilfered the corpse. The pistol resembled the ones he'd already taken from the Russian officers but with a silencer actually built into the gun. In the right coat pocket he found a thin wallet and, in a pants pocket, a thick wad of papers that seemed to be the same sort of script as that Frank used to pay the bar bill. He pocketed the wallet, the weapon, and the papers, then pulled on his coat and darted after St. Jacques across the street.

As they reached the other side of the street, Logan grinned at the Frenchman. "I gotta admit, when you dance with somebody you really sweep them off their feet."

"Thank you," St. Jacques replied. "On my part, I must admit your methods, while they lack elegance, are efficacious."

Since the rest of the group was already long out of sight, St. Jacques led Logan on a tour of the back streets and alleys of that part of Krakow, frequently slowing to obscure their trail.

Logan was thoroughly chilled by the time St. Jacques turned to climb a short flight of steps to the door of an apartment house. He turned his key in the lock then waved Logan ahead of him into a room that looked like an office, with a couple of desks and several chairs. Pacing across the room, St. Jacques stepped through a doorway into a dining room.

Sitting at the table with the former prisoners, Frank, and

Tadeusz, a dark-haired, dark-eyed woman with an oval face stared at them. The woman was beautiful, with a figure, even hidden in a bulky Polish army uniform, that reminded Logan how long it'd been since he'd seen an attractive woman.

"Logan Reid, this is Zdenka Petrovna Jeroskaya." Apparently noticing worried expressions of the people in the room, St. Jacques asked, "What is wrong?"

"Katya has not returned yet," Zdenka said. Her English had a decidedly Russian accent.

Another, older woman, stout, with graying hair, entered the room with a platter of food. Her face, too, seemed to hover at the edge of fear.

"This is Anya," St. Jacques sat in one of the chairs and introduced the woman to Logan. "Anya is Katya's aunt. After we'd been scattered by the Russian counterattack we became lost. Katya was a member of the partisan band that found us, and she led us to Polish troops and then to Krakow." His lips twitched into a hint of a grin. "More precisely, she found Frank, just as he was answering the call of nature. Both hands were occupied at the time, so there was not much he could do when he found a twelve-year-old girl pointing a Mauser rifle at him."

St. Jacques turned in his chair to face Frank. "When did she leave and where did she go?"

"Anya says she left at about noon to get potatoes at the market." Frank sipped at a glass of water. "Laura hasn't gotten back yet, either."

"Laura can watch out for herself." Zdenka's tone suggested Laura wouldn't be greatly missed. "But Katya—if anything has happened to Katya…" She scowled and her fingers touched the hilt of the knife she wore. Logan noticed it looked very much like the knife he'd taken from the Russian corporal.

Frank looked at his watch. "Curfew is in another twenty-five minutes. I'll go to the guard station and check with the guards if she hasn't gotten back by then. I'll also pull a day off so all of us can go looking for her tomorrow. Maybe she went to visit her cousin, Stefan."

"Is there anything we can do?" Reynaud asked.

"Not now, at least," Frank sipped again at the water. "Your temporary passes aren't enough to keep you out of the brig if you're caught after curfew. We'll just wait. I'll take you all in tomorrow and get you into the ORMO. It's just a temporary duty assignment until we can get you out of the country but it'll give you freedom from the curfew and let you carry your guns on the street."

Logan picked at his food but at the first bite he realized he was famished. The ham and chicken loaf was served in rather suspicious-looking, rectangular blocks but tasted very good. "Where'd you get this stuff?" he asked Frank around another mouthful.

"When the Poles rescued us they grabbed several truckloads of MREs and turned over one of them to our group. We've been using the supplies to feed the survivors of the rescue column until we could repatriate them. We've still got enough of these compact meals to last us a year."

Logan had worked his way through the meat, crackers that were apparently made of stamped steel, some passably good beans in tomato sauce, and the first coffee he'd had since before he'd been shot down. He looked up to see Frank pulling apart the wallet the Frenchman had handed him. Inside the lining was a colored fabric patch. "What've you got there?"

Frank stared grimly at the piece of cloth. "The clowns that were following us used to be ZOMOs."

"What the hell is that?" Logan luxuriated in the taste of another sip of coffee.

"The ZOMOs were the bastards that used to be the riot police and general government thugs about a generation or so ago. The old Soviet-dominated Polish government used them for their dirty work. The army always had a good rep in Poland, and the government didn't want it tarnished by using them for shit jobs. Also, the army might not be counted on to beat or shoot children or old people. The ZOMOs were a bunch of dumb bastards who were awfully loyal, especially if they got to torment people brighter than they were, which was most of the population. We think a lot of the old ZOMOs are working for the FSB, who find their character flaws useful."

Logan swallowed the last of his coffee. "That's not the first time you've hinted there's still some kind of war going on. Give."

Frank glanced at the rest of his group. "It's kind of a long story," he said.

"We've got lots of time," Steve replied.

St. Jacques smiled. "I can go to the guard station for you, Frank."

Anya brought in bowls of sliced peaches. As Logan ate, savoring the sweet taste, the minor luxury of peaches, almost certainly from dehydrated rations, brought on a bout of homesickness.

"Okay," Frank said. "It's related to Polish politics. With Warsaw in rubble, Krakow is again the capital of Poland. General Macharski could probably get away with running the country but he's a good soldier, and he wants Poland to have a legitimate government. Without one, Poland will be tied up in civil war for years. So, the military has called for a General Congress here in Krakow, in the spring. Then there'll be military and civilian authorities from all over the country coming here; in fact, some of them will be on their ways as soon as the roads will permit."

"I can't overstate the importance of this—it's like a Constitutional Convention for Poland, and it'll decide who runs the country, how they run it, and who they form alliances with. The Church is also deeply involved. Colonel Klasa, General Macharski's man here in Krakow, is working on it with Rysard Cardinal Krol.

"The FSB sees this as an opportunity to either keep Poland destabilized or get it wired with the FSB high command, which still has hopes of controlling Russia. In fact, strong FSB influence in a post-war Poland could actually help them seize and maintain power in Russia."

"So, where does the FSB come in, with regards to you guys?" Logan stared forlornly at his empty cup.

Frank again glanced at the other members of his group. The Frenchman had stood and pulled on his coat. "Tell them everything," he said, and strode out the door.

"All right," Frank said, and licked his lips. "We're part of a group—it's not a tight organization, more of a network—we call the Reconstructionists, mostly made up of junior officers and some civilians. You can see the war as the death-knell of civilization or as a second chance for civilization.

"We'd like to see it as an opportunity. We think it's in everyone's interest to let countries grow as freely and as naturally as possible, without the interference of gangs of bullies like the FSB—or the CIA for that matter. We want to see, for example, the United States come together again but free of the political bullshit and professional power-mongering that got us in this bind in the first place.

"Obviously, the FSB and similar organizations don't like the idea, and they tend to come out shooting."

"Where does this Captain Wyszynski come in?" Reynaud asked.

"The Reconstructionists are international, and he's our contact with the Polish army, just as Tadeusz, here, is our contact with the ORMO. St. Jacques has contacts with *Znak*, a Catholic intellectuals' organization that gives us an ear out to the Church."

They heard the door open and feet stamping on the heavy rug. Frank stood and paced to the door just as a blue-eyed blond woman entered the room. She was a trace taller than Zdenka and more slender. Looking at her critically, Logan thought she might not actually be more slender than the Russian but smaller in one or two dimensions.

"Laura Wessel," Frank introduced her to the group. As she dropped into a chair, he asked, "Do you have any idea where Katya might be?"

"I haven't seen her since this morning." Laura looked down at the tear in her coat sleeve and the damp spots on the knees and legs of her trousers. A bruise on her cheek was changing from angry red to sullen purple. "I had to work late at the office and someone attacked me on the way home."

"They must have been FSB," Zdenka said. "It wasn't likely they were trying to rape you. It's cold enough already."

Laura's eyes shot icicles at Zdenka. "I've already had a bad day. I don't need any crap from you."

"Take it easy, both of you." Frank again made the pumping gesture with his hands. "Are you all right?"

"I'll survive."

"When you saw Katya this morning, did she say anything to give you some idea where she might be going?"

"No, nothing." Laura sighed as she unbuttoned her coat. "And no one has reported anything to the police." Anya brought another tray and Laura nodded to her, then began to eat.

Frank watched her for a few moments, then asked, "Have you located 'Lieutenant Carter' yet?"

"No. He seems to have disappeared. The police are trying to find out who might've contacted him in Krakow before he dropped out of sight."

Frank looked around at the former prisoners. "You guys must be pretty whipped. We've got more rooms than we need right now, now that the repatriation is almost complete. We can talk more in the morning."

Smyth-Davis stood and stretched, then froze. "I've just had a disturbing thought." He turned to face the others. "Perhaps that was the reason for the prison camp—a sort of farm for false identities for the FSB to use to either escape their situation in Mother Russia, or to get agents into various other countries."

"That *is* a scary thought," Frank agreed. "How do we know we can trust you, for that matter."

"Because if you don't, I'll tear your fuckin' arms off," Logan said with a grin.

Frank laughed. "Seriously, it's a messy situation. Tomorrow, make up a list of any and all prisoners you know. That'll give us a master list we can pass on."

They all lurched to their feet and followed Frank as he led them upstairs to a barracks and a series of smaller rooms, each with only one or two bunks apiece. As Frank showed the rooms and how to operate the table lamps, he grinned at Logan. "I'm glad you and St. Jacques managed to bury the hatchet someplace rather than in each other. That Frenchie's tough and cold. Did you notice his eyes? It must come from being a sniper. I've seen him kill three men with a single bullet apiece at from five hundred to eight hundred yards."

Reynaud laughed. "I don't know if it counts the same, but I've seen Logan kill one man with seventeen rounds from twenty-five yards."

Logan glared at the Cajun. "Everybody is a comic. I'll take this room." He opened the door and stepped inside.

Sitting on the bunk he pulled off his boots and the foot wrappings the Russian troops used instead of socks and was unbuttoning his shirt when someone lightly tapped at his door. He eased back the slide on the silenced pistol he'd kept, enough to be sure a round was chambered, then asked, "Who's there?"

Chapter 5

"Laura. May I come in?" She seemed to be trying to be quiet.

Logan slipped the pistol under his coat on the chair. "Sure, come on in. He hoped her visit would be either a very quick one or a very long one. The bare wood floor felt as cold as the surface of an ice-skating rink.

Laura opened the door just enough to slip into the room. She glanced at the half-unbuttoned shirt and grinned. "Don't let me interrupt anything."

"What can I do for you?" Logan asked.

"It's more the other way around. I came by to warn you. Don't trust Frank or any of the rest of his crowd."

"Oh?" Logan arched an eyebrow. "Why not? What's the story?" His feet were getting cold and he wished Laura would get to the point quickly, before he froze.

"The polite way to say it is 'America's interests are no longer his interests.' He's Polish through and through. His oath as an officer in the United States Army means nothing to him, if it ever did. How many other Americans are in his group? What does that tell you?"

Logan decided courtesy came in second to getting warm. He finished unbuttoning his shirt and tugged it off. "Well, there's you—"

"I'm here to keep an eye on Frank to see he doesn't sell the country down the river. But who else? There's Wyszynski, who's an officer of the same Polish army that was once in the Warsaw Pact; and Woydziak, who used to be in the Polish army; a Frenchman—hell, the French haven't been solid allies since Paris was libertated in World War II; and a Russian slut. From what I understand, she used to be a tank commander in a Russian armored division. We can't be that hard up for help."

Logan had tossed his shirt over his coat, across the chair, peeled off his pants, threw them over the shirt, then climbed between the cold sheets. He waited until he could talk without his teeth chattering. "So, what damage could they do us?"

"Well," Laura said, as she sat on the end of the bed. "I could see a situation where, if they decided to take out a FSB suspect or two, it might be handy to have an American body or three to leave at the scene. If they guess wrong and hit some innocent bystander, Americans get a black eye, while Frank and his crowd could claim you just went berserk. And if they got lucky and pop an honest-to-hemlock FSB agent and leave an American body behind, they get credit for it without having to get their fingers dirty. Or they could make it look as though Russians and Americans are fighting over Polish real estate. It's the old 'heads I win, tails you lose' game."

Logan lay silent, considering what Laura was saying, then he realized she'd bent over and was pulling off her boots.

"You mind if I join you in there? The heating in this place is nonexistent, and you've already warmed up the sheets."

Logan grinned. He'd hoped this might happen. "I don't mind. Maybe you can return the favor. I hear friction is a great way to warm things up." He watched as Laura stood, her back to him, and unbuttoned her blouse. She added it to the pile of clothes on the chair, then unbuckled her belt, unbuttoned and unzipped her pants. As she bent over, pulling off her trousers, Logan admired the way the muscles of her back rippled under her skin. She was slim but fit.

As she stepped out of her pants, Logan noticed her long, slim legs, her blond hair, cut short enough it just reached the nape of her neck, and her alabaster-pale skin that gave her the appearance of fragility. She reached back and unhooked her bra, then turned to the side as she pulled it off.

Logan muttered to himself

"What did you say?" She stood poised, her thumbs hooked in the elastic of her panties.

"I was just thinking out loud. What I told myself was, anything more than a handful or a mouthful is a waste."

"Tacky, but kind of cute." She slowly pushed the panties down until they dropped to the floor. "I'll get the light." The lamp dimmed and died and he felt her climb into the bed. "Move over," she said, "It's cold out here."

Logan slid over on the bed, shivering at the touch of sheets that hadn't been warmed by his body, leaving Laura the spot he'd warmed. She slid closer and wrapped her arms around him. She was chilled but, together, they warmed rapidly.

Her hand slid down to his chest, her fingers playing in the wiry hair there. "It's too nice a body to be shot full of holes just for some crazy scheme of Frank's." She kissed him.

What had begun tentatively quickly became passionate and, despite the cold, both were soon sweating. Finally, both had achieved satisfaction and lay side by side, waiting for their breathing to slow.

When Logan had recovered enough breath to talk without gasping, he said, "Now I know why I wanted out of that prison camp so bad."

"Hey," she said, "if I'd known what I was missing, I'd have come and got you. Have you got a woman waiting for you, back in the states?"

"Probably a lot of them, but I could be convinced to move your name right up to the top of the list."

"I've had worse offers, but how about I make you a counter-offer? How about staying here in Poland with me, at least until it's summer? I'd feel a hell of a lot safer with someone like you to watch my back. As I said, I really don't trust Frank or any of his collection of cutthroats."

"Why bother to stick around? There's nothing here for us, and no U.S government for us to work for."

She backed away from him, slid off the bed, and began to dress again.

"Hey, where are you going?" he asked.

From the sounds, she'd already drawn on her panties and was trying to hook her bra. "I don't want to get you in trouble. If Frank gets jealous, he could get nasty."

"What do you mean?"

"Frank and I were lovers—some time ago. I broke it off and he's been on the rag about it ever since. If he finds out for sure I've fallen for you, he's liable to work up something so you wind up attacking an armored regiment with nothing but a stick. There are also some nasty things he can do to me." By then, she'd finished dressing. Her hair brushed his face and she gave him another kiss. He heard her creep across the floor, saw the door open and she slipped out into the hallway.

Logan lay staring upward into the darkness until the cold air on his body forced him to draw the blankets up to his chin, then he continued staring and thinking. He wasn't even aware when his eyes finally closed and he drifted into sleep.

~ * ~

Reynaud woke early the next morning. At first, he was completely lost, unsure of where he was, or whether he was free or a prisoner. The fact he had adequate blankets reassured him he wasn't back in the prison camp, then he began to remember. They'd reached Krakow. In darkness, he climbed out of bed, groped for the matches and the lamp left for him and, in the uncertain light, pulled on his clothes as quickly as possible. Taking the lamp with him, he stepped into the hallway. At least the kitchen should have a fire where he could warm himself.

Following the corridor to its end, he took the stairs down to the first floor. He tried the first door to his right, found it opened into another office. The second door opened into the kitchen, warm and fragrant with the aroma of fresh bread. Anya stood at the stove, tending a steaming kettle while Tadeusz and St. Jacques sat at a table, cleaning pistols.

The Frenchman slid a thick magazine into an automatic pistol a little more compact and shapely than the elderly .45 Colt automatic Tadeusz was reassembling. St. Jacques drew back the slide of his weapon, chambering a round, then thumbed the safety on and slipped the pistol into his left-hand holster.

Tadeusz loaded and charged the Colt, snapped the safety on, and thrust it into an old leather U. S. Army holster. St. Jacques picked up a revolver and six .357 magnum cartridges, one by one, which he dropped into the chambers, and closed the crane and cylinder. The revolver went into a right-hand holster. "Good morning," the Frenchman said. "You're up early. Most of our associates are still abed."

"What time is it?"

The Pole drew out a pocket watch, glanced at it. "It's five-fifteen. Frank will be down any minute." He paused then asked, "Do you have a pistol?"

"No, but I might be able to get one from Logan. Our group has three or four captured pistols."

"If you cannot get one, let me know. Once you are in the ORMO you can always carry a pistol."

Reynaud studied the Frenchman, who'd handled his weapons as though they were as much a part of his hand as his own fingers. "I can guess why most of the rest of your group is here in Krakow, but why are you here instead of back in *la belle France?*"

St. Jacques stared at him for a moment with that calculating gaze then he almost smiled. "Krakow is my second or third city. I was born in Nantes, lived much of my life in Paris, but I was a student—an exchange student—in Krakow. I fell in love with this place, these people, the fascinating history of this city. France and Poland are akin in many ways." He gave a Gallic shrug which seemed to convey everything and nothing at the same time.

He murmured a *"merci"* to Anya as she placed a cup of coffee before him. Anya also brought coffee for the other two of them, and slices of bread, still warm.

"I had already observed, as a student of history, that history is made by men with guns. I decided I would prefer to be a man with a gun than a student, so I joined the *berets rouges*, the paras, and was stationed abroad. Then, before the rescue, I was rotated to serve with the Franco-German brigade. I joined the rescue column because I knew the country and the language fluently. I also joined the mission against orders, so there is nothing waiting for me in the motherland but charges of desertion."

"Crazy, huh? This Frenchie is damned near the only man I know who'd desert to get *into* a fight." Frank strode into the kitchen and sat down at the table.

Reynaud poured the white powder from a couple of paper pouches into his coffee, lightening the color and take the edge off the bitterness. He took a sip and smiled in pure bliss. Anya had placed platters of some fluffy yellow mass in front of him and Frank, and the Cajun supposed the other two had already eaten. He found a tiny bottle of Tabasco sauce and sprinkled it on what he supposed were supposed to be eggs then tasted, decided it was a palatable substitute. Between that, sausages, and homemade bread, the breakfast was a feast. "Looks like you eat well, anyway."

Reynaud settled down to eating in earnest as the rest of the former prisoners and the Krakow group assembled at the breakfast table. As he ate, he noticed Logan paid an inordinate amount of attention to Laura Wessel.

"What did you find out last night?" Frank asked St. Jacques.

The Frenchman glanced at Anya then said, in English, "The ORMO had not seen her. I gave them her description and what information I could. If they have learned anything during the night they will notify the police. *Mademoiselle* Wessel can then inform the rest of us." He nodded to Frank. "While you, Zdenka, and Tadeusz take these gentlemen to the Wawel, I intend to consult some of my acquaintances of the streets and in *Znak*. I will also attempt to discover what has become of this Lieutenant Oshevsky."

"Sounds good," Frank said. "We'll meet you back here about noon."

The Frenchman stood, donned his beret and a heavy coat, and strode out. The rest of them finished breakfast, dressed for the weather, and followed Frank out into the street. The snow had stopped and the wind abated and, although it was still before dawn, the fallen snow provided a sort of dim phosphorescence to the area. The trod slowly and carefully down the stairs, using the handrail. The Frenchman's tracks were clearly visible in the otherwise flawless snow cover. Reynaud glanced down the street at a muffled sound and observed a figure pushing a cart piled with what might be cloth. "Who's that?" he asked.

"Who?" Frank glanced around then noticed the pushcart. "Just a ragman. You'll become used to them. Krakow wasn't exactly a golden city even before the war, and now, for most of the population, it's making do with what's available. Everyone in the city is entitled to three meals a day, at city expense, either in raw foodstuffs or at the soup kitchens. What they get is a little better than what you got in the prison camp. The city also allocates coal and heavy clothing. These people find rags, clean them then turn them into the city for script."

"Jeez," Logan looked after the man. "It sounds awful bleak."

"I've heard it was worse in the states," Frank replied. "Here, the people have a history of cooperation and standing in line for food and other supplies. There was a lot of rioting back in the states."

The rest of the walk to the Wawel was in depressed silence.

The city had begun to stir. They saw another ragman and squads of men in military uniform and other groups in rough clothing.

By the time they reached the imposing palace/cathedral/fortress that was the Wawel, the shifts were changing and they seemed caught in a shifting tide of men and women. Laura took her leave and walked away to the offices of the police.

"Oh," Frank said, "I suppose you're wondering who runs what. The police take care of public order and safety in the city. The ORMO, or militia, assist the police and are responsible for the military defence of the city proper. The military have their district offices here and they direct the ORMO but most of the regular troops are stationed outside the city, in the surrounding towns. There's also another small force, about two dozen men, who are the Cardinal's Guard."

He noticed Reynaud's raised eyebrow. "They're needed. Some of the old government diehards are still around, and they and the Russians regard the Church as the leader of the 'reactionary elements.' They'd like nothing better than to strike out at the church, particularly if they could make it look as though it was part of a squabble between the Church and the army, or the civilian government we're hoping for."

Reynaud glanced around the place, observing the uniforms and the people wearing them. A few wore standard military uniforms, a few others wore dress uniforms, but most were in camouflage, many of them in the old rain-drop camouflage. Many more wore camouflage with ORMO armbands, and their boots and web gear were a wild mixture, some of them even looking like NATO equipment. A scant few men were clad in workingmen's gear with armbands and most of them carried coils of wire.

"Who are they?" Steve asked, gesturing at the workmen.

Frank, who seemed a little embarrassed, rubbed his nose. "Like most European phone systems, the Polish system breaks down a lot. You ever hear the joke that if you pick up a phone in Italy, you get everybody, and in France, you get nobody? In Poland, it's more of a crapshoot. You pick up a phone here and you've got a chance of getting Nome, Alaska."

While they'd been talking, Tadeusz had approached a desk and said something to the man who'd just sat in the chair behind it. The man hardly looked up. His reply was brief and he seemed to be looking for something on his desk.

"Sergeant." Woydziak's voice, normally deep, was a bellow, and he spoke slowly enough for Reynaud to easily understand him despite his own fractured Polish. "You were taught to render a proper salute. Stand up and do so."

The sergeant stood, his face a stone mask, but red crept up his cheeks. His arm snapped up in a correct salute. Tadeusz glared at him for long moments before he returned the salute. "Sit down," Tadeusz rumbled. "Tell Captain Dabrowski that Lieutenant Woydziak is here with recruits referred by Captain Wyszynski."

The sergeant slumped in his chair and spoke into an intercom.

"Lord," Frank intoned. "I didn't know Tadeusz was that upset about Katya."

Zdenka leaned forward and Reynaud barely heard her speaking to Frank. "I am going to talk to some people here. If I am not back soon enough to find you here, I will meet you in Wyszynski's office."

Frank nodded and Zdenka strode quickly away.

Within moments the sergeant stood, saluted Woydziak, and said, "The captain will see you immediately."

Tadeusz returned the salute and they all filed into the captain's office. Woydziak saluted and the captain, a corpulent man with a ruddy face and close-cropped gray hair, negligently waved a salute. He shuffled a few papers on a littered desk and stared at the men lining the wall. "What was it that the good Captain Wyszynski wanted me to do with ... these men."

"These men are to be inducted into the ORMO and assigned to me to serve as a detached unit. Because of their assignment, they will not be issued ration chits, arms, nor will they be assigned to a barracks."

The captain had continued to shuffle through the papers on his desk. He picked up one, frowned at it, then looked up. "What do you need me for, then?"

"They will need uniforms and a release for their weapons, which were impounded yesterday."

The captain found a pen and scribbled on a sheet of paper. "Give this to the people in Supply. Dismissed."

Woydziak saluted again. The former prisoners, knowing they were now in the ORMO, did likewise, and followed Tadeusz out of the office. He led them through a maze of corridors and waiting rooms, and down a flight of stairs into the basement, to a storage area where he handed a corporal the captain's note, and the men were issued uniforms. These consisted of blouses, pants, smocks that could be worn over a heavy coat, and armbands that could be attached either to smocks or to the military blouses.

Although the warehouse was frigid, Frank insisted they change into the uniforms immediately. Some of the uniform parts needed to be returned for something closer to a fit, then the corporal handed them their weapons and ammunition, piling them on a counter.

As soon as Reynaud had finished adjusting the ORMO armband on his smock, he picked up the ancient Winchester from the counter and cranked the action open. The Poles had apparently unloaded it. He shoved four rounds into the magazine, jacked a round into the chamber, and hung the rifle over his shoulder by the sling.

"If you're finished here, we'll get you haircuts," Frank said. Tadeusz led them to another area of the basement where a "barber" ran hand-powered clippers over their heads, shearing and pulling away great masses of hair that tumbled to the floor and lay in multi-colored mounds.

"Now," Frank said, "if you're all ready, we'll go talk to Wyszynski." This time Frank took the lead through another series of hallways until Reynaud began to recognize some of the doors. Frank stopped and tapped at one of the doors and, at a muffled reply, opened the door to Wyszynski's office.

"I need a couple of days' leave," Frank said.

Wyszynski studied the armed mob of skinheads behind Frank, a faint smile under his trimmed moustache. "A war usually takes longer than two days. What is the matter?"

"The girl, Katya, who was with us has disappeared. We're trying to find her."

Wyszynski's smile vanished. "Give me her description. I will pass it along to all the ORMO units and any troops in or around the city. I presume you have already given the information to the police."

Frank nodded.

Wyszynski scowled down at his desk. "This creates a serious problem. What did she know?"

"Nothing the FSB didn't already know—except, perhaps, for our address."

"That in itself is dangerous information." Wyszynski stood and began to pace. "I have some more bad news. "Major Phillips' has also disappeared. He was scheduled for a flight to New Jersey but never appeared. Your friends think he has again changed identities. There is enough confusion at the embarkation points it would not be difficult for a man to lose himself. They are circulating a description of him now."

"Shit!" Frank slammed the desk with his fist. "It's all coming unwired at once. Have you found Oshevsky or his trail yet?"

"No, he must have vanished within hours after arriving in the city. I have an unpleasant feeling something large and ugly is being planned. Contact me every day."

As they left the office, Zdenka turned the corner at the end of the corridor. She broke into a trot until she reached Frank. "We need to talk." Her mouth was a grim line.

"Back at the apartment," Frank said. "St. Jacques should be back by the time we return."

Reynaud had gained some familiarity with the part of Krakow through which they trod and he noticed Frank led them on a slightly different route that led them through an alley behind the apartment. As they reached the corner of the building, Frank suddenly stopped and looked around wildly at the windows of the surrounding buildings.

"What seems to be the trouble?" Steve asked.

Frank pointed to a mound of snow against the building wall. "That's no natural drift. Everybody get back—or go wide around it and get clear. Zdenka, go get Anya out of the building. Give her any reason but the truth."

Zdenka nodded, a curt dip of the head and walked rapidly around the corner. Frank waved everyone else away, then crept toward the snowbank as though stalking some small, wary animal. In spite of the cold he'd begun to sweat, and he removed his gloves.

Reynaud noticed faint marks in the snow, as though someone had tried to cover tracks. This must've been done since morning, when the snow had stopped falling and the wind had slackened.

Frank carefully knelt in the snow and began to gently brush away the snow beside the building, his hands making small, slow movements. After he'd cleared away the first few inches of snow, which had been more tightly packed than drift, they saw what appeared to be a piece of plastic. Frank then probed more cautiously until he'd exposed several sections of pipe and a plastic device attached to the bundle.

"It's an acid detonator. The cold slowed down the chemical reaction," Frank said. "They probably didn't want it to go off until tonight, when they figured we'd all be there." He carefully detached the detonator and placed it in the middle of the alley then carried the rest of the pipe bomb into the apartment.

In the office, he unscrewed the end cap from a section of pipe. "Plastique. I guess we should be grateful for the contribution. Maybe we can return this to the sender."

The Deacon's long face almost cracked as he smiled. "'Tis more blessed to give than to receive.'"

"Amen, brother," Frank replied.

"What about the detonator?" Steve asked.

Frank shrugged. "There's nothing I can do about it. It operates by a simple chemical reaction. It'll be noisy when it goes off, but it won't do much damage. We've got something worse to worry about. We can guess they got our address from Katya, which means they've already tortured her. I don't know how long we've got before they—" His voice broke off as Anya entered the room.

"Anya," Frank said, "we'll need a quick lunch; just bread, sausage, and coffee. We'll be leaving again as soon as St. Jacques gets back. If he isn't here soon, we'll meet him somewhere."

"I will get food for you." Anya disappeared into the kitchen.

Frank stared after her until they could hear her working in the kitchen, then he turned to Zdenka. "What was it you had to tell me?"

Zdenka leaned forward in her chair so they could hear her murmuring. "I found out nothing about Katya but I learned Laura Wessel did not work late, last night."

Frank dropped back into his chair and stared at the floor.

"That's all we needed, a loose gun on the deck."

Zdenka patted a little German automatic she wore in a covered crossdraw holster. "A loose gun should be…secured."

Reynaud glanced at Logan and saw his knuckles whiten as he grasped the foreguard of his Russian submachine gun tighter, then Frank shook his head. "No, stupidity doesn't deserve the ultimate penalty. I'll talk to her."

"But not about things important to us all," Zdenka said pointedly.

Frank nodded. "Fair enough. If she's trying to play some game of her own, she shouldn't get to know our game plans."

They all heard the front door open and feet stamping then St. Jacques entered the dining room and sank into the chair nearest Zdenka's. "I got no information about Katya. I did describe her to some of the people I know, so if any of them see her they will take her in and notify us. I did, however, find out something interesting about Lieutenant Oshevsky. Before he vanished he was speaking with Lieutenant Barela."

Frank's head snapped up and he stared at the Frenchman. "The second-in-command of the Cardinal's Guard?"

"The very one." St. Jacques included the rest of the group in the conversation with a glance. "Lieutenant Barela is a large, surly man who owns an Italian submachine gun I covet. I went to the cathedral in the Wawel to discuss his acquaintanceship but he was not on duty today and I was unable to find his place of residence.

"It might be useful to have an animated discussion with the estimable Barela."

"Who do you want to do the job?" Logan asked.

Again the faint smile made a brief appearance on St. Jacques' lips. "It is a tradition among some of we Frenchmen to kill the Cardinal's Guard."

Frank stared down at his hands. "What bothers me is how Katya disappeared." He leaned forward and, in a whisper, told the Frenchman about finding the bomb and what they'd learned. He raised his voice to a murmur that could just be heard by the whole group. "Someone must've kidnapped Katya, but how? She wouldn't have gone to them. I'll grant there's enough places where you could grab someone, but how could they have made her not only silent but invisible?"

The silence while everyone considered the question was broken by Anya bringing in a pot of coffee and a platter of bread and hot sausage.

Reynaud contemplated the matter while he ate. Something seemed to nudge the back of his mind but was too nebulous to put into words.

"You can stay here," Frank told the former prisoners. "I don't know how much help you'd be since you don't know Katya or the area."

Each of the men insisted on joining the search. They finished eating quickly. "You might leave your long guns here," Frank suggested. "We've got a few extra pistols. Discretion is the better part of valor, and all that." He pulled open a drawer and handed a pistol to each of the group except Smyth-Davis and Logan, who were already armed with captured Russian pistols.

As they stepped out into the gloom of the street, Reynaud glanced toward the end of the street and suddenly realized what had been nagging at him. "Frank! I think I've got it!"

Frank, at the foot of the stairs, turned to look up at him and Logan, halfway down the steps, almost slipped then turned. "Well, don't give it to all of us. Walk downwind."

"Look," Reynaud explained, as he carefully made his way down the stairs, "you wanted to know how to be invisible, grab somebody, and make them invisible, too. Something rang a bell and I just realized what it was. This morning, the ragman was invisible to you. You didn't really see him until I called him to your attention, because you've gotten so used to them. And they could make somebody invisible just by tying them up, dumping them into the cart, and covering them up with rags."

"Damn, you're right," Frank snapped. "Yeah, that'd work." He paused a moment. "It may be a dry lead but it's the best we've got." He drew his pistol and checked the chamber. "Everybody who hasn't checked his or her pistol better do it now. This may be dangerous, if we find the right man."

"Maybe you'd better stay behind, if there's gonna be shooting," Logan told Zdenka.

"I can take care of myself," the Russian answered, and muttered something that sounded like Russian for "ugly American."

"Hey," Logan protested, "don't get me wrong. I got nothing

against women. Hell, some of my best friends are women."

"Enough grins and giggles," Frank growled. "We need a system. I'll talk to the ragmen—check their papers or some such—while the rest of you look through the rags and check the floorboards for blood stains."

Steve scratched his chin. "That seems a little weak."

"It's better than nothing," Frank replied, "and it's all we've got. Let's move."

For the rest of the afternoon they looked for and examined pushcarts, Frank asking the ragmen about others who might've been acting strangely, even for ragmen, or for any other information about the neighborhoods they visited. The team even crossed the Vistula, out of the old town, but found nothing. Finally, late in the afternoon, Frank said, "Looks like we're drawing a blank. Tomorrow we'll take our idea to the police, even if we have to take a chance on a leak."

As they crossed the Kosckiuszki Bridge, Logan pointed to a cart on the river bank. A man or woman, heavily bundled in rags, walked on the ice with something in his or her hand. After a single glance, Frank nodded and they hurried across the bridge and slipped and slid down the bank. As soon as they'd reached the shore, Frank, St. Jacques, Zdenka, and Tadeusz fanned out. Taking their cue from the veterans, the former prisoners also spread out along the bank, making escape impossible. The figure turned to face them and they saw it was a large man with a hatchet in his hand.

"Getting ready to do a little ice-fishing?" Frank asked, in Polish.

The man glared at the group through narrowed eyes, the hatchet half-raised.

"Put down the hatchet," St. Jacques said, also in Polish. "Do not even think of running or fighting." He drew his revolver. "If you do, I'm not going to shoot you, I'm going to shoot the ice. I have no idea whether you will freeze or drown first, but I doubt it is a question you wish to explore."

The man lowered the hatchet to the ice and, at St. Jacques' gesture with the pistol, stepped away from it. Seeing the man was secured, Tadeusz began to dig through the rags. Suddenly he whirled on the man. "You bastard," he rasped, and strode toward the "ragman."

"Be steady, my friend," St. Jacques said, "this man wishes to speak with us."

Tadeusz halted and glared at the prisoner. "Turn your back to me." In three quick steps he'd returned to the cart and snatched up a short length of wire. Striding out to the "ragman," Tadeusz seized an arm, roughly wrapped the wire around the man's wrist, then snatched the other arm, bent it back sharply enough to wring a cry from the prisoner, and bound the man's wrists together.

Frank had also rummaged among the rags. He suddenly stopped as his face paled and took on a stricken look, and he seemed ready to cry or throw up, or both.

Reynaud glanced at the rest of the former prisoners, then paced toward the cart.

"Don't," Frank said.

"This isn't idle curiosity," the Cajun replied. He moved the rags aside, steeling himself for what he'd find under them, and stared at the dead face, so battered he couldn't have told, by looking, the age or sex of the body. Reynaud closed the faded blue eyes then studied the lids. "Oshevsky did this," he announced.

"How can you tell?" Frank asked.

"He has a sort of signature. The puncture marks in the eyelids show he did it. He liked to run needles through the eyelids, so at each tiny movement it'd feel like sand in the eye."

Tadeusz had stuffed a rag in the man's mouth and tied another over it, gagging him. He walked the man around the cart, shoved him into it, and covered him with rags. After a moment's thought he pulled more rags out and began to pull them on or tie them over his uniform. "Follow me at a little distance. It would be odd to see us with this cart."

Tadeusz found where the man had brought the cart down the bank and the rest of the group helped him laboriously wrestle it back up then, with the rest of the group following at about a hundred yards, pushed the cart back to the apartment. Making sure the street was empty, Tadeusz hauled the man out of the cart and into the building.

Frank stopped at the wagon. "Jean-Marie, Zdenka, I'm going to tell Anya what happened. I want you to wait a minute or two then bring in Katya's body. We'll take it to the church tomorrow." Without waiting, he tightened his jaw, climbed the stairs, and stepped inside. Just as the Frenchman and the Russian lifted the tortured body out of the cart they all heard a shriek from the apartment and before they'd reached the door, Anya, her face distraught, rushed out, almost falling on the stairs.

When she saw the body she screamed again, then, weeping, caught the body in her arms and the three of them carried it into the building. The rest of the group filed into the dining room where Tadeusz had shoved the prisoner into a chair beside the heavy dining table. They could still hear the sounds of mourning from the back of the building, and the sounds became fainter as the dead girl was carried upstairs.

Most of the keening had stopped by the time Frank and Zdenka had returned to the dining room.

St. Jacques walked into the office. They heard him open a drawer, and a rattle of metal, and he returned holding two pairs of handcuffs. "I suggest some of you may wish to go upstairs. This interview is likely to become…intense." He unwired the man's hand then cuffed each hand to a table leg. "You may also want to find something to pound on. The sounds of hammering and other construction noises are not uncommon but screams might be noticed."

Steve and Smyth-Davis immediately left the room. Juho stood for a moment, considering, then apparently decided that what happened in this room had nothing to do with him, and turned and followed the others. Reynaud wanted to follow him but it was as though his feet had taken root in the floor, or he was paralyzed by dread but fascinated, as a bird is fascinated by the eyes of a snake.

St. Jacques leaned on the table and stared into the prisoner's eyes. "I can see you are determined to tell me nothing, while I am determined to make you reveal everything. It should be interesting to see whose will is the stronger."

The hair on the back of Reynaud's neck stirred at the Frenchman's soft, quiet tones, far more terrifying than if he'd been screaming through lips flecked with foam.

"I should warn you, however," the Frenchman continued, "that the balance is not even. I shall be assisted by my associate, Zdenka. She is a Ukrainian Cossack who is not overfond of most

Poles but called the dead girl 'little sister.' Now that we have introduced you to the unpleasant alternatives, I will acquaint you with your reward for good behavior. Friend Logan, show this gentleman the device you took from the ZOMO who attempted to follow us last night."

Logan hesitated then drew the silenced Makarov from his coat pocket.

"If you are very cooperative, you will receive a bullet in the back of the head. You may not even feel it." He waited until they heard the sounds of hammering from upstairs then pulled the rag from the prisoner's mouth. "Where did you keep her?"

The man curse in Polish.

Zdenka drew her knife. "The Turks have a ritual they call 'the death of a thousand cuts.'" She seized the man's right hand and slammed it down on the table and sawed off the first joint of the index finger, ignoring the man's whimpering as the blade sliced and grated between the bones. Using the blood-stained blade, she rolled the severed fingertip off the table and into the man's lap.

"Where did you keep Katya?" St. Jacques demanded again.

The Pole gritted his teeth and the muscles in his cheeks knotted.

St. Jacques slapped the Pole's other hand flat on the table, picked up a metal paperweight, and used it to smash the first joint of the man's left index finger. The man stifled his scream.

"Where?"

As the man only glared at him, St. Jacques waved Zdenka back. "If I might go out of turn, I believe I can illustrate something interesting." With his middle finger he flicked the smashed bone. The man winced and a shuddering moan escaped him. "You see, if you cut it off, you no longer have it to get his attention."

"I see," Zdenka said, picked up the paperweight, and smashed the first bone of the Pole's right middle finger. This time the prisoner shrieked.

"I want to thank you," St. Jacques told the prisoner in his soft tones. "I believe this is the first enthusiasm for anything Zdenka has displayed since Katya disappeared, and the longer it takes you to decide to talk, the better she will feel. I am afraid you will not share that sense of well-being, but one cannot please everyone. Now, where was Katya kept?"

"I don't know. Someone told me to meet them at an old warehouse."

Again St. Jacques flicked the man's smashed finger and the prisoner howled. "Do not tell me clumsy lies. You were once ZOMO. You have few secrets from us, and soon you will have none. And you will be dead. How painfully you die depends upon your honesty and alacrity—oh, and do not wait for the bomb that was planted to end your misery. We have already found the bomb and disarmed it."

Zdenka flicked the shattered end of his middle finger and the howl became a whimper.

St. Jacques continued. "We already know Oshevsky of the FSB and Lieutenant Barela were involved. Very soon we will find where Barela is staying, and it will be a simple trail to follow. But if you are offering your unnecessary pain as a balm to Zdenka, I consider it a splendid gesture."

Reynaud had been numbed by fascinated horror but some part of his mind, away from the flood of emotions, was impressed with how smoothly the Frenchman blended facts and speculation into his interrogation.

St. Jacques reached toward the mangled finger again then the prisoner gasped, "It was a house on *Straszewskiego,* the house nearest the Wawel."

"Very good. And how do you gain admittance. What is the signal?"

"Two knocks, then I say, 'I have a message for Rokosowski."

St. Jacques continued the questioning until they had a good general floor-plan of the bottom floor and basement of the house. The man had never visited the second floor or the attic.

"We must have someone guard him," St. Jacques said. "I do not think it would be wise to let Laura know we have him. The rest of us must decide immediately who will make the assault, because we must strike as soon as possible. We do not know, for example, if they expect him back after he has finished disposing of the body. If that is the case, they might become nervous and move their base elsewhere, and we will have lost everything."

Reynaud hesitated only a moment. "We can leave him with Juho. I'm going with you."

"We can only take a few," Frank said. "We don't have any extra silenced weapons, and we'll want to keep this quiet. I've got a chopper with a built-in silencer, and Jean-Marie and Logan have those pistols they picked up last night."

Reynaud stood. "I'll follow you in. If one of you falls, I'll take his weapon."

"All right," Frank said. "Logan, I hope you're good with a pistol." He paced to a cabinet and dug in the drawer for a moment then handed out flashlights. "You've got to be careful—these things tend to make you a target, but it beats going into the place blind."

"I can get by with a pistol," Logan said, and checked the magazine in the silenced Makarov.

Frank snapped his fingers. "Laura has a suppressed Ingram MAC-10 in her room. I'll get it for you, Tadeusz." He turned, darted down the hallway, and to the stairs while St. Jacques used the handcuffs to bind the prisoner's hands behind his back. When the prisoner was freed from the table he was hauled to his feet and propelled upstairs to Juho's room.

When St. Jacques returned he was checking the chamber of his silenced Makarov. Frank descended the stairs more slowly and, when he did, he looked worried. "The gun isn't there."

He carried a German built submachine gun with its barrel covered by the large shroud of a suppressor.

"I will follow then, too," Tadeusz snapped.

"Then let's go," Frank said. "I'd like to at least get there before curfew."

The group trudged outside, where the clouds were threatening more snow and the early evening was as dingy as the rest of the city seemed to have become. Frank led, with most of the group following closely while St. Jacques again acted as rearguard. The wind had picked up again and, through a nose that was almost numb with the cold, Reynaud caught the scent of this city now, and he wondered what scent or odor it might have once had. Now, it had that scrubbed, aseptic smell of a mausoleum and looked, in the dim light, like a city of the dead.

In the grayness, Reynaud found himself looking forward to

action, if only to prove there was still life in these gray stone canyons. The streets were all but deserted and the only figures he saw were furtive shapes driven by the cold, seen only at a distance, since strangers, to the people of Krakow, were possible dangers.

Frank had been headed toward the Wawel, whose towers dominated the skyline of most of Krakow.

Suddenly, from above and from some distance away, Reynaud heard a bugle call that stopped in mid-note.

"That's the *hejnal*," Tadeusz informed them. "It is played at noon and at dusk. It ends that way because, the story goes, a trumpeter played that call to warn the city of the approach of a Tatar army, and he was killed by an arrow in the throat, dying just on that unfinished note."

Not a good omen, Reynaud found himself thinking. The only pleasant thought he could call to mind was their enemies would also want to make as little noise as possible. This promised to be an ugly, silent skirmish.

Frank raised his hand to signal a halt then pointed across the street to a house. The bottoms of the lowest row of windows stood at about shoulder level. "As soon as we get across the street, get as near the building as you can and keep your heads down. We don't want to warn them. Tadeusz, your voice is more like the prisoner's than anybody else's here. You give the password. I'll be right behind you."

"I will follow Tadeusz," St. Jacques said. "A pistol is far better for this kind of work than your submachine gun."

Frank hesitated a moment before he nodded. "You've got it. Tadeusz, as soon as the door is open, step aside. I'll follow Jean-Marie and, Logan, you be right behind me. I want the rest of you in order after that. We don't need any crowding. Tadeusz, you follow Logan, then Zdenka, and Reynaud, then Steve. McCluskey, you're tail-end Charlie. Everyone ready?"

At the chorus of "readys" Tadeusz led the way across the street. Reynaud frowned at the house as he passed the front. It was in no way distinguished from the buildings around it and he hoped they weren't creeping up on a family preparing to share a meager dinner.

Tadeusz silently mounted the steps, St. Jacques at his heels. The Pole knocked twice and, in a low voice, said, "I have a message for Rokosowski."

Chapter 6

Reynaud, his back pressed against the frigid wall of the building, found himself sweating. The wait for someone to answer the door seemed a very long one, with each second dragging across his nerves. He'd almost decided Tadeusz should give the signal again when the door was partially opened. He heard a sharp sound, like a handclap, then the Frenchman shoved the door open and vanished into the house.

Frank darted up the steps, his submachine gun ready and, on the second step, slipped. He kept his balance enough to avoid falling but had to catch at the left side of the door frame to save himself from tumbling headlong into the apartments. He recovered and followed St. Jacques inside.

By the time Reynaud had gotten into the house, several of the group ahead of him sat in the hallway, pulling off their boots and socks or foot wrappings, and he noticed some had also shed their coats. Logan crept through the parlor toward the back of the house while Frank and St. Jacques slipped from door to door down the corridor running parallel to the street.

Reynaud lowered himself to the floor and began to tug his own boots free. By the dim glow of alcohol lamps, he could see the windows had been blacked out with dark, heavy curtains. He glanced back at the entrance as the Deacon quietly closed the front door and, for the first time, noticed the body of the man who'd opened the door. St. Jacques appeared to have shot the man in his second chin, blowing away the top of the man's skull.

Barefooted, Reynaud rocked to his feet to follow Zdenka down the corridor. Suddenly they heard footsteps on the floor above and everyone crowded into a doorway or behind whatever cover was available.

The footsteps slowed and became heavier as the man apparently started down the stairs at the head of the corridor. Then the man had turned on the landing, facing the hidden raiders. He stopped, bent down, and peered down the corridor then spun to dash up the stairs.

Light flickered at the muzzle of Frank's submachine gun

and the weapon made a sound like a stuttering belch. The figure on the landing was flung back against the wall, hitting with a jarring thump and a spray of red.

"*Merde!*" St. Jacques exclaimed, and sprang for the stairs. He gained the landing in two bounds then spun to face the upstairs corridor, his pistol gripped in both hands. The pistol again made its clapping sound as the Frenchman fired twice then he ducked and they all heard the clatter of bullets striking the wall behind him. One of the bullets whined angrily as it ricocheted.

At the other end of the house another supressed pistol was fired, three rapid shots, and a body clattered and thumped as it tumbled down the back stairs.

Frank joined the Frenchman on the landing and glanced at him then dug into a pocket and pulled out a hand grenade. At the Frenchman's nod, he crouched and, keeping himself below the level of the second floor, tossed the grenade up into the hallway. Instantly, St. Jacques rushed the stairs, Frank at his heels.

Reynaud joined the rush to the second floor. When his head reached the level of the floor he saw Frank standing in the first doorway to Reynaud's left, his subgun pointed at the second door on the right. St. Jacques had already crept past the first door on the right and moved like a shadow against the wall.

Frank's gun burped again and before the rain of cartridge cases had clattered on the wood floor the Frenchman had dived through the open door into the room.

Frank tried to shove a fresh magazine into his weapon when the door across the hall from him was jerked open and another gun belched muzzle flashes.

Reynaud saw it as though in slow motion—the flickering muzzle, the ragged holes that appeared in Frank's coat from the belly to the upper chest. Frank's face paled as he lurched against the door. A large shape slipped out of the room and dropped something metallic onto the floor then Reynaud heard the sound of another magazine being seated. Suddenly, at two suppressed pistol shots, the figure spun toward the stairwell.

The figure shambled toward the stairs and Reynaud, caught with nothing more lethal in his hand than a flashlight, pointed the beam at the man's face. The shape emitted a hideous bubbling sound and Reynaud saw blood welling from a bullet hole in the man's throat and a dark patch growing on his chest. The dying man's eyes stared wildly at nothing. He started to raise the machine pistol but it slipped from nerveless fingers and clattered on the floor.

St. Jacques stalked out of the room from which the man had come, just as the stumbling form bumped into the railing that ran from the wall to the bannister. Still moving like a sleepwalker, the dead man turned toward St. Jacques.

"*Au revoir*, Barela," St. Jacques said as he fired a final shot.

The team on the stairway were sprayed with gore then the dead man pitched backward and Reynaud saw the small black hole between the man's crossed eyes.

The rest of the team rushed up the stairs, Tadeusz pausing only to scoop up the machine pistol from the floor. Drawing back the bolt, he rushed down the hallway to check the other doors.

Reyaud was surprised to see Frank still on his feet. "How bad are you hit?"

"I'm not," Frank said, pulling open his coat to reveal a Kevlar vest, "but it was damned close. I was afraid he'd shoot me in the face before he ran out of ammo. Thanks, Jean-Marie."

He bent and picked up the grenade from the floor.

Reynaud noticed the pin hadn't been pulled and the lever was still attached to the detonator. "Did you forget to pull the pin?"

"Nope," Frank replied. "The idea wasn't to make lots of noise but to make them too busy ducking for cover to shoot at Jean-Marie."

"There seem to be no more on this floor, and Tadeusz has found the way to the attic," the Frenchman announced.

"Are you sure you're all right?" Reynaud asked Frank.

Frank shoved himself away from the wall. "Nothing wrong with me that a change of underwear won't cure. Tadeusz, you watch the way to the stairs. We're going to the basement."

St. Jacques emerged from the room in which Barela had been hiding, carrying a submachine gun about the length of two pistols end-to-end, with a very thick magazine. Across his shoulder he'd slung a belt with pouches containing more magazines for the weapon. "Since Barela is a *spectre* himself now, he won't be needing this one.

Frank took the lead going down the stairs then stopped. "We're coming down." He called out to the rest of the party downstairs.

"Come ahead, it's clear," Logan called back, "but watch out. Twice, now, somebody in the basement's tried to give us a lead enema. The last time it happened, I sprayed back a little. That seemed to discourage them."

As soon as he saw the weapon in Logan's hands, Frank snapped, "Where did you get that thing?"

"I took it off the asshole who tried to go down the 'up' stairway. What's the matter?"

Frank took the weapon, pointed out a section of wire welded to the back of the receiver to take a sling, and the foresling which had been replaced with a strap from a camera case. "This is Laura's MAC-10,"

"You mean these bastards got her, too?"

"I don't think so," Frank said. "We'll discuss this later. Have you got more ammo for it?"

"Yeah, the guy had a spare magazine."

"All right, gang, here's what we do." Frank thumbed ammunition into the other magazine for his weapon. "Spread out all through the house. Zdenka, you stay with Steve and McCluskey. Rennie, you stay with St. Jacques and I. I'll fire a burst into the floor. All of you do the same thing as soon as I stop firing. As soon as I can get the other magazine in, I'll go down the basement stairs."

"Very good," St. Jacques said, "but I'll rush the stairs. In close quarters, a pistol is a handier weapon than a submachine gun. You follow me down." As Frank looked as though he might argue, St. Jacques smiled and laid aside the submachine gun and magazines from the upstairs room. "Barela was not shooting at me. I haven't burned up my allotted adrenalin yet."

After a long stare at the Frenchman, Frank nodded. "Okay, we do it your way. The rest of you, let me burn at least half a magazine before you join the chorus."

At Frank's signal, Logan, the Deacon, and Zdenka dashed to the front of the building through the haze of dust kicked up by the earlier shots from the basement.

Frank pointed his weapon at the floor and drew a curved

line of bullet holes in the wood floor. The gun made little more noise than someone clearing their throat, and they could clearly hear bullets smashing through the floor and slamming into things in the basement or whining as they ricocheted downstairs. The racket was taken up in other parts of the building as the rest of the group with suppressed weapons opened fire then, from the front of the apartment, they all heard a scream choked off in mid-breath.

St. Jacques sprang forward into the stairway to the basement, landed with both feet on a step halfway down the stairs, and propelled himself to the floor. As he hit the floor they heard a flurry of suppressed gunfire break out downstairs. The Frenchman dropped to the floor as he fired back. Frank dashed down the stairs, firing short bursts one-handed with his own weapon. Reynaud hesitated for a deep breath then leaped down, following the Frenchman's example to present a fast-moving target.

Dust roiled the air in the basement and he could just see what appeared to be a small mountain of rags. Frank and St. Jacques had disappeared into deeper shadows, the Frenchman leaving behind a puddle of blood and red smears leading into the darkness.

Reynaud lay sprawled on the concrete floor, trying to get his bearings. Like the first floor, the place was dimly lit by alcohol lamps. Besides the mound of cloth he'd noticed earlier, the cellar was broken up by a coal bin, crates, and rolls of wire. A few feet away lay a footlocker, which could offer some cover. Intensely aware of the scuffing and scraping of his clothing against the concrete, he slithered forward and cautiously started crawling around the chest.

He froze as his hand felt another hand and he heard a moan. In the darkness, he could barely make out the form of a man lying on his side, his legs drawn up in agony. Mere inches from the man's hand lay a weapon.

Carefully, watching the wounded man for any movement, Reynaud reached for the gun then snatched it and rolled, putting a footlocker between himself and the downed man.

Reynaud looked down at the weapon, the submachine gun version of the M-16, chambered for the nine-millimeter pistol cartridge. He dropped the magazine, saw the glint of cartridges, and reinserted the magazine. The barrel seemed longer and bulkier than he remembered then he realized the gun had been modified with a supresser.

He rolled again and swung up to a crouch, the subgun pointed at the wounded man. With the flashlight switched on and lighting the man, he could see the man was dying. One bullet, probably fired from above, had shattered the man's collarbone. Another round, fired from the front, had caught him in the belly, and a third had smashed his lower jaw.

Footsteps above told him someone was moving toward the stairway then he heard Logan's voice. "Okay to come on down?"

The question tickled Reynaud's funny bone and he replied, "Yeah, we're all dressed. Just move fast and careful."

Logan pounded down the stairs then dropped to the floor. Reynaud flicked the flashlight on again, pointed at the floor. "Over here. I don't know where the others are."

Logan rushed, crouching to drop beside Reynaud, who used the light to indicate the floor above. "What was the scream up there?"

"Those clowns had a hidden exit upstairs. When we all started blasting away, we flushed one. The Russian chick caught him in the brisket with that pig-sticker of hers. She got his gun. She should be coming down in a second."

Just as he finished speaking they heard soft footfalls on the stairs. As Zdenka joined them they heard a scraping sound and St. Jacques crawled toward them. "We seemed to have killed all those still down here."

"Where are you wounded?" Zdenka demanded.

"The thigh. It is only an inconvenience."

"Let me see," Zdenka said. She stood and crouched over the Frenchman and ripped the hole in his pants leg wider to examine the wound. "Find me something to put on this," she snapped at Reynaud and Logan.

Logan found an American med kit in the jumble of cases. Zdenka tore open a capsule and dumped the contents into the wound then applied dressings and wrapped it with gauze.

As the Frenchman was being treated, Frank shouted from the other side of the cellar. "Hey, guys, come take a look at what I found."

Zdenka helped St. Jacques to his feet and supported him as he hobbled toward the sound of Frank's voice, with Logan and Reynaud following. They had to go around the pile of rags to a small room hidden by the furnace. A generator stood against the wall nearest the furnace. Once inside, the saw the space had been soundproofed with acoustic tile and was sparsely furnished with a large, complex recorder on a table and three chairs, one of them still stained with blood.

Logan stared at the recorder. "What the hell...."

Frank switched on the generator then, after a few moments, flicked the recorder on, pressed a rewind switch and, after almost a few seconds of a high-pitched hum, stabbed at another button. The voices issuing from the speakers spoke Polish and, from the static and distortions, were probably speaking on telephones.

"The only place near here they'd want to tap," Frank pointed out, "and the only place in Krakow with a working phone system, is the Wawel." Gesturing at the small room, Frank continued, "This was a listening post." He turned the machine off. "We'd better finish this in a hurry. Oshevsky must be in the attic."

Frank led them from the basement, left the Deacon to guard the front door, and had started on the stairs to the second floor when Tadeusz met them at the head of the stairs. "The attic was empty."

"You're crazier than a pet skunk, you know that?" Frank said, then apparently realized the Pole wouldn't understand the idiom. "That was a risk you took—a dangerous one."

Tadeusz shrugged. "You made enough noise downstairs no one in the attic would have heard me. There was nothing there but old, broken furniture."

"Shit!" Frank fumed. "I thought sure Oshevsky'd be here. I'll bet anything he was here within the last day or so." He considered the matter for several minutes then looked up at the others. "This must've been only a cell, a listening post. The FSB must have a headquarters somewhere else, either out of town or nearer the edge of town. With luck, we'll get some clues as to where their headquarters is stashed."

Reynaud looked around. "We could be here all night and still not make a dent in this paperwork. I don't read any Polish and recognize only a few words in Russian."

"We'll leave the paperwork for Wyszynski and his men to examine," Frank said. "They're pros at this. About the only things we'll haul out are some weapons and ammo. We'd better get what we want and make it to the Wawel. Wiktor usually works late, and we might be able to catch him there."

With St. Jacques resting on a heavy rug and covered by a blanket, the rest of them went over the house in a find and grab operation. Besides the suppressed submachine guns Zdenka and Reynaud had taken, they found another suppressed Makarov and another of the machine pistols. Zdenka also found another submachine gun she claimed for her own. The Frenchman identified it as a Finnish Jati. Logan discovered a cache of ammunition, along with several M-16 and M-4s and a number of Beretta pistols, and the Deacon found a store of explosives and materials for timers like those of the bomb planted against their apartment. Along with the plastique and the pipe bombs they found an assortment of grenades of all sorts.

"Are you sure this was an FSB cell?" Logan asked. "We're finding a lot of stuff from the good ole U S of A."

Frank looked up from sorting grenades and explosives in a backpack. "That's why they had it. If they'd wanted to pull off an assassination, they'd have wanted to ditch the weapons and wouldn't want leftovers pointing back to Mother Russia. Everybody ready to go?"

With St. Jacques leaning heavily on a thick broomstick handle Tadeusz had given him, the group moved back out into the street in a ragged file. Snow again fell, driven by wind as sharp as a knife and as bitter as a broken promise. Reaching the guard station, Frank drew out an identification card. "Captain Piotrowski and my squad. We're part of Captain Wyszynski's special detachment, and we need to talk to him immediately."

The guard picked up a phone and spoke a few words into it. Within less than a minute a squad of ORMO had arrived to lead them to Wyszynski's office. The Polish officers met them at the door and dismissed the escort. Frank inclined his head toward the door to an inner office. "Make sure we aren't disturbed," Frank said to the group, and disappeared through the door with Wyszynski.

While they were waiting, Reynaud glanced at the weapon

Zdenka had taken from the man she'd stabbed. It looked a bit like the old Sten gun with a magazine jutting from the left side of the receiver and a jacket around the barrel. The suppressor jacket gave the weapon a long, ungainly look. "What have you got there?" he asked.

St. Jacques leaned back in a chair, his feet resting on another chair. "It is a Sterling, a British submachine gun. That," he tapped the machine pistol in the Deacon's lap, "is a Czech Skorpion. It fires the relatively puny seven point six five millimeter cartridge. Frank was fortunate to be shot with one. Considering the age of the vest he wore, something larger would have penetrated."

"That little zipper might work over here, where they teach people to die whenever they're hit with anything heavier than a spitwad, but it wouldn't last you a fast Saturday night in any American city," Logan said. He caressed the Ingram's receiver as though it were a hot date. "This little monster here spits out forty-five cal pills—real punkin busters."

"It is a bullet hose," the Frenchman said. "It fires from the open bolt, degrading accuracy, and it will empty that thirty-round magazine in a second or so. A fine weapon in a crowded elevator, or if you want to shoot someone near many times with great rapidity."

"You seem awful proud of that little chopper you picked up," Logan said, pointing at the Spectre. "What makes it a wonder gun?"

"Several things. It fires from a closed bolt, which enhances accuracy, it has a high cyclic rate of fire, providing an advantage in momentary firepower, the magazine holds fifty rounds, which permits sustained fire, the design is self-cooling, and it is the only submachine gun which has a double-action mechanism, making it faster to get into action than any similar weapon."

"Jeez," Logan mumbled, "sorry I asked."

"I hate to kick a man when he's down," Reynaud said to Logan, "but don't you think you ought to replace that forestrap? It's gaudier than a Hawaiian print shirt."

"What's the matter with Hawaiian shirts?" Logan demanded.

Within ten minutes, Frank and Wyszynski joined the rest of the group in the outer office.

"Good work," Wyszynski said. "From what Frank has told me, we should be able, with the information in the files, to ferret out some of their agents for interrogation. We may even have information that will lead us to the headquarters. At worst, we have plugged a leak."

"But we did not get Oshevsky," St. Jacques retorted. "And what we destroyed was only the tail of the snake, not the head."

Reynaud nodded his agreement. "We aren't any closer to bagging Chernikov or Oshevsky now than when we first got to Krakow."

"Not true," Wyszynski replied. "There is almost certain to be evidence and a trail. My men will examine everything as soon as possible. As soon as you leave I will assign a unit to guard the building."

"While you're digging through," Logan said, "you might have somebody check the bodies and their clothes. That might give you a clue where the headquarters are located."

Wyszynski stared at him with wide eyes. "Very good. We will explore that possibility. Have you any other ideas?"

"Yeah, I have an idea I'd like to talk to the Americans at the embarkation point. Think you can work that?"

"That is easily done," Wyszynski said. "Is the matter urgent, or can you wait until we call them at the usual time tomorrow?"

Logan paused. "Tomorrow would be fine."

"What's eating you, Logan?" Frank asked.

Logan tried to look casual. "What do you mean?"

"You look like you expected us to say 'no,' and you've been keyed up all day long. I got the feeling you've been expecting us to shoot you in the back or leave you with your ass hanging in the wind. God knows, what you've been through is more than enough to make a man paranoid, but there's more to it. You were obnoxious yesterday but you weren't this wired. Give."

Logan slouched in the chair and scowled at his feet for a minute. "I had a talk with Laura last night—"

"Is she still a good lay?" Frank asked.

"What?"

"Look," Frank said, "I know Laura. If she wanted something, she didn't just talk, and she can screw you and screw you over at the same time. She's a pro at both."

Logan grinned with half his mouth. "Speaking from experience?"

"Yeah," Frank admitted. "She played head games with me—both kinds. She wanted me to support General Kroslowski's campaign. Kroslowski was a glory-hungry son of a bitch who wasn't just popping Russians, he was a right-wing bastard who'd have kept Poland at war with their neighbors for the next generation. He claimed to be pro-American but everything he touched stank. Allies like that we need like we need another set of armpits. What kind of head-trip did she take you on?"

"She said you guys had sold out America and hinted you'd be using us in a private war—or for somebody else's war. She made it sound like we'd wind up dead and you'd grab whatever glory there was."

"She's still smooth, I'll hand her that," Frank said. "So you bought it?"

Logan grinned sheepishly. "Well, I didn't exactly buy it—more like I took out an option on it. It started unravelling when Jean-Marie, here, said he'd take out Barela, when all we knew for sure was that he was in the Cardinal's Guard. If Laura'd given it to me straight, you'd have dropped the job in our laps. Then, when we raided the apartment, you'd have gotten us to do the job—sort of taken a 'we'll hold your coats' tack—but you guys took the biggest risks, and you were the ones who got hit. So, what do you think of Laura? Think she's gone over to the FSB?"

Frank shook his head. "She's not the type, but I don't think she's working alone, either. I think the best thing to do is play games with *her* head. When we get back, I'll find an excuse to get you out of the room while I throw her ass out. That'll keep your hands clean. If she gets in touch with you, play innocent and learn as much as you can from her."

Frank ran a hand through his hair. "Tonight and tomorrow are going to keep us busy. When we get back, we have to off the prisoner. The basement of our apartment is dirt-floored. We'll plant a little shit and maybe the next occupants can raise a victory garden. Wiktor, we're going to need a new place to crash. We can't count on catching every bomb the bad guys plant around the place, and one good sniper could wipe us out, one at a time."

Wyszynski opened a drawer in his desk and flipped through

some papers, finally tossed one of them across the desk to Frank. "There is a house available on *Batorego*. Most of the buildings on the street house ORMO or military, so you shouldn't be noticed. But you will have to be discreet with your berets. Take everything portable with you to the Wawel tomorrow, and I will send a truck to take everything else of importance. I will also notify the supply staff you are to receive anything you ask for."

"Besides some files, the only other things of value are the extra food rations. We'd like some of them. Give Anya what she wants from the place, including as much food as she wants. Make sure the excess goes to somebody who needs it, not some fat-cat pencil-pusher."

"Done," Wyszynski stood and paced to a corner of his office, opened a cabinet, and returned with glasses and a very old bottle. He poured an inch of a brown liquid into each of the glasses. "Brandy," he said, holding up the bottle. "Very fine brandy, in fact." He picked up a glass and raised it toward them. "To your success," he said, and tossed off the drink.

Everyone but the Deacon, who refused to drink, returned the salute. "Waste not, want not," Logan said, and drained McCluskey's untouched glass.

"'Wine is a mocker and strong drink raging—'" the Deacon recited "Proverbs chapter twenty verse one"

"'Drink not all water but a little wine for thy stomach's sake,'" Reynaud answered. "You read your Bible and I'll read mine."

"You may want to leave your new toys here," Frank said, "since we'll just have to haul them back tomorrow." He left his own suppressed submachine gun on Wyszynski's desk.

With obvious reluctance, Logan began to put the MAC down but Frank shook his head. "Bring that back with you. It's yours, now, but I'd like to borrow it briefly when I talk to Laura."

"Why?"

"Because I think it may rattle her to see the gun in our hands. Keeping someone off-balance is half the trick to getting questions answered."

In the end, the group kept the suppressed Makarovs and machine pistols but left the other captured weapons with Wyszynski.

As much as he tried to hide it, the Frenchman's wound was obviously causing him a great deal of pain. Even Reynaud found the walk back to their apartment a long and tiring march, fighting a bitterly cold wind flinging snow in their faces.

Laura sat at the dining room table, eating, when they entered. Frank glanced at Logan, who handed over the Ingram. "Logan, you, Steve, Tadeusz, and the Deacon go upstairs and bring down our houseguest."

St. Jacques leaned on his stick. "I had best start downstairs now, as I am moving rather more slowly. Zdenka, would you please assist me?

Zdenka stared at Laura with a glare that should have set her afire where she sat. For a moment Reynaud thought the Cossack would refuse then she offered her shoulder to the Frenchman and the two of them made their way to the kitchen.

Frank waited until the couple had closed the kitchen door behind them then faced Laura and held up the MAC-10. "Looking for this, bitch?"

Laura's face, already pale, looked faintly greenish in the dim light. "Where did you get that?" she managed to stammer out.

Frank sat in the chair across the table from her and laid the weapon on the table, its muzzle pointed at Laura. "We found the FSB cell. So. You really sold us out, and all that patriotic bullshit was just a cover."

"Frank, you know I'd never do anything like that. It wasn't like that at all."

"Don't try to snow me." Frank's voice snapped like a whip. "You can talk birds out of trees but we recovered this weapon at an FSB safe house,"

Laura looked down at the table. Almost absently, her left hand began to slide toward her lap.

"Don't," Frank said. "Leave both hands flat on the table or we'll have one hell of a mess to clean up."

Laura moved both hands into plain view, her palms pressed flat against the table top. "I got jumped last night—"

"Don't try to give me any crap about working late last night. Where were you?"

"I was visiting some friends—other Americans who chose to stay in Poland. Real Americans—"

Frank gripped the MAC tighter till his fingers paled. "Don't wave the flag in my face, and don't make speeches. So, you got jumped. What then?"

"They took my weapon. I thought I'd had it, then a friend of mine showed up and they ran. That's all."

"Not nearly all. Why didn't you tell us this last night, when we might've still been able to get Katya out alive?"

Laura gave no answer, only glared sullenly at him.

Frank leaned toward her. "Who are your friends?"

"I've already told you," Laura said through clenched teeth.

You haven't told me crap. I suspect your pals are CIA spooks, but it really doesn't matter." He stood, holding the gun. "Get the hell out. Logan will be down in a minute or two with a prisoner. You keep your mouth shut while he's within earshot, then you go upstairs. I'll let you get your coat, any personal items you may need—almost anything you can haul out in fifteen minutes, because I want you gone by the time we get back upstairs. I'm going to have the Finn watch you while you're packing so you don't get any stupid ideas that could get you into fatal trouble."

"That's very generous of you, Frank." Laura's voice dripped sarcasm.

"You bet your overworked ass it's generous," Frank said. "If I'd told any of the group everything I know, any one of them would've killed you with no more thought than they'd give to swatting a blood-sucking mosquito. Old times' sake is the only thing keeping you alive right now, and if I see you again, you're dead, because I'll turn it over to the others. Tadeusz thought of Katya as a daughter. The Frenchman would blow your brains out at five hundred meters without a second's hesitation or a second thought. But Zdenka would cut your heart out and slap you across the face with it—"

Frank broke off his comments as Logan and the others, keeping the prisoner bracketed among them, escorted him down the stairs from the second floor. Frank signaled for Juho to approach him and, as the others disappeared into the kitchen, pointed at Laura. "Juho, Ms. Wessel will be leaving us. Go upstairs with her and watch her pack. Make sure she doesn't leave anything behind that might tick or go boom. And you might be careful, just in case she gets any hostile ideas."

Juho nodded and simply waited for the woman to get up.

Frank leaned on the door frame to the kitchen. "So long, Laura."

"Not good-bye?"

"Bad pennies have a habit of turning up, but remember what I said." He turned and walked through the kitchen, Reynaud behind him. They walked through another door at the back of the kitchen and filed down a short flight of stairs to a landing flanked at one side by an outside door and on the other by the set of stairs to the basement.

The cellar was cruder than that of the FSB cell. The floor was packed dirt in which Logan and the Deacon, using trenching tools, worked at digging a grave. Two or three candles and two of the alcohol lamps fought a losing battle against the darkness. Back in a corner, Reynaud could just make out the coils of a crude still.

They approached a cluster of people and Reynaud saw St. Jacques sitting on an old blanket, his legs stretched out before him. Facing him sat the prisoner, his legs crossed, his arms drawn behind his back. Flanking the prisoner, Tadeusz and Zdenka glared at the man.

"All right," Frank said, "the information you gave us was correct—as far as it went. The place you told us about was just a cell. Where's the headquarters?"

"I don't know. I just did as I was told. I always met them at the house."

"Where did you live?"

"At the end of *Straszewskiego*—in the rag-pickers quarters."

"What other missions have you run?"

"There were only three others—they were the same, to put a body in the *Wisal*. Most of the time I received orders and passed them on to others."

"Don't I remember you from *Zyc, Nie Umierac!*?" Tadeusz asked.

The prisoner, after a pause, nodded. "Yes, I was there. I was told to have the others follow you back to see where you lived."

"Why us?" Frank demanded.

"I don't know. They only told me what they wanted. They did not tell me why."

Tadeusz took over Logan's trenching tool, letting the American rest while he dug the grave deeper. Steve spelled the Deacon at digging.

"I think we have all the information he has to give us." Frank said. "It's time to finish this."

"I gotta admit, I don't much like this," Logan said as he drew the suppressed Makarov.

"No, friend Logan," St. Jacques snapped, his voice and eyes cold. "He has not earned the bullet. That was a choice we gave him and he refused. Zdenka, would you finish this?"

They hardly saw the blade flash in the dim light of the cellar. The Cossack bent over the prisoner and thrust the blade, edge up, into the man's belly, the point angling down into the groin. The prisoner was too weak to do more than wail, then Zdenka jerked up on the knife, the blade making a tearing noise as it cut upward through muscle and guts until it'd torn into the heart.

Blood shot out onto the floor and the swamp-gas smell from the intestines rolled into them like a physical force. Reynaud tasted something like bile in the back of his mouth. Billy Joe's face revealed no expression but was pale in the dim light, while Logan looked faintly greenish. Tadeusz kicked the body into the hole and began to shovel the blood-soaked dirt over it.

As soon as the corpse was buried the group marched upstairs, their faces grim and set. St, Jacques murmured a request to Tadeusz and Zdenka and they helped him to his feet and up the stairs. They gathered again in the dining room, where Juho, Steve, and Smyth-Davis waited for them. St. Jacques nodded toward a chair. "Despite the annoyance," he glanced down at the bandage on his leg, "I am ravenous."

"I will bring food to your room," Zdenka said. "You need to rest."

The Frenchman smiled. "Had I known it would get you into my boudoir, I would have stepped in front of a bullet earlier."

Zdenka grinned back at him. "The only reason I am going to your room now is because I know you are relatively harmless. I doubt you can be too difficult to deal with as long as you have a bullet hole in you."

St. Jacques seemed offended. "*Ma cher*, it is only my thigh that was wounded."

Tadeusz shook his head. "Help me get him upstairs," he said to Zdenka. "Once he is in bed, I can leave and not have to listen to this."

The three of them clambered up the stairs and Frank, who was watching the Americans closely, faced Logan. "You look as though you have something to say. Say it."

Logan hadn't sat and he faced Frank, legs slightly apart and fists on his hips, a combative pose. "You're goddam right I've got something to say. This stinks. I thought we were supposed to be the good guys. I thought I knew the Frenchie, but now—Christ! And the chick is the one who gutted him." His face was still pale. "A woman for chrisakes. That's not the kind of thing a woman should even see."

Frank clenched his fists. "What is a woman's job, Logan? To cry for help? That didn't seem to help Katya any. To die? Katya did that well enough, and she wasn't only female, she was only twelve years old. This is everybody's war, so drop all the chauvinist bullshit. Men or women, we can all die, and this dirty little war belongs to all of us."

"It isn't just that," Logan said obstinately. "Okay, maybe the prisoner needed to be killed; I can understand why we didn't just turn him over to the ORMO, but the Lone Ranger never would've killed a prisoner. Neither would the Green Hornet. Even if they'd had to bump somebody off, they'd have at least made it quick and painless."

Frank suddenly looked weary and dropped into a chair. "And we aren't heroes. We aren't people reading a radio script for thirty minutes three nights a week. We're just poor damned sloggers, doing the best we can. We'd like to be out of this war but that's not possible, so we fight it the best way we can. St. Jacques is a stickler about keeping his word. If the ZOMO had talked right away, the Frenchie would've shot him. But once he made us work, once he forced us into barbarism, St. Jacques figured the guy had chosen to pay for the trip. As for Zdenka, she's a different matter."

"Yeah, I noticed," Logan said. "She gets off on using that knife.

Frank slammed his fist on the table. "You're pretty damned quick to judge. Sure, she can be ruthless. Life's been pretty ruth-

117

less to her, too. You don't know anything about her. The only one of us she got really close to was Katya, then Katya gets run through a meat-grinder by a bunch of sadist bastards. How would you have felt in her place?"

Reynaud, sitting at the table, looked up at Frank. "What I'd like to know is what you'd have done if, instead of an ex-ZOMO, the prisoner you were questioning had been another twelve-year-old kid."

Frank's weariness seemed close to exhaustion. "That's a good question," he admitted. "I don't know." He looked up the stairs as they heard Zdenka and Tadeusz coming down. "Look, you guys paid your dues in the camp. You don't owe anything to us or anyone else, so if you want to sit out the rest of the dance, that's okay."

After looking at the rest of the group, Logan shook his head and sat down. "I guess we're in for the long haul. So what do we do next?"

"The hardest job," Frank said. "We wait. We wait for Wiktor's boys to find out where the FSB headquarters is hidden, or for the FSB to try to kill us."

Chapter 7

Zdenka walked through the dining room then stopped at the kitchen door to face them with red-rimmed eyes. "Anya is cleaning Katya's body and dressing her for the funeral. We will make our own dinners tonight."

As she and Tadeusz continued into the kitchen, Logan cleared his throat. "That's all right with me. I don't have much appetite tonight, so I guess I'll just call it a night."

Frank hauled himself to his feet. "I noticed that Anya had almost everything that'd hold water on the stove, heating, so you can sort of bathe. You'll have to do it standing in the kitchen, but you can scrub down and rinse yourselves, and we've got some extra shaving kits so you can clear that shrubbery off your faces if you want to."

Logan ran a hand over the beard he'd trimmed closer. "Thanks, but I haven't had a chance to grow one of these since I got out of college. I think I'll keep it."

After what was little better than a sponge bath and a shave, Reynaud felt better and his appetite returned. He'd finally gotten the swamp gas odor out of his nostrils and the echo of the ripping sound out of his ears. He chose an MRE, cut it open, and prepared it on the stove. When the meal was ready he carried it to the dining room and stared at the collection of near-strangers.

Only Logan was unchanged. The Deacon, Smyth-Davis, and Juho were all clean-shaven, and each face seemed more like the man who wore it. The Deacon's long, bony face looked even more austere without the beard to soften the features, while Juho's square-cut face looked stronger and stonier. Smyth-Davis had a refined face with aristocratic features that had been almost concealed by the facial hair. Steve's sparse beard had been shaved away leaving only a fine moustache. Reynaud himself had left a luxuriant moustache, not as martial as Tadeusz's carefully-shaped handlebars but generous enough to be the envy of an old-west lawman.

Frank, who'd already finished eating, nursed a cup of coffee. "I feel like I need to introduce myself to you all over again."

Reynaud grinned and stroked his now-smooth cheeks. "Most of us feel like we need to be re-introduced to our own faces. I haven't seen mine for almost six months." He sobered then. "What are you going to do about Anya?"

"I'll talk to her in the morning. We're going to miss her—she's like everybody's aunt. I'll have to talk to Wiktor about her; have him find her a good place to live. I couldn't think of her living in some of the places for refugees." He drained his cup of coffee and carried the cup and his tray into the kitchen.

~ * ~

Reynaud woke slowly, basking in the languid state between sleep and waking and afraid to get out of the warm bed. He regretted, too, the knowledge he'd be leaving this place so soon. He was exhilarated at being out of the prison camp but also sensed he'd traded captivity for rootlessness; he wouldn't be able to call anyplace home until he returned to the states, and possibly not even then.

The pleasure of the waking state was crowded out by a feeling that an urgent task waited for him. Downstairs, he stood by the stove, warming himself as Anya prepared breakfast. He found himself at a loss for words and the discomfort grew until he patted her on the shoulder and trudged into the dining room.

Most of the two groups had already gathered at the table. Like Reynaud, all of them seemed to have dressed with special care and somehow the somber uniforms seemed appropriate. Eating breakfast was a duty, one they grimly performed. After the table had been cleared, Frank asked Anya to sit down.

"We are going to have to move," Frank explained, in Polish. "The FSB know where we are now. We want you to take all the food you want. I will have someone be sure you are given a safe place to live. We have enough things to trade to make the place warm and comfortable for you. We would like to be able to have you with us, but it would be very dangerous for you."

"No!" Anya shook her head emphatically. "No! I lost my Henryk to the plague. Bandits killed my son Walery, and Katya " Her face worked as though trying to wring tears out of eyes that had wept themselves dry. "Now Katya is gone, too. You have become my family. If I have no family, I have no use. I am just an old dead woman who has not enough brains to lie down and be buried."

Frank looked at the others, and most of them stared back wordlessly or gazed at the table. After a moment's hesitation, St. Jacques cleared his throat. "My leg would make me slow in the streets. I will stay here, and when you have seen the priest, one of you can bring Anya back. When the men come to take the food and a few other things to our new apartment, we will go with them. Have our friend Captain Wyszynski give his men a pass-word. Make it 'The battle of Grunwald,'" He smiled at Anya. "It is good to know I will not lose my aunt."

Frank looked relieved. "Great. We'll leave now. Logan and Zdenka can bring Anya back here. I'll feel better with everyone doubling up, working in pairs or larger groups, since we know the black hats are probably primed for us. Jean-Marie, who should I talk to at the cathedral?"

"Father Stefan Broniak. You have met him once or twice. Just be sure Wyszynski has good men he can trust to do the mov-ing. Also, have him take care of it as soon as possible. I will attend the funeral."

They gathered upstairs where Katya's body was laid out. Reynaud hadn't really looked closely at the body before, and it was a shock to see the pale girl lying on the bed, her dark hair spilling across the pillow. Her slenderness excited his sympathy and she seemed like something fragile that had been brutally shattered.

Steve picked up a corner of the sheet on which the dead girl lay. "The best way to do this is for four of us to each pick up one corner of the sheet. When we get outside, we can put her in the cart."

Reynaud moved to the opposite corner from Steve's and Tadeusz and Frank took the other corners. Reynaud was surprised by how light the body was, and he understood better Zdenka's fury. The body was already rigid, making negotiating the stairs tricky work.

The sky had cleared during the night and dawn was bright-ening the east as they trudged to the Wawel, Reynaud and Tadeusz each pulling a pole of the cart. Tadeusz steered them past the imposing cathedral to a building like the part of the castle occu-pied by the army and the ORMO. They stopped the cart and

Frank strode inside.

The rest of the group stood shivering in the chill morning until Frank returned with a young priest who directed them to carry the body inside and place it on a table in an office. The priest began to recite prayers for the dead. When he finished, he took Anya's hand. "If you would like to stay with her, just sit here. Your friends and I can make the arrangements." With the group following he trod to another office and closed the door behind them.

Frank took a chair. "We want this done right, Father. We'd like to get a coffin and have her buried in a private grave."

Father Broniak sat down behind the desk. "I can arrange for the coffin but payment will have to be made to the carpenter and the gravedigger."

"We can cover that, and a funeral Mass."

The priest held up his hand. "The other things are out of my control but no payment is necessary for the Mass. It is part of our work. But where is Jean-Marie?"

"He's been shot," Frank said bluntly. "It isn't bad but it's slowed him down. He wanted us to find out when you could perform the funeral Mass so he could attend."

"It is always a pleasure to see Jean-Marie at Mass. With Poles, I can never tell whether they attend from devotion or it is only a habit acquired in the old days when it was the best way to annoy the government and the Russians. Jean-Marie never claimed to be devout but he was usually there." He consulted a desk calendar. "We can have the Mass at four thirty this afternoon." He picked up a pen and began to fill out the paper then looked up. "Is this the girl Jean-Marie was looking for?"

Frank nodded.

"I am sorry I could not help him, but I did learn something else. One of the members of *Znak* is a playwright and director at *Teatr imienia Słowakiego*. He noticed, last week, a rat hole in the back of the closet of his dressing room. It was easy to notice because light was coming up from the basement. The basement is sealed with a government order. Then Konstantin began to check with some of the other theater companies and began to observe who came into the building during the week, when it was closed for everything but rehearsals. There were strangers entering the building who had nothing to do with the theater."

Frank leaned forward. "Can he describe any of them?"

"No, he hardly saw them. He just knew more people were coming and going than could be accounted for."

"Thank you," Frank said. "Oh, Father, you might let the commander of the Cardinal's Guard know that Lieutenant Barela will not be reporting for duty. You might also suggest a security screening of the guard might be a good idea." He stood abruptly. "We'd better go now."

"Sit," Father Broniak waved him back into the chair. "I still need the information to finish filling out this form. What was Katya's full name?"

As soon as they'd given the necessary information they returned to the room where Anya sat hunched over, her face buried in a handkerchief. Zdenka placed a gentle hand on her shoulder. "Come, Aunt Anya, it is time to go." She helped the older woman to her feet and, keeping the hand on her arm, led her out of the building, Logan following a couple of paces behind.

The rest of the group followed Frank to Captain Wyszynski's office, where the captain was conferring with a sergeant. Wyszynski stood, taking a handful of papers from the soldier. "Dismissed, sergeant." He returned the noncom's salute then waved the others into chairs. "Some of your group seems to be missing," he observed. "I hope St. Jacques' wound was not more serious than we thought last night."

"Not really." Frank explained the change in plans and the need for both speed and secrecy in moving.

Wyszynski tapped at his desk with the top of his pen. "I will make the arrangements as soon as you leave." He handed the sheaf of papers to Frank. "These are the files we have deciphered so far. There is nothing concrete in them but there are some strange references to the theater."

"What do you know about the *Teatr imienia Slowakiego?*" Frank asked.

"Only what everyone else knows, but then your friends are strangers to Poland." He stopped tapping the pen on his desk and leaned forward. "The theater is very important to Poles. In the not-too-distant past, the only way Poles could express themselves about society and the government was in the theater, and so, seeing each new play as it came out was an important bond. Because of the war and the plague, and some of the disasters which occurred because too many skilled people died, the people of Krakow must work twelve or fourteen hours a day to repair the city. Many cities are in a much more wretched state."

Wyszynski stared past them at nothing. "In Warsaw, the dead are rebuilding. The Russians, after pulling back past or around it, struck Warsaw with an airburst, flattening much of the city. Then someone, probably the Russians, set off a hidden nuclear device at ground level so the city was salted with deadly radioactivity. Many of the people dying from radiation poisoning are still working in the rubble, working until they die so the city can live again.

"I am sorry." Wyszynski dropped his gaze to where his hands were aimlessly toying with his pen. "I did not mean to talk away from the subject. The people of Krakow are too exhausted at the end of the day to do more than eat their meals and fall into their beds—those who have beds. Because of the importance of the theater, members of theater companies are relieved of construction duties for two hours a day. The city also provides a generator to provide power for the stage lights. And, on Friday and Saturday nights the curfew is relaxed until twenty-three hundred hours."

"Do you have any plans or blueprints for the theater?" Reynaud asked.

"It was built long before plans needed to be submitted to the city before building, but there must be repair records or some other information I can find. What caused this sudden interest in the theater?"

Frank explained what he'd heard from Father Broniak then said, "With what he told us, and the references to the theater in the FSB files, this sounds like what we've been looking for—a trail to the headquarters."

Wyszynski began tapping his pen again. "This is Friday. I think I can get you passes to the performance tonight."

Steve stroked his fine moustache. "It'd be a fine thing to take part in the cultural life of the city."

"Excellent," Wyszynski said. "I will get the passes after I have made the arrangements for your move. The only other matter to discuss is Chernikov. Your people have still not found him."

"Something else," Juho said. "When can we go home?"

"I can send you next week if you want to go then," Wyszynski said. "We have convoys that can get you to Gdynia— Gdansk is still radioactive rubble, and try to get fishermen to take you back to Finland. Our British friend could go along." He turned to face Smyth-Davis. "We can have you taken to Denmark, where you might be able to find a boat to take you back to England."

Smyth-Davis raised one eyebrow and steepled his fingers. "I should prefer to share accommodations with my comrades-in-arms. I shall go back when they go."

Juho looked at the Englishman, then at the others. "I will wait, too,"

~ * ~

The old apartment off *Paulinksa* stood southeast of the Wawel. The new apartment on *Batorego* lay north and a little west, almost twice as far. The group had to hurry to reach the place before the noon *hejnal*, and they found the others waiting for them.

Anya gave them bread and sausage and the Frenchman found some wine which he pronounced acceptable.

Frank washed a mouthful of food with a swallow of wine. "We'd better stop at the Wawel mess hall for supper if we're going to catch the play tonight. We can have someone escort Anya back here."

The Deacon sipped at then put down his glass of water. "It seems to me to be time wasted on unholy amusements."

Logan drained his glass of wine and leaned back from the table. "Billy Joe, there's times when I think you could curdle milk." He looked at the others. "But we don't have time to spend watchin' a bunch of limp-wrists struttin' around in tight underwear or listenin' to a fat woman screaming about her armor bein' too tight, do we?"

Smyth-Davis again raised an eyebrow. "I doubt the Krakow companies are going to be performing the work of the bard. Further, I doubt opera is on the bill. As I understand it, this is more of a reconnaissance mission, is that not correct, Captain

Piotrowski?"

"Right. When we stop at the Wawel, we'll change into civvies, so don't take anything bigger than a pistol. Logan, you try to pack that MAC with a supressor on it and somebody's going to think you're trying to smuggle in a seven-course dinner into the place. Besides wearing civvies, we all talk nothing but Polish inside the theater. If you can't speak Polish well, and none of you from the prison camp can, keep your mouths shut."

"Subtle," Steve said, "very subtle. And how do we let the rest of you know if we see something interesting?"

"Hand signals and eye contact." Frank stood. "Considering St. Jacques' leg, maybe we'd better be hitting the road now, so we can be sure to get to Mass on time. Have you had someone look at the wound, Jean-Marie?"

St. Jacques nodded. "Zdenka has seen nothing to indicate infection. She cleaned and dressed the wound just before you arrived. The fewer who know of our bullet wounds, the better."

Logan grinned at the Cossack. "What do you do for excitement around here, besides look at St. Jacques' leg?"

Zdenka smiled. "I carve little toy soldiers."

Steve chuckled. "Mister Sensitivity strikes again. I think I'd be more polite to somebody as good with a knife as she is." He stood with the others as they began to don coats, hats, and scarves. Russian-style fur hats were common enough in Krakow that both Frank and Jean-Marie wore them instead of their berets.

As he fastened his greatcoat, Logan studied the group. "You know, what this outfit needs is a little color."

Reynaud wrapped a scarf around his lower face. "We're going to a funeral, Logan. Maybe later you could go into the clothing business—go broke importing Hawaiian shirts."

Just before he slammed the door shut behind them, Logan glared at Reynaud. "What's the matter with Hawaiian shirts?"

During the walk to the Wawel, with St. Jacques leaning on a cane Logan had found somewhere, Reynaud reflected on the last few days. What had started out as a simple mission of escape and vengeance had become complicated, with other hurt people with their own needs. Somehow, he'd expected, once they'd learned Chernikov and Oshevsky had reached Krakow, they could be tracked down and destroyed like the mad dogs they were. Instead, both men seemed to have vanished into a mist, leaving no trail but bodies behind them.

At the cathedral he was surprised at how familiar the Mass seemed, and how comforting it was. Although the responses were in Polish rather than English, it was like an echo of the old days, when life was more settled. This was the second Mass he'd attended in almost a year, and the first in years to which he paid any attention. He glanced at the Deacon and saw the man was participating only as a duty.

After the Mass, they loaded the coffin onto a cart painted black and Reynaud and Logan, following Father Broniak's directions, pulled the cart northwest to a park running along the Vistula. The park had been converted to a graveyard, with clusters of individual graves spotted between mounds of earth that had been heaped over mass graves. Finally, they found the open grave, almost hidden by the driven snow.

The priest intoned a few last words over the coffin and sprinkled holy water on it, then, using ropes, they lowered the wooden box to the bottom of the hole. Anya picked up a handful of earth and tossed it into the grave, and each of the others did the same. As they filed away, an older man with an unlit pipe jutting from beneath a walrus moustache and a shovel over his shoulder approached the hole.

Anya fell sobbing onto Zdenka's shoulder and Zdenka tried to comfort the older woman while controlling her own crying. St. Jacques hobbled perhaps twenty feet away from the group and turned his back to them, and Reynaud heard painful, racking sobs. He chanced a look at Tadeusz. The Pole's face seemed even sterner than usual, despite the tracks of tears down his cheeks. Frank wiped at his face with the sleeve of his greatcoat, his face seeming decades older and weary. Reynaud looked back at the man filling the grave and his own eyes began to sting, a lump grew in his throat he couldn't swallow and could hardly breathe around, and he felt a tightness at the bridge of his nose.

Reynaud wished he'd had the chance to know Katya, felt the bitterness of loss, knowing another chance for happiness and hope to survive the war and its aftermath had been lost forever. Katya was only one of thousands, perhaps millions of children killed by the war and the plague, who'd died of cruelty or indifference, which was perhaps the worst form of cruelty.

He felt moisture on his own face and tasted salt in his mouth. Self-consciously, he wiped the dampness away. When he looked up again, the Frenchman had rejoined them, his eyes still red but with some trace of his usual languid insouciance reasserting itself.

Frank handed Father Broniak a large bundle of the ration chits that were used as currency then came back to the group.

"That was a lot of script for a coffin and a grave," Reynaud said.

Frank seemed to shrug with his entire body. "Father Broniak also knows a stone-cutter."

By the time they'd reached the Wawel again, the open mourning was done, although Zdenka still walked with her arm around Anya. They passed inside, into Wyszynski's office, where the captain paced nervously. As soon as he saw them he strode toward them. "I have news—" He stopped as he noticed Anya.

"This is Anya," Frank said. "Anya, this is Captain Wiktor Wyszynski."

Wyszynski paused a moment then offered them chairs. "I have news from Antwerp. They have found a body...they have not been able to identify the man yet."

Reynaud could guess what Wyszynski was afraid to say in front of Anya, knowing Chernikov as he did, he didn't doubt the man's face and hands had been disfigured beyond recognition.

"His papers were gone, of course. All they could tell was that he'd been an army officer. Even his rank badges and unit patches were taken."

Steve sank onto the chair he'd chosen. "That means Chernikov is on his way to America." His voice sounded tired and colorless.

Wyszynski nodded.

"Just a moment." Reynaud had suddenly remembered something, something he'd lost in the confusion and urgency of escape. "Were there any flights leaving for Texas or the southwestern states? Paulson said something about this Operation Alpha, or whatever, being set for Texas or the southwest. Would it be possible to find out who was scheduled for that flight or those flights?"

Wyszynski started for his inner office. "I can find out." He stopped at the door. "Lieutenant Reid, did you still want to talk to your people?"

Logan glanced at the others. "Nah, I'll wait to find out what's still standing in the states until we can all learn."

The Pole was gone for over a quarter of an hour and he looked troubled when he returned. "Six flights left for Texas this morning, two to northern New Mexico, one to northern Arizona. It does help narrow the search. They will try to contact me with more information by Monday morning. While I was speaking to the people in Antwerp I asked about the cities you had listed as your home cities." He looked at Reynaud and Steve and lowered his gaze. "I am sorry. Port Arthur was devastated by an airburst and Colorado Springs was apparently hit by one of the missiles aimed at NORAD. The missile was defective, and only exploded on impact."

He dropped into his chair and rubbed his eyes. "Lieutnant Symth-Davis, London was struck by two airbursts." He looked up. "Lawrence, Kansas and Asheville, North Carolina were not hit by missiles."

"Thanks for not saying the rest, Vic." Logan shoved himself out of his chair and began to pace. "But we're getting used to the idea that the plague went where the bombs didn't. Thanks for asking for us."

Reynaud felt numb. He'd avoided the thought before but it was there in his face; both his parents, his sister, his brother-in-law, and both of their kids—all gone. He felt as desolated as the city must've been. He'd never really felt the terrible effects of the plague and the war before this—he'd been too busy; first, surviving the plague then preparing for and carrying out his last combat mission and, finally, surviving the prison camp and the escape. Then he remembered he wasn't the only one worried about his family. "What about Finland?" he asked.

"No nuclear weapons were used against Finland and it was relatively untouched by the war. I do not know how badly the plague struck there."

"We'd better get something to eat soon," Frank said. "Let's see, it's Friday, so the menu is *barszcz*, which the Russians call *borscht*."

"That's all right." Reynaud said, "I'm not very hungry." The others nodded and Reynaud guessed they'd been having the same grim thoughts.

"No, it's not," Frank shot back. "You are Wiktor's guests and if you refuse to accept his hospitality, you insult him. Once upon a time, that would've gotten you into a duel. As it is, you're insulting him."

Reynaud exchanged glances with the others. "No offence intended. We just weren't clear on the rules."

"Okay," Frank said, levering himself to his feet, "it's settled. Oh, Wiktor, did you get the tickets?"

Wyszynski opened the middle drawer of his desk and drew out a handful of tickets. "These were harder to obtain than I thought they would be. I could only get nine tickets."

"That's all right with me," Logan said. "I really didn't want to go anyway."

"Think again," Frank replied. "We're probably going to have to raid the place, and if you aren't in on the recon, you'll be going in about half-blind."

"Y'know, on second thought, I've been feeling the need for a dose of culture."

The officers' mess was partitioned off but the food was the same as that eaten by the enlisted men. Reynaud spooned up some of the *barszcz* and his appetite returned. He almost felt guilty at appreciating the taste and the warmth in his belly then realized it was no more his fault he'd survived than it was his relatives' fault they hadn't, and the dead past was beyond mourning.

The *barszcz* was a beet soup, made with meat stock and, while it might profit by the addition of a little hot sauce, it was a warming meal, and a warm dinner took some of the sharp edges off an ugly world.

Wyszynski arranged an escort for Anya back to the new apartment while the team changed into civilian clothing to go to the theater. Frank dug out more of the ration chits and passed them around. "You can consider today payday. This is just in case you want to buy something or want to stop at a bar on the way home."

St. Jacques settled the Russian hat at a rakish angle. "We will visit you tomorrow, when we have formulated a plan of action."

Wyszynski followed them to the door. "I am still hoping to find something to help you."

"We appreciate the thought," Frank replied, and they made their way out of the building and into the teeth of a wind from the north. The theater stood northeast of the Wawel, a part of the old town, a roughly oval area which was bounded by thin strips of trees and grass where the old walls had once stood. The *Teatr imienia Slowakiego* was nestled just inside the northeast section of the narrow park strip.

Logan stared at the building. "How well are we going to be able to scope the place out?"

"Not very well, I'm afraid." Frank's gloved hands were thrust into the pockets of his coat. "About all we can do is try to find all the ways down into the basement. If the FSB is using the cellar as a headquarters, they'll probably have all the ways down sealed with official-looking government papers posted. Even if we could find a way to get the doors open without making one hell of a racket, we'd probably wind up in a pretty one-sided gunfight. I don't know about you, but being under-gunned in a firefight in a crowded theater isn't my idea of a fun Friday night."

Steve squinted at the building. "So, how do we get tickets for all of us?"

"You really don't know much about this place, do you?" Frank grinned. "Poland has a lot of traditions—standing in line and dealing in the black market are only two—but the theater has some traditions of its own. One of these is scalpers. The prop men and stage handlers and all that crew are probably given complimentary tickets. Unless I miss my guess, we'll see some of them outside the theater."

Reynaud was grateful for the chance to move freely, and even for the chance to see a play. With all that had happened, the resurgence of some of the trappings of civilization was comforting, a sign that the world was alive and struggling to recover.

Very faintly they heard a clopping, clattering noise then the sound became louder as a squadron of police cavalry rounded the corner ahead of them and they rode their horses, at a walk, down the middle of the street toward them. Reynaud noticed they were armed with what looked like long nightsticks and sidearms. The breaths of the horses rose, clear to see in the cold air, swirling around their heads like plumes.

Logan drew in a deep breath. "Now that's a homey smell—horseflesh. Reminds me of the farm."

Frank chuckled. "Then you should've gotten positively maudlin at the *barszcz.*"

Logan shot him a glare. "Now why did you have to go and say that? Some of us have delicate constitutions."

They rounded the corner from which the cavalry had appeared and saw a line of people forty or fifty feet long outside the theater. The line led back from a large door set in a section of wall that formed an angle to the two walls adjoining it. The theater, like much of Krakow, was impressive; a two-story structure with columns along the second floor and statuary above the columns. In the dimness they could hardly see the two cupolas flanking the façade at the front of the building.

Frank jerked his head at them as a signal to follow him and strolled along the line. At the center of the façade, the floor, at street level, was indented to provide shelter from the weather, a place of darkness and shadows. Frank stopped near a massive pillar and spoke softly with a man Reynaud could hardly see.

Reynaud had noticed the wooden signs posted outside the theater but the only thing on the sign he could read was the numeral 5. He moved closer to where Frank haggled with the unseen figure.

"Seven for each ticket is enough," Frank was saying. "To offer you more is to encourage robbery."

"Twenty apiece is almost too little," the other voice replied. "My wife's family relies upon me to put food in their mouths. Would you see the little ones go hungry?"

"Eight a ticket is all I can afford," Frank said. "Eight chits a ticket, and I will have nothing to eat tomorrow myself."

"Tomorrow is tomorrow," the Pole responded. "By tomorrow you will have found a way to get something to eat, but my nieces and nephews—they have not our resources. Twenty a ticket."

Reynaud leaned toward Logan and muttered, "Sounds like this guy is being a hard-ass. Frank's going up, but this guy's not coming down."

"Maybe I can make him an offer he can't refuse," Logan

murmured back. He reached into his pocket and drew out the wad of chits he'd received and waved them at the shadow beside Frank. Three long strides, and Logan was also in the shadows. Reynaud heard a choked-off cry and, after two or three rapid thumps, the heavier sound of a body falling.

Reynaud crowded forward just as Logan stepped out of the darkness, shaking his hand as though trying to shake out a cramp. "You just gotta know how to talk to 'em," he informed Frank. Reynaud saw a man lying at the foot of the pillar, a roll of chits stuffed into his mouth. The man moaned and rolled onto his side.

"Damned nice of him," Logan said. "He seemed to know we were from out of town and wanting to see the sights of the big city, and he insisted I take the tickets for ten chits apiece."

"Shhhh," Frank held a finger to his lips. The line, perhaps thirty feet away, had begun to move, shuffling forward into the theater. They retreated to the end of the line and eventually made their way inside, more people joining the queue behind them.

The theater was ornate but unheated and the air was thick with exhaled breath. The group split up and prowled through the lobby, examining the furnishings and especially the walls. Reynaud found a door with a printed notice pasted to its face. The door stood at the tip of a crescent formed by the lobby. Tadeusz nodded to show he'd seen it, too then led them into the theater itself and down the aisle. A glance showed Frank and the others had already taken seats, and Tadeusz slid into the same row, Reynaud following.

The first performance was a prewar play called "The Germans," which reminded Reynaud the Poles disliked and distrusted the Germans nearly as much as the Russians. During the intermission, Reynaud followed Tadeusz to the restroom. They relieved themselves and ascertained there were no doors leading to the cellar from the lavatory. As they left, Zdenka emerged from another door. Zdenka caught Tadeusz's attention and shook her head slightly.

Frank had strode forward and disappeared up a flight of stairs leading behind the curtain. As he returned to his seat he nodded and held up two fingers. Just before the house lights dimmed, St. Jacques also held up two fingers and pointed to the stage and orchestra pit.

The second play was a grim postwar presentation called "Out of the Cage." Reynaud couldn't follow it well, but it seemed to be about the country jumping from the frying pan into the fire. It was a relatively brief one-act play and was followed almost immediately by "Pandora's Box," which was only slightly longer. Reynaud understood why it had been chosen as the final performance. It showed the war and the plague as problems from Pandora's box but reminded the audience the last thing out of the box was hope for the future.

While St. Jacques and the others took their time about leaving the comparative warmth of the theater, Reynaud, Frank, and Logan hurried out and walked once around the building, finding a single outside exit from the basement.

The walk back to the new apartment was a long one, made even longer by the bitter cold. By the time they'd reached their building, the Frenchman's face, despite the cold, was beaded with sweat and he dropped into a chair as soon as they were inside.

"This operation is going to be awfully tricky," Frank admitted. "We know of at least seven exits and we'll have to block or cover them all then we have to assault the place, and that's going to be really nasty. They know the area and we don't. Also, we've got to try to keep the theater from being damaged too much and, to top it off, we want to do this as quietly as possible. Does anyone have any suggestions or ideas, no matter how wild?"

Smyth-Davis arched an eyebrow. "It sounds rather as though the best solution would be a very small, very quiet neutron bomb. Unfortunately, I'm unaware of the existence of any such device."

"Not bad at all," Frank said. "At least it's giving us a starting-point, sort of a job description."

Logan cast a concerned glance at the Frenchman, who'd stopped sweating but still looked haggard, then chuckled at a thought. "The guy we need for this job is The Shadow, who could," he spoke into his cupped hands to create an echo chamber effect like an old radio show," cloud the minds of men,"

Frank suddenly sat up and snapped his fingers. "That's exactly it! We'll cloud 'em good. Jean-Marie, have you still got your gas mask?"

The Frenchman nodded.

"Great! I think Wiktor can get us some more masks and some gas and smoke grenades. That oughta help us even the odds."

Steve nodded his thanks to Anya who brought a tray of cups of coffee. "Timing is very important. We need to hit them soon. Oshevsky's stayed a jump ahead of us, and we need to nail him soon, before he can pull something else new and lethal. Hell, for all we know, he may be trying to get out of Krakow to join Chernikov, and if he does that, we may never catch either of the bastards."

Reynaud sipped at his own coffee. "You're right about speed being important. Part of it depends upon how fast we can get the grenades, but we also have to choose the best time to attack. At a guess, the people hiding in that basement are going to be most primed during the day, when they can generally expect people to stay away. If I were using the place as cover, I'd feel safest on Friday and Saturday nights. I'd get my agents in when people were coming to rehearsals and move them out when the crews went home, before curfew. From the beginning of rehearsals until the end of curfew in the morning would be the second safest time." He paused for another sip of coffee. "Do you think they have rehearsals on Sunday night?"

"Good thought." Frank dug a pen and a pocket notebook out of his shirt pocket and began to scratch notes. "Sunday night would probably be the best time to tackle the nest."

"'Keep holy the Sabbath,'" Billy Joe flashed a rare smile. "What could be holier than destroying the minions of the Godless?"

Steve finished his coffee and set the cup down. "Can we get help from the ORMO or the military—maybe even the police?"

"I wouldn't bet the ranch on it," Logan shot back. "I kinda think we're fighting someone else's war because we aren't direct players. That about right, Frank?"

Frank sighed. "I'm afraid you're right. Obviously, there are leaks in the ORMO and the military. The FSB had to have inside help to get their man or men in to tap the lines, and lay down their own lines. I suspect the phone taps just supplemented the information they were getting from agents planted inside. The whole government is in a state of flux—the best time for spying.

Smyth-Davis stood. "No offence, chaps, but I'd feel rather more secure had we the services of an SAS detachment."

"No offence taken," Steven said. "We'd all feel better about it, too."

Logan got to his feet. "Hell, we can handle this little set-to. Most of us were fighter jocks. We're used to playing it fast and tight."

Reynaud shook his head. "This kind of thing takes different skills." He smothered a yawn and stood, then looked at the Frenchman, who was regaining some color after drinking a cup of coffee and a glass of wine. "Can I help you to your room?"

"Tadeusz and I can take care of that," Logan said. "The only good thing I've seen about this place is all the bedrooms are on the ground floor."

~ * ~

They found Wyszynski talking with an older man with a thicket of beard when the group entered his office. As the man turned toward them, Logan stode forward and thrust out a hand to the stranger. "As I live and breathe—it's Gabby Hayes."

Wyszynski and the bearded Pole looked at each other in apparent confusion then Wyszynski stood and walked around the desk. "You must be mistaken, Lieutenant Reid, this is Jacek Rakosi. He was a janitor at the theater before the war and he has offered his help. We've prepared a layout of the theater basement as it was when Jacek worked there."

Within half an hour the members of the group had familiarized themselves with the layout of the cellar. The place was a rabbit's warren but, once inside, they could control most of the area by seizing two corridors.

After the older man answered all the questions they could think of about the basement and had left the office, Frank sat down in one of the battered chairs. "We've got three good gas masks. We need five more, and all the spare filters you can find. We're also going to need all the tear gas and smoke grenades you can find us." He thought for a moment, then added, "And we'd like forged certificates identifying us as workers for the Ministry of Health. They should be obvious enough forgeries that the government can deny them but good enough to fool civilians."

"We can do that. When do you need them?"

"Sunday afternoon, at the latest."

Wyszynski began to toy with his pen. "It will be difficult but I will see it is done." He glanced at Reynaud. "Your people in Antwerp think your guess might be correct. They are transmitting the warning that those sent to Texas and your southwest be quarantined until their identification papers can be verified."

Reynaud continued to study the drawing of the theater basement. "What about the flights scheduled to take off?"

"There are none. Those were the last flights—the last airplanes available to the Americans. With the fuel shortage, the lack of spare parts, and the limited number of trained ground crew, there are no more flights scheduled to leave for America."

Reynaud's stomach seemed to drop. Their escape, bought with so many lives, had suddenly become all but worthless, a nearly futile gesture. "You mean we're stuck here?" he demanded.

If Wyszynski was offended by Reynaud's remark, he concealed it well. "Your commanders are arranging a ship convoy, using as many transport ships as they can find. This is, in fuel, far more economical. We will send you north, to the Baltic, where a ship will carry you to where the convoy is being assembled."

Reynaud let out a breath he hadn't realized he'd been holding.

Wyszynski continued toying with his pen, flipping it in his fingers, sliding his fingers down the barrel, then flipping it again. "The files you found have been most useful. An army captain has been transferred to Lublin where he will be, regrettably, shot by a Russian sniper. A lieutenant in the ORMO is being closely watched—we hope we can find his contacts and, perhaps, follow them. A third agent—an ORMO desk sergeant has disappeared, which means there is still what you Americans call a 'leak,' even in our special security group."

"That answers my question," Steve said. "No help."

Wyszynski sagged in his chair. "I am sorry. What you will be doing is too sensitive to chance warning the enemy."

~ * ~

When the group returned to the apartment they found St. Jacques cleaning his sniper rifle, a strange-looking bolt action weapon with a telescopic sight, a integral bipod, a synthetic shroud covering the barrel, and a pistol grip that looked as though it'd been added as an afterthought to a sporting rifle. He looked up from his work. "Did you get what we need?"

"We hope to have it by tomorrow afternoon," Frank replied. "Sorry you're going to have to sit this one out."

"I may not be able to take part in the attack," St. Jacques said, "but there are rat holes to watch. If I can do that, it frees one more for the assault."

"Maybe we can whip together a sled for you," Steve said. "It'd help save wear and tear on your leg. We can give it a test run when we go to Mass tomorrow."

St. Jacques grinned. "*Bien*. Frank, you will have to accompany Tadeusz, Anya, and I."

"It is not an orthodox Mass, but I will go with Anya," Zdenka said.

Seeing he was outnumbered, Frank shrugged. "All right, I'll go, if only to see Father Broniak's face."

After glancing at the others, Reynaud also shrugged. "I may as well go, too. How about the rest of you?"

Smyth-Davis' lips twitched. "It's rather higher Anglican—or different Anglicanism—than my usual religious fare, but it's an improvement over idleness."

The Finn considered the matter. "I will go, too."

Logan suddenly realized that everyone else was staring at him and the Deacon. "Jeez, I was just gonna catch some extra Zs in the morning. I'm not even Catholic. I come from the land of Methodists and moralizers."

"Very good," Billy Joe spoke up. "We can have our own prayer meeting here tomorrow morning."

Logan rolled his eyes. "Okay, gang, save a place for me in the pew."

Frank stood and stretched. "I suppose it's best to go to church. With what we have on the schedule for tomorrow night, it may be the last time for some of us."

"Aren't you just the ever-lovin' blue-eyed optimist and little ray of sunshine," Logan said, but he rubbed damp palms against the legs of his pants.

Chapter 8

Reynaud stayed near the rear of the group striding up the aisle of the theater. Frank and Tadeusz, at the head of the line, stepped up onto the stage. In flawless Polish, Frank said, "Everyone go home. See your families, drink some vodka, and celebrate the weekend."

A thin, intense young man with shoulder-length hair spat on the stage. "Fascists! Even the old government respected the theater. Now the thugs come."

Tadeusz turned red and his hands curled into fists but Frank, with some good nature, only said, "Oh, shut up. We're here from the Ministry of Health." He waved the paper, the forgery Wyszynski had provided, at the actor and stage crew. "Do you want a secondary plague? We are here to kill the vermin, or did you not know rats carry bubonic plague? You should be able to return tomorrow night for rehearsals."

The young man sputtered a bit, too rigid to conceive of the notion that he might be wrong, but some of the older people in the theater crowd were already on their way down the aisle. The long-haired actor stood and glared at them, and Reynaud was grateful Logan was still outside, guarding the outside exit of the basement. Finally the actor pulled a rough coat on over his sweater and stamped out of the theater.

St. Jacques and Zdenka, at the ends of the lobby, waved that the building was clear then chained and locked bars to the doors leading to the basement. When the doors were secured, they took positions in the back of the theater lobby where they could cover both the doors and the trapdoors on the stage and in the orchestra pit.

According to the janitor, the trapdoor on stage could be secured from the stage as well as below, and Reynaud saw Frank bend down and slip a steel pin in a slot in the floor.

Setting the duffle bag he carried on a seat, Reynaud pulled out half a dozen flashlights, snapped them on, and placed them in seats, pointing the beams at the orchestra pit. His heavy coat was too bulky and confining for the work ahead so he pulled it off and replaced it with a light jacket from the duffle bag, filled the jacket's pockets with smoke and gas grenades, also from the bag, slipped a pair of extra magazines for his submachine gun into the waistband of his pants, at the back, where they'd be out of the way. Another flashlight went in beside the magazines in case the basement lights weren't working or if the people below cut the power to the lights. Finally, he dug out a Polish army-issue gas mask.

Frank had been the lucky one, drawing on St. Jacques' mask, the face of which was all clear plastic except for the filter attachment. Reynaud pulled on his mask, adjusting the strap so it fit snugly. In the colder air of the theater the eyepieces fogged a little, cutting down what little visibility they offered. He drew several deep breaths through the mask's filter, making sure it was clear then pushed the mask up on his head.

Tadeusz gestured for him to follow and he unslung the Colt submachine gun and pulled back the charging handle then let it drop, chambering a round. He followed Tadeusz to the sealed door behind and to the right of the stage, Steve immediately behind him. Frank, with Juho, Smyth-Davis, and the Deacon, gathered in front of the other backstage door.

Tadeusz, looking grotesque and alien in his own gas mask, waited until he sensed Frank was ready then drew two grenades and hooked his index finger in the ring of one of them. Pulling the mask down, Reynaud made sure it was sealed tight against his skin. Tadeusz nodded, the canister at the front of his gas mask bobbing, and Reynaud shot into the door's lock. Tadeusz slammed his foot against the door, kicking it open, and tossed a grenade down the stairs. The second grenade was tossed down the stairs even before the first had begun to spew its gas. Tadeusz pulled the door shut and they waited twenty seconds. Reynaud counted the time off but when he reached for the door, Tadeusz held up his hand and, one by one, crooked each finger in turn, then nodded and shoved the door open again.

A bullet whined past, between them, and Reynaud simply pointed his weapon into the gloom and pulled the trigger. He was hardly aware of his weapon's throbbing recoil or the clatter of the bolt or the twang of the recoil spring under his ear.

In the swirling gray smoke below he saw an arm jerk upward and a pistol fly from the hand. He fired another burst at where he guessed the body must be, then rushed downstairs into the twilight gloom and almost fell over an outstretched arm. The man was dead, with at least three bullet holes in his chest.

Once downstairs, Reynaud slammed himself against the wall to the right. The corridor running from the front of the building to the back was clear. He chanced a quick glance down the connecting corridor, running across the back of the building, saw it was also clear, then darted across the lengthwise corridor and threw himself to the floor. When he glanced back he saw Tadeusz taking the position he'd just left.

The Pole paused only a moment then spun around the corner and stalked down the intersecting corridor, the Skorpion thrust ahead.

Reynaud fumbled in a jacket pocket and dug out a grenade, pulled its pin, and hurled it as far down the corridor as he could. The canister bounced once, awkwardly, then rolled. For a moment it simply lay on the floor then a bright violet stream of smoke shot out of the can, quickly billowing into a thick fog.

Reynaud cursed and tried to pull out a second grenade, which has snagged in the pocket. With a tug, the Cajun tore it free, checked it to be sure it was a tear gas grenade, pulled the pin, and threw it into the thick fog.

He looked around at the sound of footsteps on the stairs in time to see Smyth-Davis follow Tadeusz into the connecting hallway then he concentrated on the floor ahead and began to crawl into the purple fog.

Trying to blink away the sweat on his eyelashes, he wished he could wipe his face. Twenty feet down the corridor, he found the branch leading to the outside door. He rolled into the passage then reached out and found it was very short. Still watching the thinning mist in the corridor, he fumbled at the door until he found a bolt.

He yanked back at the bolt, which refused to budge, then tried lifting it; it swung upward easily. Reynaud pounded on the door three times with his fist then shoved it open.

Logan rushed through the door and slammed it shut behind him. Reynaud again scanned the corridor. Suddenly they heard the muffled chatter of suppressed automatic weapons from the area below the stage. After a moment they heard the single sharp report of a rifle.

"Sounds like the boys flushed one and the Frenchie nailed him," Logan said, his voice distorted and made hollow by the gas mask.

Reynaud dug out another grenade. The smoke from his smoke grenade had largely dissipated, much of it sucked out when he'd opened the door for Logan. He pulled the pin and flung the can toward the far end of the hallway. The canister landed, rolling, then Reynaud saw someone dash across the end of the corridor. He pointed his submachine gun down the hallway and pulled the trigger. After a few rounds, the gun stopped. Reynaud, still keeping his attention on the end of the corridor dropped the empty magazine, shoved in a fresh one, and pressed the bolt release.

Even before the fresh magazine was seated, two figures had charged into the passage, firing short, savage bursts. Their weapons had suppressors and in the closed space the sharp yammering of the guns made Reynaud's ears ring. Bullets droned and whined down the corridor and he could clearly hear the slapping of bullets against the stone walls. A single round hit the wall opposite Reynaud and Logan then ricocheted several times in their short branch of the hallway, making both men duck and flinch.

Reynaud thumbed the fire selector to semi-automatic and began to bring the subgun to bear when he was driven back to cover by a storm of gunfire. With a thump and a clatter, the grenade was kicked back to their end of the passage.

Reynaud could hear the slow footsteps of the men in the hallway, advancing toward them through the smoke, still firing bursts that chipped the wall near his head. He and Logan were pinned down, unable to attack or even to return the fire, until the enemy would be firing at them at point blank range.

"Fuck it!" Logan snapped, and shouldered his way past Reynaud to throw something down the corridor.

Reynaud heard something small hit the floor then, moments later, an explosion. The blast was hardly louder than a pistol shot, although in a deeper key, and a few more pockmarks appeared in the opposite wall of their branch.

A man screamed in the corridor, a shriek that made Reynaud's scalp stir, then, firing wildly, a figure lurched out of the deep red fog. The man's gas mask had fallen to his chest, and his eyes stared vacantly. Blood flowed from his mouth and nostrils but he continued to shamble forward, and the Uzi in his hands continued to bark out brief, vicious bursts of fire.

Logan leaned forward and the Ingram belched out a flickering gout of fire licking at the man with the Uzi. The man spun and was flung against the opposite wall, where he left a rough silhouette in blood, then crumpled.

Logan stepped back to change magazines and reload the empty while Reynaud looked around the corner. The other gunner, or what was left of him—or her—lay like a mass of bloody rags on the floor. The man Logan had shot was obviously dead, a shattered Uzi inches from his left arm, which had almost been torn away. "Lord, Logan, what'd you hit them with? It looks like you found that pocket nuke the Brit wanted."

Logan continued loading the magazine. "When we did clean-up at the FSB cell, I found some grenades about the size of golf balls. They were small, so I took two. Then I turned the rest of them over to Frank." He looked out at the body, which lay so they could see its back had been largely shredded by the grenade. "Take two of those, and you won't need to call the doctor in the morning."

From the end of the corridor, upstairs, they heard the burp of a suppressed subgun and bullets hammering at wood. The racket of a second burst was fainter then a body thumped and clattered its way down the stairs.

"Three up and three down," Logan said. "There's a door on the opposite wall about twenty feet up the corridor. You feel ready to hit it?"

Reynaud readied another smoke grenade. "Okay, cover me. I'll try to pop the door and put this inside. You stay at the door while I go in."

Logan ran his hand across his gas mask, apparently forgetting he wore it and had no way to wipe the sweat off his face. "Why should you have all the fun? As soon as you dump the 'nade, duck back and cover me. I'll do the canvassing."

Reynaud peered down the corridor then crept across and sidled along the wall until he reached the door. His right hand gripped his submachine gun and the ring of a smoke grenade, while his left hand twisted the doorknob. He shoved the door open, snatched the grenade, and tossed it inside. As the grenade began to hiss he darted across the opening and held up his hand to Logan. "It's darker than the inside of a cat in there."

Reynaud watched the far end of the corridor and the other door on the inner wall, a good forty-five feet away.

"Ready," Logan said. As he stepped to the door he held out his flashlight, bound with bootlaces to the buttstock of the ruined Uzi.

Logan had just vanished into the green fog when Tadeusz appeared at the near end of the corridor. "The stage area and dressing rooms are clear," he said in Polish.

Reynaud chopped his hand down to signal silence then gestured that Logan had gone into the room. As Tadeusz crept forward, Reynaud motioned for him to take over watching the hallway then prowled into the room after Logan.

The room was closed but, as he snapped on his own flashlight, Reynaud remembered this was a furnace room and the smoke had cleared enough to let him make out a dim glow ahead, which must be Logan's flashlight.

As he started toward the glow, a suppressed pistol coughed twice.

Logan's MAC made its farting sound and a body crashed to the floor.

Reynaud flinched at the noises then trained his flashlight at where he'd heard the body fall. A streamer of green smoke drifted away, revealing Logan trying to shake loose an empty magazine then Reynaud saw another man, just beyond Logan, raise a metal bar to strike.

He couldn't fire without hitting Logan, and Reynaud had only time to scream, "Asshole at three o'clock!"

As quick as a cat, Logan dropped his flashlight and spun to his right, bringing up the Ingram, left hand gripping the suppressor, to block the descending bar. The clangor as the two pieces of metal slammed together made a hollow sound and the suppressor was bent.

"Dammit!" Logan shouted. Instead of dropping to the floor to give Reynaud a clear shot, he dropped the gun and sprang at the other man. His fist crashed into the man's throat, while a knee caught him in the groin.

"Do you know how hard those things are to find?" Logan roared as he drove a short punch in just under the man's heart. The man staggered with the impact, dropping the bar. Logan caught the bar as it fell, whipped it behind the man's back and, using the bar, bent the man backward over the bar until Reynaud heard a sickening crunch and a scream.

As the man crumpled, Logan dropped on him, driving his knees into the huddled figure. Reynaud heard another crack and moved forward as Logan stood. The man's head lay at an unnatural angle, but he still moaned. With back and neck broken, the man was still, painfully, alive.

Reynaud hoped he wouldn't vomit in his gas mask, raised the Colt and shot the man through the head. At last the moaning stopped.

Logan scrambled around on the floor until he found the Ingram. In the beam from Reynaud's flashlight they could see the suppressor was badly dented and bent into a shallow V, but the gun was undamaged. Logan muttered curses as he unscrewed the suppressor then dropped it on the floor. He changed magazines and pulled the bolt back.

"I'm going to have to stop putting all my pills in one casket," Logan muttered. He gazed around the area, at the coal bins and the massive furnace. He waved at Reynaud to move left while he, after he'd recovered his flashlight, flanked the furnace to the right.

Reynaud had only moved three paces when he heard another door across the room jerked open and a grenade rattled on the floor. "Hold it!" Reynaud screamed, "It's us in here!" then realized his voice was muffled by the mask. Thick, green, oily-looking smoke shot out of the grenade and, within seconds, he was unable to see the floor.

He lurched forward two more steps then stumbled over something on the floor. He dropped the flashlight as he fell, and the glow was lost in the heavy smoke. Afraid of dropping his gun, he twisted as he went down. His hand slipped on something slick and wet and he slid into something soft and moist.

He tried to fight down nausea and panic as he realized he'd fallen over the body of the man Logan had shot.

The panic grew stronger than the nausea. He was effectively

blind and lost. The only directions he could even guess at were up and down. He wanted to claw the mask from his face, to spring to his feet and run out of this oversized closet, but escape was impossible. His strongest impulse was still to run but he forced himself to stay down and wait.

Eternities passed before the smoke thinned enough for him to see the glow of his flashlight. The smoke was thinner near the floor, so he stayed in a crouched position.

Logan's voice came from somewhere to Reynaud's right. "If you come in, don't come in shooting. We're still here in the gallery."

Frank's voice was so distorted Reynaud couldn't immediately recognize it. "Are you in there alone?"

"Rennie's in here, too." Logan replied.

Reynaud heard footsteps and listened for other sounds, any hint an enemy was creeping through the fog. Apparently, Logan was also remaining motionless. The footsteps stopped and Frank chuckled, an odd sound through the mask. "Logan, green is definitely your color." After a pause, he added, "How bad are you hit?"

"The red stuff is somebody else's," Logan said. "Where the hell did Wyszynski get these grenades, from militant interior decorators?"

The smoke cleared enough for Reynaud to see the two men, a third, still indistinct, behind them. "These are mostly grenades used to mark an area for a landing zone or an artillery barrage. Stop bitching. Regular combat smoke grenades can start fires and have no character—usually they're just white or gray."

Making sure the man behind Frank was one of theirs, Reynaud stood and walked toward them.

"Damn!" Frank exclaimed, "I hope all that red stuff is somebody else's, too."

Reynaud stared down at the blood smeared on his hand and jacket. "I fell into a mess Logan left. Some people just never seem to learn to clean up after themselves." He turned the beam on the body he'd fallen over. It was the one Logan had emptied a thirty-round magazine into.

"Sonofabitch," Logan said. "He looks like he's been chewed up and spit out." He bent over the corpse and picked up a .22

Ruger pistol with a suppressor over its barrel and slipped it into his belt.

Frank looked over Logan's shoulder. "Let's get this over with." Through the murk, he looked a little greenish himself. He turned to Juho and the Deacon, who'd followed him in. "We'll start at that wall," he nodded to the back wall of the furnace room. "We just walk from there to the opposite wall."

Reynaud and Logan joined the skirmish line that examined the furnace room. Frank found the other body Logan had left. "This one didn't even have a gas mask or a gun. Looks like we caught a few of them with their pants down."

"What happened back there?" Reynaud asked, pointing his thumb over his shoulder at the rear of the building.

"Tadeusz got one, and another one tried to get away through the orchestra pit but Jean-Marie nailed the lid on his box. They'd set up a 'war room,' with maps and everything in one of the basement dressing rooms. On our side, they'd set the dressing room up as an office, with lots of files. We had to kill the woman there; she damned near got the Deacon before he got over a near-fatal case of chivalry. We also took some fire from the front of the building but Steve got one and the others are pretty much pinned down. This room is clear. Let's move."

Reynaud and Logan slipped out of the door they'd come through and saw Smyth-Davis standing beside the next door. Before they reached him he pointed into the room. "Tadeusz is inside. It's time for the changing of the guard. I'm going to help him."

Reynaud glanced into the dimly-lit room, where racks of clothes stood like ranks of empty soldiers. "Looks like a costumes and prop room." He tapped Logan on the shoulder. "You stay here and make sure the bad guys stay away. It's my turn to get into trouble."

Logan leaned against the wall and fished in his pocket for more ammunition. "I've got to load up another magazine anyway." He followed Smyth-Davis into the room then, using the doorway as cover against fire from the front of the building, kept watch on the passage while reloading a magazine.

They found Tadeusz and the three of them began to stalk down the rows of costumes, shoving the clothes aside. Halfway down the row, Reynaud dropped to one knee and peered under the costumes. Too many robes and cloaks hung only inches from the floor for him to be certain, but he thought he saw a pair of boots.

He slid to his belly, pointed his weapon at one of the boots, and squeezed off a shot. The boots reacted violently and Reynaud shouted, "Headed your way!"

"Tally ho!" Smyth-Davis exclaimed, and fired his pistol twice.

At the second shot the body spun and fell, thrashed in a heap of costumes as though searching for a proper shroud, then crumpled to the floor.

Reynaud froze, watching for any more boots or for movement, saw neither, and pressed ahead. They found no one else in the room and Reynaud found himself wishing he could spend more time examining the costumes and props, some of which were remarkably elaborate. By the time he'd returned to where the body lay, Smyth-Davis and Tadeusz were already leaning over it. Smyth-Davis' shot had hit just behind the right ear. They found no other wounds on the body although a boot heel had been almost torn away by a bullet.

As they pulled the costumes away, they saw the body wore an American uniform and carried a Beretta M-9. The man had been young and blond.

"Does this make sense?" Reynaud asked.

"None of it does," Tadeusz said. "We must finish this quickly."

Back in the passage, Tadeusz took the lead to the cross hallway. The body at the foot of the stairs was that of a woman, perhaps thirty years old. Tadeusz checked the hallway then stepped out and brought back a submachine gun like Frank's. He handed it to Smyth-Davis. "You need this."

Reynaud ducked out to study the hallway which was, fortunately, straight rather than following the curve of the lobby. The far wall ended in a set of stairs leading up and he counted three doors facing the front of the building.

Tadeusz showed Smyth-Davis how to operate the submachine gun then motioned for the Brit and Reynaud to move across the corridor to provide cover while he and Logan crept toward the nearest door. Before Logan and the Pole had covered more than half the distance to the door, Frank appeared at the other end of the hallway. They could recognize Frank by the French gas mask he wore, and could only hope he recognized the armed and masked figures he faced were part of his team.

Frank halted and studied them a moment, then waved.

Tadeusz and Logan reached the door and stopped for a moment then Tadeusz sprang into the room, Logan immediately behind him. Several long, silent moments passed before Tadeusz slipped out the door. Frank's team had apparently cleared the far room by then, and Frank and Tadeusz approached the central door at the same time but from opposite directions.

Logan had stayed at the door, using it for cover. He shouted, "Give it up. We've got you cold."

"What the hell—are you Americans?" demanded a muffled voice from the center room.

"Most of us are," Logan shouted back.

Reynaud heard feet pounding as someone dashed down the far corridor and Steve turned the corner, waving a book. "These codebooks are in English," he shouted.

Frank muttered something that sounded like, "Holy shit," then raised his voice to shout into the room. "If you're Americans too, who won the World Series back in seventeen?"

After a pause, the stranger's voice shouted back, "How the hell should I know? I'm a football fan."

"He's an American, all right." Frank said, then, more loudly, "Okay, come out here, hands on your heads."

"One of you come in here and we'll talk about it."

"No games," Frank replied. "We're holding all the aces in this hand, and we're calling." After a pause, he added, "Is Laura in there with you?"

"She got called out of town on business," the voice said. "So, now that you know who we are, why don't you just go away? The best thing you can do is just get out of here and forget about all this."

"Forget it," Frank snapped. "You've got two minutes to get out here with your hands up or we waste you and cry about any little mistakes later."

Reynaud waited until he was sure the hardest part of the

battle was still ahead when two men in gas masks slowly marched out of the room, their hands on their heads.

"Against the wall," Frank waved his submachine gun. "Assume the position."

As the men leaned, spread-eagled against the wall, Frank handed his weapon to Tadeusz and frisked them quickly but efficiently. Logan emerged from the room. "They clean?"

"I wouldn't go so far as to say that," Frank replied, "but they aren't packing any weapons." He took his submachine gun back from Tadeusz and gestured with it. "Okay, you guys can relax now. Take off the masks." Both men pulled off their gas masks and, when they showed no sign of choking, Reynaud did the same. The air seemed a little thick, with a sharp, acrid odor, but was fresher than the rubber-scented air in his mask. He wiped the sweat off his face with his left sleeve.

"All right, fellows," Frank said pleasantly, "where's the detonator?"

One of the prisoners, a tall, bear-like man with a full beard and sand-colored hair, shook his head. The other prisoner, smaller and darker, seemed surprised by the question. "What are you talking about?"

"C'mon," Frank's voice betrayed his exasperation. "I told you, no games. We've disarmed the packages you left up front. Even if part of the place blows, all it's going to do is lower property values in the neighborhood and leave a lot of American fingerprints on the damage. You don't want to embarrass my friends and I—not to mention yourselves, do you?"

The two men looked at each other then the big one said, "The phone on the desk. But don't take the receiver off the hook, just pull out the jack."

When Frank ducked into the room to disconnect the detonator, Logan stepped closer to the prisoners, his MAC held loosely. "What're you guys doing skulking around here? Jeez, we thought you were FSB. Hasn't anybody told you the war's over?"

"Not for the FSB," the smaller man snapped.

"And not for hard-core mental cases like these guys, either," Frank said as he emerged from the room. "Stay the hell back from them, Logan. Either one of them could've jumped you, grabbed your weapon, and shot you with it."

"They could've tried," Logan said, but he took two steps back from the prisoners. "What the hell, man, these guys are Americans."

"The real kind," the shorter man interjected. "If you're really good Americans, you'll just get the hell out of here and forget about this evening, like I said before." His eyes narrowed "You must be the ones Laura talked about. I didn't think you'd really turned your coats, although you must've bought a load of crap."

"Frank, what the hell is this guy talking about?" Logan demanded.

Frank ignored the question and addressed the prisoners. "Like Logan said, we were hunting FSB. This is really awfully embarrassing." He turned to face the others. "Let's get ready to move out." When he swung to face the prisoners his gun suddenly swung up and farted fire from the muzzle,

The smaller man spun and went down but the bigger prisoner staggered toward Logan, the nearest of the group.

Tadeusz's Skorpion rattled and the man grunted but continued to stalk toward Logan, his eyes wild.

"Shit!" Logan screamed, and swept up him MAC. The roar from the unsuppressed weapon was almost deafening in the closed cellar. Bullet holes appeared in the man's jacket then his face dissolved into a red mist.

As the body fell to the floor, Logan turned on Frank. "What the fuck was that all about? They were on our side."

Frank inserted a fresh magazine into his Heckler and Koch. "Not hardly. Those were CIA spooks. They aren't on anyone's side. They're just as responsible for the plague and the war as the FSB." He bent down and tore open the man's jacket and shirt, most of which had been shredded by gunfire, to show a Kevlar vest. Besides being almost decapitated, the body also had a smashed right elbow and two bullet wounds in its left upper arm, as well as a single hole from a bullet that'd found the armpit opening in the vest.

"He was a rugged bastard, I'll hand him that," Frank said. He looked up from the body. "Smyth-Davis, go upstairs and let Jean-Marie and Zdenka know it's finished down here. The rest of you, let's follow the wires from the wall mount. We have no idea what kinds of goodies they had rigged in this place. Work in teams, because a lot of wires are going to be threaded through the walls, and we need to check them all. Rennie, you stay with me."

As Frank and Reynaud went from room to room, with Frank disarming charges found by the rest of the group, Reynaud finally asked a question that had been bothering him, "How did you know about the detonator?"

"Bluff and guess," Frank replied, as he carefully detached a wire from a blasting cap sticking out of eight sticks of dynamite and removed the cap. "I guessed they were spooks when they knew Laura, and spooks are paranoid enough to wire a place like this for sound. It was a gamble, but not as big a gamble as storming that arsenal would've been. You'd better believe that one or the other of them had their hand on that phone. Mostly, we were lucky."

"Some luck—blowing away fellow Americans, and we still haven't got a clue where the FSB headquarters is."

"Don't lose any sleep over this gang." Frank wiped his sleeve across his forehead. He'd just finished clearing the last charge and they sank against the wall to rest. "FSB or CIA, they're just different breeds of rats. Look, there might've been some good people in the CIA—hell, there might've been a few in the FSB; it's a big organization—but anybody still dicking around and fighting the last war is an enemy of everyone who just wants to get on with life."

Reynaud sat, resting his head on his forearms until he could feel his muscles stiffening from the cold. "Was that last room we took really an arsenal?"

Frank shoved himself to his feet and Reynaud did the same. "That's what it looked like to me." They trudged back and joined the rest of the group who were already stacking the weapons that looked most useful. Among those were three suppressed Ruger .22s and another suppressed Skorpion. The Deacon had added a bandolier of grenades for the launcher mounted on the AK he'd captured before. Most of the remaining guns were Russian, Polish, or Czech. The submachine gun Reynaud had supposed was an Uzi was actually a Czech Model 24. They found two more of them as well as a suppressed Model 25, which was the same gun but chambered for nine millimeter.

The rest of the weapons were mostly still racked and ranged

from Polish Model 63 machine pistols to machine guns, sniper rifles, and even a couple of rocket-propelled grenades. Russian RPG-16s.

"They had them for the same reason the FSB goons had allied equipment," Frank explained. "We'll take everything with a suppressor and leave the rest."

"What about the files?" Logan asked.

Frank considered the question. "I sure as hell don't want to try to lug them all back tonight. I'll check with Wiktor but I suspect some of us are going to be bogged down trying to dig out useful information for a helluva long time. Wiktor's team would have the same trouble with them that we had with the FSB paperwork."

Hauling the booty weapons upstairs, they rejoined the others in the lobby. "Anybody get curious about the noisy party?" Frank asked the Frenchman.

"This is a very thick building," St. Jacques replied. "We hardly heard most of the shots up here. I doubt anyone twenty meters from the building would have heard anything."

"Seems like a clean operation," Frank said. "Let's go home. I'll talk to Wiktor in the morning."

Taking turns dragging St. Jacques' sled, they made their way across and out of the old town and to the new apartment. By the time they stumbled, stamping the packed snow off their boots, through their door, the adrenalin rush had long burned out.

Before he sat down to eat, Reynaud took some rags and a pan of warm water to his room, undressed, and washed other peoples' blood off himself. When he was satisfied with the rough cleansing, he dressed in a clean uniform. He was surprised he had an appetite and supposed he'd become hardened, as opposed to the emotional numbing of the prison camp.

Anya had fussed over them when they returned then had prepared MREs. After they'd eaten they rested in their chairs, sipping at coffee or wine. After a single glass of wine, the Frenchman limped to his room. The rest of the Krakow group, one by one, drifted off to bed until only Frank was left with the former prisoners. He leaned back in his chair and crossed his arms, appeared to be dozing then, without opening his eyes, asked, "After you guys get Chernikov, what then?"

Reynaud, who'd up so late simply because he hadn't found the energy to get out of the chair, took another sip of wine. "Hell, I don't know. Why?"

Frank opened his eyes and stared at each of them in turn. "Because the Reconstrucionists really can use all the help they can get, and good help is hard to find. Besides the odd FSB agent, the old U S of A is crawling with renegade CIA ops who'd like to build private empires, two-bit warlords with the same ideas, and assorted other crazies and thugs, some of them pretty lethal."

He sipped coffee and stared before him like a dazed man. He roused himself and continued. "They call the kind of work you'd be doing 'recon,' although you wouldn't have any army behind you and you'd have to take care of the problems your-selves. "It's mean work, with lousy hours, no pay but booty, and there's no retirement plan because a lot of you won't live to retire."

Logan snorted. "With a recommendation like that, how could anyone turn you down?"

Frank's grin was awkward. "You don't have to play. You can forget the whole thing, or you can stop Chernikov then forget the whole thing. You can pull out at any time. This isn't like an army or a government but, the way I see it, what's left of the country needs people to help it heal—work toward reunification and a new government a lot cleaner and a lot more responsive to the people."

"Okay, okay," Logan drawled, "put away your soapbox. You've sold us."

Smyth-Davis was drinking tea and took a sip before it cooled too much. "What of Mr. Tartakainnen and I? I don't believe either of us would care to emigrate."

"You wouldn't have to. We'll get Juho back to Finland with a radio frequency and a code name. If he gets the urge or feels the need, he can get in touch with us through Wiktor. As for you, if you're willing, we can give you some contacts in England. There are people in almost every country who're trying to rebuild."

"What do we have to do to join up?" Steve asked.

"Right now, all you have to do is choose a name for your group."

Steve finished his coffee. "What's the codename for your

group?"

"Commando Krakow."

"Hey," Logan said, "how about Recon 9?"

"Where'd you come up with that one?" Reynaud asked.

"Well," Logan explained, "we're working for the *recon*struc-tionists, and we'd be doing *recon*naissance for them. As for the 9, I once saw a movie called 'Plan 9 From Outer Space.' It was a real hoot." He grinned at Reynaud. "Do you wanna be Tor Johnson or Bela Lugosi?"

"I'll pass on the casting," Reynaud said, "but I suppose it's as good a name as any. Anybody have any better ideas?"

"I like it," Steve said. "It has dash, a touch of the melodra-matic, and it's misleading. It seems like the perfect name."

Billy Joe sipped slowly at his coffee, as though he hadn't yet decided whether drinking coffee was a vice. "It would seem presumptuous to call ourselves 'God's Chosen' or 'The Elect.' His ways are His own, and not revealed to us."

Reynaud grinned. "I'm kinda partial to 'The Saints,' myself, but it'll do."

"Great!" Logan said. "I'll work out the secret handshake and call the shop to have the bowling shirts printed up right away." He shoved himself to his feet. "Time to turn in. Pity you had to cut Laura loose, Frank, I could use a little action."

Steve rolled his eyes. "If you see her again, you'd better be thinking of something besides screwing, or you'll be screwed. If she ever finds out we helped waste her boyfriends...." He stood and shambled to his own room.

Everyone but Frank and Reynaud had finally gone to bed. Reynaud knew he had to get up and go to his room, but it took a minute or three for him to convince his muscles to make the attempt. Finally, with a grunt, he levered himself out of his chair.

Frank slowly stood and faced Reynaud. "One more thing. Every group needs a leader. I think you should run Recon 9."

Reynaud stared at him. "Why me? Steve's better educated, and most of them are better in a fight than I am. This is going to be a fighting outfit, remember? There are lots of people with bet-ter qualifications. The Finn is a goddam rock; nothing ever rattles him. And Logan would rather fight than eat. Hell, there's times when I think he'd rather fight than screw. Every time I'm in a gunfight, I'm scared shitless."

Frank was obviously too tired to punctuate his remarks with his usual gestures but his gaze was steady and intense. "Look, Rennie, I've got to change my underwear a lot after firefights, too, but I run Commando Krakow. St. Jacques is the best man in a fight, and Zdenka is almost as good with weapons. And Tadeusz, in combat, is as steady as the pope at Mass.

"Being the leader of this group doesn't mean being the toughest mutha in the valley. You've got excellent qualifications. You seem to be the conscience of your merry little band. You're a little paranoid, which is useful when there really are bastards out to get you. You're cautious—you seem to plan more and leave less to chance but can still adapt quickly." He started for the door. "You don't have to decide just this minute, but think about it, will you?"

Chapter 9

Reynaud woke late the next morning. When he finally got up and dressed, he stumbled to the kitchen and found Frank had been gone for almost an hour. Steve still sat at the table while, in the living room, St. Jacques and Zdenka showed Logan, Juho, and the Deacon how to field-strip and clean their weapons and how best to use them.

Reynaud ate slowly, savoring the food. When he finished, he accepted a second cup of coffee and St. Jacques sat at the table for another cup. Reynaud gestured toward the group in the living room. "How did you guys ever wind up with a Russian on your team and, from what I hear, how come she's still here when there are revolutions going on in the Ukraine?"

The Frenchman leaned back in his chair, favoring the leg he was resting on another chair. "It is a long but interesting story. Her grandfather was a Cossack who, like many others, fought with the Germans in World War II. After the war, he was shot and his family was 'relocated' to Siberia. Zdenka's father, Piotr Dmitrovitch Jerosky, became an important man and, supposedly, re-educated enough Zdenka was allowed to attend the university in Moscow.

"I believe she'd been considered for the consular service. She speaks French even better than English and knows Spanish and German. She was also in the reserves and was called up when the plague broke out. Since she was a trained tank commander, she was sent to the front—the Russians committed most of their armor to the front—where she fought the Germans."

"Isn't it unusual for a woman to be a tanker?" Reynaud asked.

"You have never been in a Russian tank," St. Jacques said. "They are very cramped, and so smaller people are preferred for tank crews. There were no women in the regular army armored corps, but the reserves were another matter.

"Her loader died after having his arm torn off by the automatic loader—again, a not-uncommon occurrence with Russian tanks, and her tank was disabled. She managed to make her way to our relief column. At first, she was a prisoner, but she took over command of a British tank after most of the crew had been killed, when the Russians attacked us. When the column broke up, she stayed with us.

"She is Ukrainian but has not spent three months in Ukraine, so she has no contacts to join the Ukrainian resistance to the Russians, and it would be worse than impractical for her to attempt to return to Siberia."

Reynaud finished his second cup of coffee. "How soon do you think we'll get a fix on the FSB headquarters?"

St. Jacques performed another Gallic shrug. "That is a very good question."

They heard the door open and heavy footsteps headed for the kitchen. Frank strode into the room, flinging his gloves at the table. "Sorry, fellows, I've got bad news. Another glitch in the plans, and some dirty work for you."

Dropping into one of the chairs, Frank said, "Better dress warm and wear your ORMO gear. Colonel Waskewiesz has just come in from Silesia for the Polish congress and the ORMO has drawn security detail. The regular ORMO is providing direct security for the colonel and clearing the part of the old town nearest the Wawel. The police will mount patrols in the area to replace the ORMO who've been reassigned but they've turned another job over to the ORMO reserves and detached units. They want you to continue the sweeps started from the old town outward."

"Any chance we'll run into FSB cells?" Logan asked.

"It isn't likely. Tadeusz will be with you and he'll give you any information as it comes to him. I'm not sure, myself, what these sweeps are to accomplish."

Reynaud assembled his gear and was headed for the door when Frank stopped him and pointed to the old Winchester '95. "Are you really taking that antique?"

Reynaud hefted the rifle. "Yeah, I'm a lot more comfortable with it than I would be with a chatter-gun. I'm afraid if I took one of the choppers I'd be more dangerous to our guys than the opposition. I'd feel even better with a shotgun, but there don't seem to be any available."

"Tadeusz, when you report for orders, get him a shotgun," Frank said. He gestured at the Winchester. "Rennie, you leave that relic of 'the Great War' here."

"What're you going to be doing?" Logan asked, as he pulled the ORMO smock over his coat.

"Wiktor is supposed to be sending the CIA files over later this morning. Jean-Marie and I will go through them."

As they stepped outside, Reynaud observed the sky had cleared and the day was cold but clear. The city looked more lively than he'd seen it before, with people toiling to clear snow from the sidewalks and opening lanes in the streets. He also saw more troops than he'd seen before, except inside the Wawel. Most of the soldiers were ORMO, with a scattering of police, and almost all of them were carrying shoulder arms.

"Jeez," Logan said, "it looks like there's a war brewin'."

They assembled, with over four hundred other ORMO, in the courtyard of the Wawel. Tadeusz forced his way through the mob of troops and disappeared inside. Reynaud and the others found places to sit. The cold and the damp uniforms became annoyances then sources of anguish as they waited. Half an hour later, Tadeusz returned, carrying a pump shotgun, a twelve gauge Mossberg with the barrel cut off the same length as the magazine tube.

Opening the box of shells, Reynaud stuffed five rounds into the bottom of the receiver, worked the action, and loaded in a final round then thumbed the safety back.

While Reynaud loaded the shotgun, Tadeusz told them about their mission. "We are to form up with other groups with their own officers or sergeants. Our task is to help clear part of a section of the city called *Nowy Swiat,* from *Straszewskiego* to *Al. Zygmunta Krasinkiego.* We are to verify the identity papers of everyone in any building we enter or in the streets. Anyone who is not registered for the address is to be detained. If their identification is in order, the officer in charge may re-register them and they may return. Anyone without identification or with forged identification will be retained and they may or may not return. Anyone found with contraband will be detained. They will not return."

"What's contraband?" Steve asked.

"For anyone not in the ORMO or the police, rifles or automatic weapons. Pistols and shotguns are not prohibited. Also, any explosive devices are prohibited. We will probably not find anything like that. Other contraband is any petroleum fuel over a two-gallon allotment for cooking or light, more than sixteen packs of cigarettes, or more ration chits than are needed for the family for one month.

"We simply want to provide security to the area and to stop the black market. The officer in charge wants me to remind you we are dealing with civilians, who are probably citizens, so we are instructed to treat them with every courtesy."

"I think I just died and went to Hell," Logan groused. "All I needed to make my life complete was to be a glorified traffic cop in Poland, where I don't even speak the language worth a damn."

After waiting another thirty minutes for their officer, Steve shrugged. "It may be Poland, but the army's the same everywhere—hurry up and wait."

Finally, several officers emerged from the Wawel and Tadeusz waved everyone to their feet. As they walked to where they'd begin their sweep the group, of which they were a part, was organized into four teams, each of eight to ten troops, to search. One team was held in reserve to guard prisoners.

At the first home on their sweep, Tadeusz rapped at the door, waited, and rapped again before it was opened by a middle-aged woman. While Tadeusz questioned the woman the rest of the group went through the apartment. Two other women shared the bare rooms, which contained only the most necessary items.

Reynaud felt like a thug as he walked through the place and he was acutely aware of the women's contempt. He wanted to leave a few extra ration chits but was afraid they'd be seen as an insult and knew, also, it was impossible to help everyone in need in Krakow.

By the time they'd searched their third apartment the members of the team were performing their functions by habit, with grim efficiency. Their morale sagged with the odious work and the disdain of the people whose lives they were having to invade. Their weapons had become only dead weights, impediments to doing an ugly job as quickly as possible.

After searching their sixth building they were rotated to guard duty, standing and watching a herd of sullen men and a few women. The captain in command of their part of the operation arrived with three more prisoners, then blew a whistle, a signal they could hear repeated back to the Wawel. As they waited for a truck to pick up the prisoners, Reynaud studied the men.

Tadeusz noticed his interest. "I doubt if any of them are FSB or CIA," he said, in English. "Most of them are probably deserters. One or two of them might be—" he stammered for a moment, trying to find the correct word "—gangsters."

"What'll happen to them?" Steve asked.

A truck swung around the corner and drew up beside them. The captain examined the driver's credentials then the prisoners, with the urging of the group and the truck guards, climbed into the bed of the truck. The driver gunned the engine and the truck lurched away.

Tadeusz rubbed at his nose. "Any deserters will be sent to the army's prison farm or prison factories to serve out their terms then they will be given discharges. Any black marketeers will be assigned to dangerous or especially unpleasant work. That is why our orders are to shoot to kill prisoners who try to escape. If we only wound them, they take medical facilities from people who are willing to work to make Krakow and Poland great again."

One of the other group of ORMO reservists brought in more prisoners and Tadeusz's team was rotated back to examining papers and searching for contraband.

The light was fading when the last bunch of prisoners had been taken away when another truck arrived and the crew in the back tossed sleeping bags into the street. The search crews lined up and each member was given a bowl of warm *barszcz*, a thick slice of bread, and a canteen of water.

As they downed the rations, Logan glared down at the soup and bread. "This reminds me of the camp."

Reynaud dipped his piece of bread in the *barszcz* and ate it. "We've been spoiled. This is what life is like for most of these people." He looked at the sleeping bags then at Tadeusz. "Where do we sleep tonight?"

"The next place we search. We will request space inside."

"And do this all over again tomorrow?" Steve asked.

"We are little more than a third of the way through our sweep, so we sleep here and finish it tomorrow. We will also have to provide guards to watch the street, to make sure no one slips through the cordon."

The man who answered Tadeusz's knock was in his late thirties or early forties, with broad, strong, worker's hands. "We must examine your papers and this house," Tadeusz said.

The man stepped aside and allowed them to enter but he glowered at them and spoke only when answering questions. The man shared four rooms with a woman, slightly older, a girl of about Katya's age, and a boy who appeared about eight years old.

The family had just finished dinner when the group entered. It was the work of only a few minutes to search the apartment. Logan found the man's shotgun, an old double-barreled gun that looked as dangerous for the shooter as for the target.

Reynaud wracked his brain for some way to sugar-coat the forced hospitality or avoid an outright refusal by the man. He returned to the front room where Tadeusz still examined the family's papers while the captain checked the names against the list. Finally, apparently satisfied, the officer left.

Reynaud approached Tadeusz and sketched a salute and, in English, said, "The place is clear." He glanced at the man whose face, for the first time, showed something besides controlled anger. The Pole stared at Reynaud with a glimmer of interest. Again speaking English, the Cajun said, "When you ask him if we can stay for the night, you might suggest Poles have a reputation for hospitality."

"Americanski?" asked the man. At Tadeusz's nod, the man spoke a rapid burst of Polish, the only word of which Reynaud understood was "Detroit."

"He wants me to ask you if you have been to Detroit," Tadeusz said, translating.

Reynaud shook his head. "*Nie.*" He glanced at Tadeusz, then spoke directly to the man. "Does he have relatives in Detroit?"

The pauses while Tadeusz translated back and forth from Polish to English and back were awkward but Reynaud guessed his own accent might sound Russian, and he'd heard Poles had an interest in people from other countries.

"Yes," Tadeusz translated the man's answer, "his uncle Jozef." As an aside to Reynaud he said, "Thank you for making it easier to ask for a place to sleep." He turned to the man and asked if he and his men might sleep in the living room.

The man paused only a moment before he agreed. They brought in the sleeping bags and spread them on the floor.

"We must have guards," Tadeusz said, "We have enough people for each of us to only stand guard for an hour. Since one system is as good as another, we will stand duty by the alphabet. "Dechaine, you will be first." He assigned one of the Poles with them to the second watch. "I will be last."

As he prepared to leave for sentry duty, Reynaud checked the chamber of his shotgun then stopped to watch Logan get ready to bed down. He'd laid the AK by his sleeping bag, taken off his coat and pulled off the MAC, which he wore on a sling so it hung just above his waist, unbuckled and removed his holstered Makarov and laid it beside the rifle, drew the suppressed Makarov from an inside coat pocket, added it to the heap of firepower, and finally slid a bayonet out of his boot and stuck it in the floor beside the other weapons.

"What the hell were you expecting to run into," Reynaud inquired, "a Russian division?"

"Better to be overdressed than underdressed," Logan said. "It's the Boy Scout in me, being prepared."

Still shaking his head, Reynaud stepped out into the darkening street. Within a few minutes, other guards emerged from the buildings around theirs. He found shelter from the wind on the lee side of the stairs, crouched, and stared out at an empty street. The hour dragged by, during which the only things he fought were the cold and his own boredom. The only movement he saw during his watch were the streamers of exhaled breath along the street where the other guards had taken their places.

He was battling an attack of trembling when his relief stepped out the door. Reynaud groaned as he struggled to stand then dragged himself inside.

With only the light of a single candle to illuminate the room, Reynaud had to pick his way carefully through the mass of sleeping bags to reach the kitchen. The stove was still warm when he approached it and he peeled off his gloves and warmed his hands. Tadeusz, who'd been sitting in the shadows at the foot of the table handed him a cup of warm water. He wrapped his hands around it and sipped, grateful for the warmth.

"When you are warmer, you may drink half of what is left in

this." Tadeusz handed him a small flask of vodka. "The other half is for the man who relieved you, after he has finished his guard turn."

Reynaud finished the water, drank his share of the vodka then stood and threaded his way back to his sleeping bag. "Where'd the booze come from?" he asked Logan, who lay in the sleeping bag to his left.

"You think artillery is the only thing I pack for emergencies?"

"Well, God bless your scoutmaster."

The Pole, in whose apartment they were sleeping, who'd also been in the kitchen, followed Tadeusz to his bag and sat, cross-legged, draped in a blanket, between Tadeusz and the Cajun. Reynaud thrust his hand out to the Pole. "Reynaud Dechaine."

The Pole shook the proffered hand. "Maciej Slanski." He turned to Tadeusz and spoke rapid Polish.

Reynaud studied the man as he spoke, not even trying to understand what he was saying, knowing Tadeusz would translate. The man's voice sounded sympathetic and concerned.

"He said 'It must be hard for you to be so far from your home and family so near to Christmas.'"

Reynaud was struck by a sense of time returning with the force of a collision with a brick wall. Most of the prisoners in the camp had kept some record of the days and dates, less as a method of looking forward to anything than as a sort of tally of victories, for each day survived in the camp deserved some notice. "What's today's date," he asked Tadeusz.

"Monday, December twenty."

Reynaud tried to add up the days in his head but kept losing them in the pleasant fog from the vodka. "So Christmas must be—?"

"Saturday."

Reynaud digested the thought for a moment or two. Until Maciej had mentioned it, he'd been numbed to the loneliness but now it returned as a pang. "Tell Maciej he is fortunate to have such a fine family."

Tadeusz translated then, softly, said, "They are not what you Americans call a family. His wife and older son died in the plague. The younger boy is his son, but the woman is his wife's sister and the girl is the woman's niece."

Maciej's face was a mask, hiding any feelings.

"Ask him," Reynaud said, "whether we might spend Christmas with his family—if we are able."

As Tadeusz interpreted the question, the Pole nodded and spoke.

"He said he would be honored."

The candle had burned down to little more than a puddle. The man offered them a good night and stumped off to bed.

Reynaud had already laid his shotgun by his sleeping bag. Now he pulled off his smock and coat, tugged off his boots, and burrowed into the bag,

"What were you planning to do on Christmas?" Tadeusz asked.

"We've got more rations than we need and the people here are going hungry. The least we can do is try to put a dent in the problem."

Logan squirmed in his own cloth cocoon and mumbled, "Rennie, if you're not careful, you're gonna give Billy Joe a run for his nickname." But he didn't argue.

~ * ~

Breakfast was another cup of warm water, a bowl of thin potato soup, a small piece of sausage, and a small piece of bread. As soon as they'd eaten they gathered their weapons and returned to the odious job of searching. They'd heard a loudspeaker mounted on a truck blaring out the message that the people were to remain in their homes except for food lines.

The first house they approached looked like the others they'd searched but Tadeusz's knock at the door was unanswered. The tried a second time, and a third, then strode out to the street and returned with a sledgehammer. After a last series of raps, he smashed the lock, shoved the door open, and marched in, leaving the hammer at the door.

A heavyset man with thick, tousled hair pushed open a door to one of the rooms and glared at them. "ZOMOS!" he shouted. "Thugs! Nazis! Stormtroopers!" Reynaud could hardly understand the words and the stream of invective that followed was incomprehensible.

"What is this asshole calling us?" Logan asked, in his badly accented Polish.

"Russki!" the man screamed, and followed it with a fresh torrent of abuse.

"You do not want to know," Tadeusz replied then shouted for the man to be silent.

Logan seemed to have completely ignored the Pole's outburst after his question to Tadeusz. He strode toward the door and the man sidestepped into his way.

"Please step aside, sir," Logan said in his fractured Polish, giving an ironic twist to the title.

The Pole shouted "ZOMO!" again, and pushed at Logan.

Logan's knee swept up and smashed into the man's crotch and his left fist buried itself in the man's belly just above the belt buckle. As the man jack-knifed forward, Logan brought up his knee again, slamming it into the Pole's face. As the man was flung upward and back, Logan drove his elbow into the side of the man's head. "Excuse me, sir" he said and stepped over the man's body.

From the room they heard Logan's chuckle then, in his terrible Polish, "Your papers, madam?"

The man on the floor groaned and stirred, and Steve and Smyth-Davis bent over him and hauled him to his feet. "Sorry about your fall, sir." Steve said,

Smyth-Davis twisted the man's arm behind his back and propelled him into a chair. "Perhaps it would be best to take a seat, sir. An aggressive individual, as you seem to be, who rushes willy-nilly into things tends to be accident-prone." He smiled at Tadeusz. "Would you kindly translate that properly, Lieutenant Woydziak?"

"I think he already understands," Tadeusz said, with a grin.

The Deacon marched into the room behind Logan, sniffing. "There's a funny smell in here," he announced.

Logan laughed. "Yeah, they've been screwing like rabbits in here. What do you think, Tadeusz, think we caught this guy making it with somebody else's wife?"

The woman was rapidly dressing herself and shrieking more Polish at Logan.

"No," Billie Joe insisted. "I smell something like gas in

here."

Leaving Zdenka to guard the couple in the living room, Tadeusz led the rest of the group into the bedroom and began to ransack the closet. The Deacon paced around the room, trying to find where the scent was strongest. Steve began to pull drawers from the dresser while Reynaud and Smyth-Davis pawed several boxes out from under the bed and tore them open.

Juho, who'd been standing at the door watching the Deacon, suddenly paced to the bed and pointed to marks on the floor, showing where it'd been moved. He waved Reynaud and the Briton away and shoved the bed into the center of the room, revealing a few boxes he shoved aside, stared at the floor a moment, and pulled three planks from the floor.

Reynaud drew his flashlight and snapped it on then played the beam into the opening. They could all see several Jerrycans and a small box. He lifted the box out of the floor and forced it open to reveal several stacks of ration chits and a small treasure trove of watches, rings, and small pieces of jewelry.

Logan whistled at the hoard. "Better call the captain, Tadeusz, it looks like we have a live one here."

Tadeusz strode to the door and shouted outside. A call on the whistle they hadn't heard before was relayed down the street and by the time they'd dug out all seven Jerrycans of kerosene, the captain had entered the apartment.

They escorted the couple to the street, along with the contraband then returned to the apartment and examined it closely but found nothing else that could be considered contraband. The captain tacked a government form on the door, and the group continued its sweep.

Lunch was a piece of bread and a piece of cheese, washed down with water from their canteens, and it was eaten as they continued to search. After the brief excitement of their discovery had died they again fell into a dull routine. A few more Poles cursed them or spat at them, while most only showed a sullen disdain that was almost harder to bear.

"It seems like we've been doing this half our lives," Logan groused, as they marched to another apartment. "How much longer are we going to be doing this? Do we have to put up with another night of sleeping on somebody else's floor? It's late afternoon now."

Tadeusz gestured at the buildings before them. "In two more blocks of houses we will be finished. The captain wants all the houses on our sweep searched before nightfall, then we will be released from this duty. The police patrols will guard the streets of this area tonight."

The woman who answered their knock on the door at the next door stood aside for them to enter then hurried ahead of them to take her papers from a bureau and hand them to Tadeusz. The captain entered minutes later with his clipboard.

"According to the registry," the officer said, tapping the top sheet of paper on his clipboard with the cap of his pen, "your nephew also lives here. Where is he?"

"He is working," the woman replied. "He is a salvager who trades with some of the farmers."

The captain tapped at the paper harder. "Did he not hear he was to remain at home?"

"He was not home yesterday. Sometimes he must stay with friends or with customers, when he works too near curfew."

The group had fanned out through the apartment. Reynaud, Smyth-Davis, and Juho had gone to the bedroom, which appeared to have been recently repainted. Smyth-Davis, who'd become pale with the day's exertions, paced along the wall to examine the wardrobe, while Reynaud looked under the bed. Juho watched the Briton walk along the wall, then moved to the door and waved for Tadeusz to join them.

"Walk again," Juho said, and, as Smyth-Davis returned and retraced his way along the wall, pointed down to where the floor met the wall. As Smyth-Davis trod on the floor planks, they sagged, opening a small but visible crack between the base of the wall and the floor.

Juho strode past Smyth-Davis to open the door of the woman's wardrobe. He pushed the dresses aside then pulled them out and tossed them onto the bed, to run his hand against the back wall of the standing closet. With the groan of a spring, the back of the wardrobe swung inward.

"Ask Logan to come in here," Tadeusz said, quietly and in English.

When Logan had joined them, Tadeusz, still speaking

English, pointed to the wardrobe and said, "I want you and Reynaud to follow me in."

Logan nodded at the AKM Tadeusz carried. "It's liable to be a little close in there for you to use that musket. He set down his own AK and drew out the MAC. "This chopper of mine is a lot more compact. Let me take the lead, and Rennie can cover me with his scattergun."

Tadeusz considered it, finally nodded. "Do you have any more of those assault grenades?"

"Yeah, I've got another goofball in here somewhere."

"Try not to use it. Remember, we'd prefer to recover any contraband intact."

"Okay, okay," Logan said. "It's time for me to step through the looking-glass."

"Actually," Smyth-Davis observed, "you're going through a wardrobe, which is the way to Narnia. Watch out for a lion and a witch."

Reynaud grinned. "I've heard of the book but never read it. Do you suppose we need a passport for Narnia?"

"I've got my passport in my hand," Logan said, as he worked the bolt on the Ingram. Keeping the MAC in his right hand, Logan reached out with his left, shoved the hidden door open, and shouldered his way through the narrow passage.

Reynaud immediately followed him. The apartment room had been dim; the passage was as dark as a tunnel. He reached out and lightly rapped the false wall and felt it give slightly. Groping out the Russian bayonet in his belt, he slashed at the wall, which crackled and ripped. It was apparently a piece of canvas stretched on a wooden frame and covered with light layers of plaster and paint.

In the dim light admitted by the hole, he could see the false wall ended at the outside wall. In the other direction, extending toward the living room, the passage led to a hole in the floor. Again using his flashlight, Reynaud peered into the hole but all he saw, about two feet below, was dirt.

Logan, ahead of him, leaned back and murmured. "It's the crawlspace under the house. We could sure use some gas grenades and masks about now."

"Want me to pass it on to Tadeusz? He can probably get

what we need."

Logan shook his head. "Nah, it'd take too long. I want to get this over with and get home to a real bed. It looks like there's some kind of frame around the opening. I'm gonna crawl along it and drop. As soon as I get down on the frame, pop a couple rounds into the floor then give me a slow count of fifteen before you come on down."

Reynaud turned in the passage and waved Tadeusz back and, as soon as Logan was ready to drop into the hole he fired a shot almost at his feet and a second shot four or five feet away.

His ears rang with the roar of the shots and he hoped anyone hiding under the house would also be momentarily deafened and distracted by the noise and the dust the shots would stir up.

Reynaud heard Logan grunt as he dropped to the dirt. "Follow me ten seconds after I drop," Reynaud told Tadeusz, pocketing the flashlight, then crawled to the edge of the hole, staring into the darkness, counting to fifteen. Like Logan, he crawled as far over the hole as he could, then dropped. As he fell, he twisted, trying to land on his back and keep the muzzle of the shotgun out of the dirt. As he turned in the air, his head nicked the side of the opening and the blow, even cushioned by the fur hat, stunned him, then he hit the ground on his left side and doubled over in pain as the wind was knocked out of him as the flashlight was driven hard against his ribs.

He wasn't sure how his legs got through the opening, he only knew they were drawn up against his chest in his agony. He panicked for a moment as he couldn't draw in a breath then the pain began to ebb and he scrambled away from the hole just as Tadeusz dropped in after him. Reynaud was shocked by the sudden glare of a muzzle flash and an explosion.

In the closed space under the floor, the concussion from the shot was a physical force that hit him like a blow from a fist.

Even as Reynaud started to swing his shotgun, he realized the shot had come from beyond Tadeusz then Logan touched off a short burst. Reynaud almost screamed at the pain battering his ears and when he closed his eyes he could still see the afterimage of the flashes. He crawled to where Tadeusz lay but the Pole whispered, "Move away. There may be more of them."

The darkness, to his temporarily night-blind eyes, seemed

even deeper. Crawling a few feet, he blinked. Still he saw nothing. With his hand, he felt the earth ahead of him, trying to find depressions that could offer some cover. He wanted to stay as low as possible and would've flattened even more but his buttons were in the way.

As he inched forward, something thread-fine scuttled across the back of his hand and he shrank from the touch, suddenly imagining a cluster of poisonous spiders. He could sense the weight of the building above him, seemingly pressing down on him while he was caught in a space too low to even get to his knees, much less stand, in the darkness with God only knew what sort of vermin.

At least he could do something about the darkness. Moving slowly, he reached into his coat pocket and pulled out the flashlight. He transferred it to his right hand, extended his arm to the side, and snapped the light on. Immediately, he dropped the light and grasped his gun.

Seeing sudden movement he snapped off a shot, heard a squeal, and rolled frantically to his left, working the action. As he rolled, a gun barked three times and he heard one of the bullets smack into something solid to his right and another slap the dirt where he'd been. He fired again, this time pointing at the area of the muzzle flashes, rolled again, and, when no more shots were fired, crawled back toward the flashlignt.

He felt something wet running down the side of his face and the outer edge of his left eyebrow stung. Gently, he examined the wound with his fingers. The area over his eye was swelling but he found no serious damage and, closing his other eye, could still see. Doggedly, he continued crawling toward the light.

When he could reach the flashlight with the toe of his boot, he nudged it around to point it where the shots had come from but saw nothing. Leaving the light, he flanked wide around the beam, hoping Logan was also covering the area.

He almost fell into the hole before he saw it. By the dim reflected light, he could see two bodies in the hole, one of them still breathing raggedly. He fumbled in a pocket for more ammunition, stuffed two more rounds into the tube magazine. He pointed the shotgun at the man in the pit who was still breathing, sheltered himself as best he could against the concussion, and fired.

As the shotgun roared he sprang away from the pit then flung himself forward to slide into the hole. The sides were steeper than he'd thought and he fell with bruising force onto some boxes, dropping the shotgun as he fell. Even stunned, he knew no more shots had been fired.

He fumbled out the .45 automatic he carried and cautiously crawled across the boxes, which wobbled alarmingly under him, to where the bodies lay, where he could finally get to his feet. "Hey, Logan," he called, "I think we've cleaned them out."

"Looks like," Logan's voice came from the darkness. "Where are you?"

"There's a hole back here stocked with goodies and two corpses in it." He found his shotgun but left the action closed and thumbed the safety on. "See if you can get more light down here, and have somebody check Tadeusz. He had a lot of blood on his coat."

"What about you?"

"I'm a little bloody but nothing serious."

Logan crawled back to the opening and shouted up for flashlights. As the first light was handed down to him he snapped it on and studied Tadeusz's wound. Reynaud, with the light as a beacon that gave him some view of what lay between himself and the opening, crawled out of the pit and toward Logan, making a slight detour around the rat he'd killed.

When Reynaud was close enough to see Tadeusz, he observed the man's face was pale and slightly yellow in the flashlight's glare, with the upper chest of his coat soaked in blood. Logan had pulled open the coat and the shirt beneath.]

"How bad is it?" Reynaud asked.

"I only found the one hole," Logan replied. "It looks like the bullet clipped his collarbone and broke it, then drilled through the muscles between the neck and the shoulder. I'm no doctor, but I think he'll make it, although I'll bet it smarts like a bitch."

Steve stared down at them through the opening. "Can you hand him up here?"

Logan and Reynaud, working as carefully as possible, wrestled Tadeusz around and lifted his shoulders to where Steve and Juho could pull him clear of the hole. The Pole clenched his teeth, and twice they heard sudden indrawn breaths, but he never screamed. When Tadeusz was clear of the passage, Juho slipped through the opening with more flashlights and they all crawled to the pit.

The two bodies had their faces blown away by shotgun blasts and one of them had two bullet holes in his chest.

"That explains why I didn't find the body where I was shooting," Logan said. "I did find a wet spot and a rifle. It felt like an old bolt-action." The two of them dropped into the pit and Reynaud found a semi-automatic that looked like his Colt .45 automatic, but somewhat smaller. He dropped the pistol's magazine and jacked back the slide to clear the chamber then dropped both the pistol and the clip into his coat pocket.

Both the bodies had been tall, strong men. "Look like enforcers," Logan said, and began to rummage through the boxes. Ration chits, jewelry, bottles of vodka, and cans of food were all stored in separate boxes, with some machine tool parts and engine parts in a large wooden case. Most of the fuel cans, which were carefully sealed, held kerosene but two of them were marked with the Polish word for gasoline.

"Well," Logan said with a grin, "we can't tell 'em we've got a live one for them this time, but we've got enough goodies here to make it worth the trip."

They began moving the cans and boxes toward the opening, working in relays, with Juho shoving them up the opening to the men upstairs. The last things they took out of the pit were the bodies.

After the Finn followed the second corpse upstairs, Reynaud gestured toward the opening. "Go ahead," he told Logan.

"After you," Logan replied. "You've been getting antsier down here than a whore in church."

Wasting no time in argument, Reynaud scrambled out of the hole and made his way through the huge opening that'd been torn in the false wall. He was trembling with fatigue, tension, and the draining effects of having survived a gunfight. "Where's Tadeusz?" he asked.

The Deacon, returning from hauling cans outside, said, "He's already been taken to the aid station."

Reynaud handed the captured pistol and magazine to the

captain, who identified it as a Vis then, speaking slowly and distinctly, said, "Go to guard duty as soon as the contraband is gone."

Logan ignored the hole in the wall to emerge from the wardrobe with a grin almost splitting his face. "No witches, and no white rabbits, but Rennie wasted the dormouse and we got a couple of cards. Speaking of a mouse, that's one helluva knot you've got over your left eye, Rennie. What happened?"

Reaching up and cautiously touching the swelling, Reynaud found only a little blood on his fingertips. The wound had apparently stopped bleeding. "I don't know. I must've dinged my head on the gun barrel when I was trying to roll and work the pump at the same time." He worked the Mossberg's action several times until he was certain the gun was empty then, with the action open, peered down the bore, which was plugged with dirt.

He borrowed a cleaning rod from Steve and cleared the dirt from the barrel, tapped the barrel against the floor a couple of times to be sure the dirt had been knocked out, then reloaded the weapon and followed the rest of the group outside to guard the contraband.

The captain blew the odd signal again and, within minutes, a truck arrived to haul away the contraband, the bodies, and the woman.

The sun had just disappeared below the horizon when the sweep was finally completed. A truck picked up their teams and dropped Reynaud's group off on the way back to the Wawel, leaving them a few blocks to walk.

So exhausted he almost leaned against the cold wind for support, Reynaud stumbled forward against it. He noticed Smyth-Davis was also weaving and lurching like a drunk by the time they reached the apartment.

They collapsed into chairs and explained to Frank and St. Jacques Tadeusz had been wounded and taken to an aid station. Anya started dinner, then fussed over Reynaud and Smyth-Davis like a mother hen. Using a soft cloth and warm water, she cleaned Reynaud's cut and Frank carefully daubed it with an antiseptic cream from a med kit.

"I have more news for you guys," Frank said.

"I don't think I can take much more news today," Reynaud

said, "I'm ready to crash and burn."

"It's mostly something to think on." Frank put away the med kit. "It looks like the FSB and the CIA have the same general plans and programs, just different beneficiaries. For instance, Barela was obviously planted in the Cardinal's guard to either assassinate him or set him up for assassination when the time was right, with the object of framing the CIA and elements of the new Polish government. They probably intended to make it look as though the new government was a pawn of the CIA

"From the papers we found at the theater, it looks as though the CIA had the same idea, only they wanted to make it look like the FSB was pulling the strings."

Anya brought food to the table and Reynaud decided rest could wait until he'd eaten, and he wondered how the Poles survived on their meager diets.

"Why's the Cardinal so important?" Steve asked.

"He's not the only target, of course." Frank chewed a piece of meat then swallowed and continued. "You have to realize the Polish culture stands on three legs; the government, the army, and the Church. The real temporal power right now is in the hands of the army, but General Macharski is eager to turn power over to a regular government, which will depend upon the Church for some of its legitimacy. That's what this Polish congress is about—how the government is set up.

"If Cardinal Krol is assassinated, and if the murder can be pinned on elements of the new government, General Macharski will have no choice but to keep control, and it's always easier to get people to resist a military government than a representative one."

Logan looked up from stoking his internal furnace. "So, what's the CIA doing shit like this for? Seems to me we'd want a real government here in Poland."

Frank paused, a forkful of meatloaf halfway to his mouth, and stared at Logan. "Has anyone broken the news to you about Santa Claus and the Easter Bunny? And the terrible things they've been saying about the tooth fairy are true. Look, anyone still carrying on the CIA program is hardcore, and they've been destabilizing governments and supporting dictators for ages. They'd set up General Macharski for assassination and try to make sure the next man in line is Adolf Hitler's grandson."

"Okay, okay, so where does this lead us?" Reynaud bit off a piece of cracker smeared with peanut butter. He glanced at Smyth-Davis and noticed he hadn't eaten at all.

"Nowhere, directly," Frank admitted, "but I wanted you guys to know what's at stake here."

Steve swallowed a mouthful of coffee and cleared his throat. "We always had a pretty good idea about that. What have you got to help us deal with our immediate problems?"

"As a matter of fact," Frank said, "Wyszynski's boys came up with a clue about where Oshevsky might be hiding."

Chapter 10

Into the sudden silence Logan interjected what everyone was thinking. "How good a clue?"

Frank leaned forward. "They found something wedged between the soles of the shoes two of the men were wearing. It was straw and manure. Does that ring any bells with any of you?"

"Yeah," Logan snapped. "It means we shot up a couple of ploughboys. So what? In case you haven't noticed, the whole damned city is surrounded by farms."

"Maybe," Frank said, but those clowns wouldn't be outside the city. They've got to keep their command structure a lot closer to the action than that. Wiktor gave me a list of places where farms have been set up in what used to be parks." He unfolded a sheet of paper and a map of the city.

He tapped the printed list. "There are a few places we can disregard right off the top, like the parks that replaced the walls of the old town; they've been converted to graveyards. Jordan Park, Krakow Park, and *Warszawakie* off *Rakowicka* are all either military or police farms, which are tended by captured deserters and criminals. That leaves the observatory—we can exclude that; it must be a mistake—*Ludwinow*, *Podgorze*, and *Park Bednarskiego*, as well as three, four smaller areas."

"That's still a lot of area to cover," Logan said, "and we'll get a damned sight further along after a little sleep. Jeez, I miss Laura. Until I got dumped in a P-camp, I wasn't much used to going to bed alone."

Reynaud snorted. "You must've gone to bed with a lot of ugly women."

Logan laughed. "Nope. I never went to bed with an ugly woman. I woke up with quite a few of them, but they always looked as good as a paycheck the night before."

Steve stood. "You need to eat more carrots. Helps your night vision. Well, I'm going to turn in."

"Carrots! Shit!" Logan growled. "You guys are trying to take all the mystery and romance out of sex."

~ * ~

Reynaud was up well before dawn and found Frank in the kitchen. "I forgot to tell you last night—we got an invitation to spend Christmas with a Polish family."

Frank simply stared at him while he sipped coffee.

"You'd have done the same," Reynaud said. "They're good people. I thought we might play Santa Claus; take them some food, along with anything else we can make or scrape up. Could we get another shotgun, for instance?"

"Yeah, I think we can do that. I'm getting ready to go see Wiktor and I can ask him about it. I also want to see how Tadeusz is doing, and try to find out how we can get to the FSB."

"Why don't we just have the army raid all the farms at once?" Reynaud accepted a cup of coffee and a plate of bread and sausage from Anya.

"Too many chances for a leak. If someone in the army talks, or if there are more FSB plants, the FSB will just burrow deeper underground. I'd rather have them overconfident than warn them."

Logan and Steve had come into the kitchen while Frank and Reynaud were talking. "You have an answer in your hip pocket," Steve said. "We've still got those phony Ministry of Health cards, haven't we? Why don't we just flash the papers and tell the people at the farms we're checking food storage or vermin control, or some such excuse?"

"That's one hell of an idea," Frank said. "Sounds good to me. I'll be back in a couple of hours and we'll hit the list."

"I want to go with you, especially if you're going to see Tadeusz."

Frank stood. "Then grab your coat and hat, because I want to be on my way right now."

The sky was gray and overcast but the wind had stilled. The long walk to the Wawel was more pleasant than Reynaud had expected it to be. Wiktor had arrived at his office only minutes before they arrived.

As soon as they'd closed the door, Wyszynski waved them toward chairs. "I just received the news this morning. They finally identified the body of the dead man they found in Brussels. He was scheduled to leave on a flight to Texas. They're trying to find Chernikov there now but the matter seems to be slipping through our fingers just as we reach out to catch it."

"Is Tadeusz all right?" Frank asked.

Wyszynski leaned back in his chair. "He will recover. They will keep him at the hospital for several days longer. Have you considered how to find Oshevsky?"

Frank explained the plan to use the Ministry of Health credentials to get into and examine the farms.

Wyszynski nodded. "That might work. The list of farms I gave you also has the name of the man in charge of each of the farms. It seems a rather unlikely chance, though."

"What other ideas do you have?" When the Pole said nothing, Frank continued. "Any plan is better than no plan. Can we get a ride to the hospital to see Tadeusz?"

Wyszynski picked up the phone and barked orders into it. When he replaced the receiver he grinned at the Americans. "I have put a car and driver at your disposal. Tell Tadeusz I will expect to see him when he is out of the hospital. And, before you go," he turned to Reynaud, "I need a written report of the action in which Tadeusz was wounded. Your captain has already filed a report but we also need a report from a man who was involved in the action."

Reynaud hurriedly scribbled a report and Frank just as quickly translated it then the two of them made their way to the Wawel courtyard, where they found a small, black Polski Fiat and a driver waiting for them.

Reynaud learned again the meaning of fear as the driver, an ORMO sergeant, drove the Fiat at breakneck speed despite the snow and ice covering the streets, shouting and gesturing at pedestrians slow to get out of his way. After having braced himself, for the fourth or fifth time, for a crash, Reynaud leaned toward Frank. "Could you tell him we're just going to the hospital to visit a friend, that we're not trying to be patients?"

"Maybe he thinks you're pregnant," Frank replied.

When they finally arrived at the hospital, Frank dismissed the driver and they entered the building, found the nurse's station, and got directions to Tadeusz's ward. The ward was over half empty and the few beds occupied held men of military age, all of them with casts or bandages. They found Tadeusz scowling at the ceiling, his left arm taped to his chest and more tape holding his shoulder in place and binding his chest.

Reynaud approached the foot of the bed. "If Logan were here, he'd comment on how you look like the mummy. How's your arm?"

"There is nothing wrong with my arm. The bullet broke the collarbone and tore some of the muscles in my shoulder. They want to keep the shoulder immobile. They have succeeded."

Frank found a chair, pulled it up beside the bed, and sat. "Are they treating you all right?"

"Except for the food. If they fed that to prisoners, the cook would be hanged for war crimes."

"Does the shoulder hurt much?" Reynaud asked.

"Only when I breathe—or hold my breath."

Frank brought the Pole up to date on the search for the FSB, including their plan to use the forged papers.

"Will you know what you are looking for once you are in the farms?" Tadeusz asked.

Frank shrugged. "We'll just have to take our chances. The opposition can hide a lot, but we can try. Oh, sorry you won't be able to spend Christmas with the family Reynaud mentioned and the rest of the gang. Can you suggest anything to take the family besides food?"

Tadeusz stared at the ceiling. "I didn't see a crèche in the apartment, so you might carve them one. If you take food, it should not be given until after the *wigilia*, because it is the responsibility of the host to provide food for it."

"What's a *wigilia*?" Reynaud asked.

"It is a Christmas eve supper, and it starts with the appearance of the first star, so you must arrive early. Maciej will probably break and share the *oplatek* with you and exchange good wishes then they will serve an odd number of courses of meatless dishes. After dinner, they will all sing carols, and I think you will go to midnight Mass. That would be the best time to have someone bring in the gifts—while the family is at Mass."

Reynaud snapped his fingers. "We forgot to ask Wyszynski for another shotgun."

"Don't worry," Frank said, "I'll take care of it tomorrow morning when I try to get the latest report on Chernikov."

Reynaud stood. "I supposed we'd better be going, if we're

going to get in any search time today." He shook Tadeusz's hand. "Take care of yourself. If we aren't in to see you before then, we'll make a special trip on Christmas day."

"The best Christmas present you could bring me," Tadeusz said, "is Oshevsky's head. If you cannot bring that, bring me some real food."

Frank stood and moved the chair back to where he'd found it. "If you come up with any ideas about our problem, let us know."

The hospital lay west of the apartment on *Batorego*, and near enough for an easy walk, which spared them the dangers of riding again with the ORMO sergeant.

While the group downed a quick lunch, Frank took out his map of Krakow and pointed out *Park Bednarskiego* and *Stadion Korona*. "This is the biggest park not being used by the military or the police. Its base is the stadium, where the cooperative committee keeps its offices. In many ways, this park is going to be the most difficult to search, so we should probably check it out first, since it's the most likely."

They managed to reach the park in less than an hour only because they were able to ride most of the way on ORMO patrol trucks.

Janusz Michalowski, the head of the cooperative, was obviously proud of the beginning his group had made in self-sufficiency. A veteran of the early clashes on the Polish-German front, he'd formed the cooperative early enough in the summer they'd been able to harvest crops before the onset of bad weather. He pointed out how strips of park had been left between the crops and the storage facilities and offices of the group had left most of the stadium available for other uses.

The people who farmed the park lived in apartments around the area. Frank and his group were able to make only the most cursory examinations of the apartments and prowled through the stadium but found nothing to excite suspicion.

As they returned to their apartment that night Frank considered the day largely lost. He couldn't even be certain the FSB hadn't been watching the search but there were still many farms to inspect.

That night they began to carve a crèche. Juho, they learned, could carve better and quicker than any of the rest of the group. He seemed to sense the shapes hidden in the blocks of wood and could swiftly pare away the obscuring wood. He was left to do the human figures while the others carved the animals and rough-cut the manger and stable.

~ * ~

Frank returned from the morning visit with Wyszynski with another shotgun but no new information, except that Chernikov had apparently vanished in Texas.

The group spent most of the day examining the farm at *Podgorze*. As in their search the previous day, they discovered nothing amiss, and returned, tired and discouraged, to their apartment two hours before dark.

They cleaned themselves as best they could, gathered together their presents, including over a month's food supplies and, with Anya, set out for the family's apartment, the gifts stacked on the sled.

As they neared the apartment, Frank looked at the sled then stared at the other buildings on the street. "We can't take this stuff in with us, and there's no safe place to leave it."

"Sure there is," Logan replied. "Three doors past Maciej's place, where we found the first stash of contraband. Remember? The captain sealed it but we're part of the government now. We can just leave it there."

Frank squinted at the building for a moment then said, "We'll have to leave a guard with it. The place is going to be cold, so I don't want anyone to spend more than an hour with the stuff. I can tell our host—Maciej, you said his name was—I can tell him we're having to do some kind of guard duty for the ORMO. Who wants to take the first watch?"

"Better to get it done earlier than later," Smyth-Davis said.

They unloaded the food, clothing, and the shotgun, and even hauled the sled itself into the apartment then walked the short distance to Maciej's building.

The Pole met them at the door. "Please, come in. Will Lieutenant Woydziak recover? I had heard he was badly wounded."

As the group trooped into the small dining room, one end of which was dominated by a Christmas tree, Frank nodded. "He was only slightly wounded, and he should be out of the hospital by the middle of next week." He introduced himself, Anya, and St. Jacques. When he mentioned the Frenchman's name, Maciej smiled broadly.

"*Comment allez-vous?*" the Pole asked.

"*Bien, merci, et vous?*"

"*Bien aussi,*" Maciej replied, then, in Polish, "I worked at the university before the war. It is a pleasure to see you again and hear French spoken once more." He introduced his family to the group, then led them to two tables laid end-to-end. Somewhere, he'd found enough chairs to seat everyone. "There is another of your group missing," he observed, as they all took chairs at the tables.

"Smyth-Davis is on guard duty for the ORMO." Frank stretched the truth only a little. "Juho will have to relieve him, later, and each of us will have to be gone for some little time this evening."

Logan carried the one box the group had brought into the apartment to a sideboard, opened it, and began to place the figurines of the crèche on the buffet, while St. Jacques held up two bottles of wine that had been packed in rags.

Walery, Maciej's son, had been going to the door and looking outside every few minutes. Suddenly, after one of his trips, he dashed into the room. "The first star! The first star!"

Maciej broke the *oplatek*, the blessed wafer, and passed out pieces to each person at the table, with exchanges of hugs and good wishes, and left a piece of the bread on a dish by the crèche. To Reynaud, the wafer reminded him of the Communion host given at Mass.

After the exchanges of friendship the woman and the girl brought in the first course, small bowls of *barszcz*. When they'd finished the beet soup, Frank caught Juho's attention then glanced down at his watch.

Without a word, Juho stood, strode to the corner where the longarms were stacked, slung his rifle, and went out into the darkness.

Smyth-Davis arrived at the same time as the next course, which was some kind of noodles stuffed with farmer's cheese. Maciej gave the Briton the bit of *oplatek* he'd saved for him then

Smyth-Davis nibbled at the three *pierogi* they'd each been given. He sipped once at his wine then ignored it.

The next course was some sort of fish, and everyone received a small piece of it. Reynaud sawed at his morsel, which seemed to have the consistency of a mud and snow tire. Logan had finally whittled a smaller piece of his serving and seemed to be making a career of chewing it.

"What do you think it is?" Reynaud whispered. "Gar, maybe?"

Logan finally managed to swallow what he had in his mouth. "I'm not sure, but I think maybe they caught a Russian sub." He washed down the bite of fish with a sip of wine.

When they'd finished the meal, the plates were cleared from the table and Maciej began to sing *"Adeste Fidelis."* One by one, the rest of them took up the song, Reynaud's altar-boy Latin coming back to him in bits and pieces. As the carol died away, the Deacon began it again, in English, and, in their turns, Frank, Jean-Marie, and the family sang it in Polish.

As the song ended, Frank leaned across the table and tapped Reynaud's wrist with his watch. Reynaud stood and paced to where the weapons were stacked, picked up his shotgun, and stepped outside. As he went out the door he heard them begin "Silent Night" in Polish.

The night was clear, though bitterly cold, with the brilliant stars looking like they were frozen in the sky, and he could hear voices from each building along the block, singing. Someone in one of the buildings was playing a piano and, as he neared the building where the gifts were stored, he heard a few chords being played on a guitar. He climbed the stairs and, after a knock on the door, entered the apartment.

Juho nodded to him then left, and Reynaud was alone. He found where Juho had sat and dropped into the still-warm chair. It suddenly occurred to him he'd spend an hour alone on Christmas eve. He began to sing "Silent Night" to himself, quietly, until his voice broke. For a time, he remembered his family and felt intensely alone. Joy to the world. He snorted. Little enough joy was left in the world unless one were a sadist or a masochist.

He began searching the floor around his feet, wondering if Juho had perhaps had a candle against the darkness, and his fingers brushed wood shavings. He continued to grope on the floor until he found a small figurine carved in wood. Not wanting to dig out his flashlight, he tried to hold it up against the ghostly faint gleam of the window but the darkness was too deep to make out more than a vague shape.

He ran his fingers over it slowly and carefully and discovered it was a figure of a woman. Somehow, it made him feel better, knowing the Finn, so grim and strong, also felt the aloneness; it made him somehow more human. Reynaud slipped the carving into his pocket and waited, sometimes humming along with occasional snatches of melody he heard from outside.

The door opened and a bulky shape stepped into the room. "Your hour is ended."

"Don't make it sound so morbid," he said to St. Jacques. "I've become superstitious."

"War does that to one," the Frenchman replied.

By the time Reynaud had returned to Maciej's, most of the carols had been sung and Logan was attempting a rendering of "Jingle Bells Rock" and was pretty effectively rending it.

When Logan had finished, Reynaud grinned at him. "That damned near brought tears to my eyes. I used to be a music minor. Don't you know better than to make noises like that when your audience is armed?"

Logan glared at him. "Everybody's a critic. Why don't you lay something from the bayou on us?"

Reynaud shook his head. "The only appropriate way to follow that act is with an alligator roaring."

"Do alligators roar?" Steve asked.

"Only when they're feeling romantic, or when they're brought to a boil."

Frank had translated the exchange for the Poles, who looked puzzled, and Maciej asked how one brought anything as large as an alligator to a boil.

Reynaud's off-the-wall and convoluted answer inspired more jokes and tall tales until Zdenka had to leave. They waited for the Frenchman to return and finally Steve stared at Frank. "Do you think they had some kind of trouble?"

"We didn't hear any shots," Frank replied.

"Hey, maybe he's getting lucky," Logan said. "Hell, it's

Christmas. Keep a happy thought for the poor guy."

"Well, we'll have to leave pretty soon for the midnight Mass," Frank said. "Logan, you and McCluskey stay behind." He told Maciej, in Polish, that they'd leave McCluskey to guard the apartment while Logan was on duty.

"Time for me to saddle up, I guess," Logan said, and, after preparing for the cold and checking the chamber of his weapon, "If I see the kids, I'll send 'em along."

The family prepared for the walk to St. Mary's Church, bundling themselves against the cold, and St. Jacques and Zdenka returned just before they started out the door. The group left its shoulder weapons at the apartment and joined the people who began to appear in the streets. The crowds grew thicker as they neared the church and they were hardly able to find standing room inside.

They had to wait almost an hour, with a crowd around them continuing to swell. Maciej leaned toward Frank and Reynaud heard him mutter. "They will have to serve another Mass outside, in the marketplace."

Reynaud was grateful for the relative warmth of the church, relieved he and his friends weren't among the throngs outside, shivering in the cold night. He glanced at the others and noticed Smyth-Davis seemed pale and a little unsteady. He leaned closer to the Briton. "Are you all right?"

"It just seems a bit close," Smyth-Davis replied.

Finally the Mass began. Reynaud followed the responses mechanically, watching the Brit closely, but saw nothing other than the pallor to suggest the man was suffering from anything other than the crush of the crowd around him.

Almost an hour after Mass had ended they were finally able to make their way outside and return to the apartment, where Logan and the Deacon opened the door at their knock. "You had a visitor while you were gone," Logan said. "Sort of a tubby guy, wore a red suit, and had whiskers down to here." He held his hand at about mid-chest.

A few gifts had been placed under the Christmas tree before, but now the floor around it was heaped with MRE packets, a bright-colored bundle of clothing, and the shotgun. When the girl opened the bundle, she held up embroidered clothing that had belonged to Katya.

"I cannot accept all this," Maciej protested.

"You couldn't if we'd given it to you," Frank replied. "We would not insult you like that. But to refuse St. Nickolas—I'm not sure that wouldn't be a sacrilege."

Maciej stared at Frank and the others then saw his "daughter" holding a skirt to her waist, obviously pleased with the bright colors, and he laughed. "You are right. No good Pole would insult a saint." He hugged each of the group then hurried to the kitchen and returned with two bottles of vodka. He held one of the bottles up and even in the dim light they could see a long strand of grass in the bottle. "Buffalo-grass vodka from before the war. This is the really good vodka."

Reynaud accepted a glass and sipped. The vodka was ice-cold and as smooth as water, without the slightest taste of alcohol.

Frank raised his glass to the family. "*Sto lat,*"

Maciej raised his own glass. "*Sto lat,*" he replied.

Frank sat at the table and took a deep drink of the vodka. "Anya will stay with you for a day or two. She has some practice cooking the meals in those bags. We'd better get ready to leave."

"Not until you have warmed yourselves, both inside and outside." Maciej refilled the glasses, although the Deacon hadn't touched his, and Smyth-Davis had hardly sipped at his.

"The man is a veritable sage," St. Jacques said, and drank most of his second glass of vodka.

"You keep that up," Frank said, "and you won't be able to walk at all."

They moved the party to the kitchen and warmed themselves by the stove, which still held glowing embers, and drank and talked. Reynaud learned Maciej hadn't really known St. Jacques but recognized him from chance meetings on the campus. By the time the two bottles held only happy memories, they were warm enough to brave the trip back to their apartment.

As they prepared to leave, Smyth-Davis reached for his AKR with his left hand but the weapon slipped from his grasp and clattered on the floor.

Smyth-Davis saw Reynaud staring at him. "I seem to have had a bit too much to drink. I could never tolerate more than a taste." He bent down and picked up the submachine gun with his right hand.

Reynaud picked up his shotgun and followed the Briton out the door. Something was wrong but he couldn't be exactly sure what the problem was. The Brit had always been reserved, so it was difficult to guess if he'd become more withdrawn. The bullet wound to Smyth-Davis' head could cause some of the physical problems he'd observed but he had no idea how dangerous it was. He shook his own head, trying to force the vague ideas to unsnarl themselves and stand out clearly but nothing seemed any sharper.

"Hey, Frank," Logan asked, "what was that toast you and Maciej swapped? It sounded like Polish for 'one hundred years.'"

"That's just what it was," Frank said. "It's sort of a Polish *'aloha.'* It's kind of an all-occasion best wish. A hundred years of health, or happiness, or whatever. They use it for Christmas, New Years', weddings, whatever. *Sto lat.*"

Reynaud put his hand into his pocket and felt the wooden figurine. Juho had fallen back to the tail of the line and Reynaud dropped back to walk beside him. As they walked, Reynaud handed the carving to the Finn. *"Sto lat."*

The Finn looked at the carving with surprise, then took it, touched it lightly with his fingertips, and put it in his pocket. He flashed a rare grin. *"Sto Lat."*

~ * ~

They all visited Tadeusz at the hospital and smuggled in a few MREs. He slid the rations under the blankets. "I am supposed to be released from the hospital tomorrow or Tuesday. Have you found any other information? Are you any closer to finding Oshevsky?"

Frank scowled. "Not yet. We're pretty sure the first two places we checked are clean. Don't worry, we'll nail him."

"Perhaps we're using the wrong voice," Smyth-Davis said, "passive instead of active."

"What do you mean?" Reynaud asked.

"I'm not sure, yet, but an idea does seem to be percolating."

Logan had, along with the rations, smuggled in a bottle of vodka and they passed it around.

Chapter 11

Smyth-Davis, when handed the bottle, simply passed it on to Dechaine. Drinking made his already-upset stomach even worse. The pain in his head was back, making his thought process slow and clumsy, something that frustrated and annoyed him. The headaches had improved slightly until the battle in the Polish town, although he still wondered if he hadn't rushed toward the mayor's kitchen to have it finished quickly. Then, when the grenade had exploded behind him, the pain had returned, worse than ever. Since then, he'd had no relief from the headaches or the bouts of numbness on his left side.

There seemed no end to it but death, and death was no longer something to fear. With the world flung into a garbage heap, there was no reason for him to continue.

The months in the prison camp had been an acid, eating away at his allegiances—what few remained. His family had survived the blitz in London, and they would've remained in London this time, but no one would've survived in London in this war, with the bomb and the plague, like two horsemen of the apocalypse in a race to gather souls.

The nearest he'd come to establishing relationship or an allegiance was the comradeship, almost a kinship, he felt for the men around him. Liking them had nothing to do with it. Reid's almost calculated abrasiveness, McCluskey's dour disapproval of almost every amenity, or St. Jacques' ever-so-faint air of superiority all annoyed him, but he knew each of them would stand beside him in mortal peril. If they might not give their lives—lives which still had meaning for them—for his, they'd certainly risk those important lives for his.

There was an irony there which, because of the pain in his head, he couldn't really appreciate.

The only other relationship that could move him was the deep and abiding hatred he felt for Chernikov and Oshevsky, and he'd be willing to give his life—such as it was—to know that either or both of them were feeding worms. That was the idea that kept eluding him. He was sure the exchange might be possible, but the details of how to arrange the transaction remained just out of reach.

Certainly, they were accomplishing nothing with their sweeps of the farms. Even if they found some clue, how many days or weeks would it take? And each day was another opportunity for them to slip beyond reach, perhaps forever.

He hadn't been paying attention to where he was walking beyond the few feet in front of him and he realized, with something like surprise, that Piotrowski had begun to climb a set of stairs. They'd returned to the apartment.

The mild shock of surprise caused a series of connections to be made and he suddenly realized how they might find Oshevsky. With the others, he stamped snow off his boots but kept his coat on because the apartment was frigid. Frank started a fire and set a kettle of water on the stove.

For several minutes, Smyth-Davis sat staring at nothing then cleared his throat. "Lady and gentlemen, I believe I have an answer to our difficulty."

Dechaine stared at him intently. "What's your idea?"

"If I permit myself to be taken by Oshevsky's confederates, it should be a simple matter for you to trail them to their lair."

"You're crazier than a pet skunk!" Reid exclaimed. "Way too many problems. There isn't even a newspaper to take out an ad in. And once you're in the bag, how're we gonna be able to tail you? You gonna leave a trail of bread crumbs? And you're counting on us to make the raid in time to get you out before Oshevsky's made you look like you took a vacation in a Mixmaster. Not to mention the fact they might just pop you off if we don't hit hard and fast enough. Finally, why you? I think I'd have the best chance of any of you of being able to stomp Oshevsky's guts in if you all stop for a coffee break."

Piotrowski stood. "Don't go off half-cocked, Logan. The plan may have some merit." He walked to the cupboard where he took down several cups, emptied packets of instant coffee in all of them but one. In that cup he placed a tea bag, then poured hot water into all the cups. He picked up a cup of coffee and the cup of tea, carried them to the table, and set the tea before Smyth-Davis. "Merry Christmas. I managed to score a few of these at the hospital."

Smyth-Davis smiled. "I suppose that explains the tea being in surgical dressings. I appreciate the consideration."

St. Jacques limped to the cupboard and returned with two cups, one of which he placed before Zdenka, then sipped at his own coffee. "I would be the more logical choice to be the one captured, since I'm already limping a bit." He sipped again at the coffee. "How did you plan to be captured?"

Smyth-Davis leaned back in his chair. "It only occurred to me on the way back from the hospital. Surely it was not by accident that the former ZOMO thugs saw us at the pub. They were either following you or they knew you frequented the place. Would that latter be a correct assumption?"

Piotrowski simply nodded.

"Now, the only questions to remain are whether this item of information was known to the FSB headquarters or only the cell, and whether they'll still be maintaining a watch on the place."

Piotrowski slowly drank his coffee, staring into it as if the answer might be printed on the bottom of the cup. The others were also silent, each apparently harboring their private thoughts and doubts.

Piotrowski finally broke the silence. "All right, we'll do it, but with a few amendments. The first is; we find some fair way to decide who takes the risks. Another proviso is we have some safety nets. It'll take until tomorrow to set that up."

Smyth-Davis considered the options for a moment then got to his feet, paced to the cupboard, and returned with a handful of wooden matches. He turned his back to the group then sat and extended the matches to the others. "I've shortened one. The lucky soul who draws the short match will be the sacrificial lamb."

Piotrowski drew the first match. One by one, each of the others drew a matchstick. An almost preternatural sensitivity struck Smyth-Davis and he could read relief struggle with disappointment on each face, and he knew two or three of them were considering snapping the matchsticks they held. As Jeroskaya drew one of the matches he saw St. Jacques relax and take a match, leaving only the one for Smyth-Davis.

Smyth-Davis had some experience with sleight of hand and slipped the end of the remaining matchstick under a long fingernail. He pointed to Reid's stick. "Isn't that match a bit—oh, never mind." In the split-second of the others' distraction he'd snapped the matchstick in his hand, keeping the broken end captured under the nail. "I seem to have had the luck of the draw." He held up the broken match.

He saw Dechaine staring at him with an expression of intense concentration and he knew the Cajun had guessed what he'd done. He stared steadily back, and Dechaine gave a barely perceptible nod.

~ * ~

Reynaud took a swallow of lukewarm coffee, still thinking about Smyth-Davis. He wasn't sure why the Brit had insisted upon taking the gravest risk but it was time for him to trust the man.

Frank left the room for a moment then returned with a pencil and several sheets of paper and began to draw a series of lines. "All right, this is the bar." He darkened the central rectangle and emphasized the lines beside it. "*Paulinska* ends at the park cum cemetery. They aren't likely to take Smyth-Davis that way, although the trees that are left do provide a hidden way to the streets north and south. Jean-Marie, you and Zdenka take positions there."

He continued to sketch, assigning members of the group to various sites around the bar until the area was surrounded by pairs of watchers. "This gives us a good chance to follow them back to the headquarters but, just in case, I want to have ORMO teams picked by Wiktor to watch all the farms, just in case they get away from us. We can always use the song-and-dance that we think some of the places may be smuggling contraband."

"Isn't that a little risky?" Steve asked. "I thought we were trying to keep the ORMO out of this."

"In the first place," Frank held up his index finger, "this will come from a different angle, so it won't seem so suspicious. In the second place," he raised another finger, "this is only a precaution. The primary responsibility for the job rests with us." He held up a third finger. "Finally, how many of you want to let Smyth-Davis risk falling into Oshevsky's hands because we didn't take all possible precautions?"

No one spoke.

"Then let's use the rest of daylight to recon the area, be sure of our positions, set up any additional cover any of you might need, and make sure we don't overlook anything. I don't want a doorway or an alley that isn't in someone's view. Jean-Marie, you stay here. I'm not crazy about leaving this place completely undefended. Zdenka can get the information the two of you will need."

"I can stay behind with *Monsieur* St. Jacques," Smyth-Davis said with a faint smile, "since I'm already certain of my position."

"Do it." Frank bundled himself against the cold.

After the long trek to *Paulinska*, Reynaud wasn't surprised to see the bar was open. Too many Poles were alone, their families wiped out by the plague, and now they only had the artificial families in places like the bar.

Frank dispatched the members of the group to the positions they'd been assigned and checked to be sure they could remain out of sight while still able to observe anyone leaving the bar. After they'd been paced through two or three of the possible escape routes, Frank nodded. "Lookin' good. Just remember, it's going to be dark when this goes down."

On a sudden impulse, Reynaud said, "I've developed a thirst. How about the rest of you?"

Frank pursed his lips and stared at the bar through narrowed eyes. "It's risky...but let's go for it. I'd like to scope the place out for myself."

The inside of the bar was a deep twilight and they had to wait for their snowblind eyes to adjust before they threaded their way through the crowd. The table they'd used on their first visit was occupied, and so they stood at the bar.

The bartender poured vodka for Frank. "Where is the Frenchman who always come in with you? Or Tadeusz?"

Frank turned the glass with his fingertips. "St Jacques and Tadeusz had some business to take care of, but St. Jacques should be in tomorrow night. Be sure to have good wine for him. He will probably come in with a friend of ours, an Englishman. Do you have any gin?"

"Only schnapps."

Reynaud ordered a beer and drank it. He'd been able to follow Frank's conversation with the bartender and he glanced around the room, wondering who else in the bar had also been listening. He looked over the men and the few women in the place. As before, most wore military uniforms and almost all of them had ORMO armbands. The rest all wore work clothes. The few civil-service types that had been the bar before were either absent or dressed for warmth and comfort rather than to satisfy a fading sense of fashion.

Each of the group had finished his or her drink and left a wad of chits on the stained wood of the bar. Frank jerked his head toward the door and they filed out.

Logan hurried to fall into step beside Frank. "Looks like you planted the seed back there."

"That was the idea," Frank said.

"Let's just hope we can reap what we've sown," the Deacon intoned, as Frank took a crooked trail back to the apartment, all watching for people following them.

~ * ~

Smyth-Davis sat quietly, wishing he could feel as calm as he appeared to the rest of the group. Piotrowski had returned with the assurance that Wyszynski would have ORMO teams watching the farms on their list. The headache seemed even worse with the tension, and he wished he could convince himself it didn't matter whether he was rescued or not. Even knowing death would at least end the pain behind his eyes couldn't settle the fluttering in his stomach.

"All right," Piotrowski said, "we go over it one last time. We go in in three waves. Rennie will lead the first group and they'll have ten minutes to scout and set up. I'll lead the next section. We'll get into prepared positions. Smyth-Davis, you're in St. Jacques' group. He's in charge and he'll decide when you go into the bar.

"Once you're inside, let it be known you're waiting for St. Jacques to show up. It sounds strange to say this but, with any luck, you'll be grabbed almost immediately. Don't resist. If they give you a song and dance, pretend to buy it. If they clip you, go down right away; don't stay up and take more punishment."

"All this is obvious," Smyth-Davis said.

"I know. I'm just going over it one more time so I'm sure everyone understands it. Now, once the grab is made, the teams coordinate with flashlight signals but be careful. I don't want to alert the bad guys." Piotrowski looked at his watch. "We've got two hours to get ready. Use the time for a last weapons check. I'd prefer suppressed weapons but I'm not going to be fanatical about it. Just be sure we spring Smyth-Davis before you start making a lot of noise."

"I believe I'll take a nap while we're waiting," Smyth-Davis said, and walked out of the dining room back to the bedroom he shared with McCluskey and Tartakainnen. He finished the preparations he'd begun earlier then lay down. He knew he'd have trouble resting, but the pain was almost blinding him. He closed his eyes and forced himself to breathe slowly and steadily.

Someone shook his shoulder. "It's time to go," St. Jacques said.

Smyth-Davis rolled off the cot and strapped on the Beretta. It'd never do to go unarmed—it'd make his captors suspicious—but he'd take no extra ammunition. He pulled on the Russian greatcoat and fur hat then threw on the ORMO smock over it.

Snow was falling again and a bitter wind was driving it into knee-deep drifts. He concentrated on simply walking. St. Jacques was two or three paces ahead of him and Reid strode grimly to his left. "I can still take this mission," the Frenchman said, as they turned onto *Paulinska*, the pub before them and to their left.

"How long will you and Reid need to take cover before I enter the bar."

St. Jacques frowned. "Until you can no longer see us."

Smyth-Davis watched the Frenchman until he disappeared into the few trees in the dimness, then he trod to the door, opened it, and stepped inside. The place was crowded and he was jostled as he made his way to the bar.

"I am looking for a man named St. Jacques," he said to the bartender in his badly broken Polish.

"He has not come in yet," the bartender replied, "but your friends came in last night. For five chits, I can give you gin. For ten, you can have real Scotch whiskey."

"Gin."

He'd only tasted the drink before a man in work clothes stepped up to the bar. "Did you say St. Jacques?" the man asked in Polish.

"Yes. Has he come in yet?"

"Not yet, but my friend and I am also waiting for him. You may come to our table and wait with us. It would be more comfortable than standing here."

"I am tired," Smyth-Davis admitted and allowed himself to be led to the table. As he sat, he studied the men. The man who'd met him at the bar had calculating gray eyes. He was slender, and more fit than any Polish worker could afford to be. The other man was powerfully built, obviously very strong, but he had an air of truculent stupidity about him and had his brow been any lower it would've overlapped his eyebrows.

Smyth-Davis nursed the gin for twenty minutes then the lean man stood. "I will buy the drinks this time." He left and returned with three glasses, one of which he placed before Smyth-Davis.

Smyth-Davis knew the drink was almost certainly drugged but as he sipped it he realized that, with the effects of the head wound, he couldn't have been able to taste the difference if they'd cut the gin with diesel fuel. The man raised his glass. "To our friend, St. Jacques."

He obediently raised his glass and drained it. "I will get the next drinks," the ape wearing clothes said, and bulled his way to the bar.

"Isn't that our friend?" the lean man asked, pointing.

Smyth-Davis turned and saw a Pole wearing a red beret, but he wore it in the Anglo-American fashion, tilted to the right. Smyth-Davis' eyes couldn't seem to hold their focus. "I don't think so," he said, and tasted the drink the ape had set before him.

"Is St. Jacques still staying at the old place?" the lean man asked.

Speech seemed difficult, but he was able to get out the words, "What old place?"

"I had just heard he had moved recently. Is he still working with Piotrowski?"

Apparently, these men knew more about the group than even most ORMO would know without investigating. He allowed his words to slide into unintelligibility, mumbling sounds rather than words. He leaned back in his chair but had trouble holding his head up. For several minutes he simply sat awash in a sea of noise, unable to distinguish the sources of the sounds around him. Weariness washed over him like a tidal wave and he leaned forward, his head resting on his arms, then the sounds and the dim light faded to nothing.

Chapter 12

Reynaud froze into immobility as two men, carrying a third, walked by the entrance of the alley in which he and Logan were hidden. He even held his breath, so the men couldn't see the fog of exhaled breath. The men stopped and, for a moment, Reynaud was afraid they'd seen Logan's tracks, but the men had only stopped to shift Smyth-Davis' body as the larger man bore him over his shoulder in a fireman's carry then the two continued down *Paulinska*.

Waiting until the men were only dim shapes in the driving snow, Reynaud, covering the lens of his flashlight with his hand and using the wall of the building across the alley for cover, flashed the signal, making sure it could be seen from the alley across the street and from the last building in the row, where Juho or Steve would relay it to the watchers in the park.

Logan had already stalked after the figures and Reynaud moved after him, cautiously, but as quickly as possible, hoping the others were following. The tracks they followed vanished even as they paced along them. Reynaud hurried a bit more, his fear of being seen by the kidnappers competing with the fear of losing track of the enemy. From *Paulinska* the tracks took a left turn onto *Augustianska*, cutting diagonally across the street to turn right again at *Josefa Dietla* then the trail stopped.

He and Logan dashed forward and found, partly obscured by the snow, a hatch for a coal chute. The hatch had been raised only minutes before, otherwise they couldn't have seen it for the snow. Reynaud glanced above the hatch and saw it must lead into the basement of a burned-out shell.

Hesitating only a moment, Reynaud climbed into the chute and slid into the basement.

He listened closely but heard nothing, then used his flashlight to grope across the cellar blocked, here and there, with fallen timbers and other rubble. He heard Logan's voice at the hatch then a scraping sound as Logan slid down the chute after him.

"Rennie?" Logan whispered.

"Over here." Reynaud crouched, a flashlight in one hand

and a pistol in the other.

Logan moved a step or so away from the hatch in a different direction. "Frank'll be down in a minute. He's sending Juho around the building to try to pick up the trail. He thinks the bad guys went out the other side."

Logan moved a few feet then they both heard a scraping sound. "Shit!" Logan exclaimed, "I just snagged a foot on a wire or string."

Reynaud studied the floor between them. He saw a board with nails pointing up. Going around the trap he crept closer to Logan and, in the beam of the flashlight, saw a piece of cord tied to the base of a timber, stretching to the toe of Logan's boot and vanishing into the darkness beyond. Reynaud moved around Logan to where he could see the other end of the string, which was tied to a grenade which had been pulled halfway out of a can.

"Whatever you do," Reynaud said through teeth gritted to keep them from chattering, "don't move or they'll wipe us up and bury us in a sponge." He almost jumped as someone else slid down the coal chute.

"Stay by the chute," Reynaud snapped, "and tell the others to stay topside."

"Private party?" Frank asked.

"Hell no," Reynaud said, "any number can die." After finding a piece of wire amid the rubbish he knelt by the can and grenade. Cautiously, with hands that wanted to tremble, he reached down and caught hold of the grenade as though it were a live snake. Holding the lever tightly against the grenade, he pulled it from the can, carefully threaded the wire through the holes for the ring, and used the ends to tie the lever to the body of the grenade.

He released a long, shuddering breath. "Okay, Logan, you can dance again."

"Booby trap?" Frank asked.

"No," Logan replied, his voice dripping sarcasm, "some kids were playing down here and forgot where they'd left their pull-toy grenade."

Reynaud played the light around the cellar, noticing several timbers leaning at odd angles against other beams. "This whole damned place is one big booby-trap. Let's get out of here while we still can."

"How do you plan to do that?" Frank asked.

"Same way we got in. I'm not about to go digging around for other exits. Logan can give us a boost up, and we can pull him up by using belts buckled together. If we try to look for the door the bad guys took," he swung the flashlight's beam around the cellar again, "they won't even dig us out, they'll just put the head-stones by the coal chute."

Logan had his own flashlight out and followed Reynaud back to the coal chute. Together, they gave Frank a shove up the chute then Reynaud followed him. By the time the two of them were outside, Steve had attached some belts. They tossed one end down and Logan was pulled up.

Juho joined the rest of the party, shaking his head. "The trail is gone. No more tracks."

"Well," Reynaud said, "we did it. We lost them."

"Maybe they're still inside," Logan said.

"You've been in there. Would you stay in a place like that?" Reynaud shook his head. "This place was just a convenient place for them to lose a tail; it was a set-up. We screwed up and Smyth-Davis is screwed. We'd better get in touch with Wyszynski and find out what the observer teams found out."

"Let's at least check the streets on the other side of the building," Frank suggested. The group spread out in a line, each of them able to see only the figures to their immediate left and right. For half an hour they prowled the streets, ranging further and further away from the booby-trapped building, but found no sign anyone had been on those streets.

Dispirited, they made their way to the Wawel and an orderly was sent to find Wyszynski, who looked as though he'd been preparing for bed.

"They got Smyth-Davis," Frank said, "and we lost them."

Wyszynski rubbed his eyes and suddenly seemed very much awake. "I will call in the ORMO teams and get their reports."

"Not this soon," Frank said. "They might take their time about getting Smyth-Davis to their headquarters. We don't want to pull the patrols too soon and have them sneak our man in between the time we call our teams in and dawn. Besides, aren't the teams supposed to report as soon as they see someone or anything going into the farms?"

Wyszynski nodded.

"If you don't mind," Frank said, "we'll stay here until the teams report."

Wyszynski walked around his desk and sat in another chair. "Unless they see something unusual, the teams will not report until after dawn, and it is still early." After glancing at a clock on a filing cabinet, which showed it was a little over an hour to midnight, he said, "Go home. If I get any reports, I will send a truck for you."

Frank paced back and forth in front of Wyszynski's desk, driving his fist into his hand. "There has to be something we can do."

"I do not want you going out to visit the farms tonight. That might destroy the purpose of the surveillance."

"All right," Frank growled, "you've convinced us." He turned to go then wheeled around. "What about Tadeusz? You want him to meet us here in the morning?"

"I will call the hospital and have him sent home by car. He should be there by the time you are ready to come in for the dawn reports, unless I learn something before then."

"If you have him sent by car," Reynaud said, "you might find a different driver. There's no percentage in getting Tadeusz out of the hospital just to put him back in again."

Wyszynski looked surprised. "Edmund is a very good driver. He has never had an accident."

"Then the crashes were on purpose," Reynaud said. "I'll bet he's never had a heart attack, either, but he's probably given his share to other people."

Wyszynski shrugged. "I will send someone else, if I can."

The long walk back to the apartment seemed even longer and colder, and St. Jacques was limping badly by the time they gathered in the kitchen and Frank started a fire. For a time, they just sat, slumped in their chairs and their depression then Steve stood.

"I'm not hungry. I'm going to bed. Wake me if you hear anything." He picked up a coal-oil lantern, and trudged to his bedroom.

He'd hardly stepped through the door before he shouted, "Hey, come here! Come take a look at this!"

Reacting to his urgent tone, the rest of the group sprang to their feet and rushed back to the room he shared with Juho and Smyth-Davis. Like almost everyone else, Reynaud had drawn his pistol but holstered it when he saw nothing dangerous. "What's the fuss?" he asked.

Steve pointed to Smyth-Davis' footlocker at the foot of his bunk. It stood open and the contents were neatly laid out in tidy rows, some of them tagged with pieces of paper.

"I noticed it when I came in to wake him," St. Jacques said, "but I attached no importance to it. Should I have?"

"Looks like he's got it all ready for an inspection," Steve said. "What do you think it means?"

Logan saw a slip of paper with his name on it and picked up a small, dark bundle. He unrolled it then held up a pair of socks. "Wool socks! Real wool and honest-to-God socks instead of those goddam Russian foot diapers. Wonder where he scored these?"

Reynaud had been staring at the equipment and weapons, all carefully cleaned and oiled or polished. "Gang," Reynaud said, "you know what this is? This is the closest thing we're going to find to a last will and testament."

Logan had sat down at the foot of Steve's bunk and pulled off his boots. He'd already unwrapped his right foot and was poised to pull on the sock when Reynaud's words soaked through to him. "Say what?"

Reynaud pointed at the footlocker. "It looks like he knew he wouldn't be coming back, so these things are laid out to be taken by whoever needs them."

Logan looked at the sock in his hand then re-rolled it with the other one and a flush spread across his face. "That goddam limey! He's trying to play hero!" He re-wrapped his foot and pulled his boots on then stood and stuffed the socks in his pocket. "I'll be damned if I'll take these. We're going to find him and I'm gonna give these back to him if I gotta put 'em on his feet myself. And if he gives me any shit, I'm gonna stuff them right down his pipe-cleaner neck. Who the hell does he think he is?"

Reynaud sat on one of the other footlockers. "I think he thinks he's someone who's dying."

"What do you mean?" Frank asked.

"Didn't you notice how he dropped his weapon, back at the

wigilia? And he wears out awfully easily. It must be that head wound of his. It must've been worse than we thought. And maybe he thinks it's worse than it is."

Frank leaned against the door frame. "That could be. The damage could cause depression and poor judgement and, if he were in pain, he might decide his life was as good as over."

"So, what do we do?" Logan demanded.

"The most difficult task," St. Jacques said. "We wait."

~ * ~

Smyth-Davis became aware of his surroundings and the sound of voices speaking Russian. As consciousness slowly returned, he felt ropes tightly bound around his right arm. As often happened, his left arm was numb. The bindings held him in a chair and he knew, then, that his body was sagging against the bonds and his head was bent forward. Despite the discomfort, he continued to let the ropes bear his weight.

"I told you to be sure not to give him too much," one of the voices said, and it seemed a familiar voice. "I also told you not to start the interrogation until I was present."

Smyth-Davis tasted something salty in his mouth and felt something wet and sticky on his chin.

"We only gave him a single packet," protested another voice, also speaking Russian. "We were afraid he had died. When we stopped at the second safe hole, he was hardly breathing. We could see he was breathing only by holding a mirror to his mouth, and we could not find his pulse."

"It is a very good thing he is alive." The observation was partly threat, and Smyth-Davis recognized the voice as Oshevsky's.

"Are you sure you were not followed?" Oshevsky demanded.

"Jerzy thought someone might have tried to follow us but we went through the safe hole on *Augustinianska*. We did not hear either grenade explode, so it is likely Jerzy was just nervous."

"Tell him to continue to be nervous, and you learn to be nervous, too." After a pause, Oshevsky said, "No, he is still unconscious. I will be back in half an hour. I repeat, you will not start the interrogation until I return."

Somehow, without knowing how he'd done it, Smyth-Davis had managed to buy time. He knew once Oshevsky started questioning, he'd be able to break any man. Now, every second bought was a separate victory. He knew even his constant pain was no defence against the agony Oshevsky could inflict. Victories, tiny ones, would come from minute to minute, for each minute he could endure was another minute the group could use to try to find this place.

Was he only fooling himself? He was lost. The group had certainly lost the trail, and even he had no idea where he was being held. If, as he supposed, the group had lost the trail, then only the slimmest of chances remained they could find the trail anew. The ORMO teams watching the farms had been a good idea—or would've been, had the mission not taken place after dusk and in a driving storm.

His own idea had seemed so good, so reasonable at the time. The best-laid plans of mice and men.... Plans were all very well, but now all he had was improvisation. Escape was impossible, as was finding some way to contract the group. Perhaps he could find some way to force Oshevsky's hand, cause him to make some move that would give away his positon.

Chernikov's mission, whatever it was, was important. If he could get Oshevsky to talk about it—forget it, he told himself. Oshevsky would ask questions, not provide answers, even to boast. The man was too professional for such an error. Still, it gave him something with which to taunt Oshevsky. He also harbored no illusions about being able to make Oshevsky angry enough to simply kill him, even by accident.

What else could Oshevsky want? The CIA? It was worth playing. As a card, it might be only a fool—what the Americans called a joker—but even a fool was better than no card at all.

Oshevsky would certainly want to know where the group was based and it was possible, though unlikely, that he didn't know Wyszynski was their contact with the Polish army.

He heard heavy footsteps approaching. "Is he awake yet?" Oshevsky asked.

"He has not moved yet," another voice said.

Oshevsky swore, then Smyth-Davis felt a needle jabbed into his right arm. Reflexively, he flinched. "He is awake," Oshevsky snapped.

As Smyth-Davis opened his eyes and raised his head, the thin man he'd met at the pub slapped him, a stinging, bruising blow on the cheek. Fury at the cowardice and unfairness of the blow flooded through Smyth-Davis and he glared at the Russian.

"Fool!" Oshevsky roared. He struck the man across the face with a back-hand blow hard enough to stagger him. "If you do anything more, unless I order it, you will wish for a transfer to a penal battalion. Stand there and learn. You never simply strike a man. Do you see the rage in his eyes? You have made him stronger, better able to resist. When you punish a prisoner, it must be so painful it inspires only fear."

Oshevsky caught Smyth-Davis by the chin and raised his head so the Englishman stared into Oshevsky's black, reptilian eyes. Smyth-Davis had hoped to never again see that face with its narrow eyes, hooked beak of a nose, and thick, brutal lips, except over a gunsight. The Briton explored his mouth with the tip of his tongue and felt a loose tooth, and he tasted blood again. "Lieutenant Oshevsky, you've risen in the world." He spoke English, knowing Oshevsky understood every nuance. "I can't say this is either unexpected or a pleasure. I've a message for you."

"Say it then."

"Chernikov managed to reach Texas before he was shot down like the filthy dog he was, and I've been sent to demand your surrender." He wondered, for a split-second, whether Oshevsky would laugh or fly into a rage.

Oshevsky remained impassive. "Strip him and put him on the table," he said, in Russian, in a cold, precise voice.

Hands loosened the ropes binding Smyth-Davis to the chair, then he was hauled to his feet and his clothing was torn away. His pilot training had touched on the possibility of falling into enemy hands, and the months at the prison camp had been a postgraduate course. He knew stripping a prisoner had the effect of humiliating him and making him feel vulnerable. Knowing the secret did not, however, lessen the effect.

They manhandled him onto the table. He noticed a long, thin line of blood running from a puncture wound on his left arm, and he realized how Oshevsky had been deceived—he'd pricked Smyth-Davis' left arm and the numbness that meant he was already dying had helped postpone his torment.

Someone drew Smyth-Davis' arms over his head and cuffed them in place and the thin man shackled his ankles, his legs spread.

Oshevsky leaned over him. "I want to know where your companions are hiding."

As Smyth-Davis hesitated, Oshevsky lit a torch and held it to the Briton's right foot. The pain was incredible as the burning in his foot seemed to travel up his nervous system to the brain. He clenched his teeth but still screamed as he writhed on the table, straining against his bonds. He could smell the sickening odor of burned flesh and the pain continued, even after Oshevsky had set down the torch and again leaned over him.

"That, or worse, will happen to you each time you hesitate or lie to me. Lie to me or refuse to speak as often as you like. I enjoy providing...negative incentives. It is always a learning experience to find out what will break a man. Each one is different. Most men break when I apply electricity to their genitals. Most artists are unable to bear damage to their hands." He leaned closer and grinned, a horrid, ghoulish rictus. "I will take great pleasure in learning what will make you snap like a twig."

Smyth-Davis suddenly felt very cold but his mind seemed to work with incredible speed. "Did you know we raided the CIA headquarters?" he asked, in Russian.

Oshevsky scowled. "Yes. You removed a minor inconvenience to us, but also deprived us of a very convenient whipping-boy."

Still in Russian, Smyth-Davis continued. "We also took their records and we are breaking the code."

"Are you offering us information?"

Smyth-Davis drew a deep breath. "The most important information; they had found your headquarters and, as soon as the code is broken, my friends will eliminate you. You had best surrender while you have the opportunity."

Smyth-Davis noted, with a certain satisfaction, that his statement seemed to agitate the thin Russian, but Oshevsky never blinked. He reached behind him and held up a pair of wires. He touched them together and Smyth-Davis heard a faint pop.

"The battery is weak—too cold." Oshevsky growled to the

other two men. "I told you not to store them near the outside wall. Get me another battery."

The thin man, who'd been watching Smyth-Davis, looked up at Oshevsky. "The only other batteries we have are the back-ups for the generator."

"Bring me one."

The big man called Jerzy stepped into the field of Smyth-Davis' vision. "Are you sure you want me to do that? If anything happens to the generator—"

Oshevsky spun and slammed his fist into the man's face. Smyth-Davis heard the impact of the punch and the sound of the big man falling to the floor. "Get it." Oshevsky's voice was still cold and precise.

The big man scrambled to his feet and dashed from the room.

"What if he is right?" The thin man pointed at Smyth-Davis. "What if the men who were with him are coming here, or if they alert the ORMO?"

"Fool," Oshevsky snapped. "had they known we were here they'd have tried to attack us themselves."

"Yes, sir," the thin man said, but his voice lacked conviction.

Jerzy returned, his footsteps slow and heavy. Oshevsky leaned away, out of Smyth-Davis' view. When he straightened, he held the wires again. He touched them together, creating a spark and a pop that sounded like a pistol shot. "I told you what would happen if you lied to me." Oshevsky bent forward and Smyth-Davis couldn't repress a moan as he felt one of the wires being thrust into his scrotum over his right testicle.

He tried to brace himself for the pain but the agony as the second wire was driven into him turned his world red, a wrenching torture far worse than dying. He heard a voice screaming and realized it was his own, then blessed blackness rolled over him and carried him away.

~ * ~

Reynaud had dozed off in the chair in which he sat. A sudden noise at the door brought him awake in an instant. St. Jacques was already pacing to the front door, his revolver in his hand. He snatched the door open, then, "Tadeusz!"

The Pole stepped in onto the rug and stamped his feet. "There is a truck outside waiting for us," he said. "Wiktor wants to see us all as soon as possible."

Logan sprang to his feet and strode to the back room, where Steve and Juho had taken to their bunks. "Red alert! Hit the floor runnin'!" he roared then returned to the parlor and began to pull on his coat and hat.

Reynaud shoved himself out of his chair, finding aches and stiffness had crept into his neck and back. By the time he'd drawn on his coat most of the rest of the group were snatching up their weapons and Juho and Steve had emerged from the bedroom, grim and ready. Before everything had completely registered, Reynaud found himself climbing into the back of a truck.

Frank sat beside Tadeusz at the front of the truck bed. "Did Wiktor say why he wanted us?"

Tadeusz shook his head and Reynaud, after making sure his shotgun's barrel was pointed in a safe direction, checked the chamber and the magazine then did the same with the silenced AR-15. All around him he could hear the clatter as the rest of the groups checked their weapons.

The distance from *Batorego* to the Wawel wasn't great but they seemed to be riding in the cold bed of the truck for hours, and Reynaud began to wonder if he'd died and been condemned to ride for eternity, rattled and frozen, in the back of the noisy truck, breathing in the fumes from the exhaust that somehow found their way into the back of the truck.

At last the time in Purgatory ended as the truck jerked to a stop. Two at a time, the members of the group bailed out, except for Tadeusz and St. Jacques, who had to be helped out. Reynaud noticed the Frenchman carried both his submachine gun and his sniper rifle. They walked across the courtyard and displayed their identification to the guard, and a team of ORMO escorted them to Wyszynski's office.

Wyszynski picked up his phone and spoke into it as they filed through the door then he waved them into chairs. "I have ordered a pot of something resembling coffee be sent up, and breakfasts as soon as they are available." He returned Taduesz's salute then shook his hand. "It is good to see you again."

Frank asked, "Have the ORMO teams watching the farms reported yet?"

"Not yet," Wyszynski said, "but it was logical to call you in as soon as Tadeusz was released and use the same truck for both missions. The groups should begin to report within the next hour. I assume you are all ready for an assault."

"Nah," Logan said sarcastically, "we just brought all the guns in case there was an inspection. Okay, we're here. Now, what do we do until the ORMO get here—play checkers?"

"Take it easy, Reid," Frank snapped. "Everyone's doing everything they can." He stood and began to pace, and Reynaud observed almost everyone was nervous and most were irritable. Frank marched back and forth across the room three times then turned to face them all. "In his abrasive way, though, Logan is right. There should be something we can do while we're waiting. Do you have a map of the farms, Wiktor? We could at least try to plan an assault."

Wyszynski opened the right bottom drawer of his desk, ruffled through some papers, then tossed a map on his desk and spread it out. He pointed out all the park areas were marked in pale green.

Frank bent and pored over the map, identifying the farms they'd already visited then noticed a very large green patch in the upper right of the map. "I don't recognize this? What is it?"

Tadeusz looked where Frank pointed. "That? That is the observatory, with its botanical gardens." He stared at Frank. "You did not know of this?"

"It was on my list to you," Wyszynski reminded Frank. "In fact, I put it at the top of the list because it is one of the largest of the cooperative farms, and also because of its other features."

"And those are—?" Frank asked.

"The observatory is away from the center of town or the heavily settled areas north of the *Wisla*," Wyszynski pointed to the lines around it on the map. "It is located with major streets running both north-south and east-west, making communication and escape much easier, and, while it is away from the old town, it is still nearer to the Wawel than most of the other farms, and it is not cut off from the Wawel by a bridge."

Frank dropped into a chair as though stunned. "God. And

we didn't have an ORMO team cover the place—" He was interrupted by a knock at the door.

Before the man with the tray holding a pot of coffee and nine or ten cups had stepped into the room he was covered by half a dozen weapons. Embarrassed by their display of nerves, the members of the group set their weapons down or pretended they were merely checking the guns. The corporal almost dropped the tray but recovered and carried the tray across the room to set it on the edge of the desk.

"Have a cup of coffee," Wyszynski invited.

"I am on duty, sir," the man replied.

"Consider it an order," Wyszynski said.

"Thank you, sir." The man poured a cup of the stuff and sipped it, obviously relishing it, until he'd finished it. He snapped a salute to Wyszynski then marched out of the office.

St. Jacques raised an eyebrow. "A drafted poison-taster? Is there that much danger even here, in the Wawel?"

"Probably not," Wyszynski replied, "but it is, as the Americans say, 'better safe than sorry.' You can be sure the FSB has agents, witting or unwitting, in the Wawel, and if they know what my function is, they will not hesitate to attempt an assassination."

"Jeez," Logan said. "I never thought of that. Why don't you crash—I mean stay—with us?"

Wysaynski shook his head. "My work is here. If we stop doing our work because we fear the FSB, they have succeeded. The best thing we can do is take reasonable precautions and do our duty as best we can." After pouring everyone a cup of coffee he opened a file cabinet.

"I have a feeling about this," Frank said. "I suspect I screwed up royally. Let's operate on the assumption the FSB is using the observatory for their headquarters. What can you tell us about the place?"

Wyszynski returned to his desk, leafing through a book from the file cabinet. He laid it, open, on the desk. "This is a photograph of the observatory, with the botanical gardens in the background. This was taken before the war. When I last saw it, they had cut down most of the trees, so there is less cover on the grounds. As you can see, the building has a flat roof with railings.

It would be safe to say there would be a sentry on the roof, possibly two or more of them."

Frank ran his forefinger along the lines representing streets. "Can we get an army of ORMO units to block these streets to cut off a possible escape attempt? Could we get away with telling them we're making a raid for contraband?"

"We could block the three major streets in places with wide fields of fire, but I would prefer to be as discreet as possible. It will be your responsibility to keep all the gunfire inside the building. There are several other problems, too. The FSB will have hostages; there are many innocent Poles who work at the farm. The FSB will probably use them to hide behind if they are raided, just as they would hide behind them if they were investigated."

"They've got another hostage, too—our friend Smyth-Davis," Reynaud said. "That's a good reason to make the raid during daylight hours; so we can be sure we're shooting at the right people. Also, I don't think Smyth-Davis can survive FSB interrogation until tonight."

Frank studied the photograph of the building and the map again. "We need just enough of a diversion to get one man inside to take out the guards. That'll be me. I trained for Delta before being assigned to a B-team. Wiktor, how close can the rest of the group get to the building without being seen?"

Wyszynski sank into his chair and closed his eyes, visualizing the building and the area around it. "The last time I was there, they had left a tree standing near the center of the botanical gardens." He pointed out the tree in the photo. "It is not an evergreen and its branches would be bare but it would still provide some concealment. Using it and a small fold in the ground that runs across the garden in front of the building, you should be able to move to about two hundred meters from the front of the building."

"I can cover the back," St. Jacques spoke up. "No one will escape from the back of that building."

"We need an excuse for getting several people in the front door," Frank said. "Four of them will not be part of the assault. Wiktor, would you do it, with Tadeusz? I know there are risks—"

Wyszynski waved away the warning and turned to Tadeusz. "Are you ready to help?"

Tadeusz nodded. "But why may we not take part in the assault?"

"Because I don't want the assault team to have to worry about anymore hostages than the ones the FSB already has. As it stands now, when the raid begins, we can kill anyone who's armed." He leaned back and looked around at the other members of the group. "I'd a whole lot prefer we not make any unnecessary noise until we know Smyth-Davis is free, but if it looks like another hostage will buy it, or we get pinned down and the assault is stalled, then Smyth-Davis will have to take his chances along with the rest of us. Wiktor, I want to start on this as soon as we can."

Wyszynski frowned. "Should we not wait for the ORMO teams to report? If we start the raid and then discover we are wrong, it will be worse than embarrassing, and we will not be able to excuse ourselves with a simple apology."

"Right," Frank said, "and in case our guess is correct, how do we give Smyth-Davis a simple apology?"

Wyszynski stood. "We should eat before we go, and it will be quicker if we eat in the mess hall." They followed him to the mess hall where, among the ORMO he found two men he trusted. He stopped at their table. "Eat quickly," he told them, "then come with us."

Reynaud quickly made himself a sausage sandwich and wolfed it down, and the hot liquid, although it resembled tea no more than it did coffee.

As soon as the group had eaten, they marched to the motor pool, where Wyszynski selected two vehicles, a UAZ-469 "Jeep" and a truck. "Work crews are sometimes sent by truck," he explained. "It would be more subtle than your personnel carrier. Jacek," he said to one of the ORMO he'd drafted, "you drive. We are going to the observatory. Take the *Lubicz* route."

Frank passed his suppressed submachine gun to the Deacon. "Use this, or leave it in the truck." He turned to St. Jacques. "Have you still got that suppressed Makarov?"

St. Jacques handed over the pistol and Frank slipped it into his waistband then loosened the knife he wore in a belt sheath. "When I've taken out the sentry—or sentries—I'll give you a signal. When you see me stand up and raise my arms, rush the building. The first team should be clear by then."

"We don't have a plan of the building or anything; we're going in blind," Reynaud said.

"Hell," Logan replied, his grin more predatory than humorous, "we've got the ground rules. We kill anybody we find with a gun."

~ * ~

Smyth-Davis heard someone moaning then realized he was making the sound himself.

"I recognize you from the camp," Oshevsky said. "What is your name?"

"Richard Smyth-Davis, Royal Air Force." He started to open his eyes and the pain was almost enough to make him faint again. While he was unconscious, Oshevsky had used one of his favorite tricks; the needles through the eyelids.

"You have noticed, then," Oshevsky said. "Good. This is to remind you I can cause you more pain than you have ever known. You are helpless. Your life is in my hands. More importantly to you, your pain and the end of that pain is also in my hands. You will beg me to kill you many times before you die. Who escaped with you?"

"The other men in the woodcutting detail." That was information Oshevsky already had. The pain in his right eye was like a flash of sudden lightning as Oshevsky pulled the needle out.

"You see, I can ease your pain, too."

Oshevsky pulled the second needle out of his left eyelid and again Smyth-Davis experienced the sudden lightning-flash of agony. His eyes blinked open but his vision was blurred and Oshevsky's face was almost lost in a sea of red.

"How many of your group died in the escape?"

"Just one. Franz Schiller." There was no point in lying to Oshevsky and risking punishment over something the Russian probably already knew.

"How many of you were seriously wounded?"

"Two. Michael Teller and myself."

Oshevsky moved out of Smyth-Davis' view and the room was silent. At first, Smyth-Davis felt totally alone, more vulnerable than ever, and he began to anticipate the questions Oshevsky might ask and the pain he might inflict. Suddenly he realized this anxiety was exactly what Oshevsky had intended. He forced himself to relax and used the time to rebuild his reserves of will. And he saw a delicious irony; Oshevsky had gambled and lost, giving Smyth-Davis another tiny victory. He kept his face impassive, certain the least sign of pleasure would bring him more abuse.

Oshevsky finally broke the silence to ask, "Who did you meet outside the camp?"

"No one, until we had crossed the Polish frontier."

After only the briefest pause, Oshevsky asked, "What does Operation A mean to you?"

Smyth-Davis tried to think quickly. Would admitting so much ignorance weaken the illusion of power and knowledge he'd tried to create? For that matter, how much did Oshevsky know about Operation A?

Oshevsky leaned over him. "I told you to answer quickly. Do you know what a 'dry submarine' is?"

"No."

"You will learn." Oshevsky held up a black plastic bag then pulled it over Smyth-Davis' head and twisted it tightly around his neck.

Smyth-Davis was overwhelmed by panic. He couldn't see or breathe through the bag. He strained against the bindings. His lungs heaved they frantically tried to pump the air he couldn't draw in, and his heart pounded as though trying to hammer its way out of his ribs. He twisted the handcuffs and pulled but the unyielding metal held him fast. The bag tightened around his face and he felt himself weaken until he slid into unconsciousness.

He could breathe again! He drew the delicious air into his chest and realized he was still alive, and he knew he'd probably never been closer to dying. That strangling foretaste of death was so vivid he shuddered uncontrollably. Death no longer seemed a refuge from pain and terror, but something to be avoided at nearly all costs.

"What do you know about Operation A?"

"I know Chernikov is in charge of it, that he was in Texas—" he suddenly remembered his earlier lie "—where he was killed."

Oshevsky turned his head to speak over his shoulder to someone else in the room. "They insult us by sending such incompetent bunglers." He stared down at Smyth-Davis. "You and your friends are amateurs, children playing at soldiers and spies. You tried to find us by offering yourself, and you failed. All you accomplished is to give us a source of information. Now that we have you, we will simply kill your friends, one at a time." Again, the ghoulish delight passed across his face. "Which one should we kill first?"

Smyth-Davis had finally caught his breath and his breathing had slowed to a normal rate. "You want me to choose your victim for you?"

"That is correct."

Smyth-Davis suddenly realized Oshevsky wanted him to give the name of at least one member of Commando Krakow, guessing that Smyth-Davis would be more prepared to sacrifice them than the men with whom he'd escaped.

"Quickly," Oshevsky barked, and held up the wires, letting them brush together so they snapped and threw a spark.

Smyth-Davis closed his eyes and clenched his jaws, trying to steel himself against the pain to come. One of the wires touched the nipple of his right breast, then a jolt of electricity jarred him, the shock making him convulse.

"Choose!" Oshevsky shouted.

"Logan Reid." It was the first name that came to mind, and it seemed an apt choice. Anyone who tried to kill Reid would, if they survived, bear the scars of a real battle.

"Who is your contact with the Polish government?"

Smyth-Davis knew he was weakening, that each answer he gave, each moment of abuse he sustained brought him nearer the point where he could no longer resist. He clamped his jaws shut and prayed he could last just a little longer. Again, the wires were thrust into his scrotum and the charge overwhelmed all his senses. He screamed and dropped into a bottomless abyss. As he fell into the pit, he thought he smelled the sickening odor of burned flesh.

Chapter 13

St. Jacques waved for the truck to move on then darted into the cover afforded by a fringe of evergreens between the street and the bare field which had once been a botanical garden. Among the trees, he studied the way ahead. He could see the building, four hundred meters away, and he was sure he could make a hit at that range, but a rise in the ground between the trees and the building hid the lower floor, and he'd promised no one would escape from the back of that building.

Raising his rifle and using the scope, he scanned the roof. A sentry crouched or sat behind a railing at the northwest corner of the building and he could assume another man was posted at the southeast corner.

Lowering the rifle, he studied the ground ahead of him. He saw no wires and, among the trees, the ground was only lightly crusted with snow. Creeping forward, he avoided any patch of ground or snow that might conceal a mine, generally following the veins of the roots. As he neared the edge of the windbreak he went down on his belly and began to inch forward.

It was impossible to cover his trail and he could only hope the glare of the snow would prevent the sentry from noticing the unevenness. It helped that the ground cover over which he crawled was still heavy with stalks and he could follow the line of an old furrow.

The cold and dampness chilled him through, and his leg began to ache, but he continued until he could see the base of the building. Still moving only inches at a time, he extended the legs of the FR-F2's bipod and set himself, the scope's crosshairs centered on the gap between two rails, where he could make out the almost-flat top of the sentry's hat. Then he waited.

~ * ~

After they'd stopped in front of the observatory, Wyszynski left the driver with the UAZ and led the other three men up the stairs to the observatory's main entrance. After his knock, three men met them at the door; a bespectacled man of late middle age with the air of a scholar and two younger men, one lean and with a hatchet face, the other a large, pasty-faced blond.

"Come in," the older man said. "How may we assist the ORMO?"

"We want to see your records," Wyszynski said. "There have been black market sales of grain."

"Surely, you don't think we—?"

"It is not my job to think. It is my job to check records." Wyszynski fixed the older man with a cold stare. "You have your records available for inspection, do you not?"

"Yes, sir," the man said, faintly nervous and a little annoyed by Wyszynski's officious manner. "Follow us, please."

The antechamber was a sort of lobby, with a large oil painting of Nikolaj Kopernik and glass display cases holding photographs and bits of meteorites. From there they passed into a corridor. Frank glanced both ways and saw marble stairs at both ends. The men escorting them headed for an opening that must lead to offices, but the area to the right was occupied by a large expanse of wall with double doors set in the center.

"What is that?" Wyszynski asked, indicating the large room.

"That is the theater, which was once used for films and for star displays," the older man replied. "We have sealed it, since we do not have the power to use it, and no one for whom the shows have any interest these days." The man stopped, removed his spectacles, and cleaned them with a handkerchief. "War and the plague seem to have ended what Kopernik began. Science seems as dead as any other dream, nowadays." He replaced his glasses and started back toward the opening in the wall.

"What is the area beyond the theater?" Frank asked.

"That? Oh, it is a small exhibition hall, with some early astronomical instruments and a mock-up of the Soyuz capsule and some crew suits."

"I would like to see that, captain," Frank said. "My cousin was trained to be a cosmonaut."

Wyszynski negligently waved a hand in the direction of the hall. "Very well. Join us when you have finished."

"I will accompany him, captain," the hatchet-faced man said. "There are several offices back there, and it is easy to become confused in this place."

Frank unzipped his coat as he strode down the corridor then stopped in front of the life-sized model of the Soyuz. "This thing is very small." He opened the crew door and observed the mock-up was hollow. Glancing around, he seemed to notice the stairs for the first time. "What is on the next floor?"

"Rooms for the men and women who work the farm." The lean man placed himself between Frank and the stairs.

"And above that?"

"The third floor is sealed. It held the photographic laboratories and other things." After a momentary pause, the thin man added, "We should rejoin your officers."

Frank turned his back on the stairs and began to examine one of the flight suits. If the cosmonauts actually wore suits like this, they hadn't been as well-equipped as American fighter pilots. "I suppose the fourth floor is also sealed. It held the telescopes?"

"And a classroom." The man seemed to relax a bit and took a step toward Frank but still stayed well out of reach.

Frank continued to pretend to examine the suit, while cursing inwardly. He couldn't have counted on killing the man with a single, unarmed blow, even if he'd been within reach, and the man stayed too far away from him to even let him use his knife.

They heard footsteps and turned to see Tadeusz striding toward them. "Captain Kowalski is almost ready to leave," he said to Frank.

"I was just leaving." As Frank turned his back on his guard, his hand flashed to the suppressed pistol in his belt. He spun, bringing up the weapon. The man stood two long paces behind him. As soon as the sights centered on the man's face, Frank pulled the trigger. A hole appeared under the man's left eye. His eyes rolled up in his head and he jerked back then pitched for ward.

Tadeusz's cough almost covered the sound of the muffled shot. Catching the body under the arms, Frank dragged it to the capsule. "Open the door to that capsule," he snapped, then, as Tadeusz wrenched the door open, Frank stuffed the corpse into the mock-up. As he released the body, it slid deeper inside and clattered against the base. Both men froze, and Frank thought he heard footsteps on the floor overhead but, after a second, the sound faded again.

After Frank had released a held breath he jerked his thumb in the direction of the sealed theater. "Except for that, I think we've checked out the ground floor. I wish we had some way to let the assault team know not to waste their time down here."

"We may be able to alert them," Tadeusz said. "Do you want me to say you've gone outside?"

"Good."

~ * ~

"Good luck." Tadeusz turned and strode back to the office. The former professor hovered anxiously over the desk while Wyszynski sat in the chair, pretending to examine the record book before him. The blond young man leaned against the back wall of the office, looking as solid and composed as the file cabinet beside him.

"Lieutenant Dabrowski has gone outside and is waiting in the UAZ." Glancing at the blond man, Tadeusz added, "Your friend went upstairs."

The man stared coldly at Tadeusz, and he had the sense he'd been caught in the lie. With a faint nod to Wyszynski and another glance at the blond man, he said. "I presume the records are correct."

"Yes, they are." Wyszynski reached across with his left hand and slammed the book closed then his right hand, holding a suppressed Makarov, appeared just above the desk and the pistol popped. The blond man stared stupidly down at the spreading spot of red on his chest. He stumbled forward and his chest heaved, as though he were trying to draw a deep breath. His right hand jerked up and fumbled at his shirt around his waist then blood poured from his mouth and his knees buckled. The man pitched forward onto the floor, dead.

"Oh my God," the professor said. "they'll kill the others."

Wyszynski bent over the body and found the pistol hidden in the man's waistband. "Not if you help us," he said, "but we need your help. Is the rest of this floor clear?"

The professor, still staring with wide eyes, at the corpse could only nod.

"Very good." Wyszynski said. "Just do as we tell you."

~ * ~

Frank watched Tadeusz until he'd turned the corner to the opening then darted up the stairs, stopping as his head came level with the second floor. In the dim light he could see a row of doors, all closed, and a single open door at his end of the corridor. He also noticed a third stairway in the middle of the hallway. Creeping up the stair, he paced quickly and quietly around the landing then padded up to the third floor.

The third floor was darker and all the doors seemed to be closed. He paused only a moment before moving to the next flight up. As he mounted the stairs he heard a faint, regular sound he had to listen to for a moment before recognizing it as the noise made by a small motor, well muffled. Listening intently for any other sounds, he heard none, and prowled up to the fourth floor. The stairs ended at the top floor and he crouched in the stairwell, examining the way ahead of him.

The engine noise seem to come from one of the near rooms on the right side. The third door to the right was featureless and heavy-looking, with a plain knob and a plain lock. After pausing to catch his breath, he crept forward then, staying close to the wall, sidled toward the first door.

Passing the first door, he listened a moment. Nothing. Another fifteen side-steps brought him beside the second door and he didn't need to press his ear against the door to know the motor was in that room. Another dozen side-steps and he stood beside the heavy door. Listening, he heard nothing but colder air blew against his cheek.

Grasping the knob, he slowly twisted it then pulled the door open. The passage was so dark he could hardly see the steps leading to the roof. Slipping into the stairway, he closed the door silently behind himself and began a step-by-step progress up to the door, outlined in pale light, at the top of the stairs.

Twice he stopped to listen but heard nothing but the muted whistle of the wind as it forced fingers through the openings around the door. He hoped the rest of the diversion team was clear of the building. Finally reaching the door, he slowly turned the knob and opened the door a crack. Peering outside, he saw nothing but one of the domes and the chimneys. He opened the door still further and slipped through the narrow opening, shoving the door shut behind him.

Stopping a moment to get his bearings, he saw he stood near the middle of the roof, his back against the passage, the outer shell of which sloped down to the roof. He chanced a quick look around the wall at his left and saw, near the southeastern corner of the building, a man sitting by the stone railing.

The man's head was below the level of the top of the railing, staring downward through the rails.

Frank ducked back behind the wall and visualized what he'd seen, like examining a mental photograph. The man had an AK cradled in his lap and he'd been holding a radio.

Taking a final look around the roof, Frank could see none of the corners, and most of the western end of the observatory was hidden behind the dome. Glancing around the wall to his right, he saw the northeastern corner was clear. Moving soundlessly, he crouched behind the slope of the passage and looked around. The other dome stood between him and the sentry, and he reexamined his memory of the man's position. The sentry's position was such that it'd be almost impossible for Frank to creep near enough to use his knife.

Like a hunter stalking wary game, Frank crept toward the dome and started to slip around the north side then, looking back, froze motionless as he noticed another sentry at the northwest corner of the roof. The man, staring down at the tree line beside the street, had failed to see him. Frank slowly moved to the south side of the dome until he was out of the other man's field of view and concentrated on the nearer guard. Shifting the pistol to his left hand and keeping his back to the dome, he edged around it.

He stopped again as he heard the radio click then heard it click again. He could guess the man had signaled someone inside the building the ORMO car was leaving. Frank waited, in case there were other signals, then a little longer for the man to set the radio down.

Steadying himself, he counted to ten, then sprang out from behind the stone and fired three rapid shots into the sentry.

As the first bullet hit him in the chest, the guard jerked, almost as though he were going to jump to his feet, then he slumped, the rifle sliding off his lap to clatter softly onto the cleared section of roof. The radio, still in his hand, slid from limp fingers and fell to the man's lap.

Pausing, Frank listened for any sounds from the other guard's station then, hearing none, he darted forward in a crouch and picked up the radio. The switch was set on "off." Frank carefully laid the radio beside the body then, staying low, ducked back behind the dome.

After watching and listening for another few moments, he cautiously made his way across the roof to the other dome.

A glance around the dome assured him the second sentry still watched the trees, probably daydreaming, not even seeing what lay before him.

Going down onto his hands and knees, Frank moved across to the railing, to approach the man from behind. As he half-rose to a crouch, he slipped his pistol back into his waistband and drew his knife.

With infinite patience, Frank crept forward, concentrating on each step, making sure he wouldn't slip on a patch of ice or step on crusted snow that would crunch beneath his foot. He had to remind himself to relax, as his world narrowed to the guard and the six feet of rooftop that now separated them.

Moment by moment, the distance shrank then Frank coiled himself to strike. Suddenly, he was atop the guard, his left hand covering the man's mouth, smothering any screams he might make, his right hand driving the blade through the sentry's neck, behind the windpipe.

A quick, wrenching movement, and he'd cut through the front of the neck and the throat.

As Frank had struck, he'd felt the man tense, then the dying guard thrashed about until Frank struck again, this time stabbing down, just behind the collarbone and into the heart. Finally, the guard relaxed and Frank set the body down on the roof. Glancing out across the fields, he couldn't see Jean-Marie, who, he could only hope, was in position to cover the rear of the building.

As he looked out and down, he noticed a black iron railing and followed it with his gaze to where the two fire escapes zigzagged their way down the back of the building. After considering the nearer fire escape a moment, he turned away and crossed the roof, where he held up his arms to the assault team, then returned to the covered stairwell and crept down.

~ * ~

Smyth-Davis returned to consciousness hearing Oshevsky arguing with the thin Russian. From what he could gather, an ORMO team was downstairs, inside the building, and he felt a surge of hope. The thin man's voice was tight with nervousness. "But if he was telling the truth—"

"He was lying." Oshevsky's flat, unemotional voice made the assumption a statement of fact. "If you are so frightened, go downstairs. You are no good to me here. You cannot interrogate a prisoner when you are more afraid of him than he is of you."

As the man's footsteps receded, Oshevsky spoke to someone else. "Vasily is losing his nerve and will be no further use to us. Kill him tonight." After a pause, he lightly slapped Smyth-Davis' cheek. "Ah, awake again."

Smyth-Davis simply stared at him.

"You are a sorry soldier," Oshevsky said. "You are going to die without accomplishing anything but providing me some pleasure. You might as well tell me who your contact is—I already know and I am just waiting for you to lie to me."

Smyth-Davis had felt the tension twist his muscles and set his nerves on edge. Suddenly, he laughed, and it felt good, a release. "You're becoming desperate, Oshevsky. You've given the order to kill one of your own men. You've lost control of the men under you."

Oshevsky struck Smyth-Davis across the face but despite the pain and the taste of fresh blood in his mouth, the Briton only smiled. "You've lost control of the situation and you're even losing control of yourself. You'd never just strike a prisoner if there were any way to extract more pain." Oshevsky swore and took a step toward the table but, before he could answer, they all heard a single rifle shot. As though the shot had been a signal, the lights flickered and dimmed to darkness.

~ * ~

After making their way carefully from the truck to the small knoll, Reynaud and the rest of the team had been watching the roof of the observatory, for hours, it seemed. At last the front door opened and Wyszynski and Tadeusz emerged from the building and climbed into the Russian Jeep. He looked back up at the roof as the car started and pulled out of the drive. He feared Frank had given the signal but he'd missed it, but the rest of the team still waited. He thought he saw movement on the roof but couldn't be sure because of the stone railing around the top edge of the building.

Reynaud began to worry Frank had been captured or killed, then he saw a figure on the roof approach the railing and raise its arms. He was already rushing forward when Logan hissed, "Scramble! Go! Let's take 'em!"

Reynaud had forgotten just how great a distance two hundred yards was, and he felt, at every step, as though a bullet would smash into him. His lungs burned with the cold, dry air they'd drawn in, and his legs ached with the long wait in the cold and the sudden jump and run.

Panting heavily as he closed on the building, he almost slipped and fell as he dashed up the steps to the door. He was ready to force his way through when he saw it stood slightly ajar.

He snatched open the door and almost shot the man standing just inside before he could see the man's hands, open and empty. The man had graying hair and wore glasses. Reynaud plunged into the building, drawing the man after him.

The man held a finger to his lips to signal silence then, as the rest of the team crowded into the antechamber, he pointed upward. "The hostages are on the second floor," the man whispered urgently. His eyes were wide and staring in a pale face, and he kept wiping his hands on his trousers. "You can get up there using the stairs at the ends of the hallway." He took a deep breath. "Please, be careful. They have loaded the place with explosives."

Reynaud gestured to the others. "Logan, Steve, you come with me. You others, take those stairs." He pointed at the stairway at the eastern end of the building.

Without waiting to see if the rest of the group were following his instructions, he moved down the corridor, taking care to make as little noise as possible. He'd started up the stairs and had just reached the landing between the first and second floors when he heard someone pounding down the stairs from the floors above. He stopped, motionless, his feet seeming to have taken root in the stairs as the feet stepped off the stairs at the second floor, and Reynaud crouched.

"Be alert," said a voice speaking Russian. "There may be trouble downstairs. Find out what is going on."

Reynaud heard the sound of a chair scraping against the floor and the voices of three more men, one of them thick with sleep, and he heard them moving around in the room at the head of the stairs.

Another voice, speaking Russian with a Polish accent, said, "We received the signal about ten minutes ago that the ORMO had left. There has been no alarm."

"Then there is no reason you can't go down and investigate," the Russian answered, then, after a pause, "Give me the key to door three." A moment later, one set of footsteps moved down the hall, away from his set of stairs while another approached his set of stairs.

Reynaud raised his suppressed submachine gun to his shoulder and, as the heavy footsteps neared the stairs, stood and opened fire as soon as he could see the nearer man.

The figure held a suppressed pistol in his hand but the weapon fell from his fingers as a stream of 9 mm bullets ripped across his chest. The man twisted and stumbled then pitched forward and slid down the stairs to the landing.

Logan's suppressed Makarov popped and a second man groaned and clutched his head then fell to the floor. Reynaud charged up the stairs as soon as his enemy fell and he leaped to avoid the falling body. A third man hurled himself at an open door when Reynaud lashed him with a whip of bullets. The man's right leg folded under him and his hand gripped the door frame. Reynaud raised the barrel higher and fired another burst into the man's body.

Blood flecked the door and frame as the man convulsed then hit the floor in a heap.

A figure appeared at the other end of the corridor and waved a weapon then Reynaud recognized Zdenka's build. Reynaud spun and gestured up the stairs leading to the third floor. "Steve, cover the stairs." Steve nodded and knelt at the foot of the stairs, a suppressed pistol in his hand.

Logan bulled his way past Reynaud and over the body to step into the room. By the time Reynaud had caught up with him, Logan pointed to a button set on the wall. "Do you think it's for explosives or an alarm?"

Reynaud shrugged then looked closely at the bodies. He recognized none of the men, all of whom were large, perhaps ex-ZOMO. He swung the barrel of his chatter gun at the door. "There's at least one more out there, somewhere down the hall in one of those rooms."

Reynaud had just reached the door when he heard the voice of the Russian, speaking Polish. "I have a hostage," the Russian shouted through one of the doors. Kneeling at the doorway, using the frame for cover, Reynaud pointed his weapon down the hall-way. He tried to guess from which door the voice had come then realized that all the rooms' doors were secured by hasps and locks except the second door to his right.

"I am coming out with the hostage," the Russian shouted. "If you fire a shot at me, the hostage will die first."

The door without a lock swung open and dim shadows danced on the walls then a tall, lean man forced a young, dark-haired girl out of the door ahead of him. The man's arm was around his prisoner's shoulders and he held a pistol to her head.

"Step out, all of you. Put your weapons on the floor and step away from them."

~ * ~

Juho had been only a step behind Zdenka as they stopped on the stairs, just below the landing, when they heard footsteps at the other end of the corridor. Juho had clipped a bayonet on the SVD sniper rifle, and he gestured with it.

"Wait," Zdenka whispered. They heard a voice speaking Russian, but it was too far away to be able to distinguish the words. Zdenka leaned toward McCluskey. "As soon as we reach the second floor, you guard the stairs to the floor above. Juho, you come with me." The voices had stopped and they heard a light, metallic rattle, then the sound of a door being open then closed.

As they charged up the last few steps, Juho saw an open door to his left and followed Zdenka into the room. Zdenka fired a burst as she sprang through the door.

Her burst caught a man just as he shot to his feet, a pistol in his hand. The bullets chewed into the man, sending him sprawling backward, and the pistol in his hand popped once, the shot going into the ceiling. The crash of the chair and the body were only slightly louder than the burp from the Sterling.

A second man reached into his shirt as he leapt toward a button on the wall. Juho was also moving and he swung the rifle. The bayonet took the man in the upper belly, just below where the ribs met the breastbone. Juho wrenched upward, as though swinging a forkful of hay, and the man, making a choking sound, was lifted from his feet and flung against the wall.

Juho twisted and tugged the bayonet free then, having a split-second in which to aim his second thrust as the body began to tumble forward, rammed the bayonet through the man's mouth.

He took the dead man's weight on the bayonet and lowered the body to the floor. He'd just put his foot on the man's face to pull the bayonet loose when a door at the back of the room swung open and a man stared at them. His hair was tousled from the pillow and his shirt hung loose over his belt, but he swung a pistol toward Juho.

Zdenka's gun burped again and the man was slammed against the door frame then collapsed like a figure made of paper. Zdenka sprang the half dozen paces to the door then swung around, her weapon pointed up. "There are no more."

She hardly spared a glance at the body of the man Juho had killed but she nodded once. "Good."

They both started toward the door when they heard a man shouting in Polish, his voice muffled. The man's words were difficult to understand but Juho understood the word for "hostage."

He stepped into the corridor, then a door swung open and he heard the man's threat to kill his hostage.

Juho continued to side-step across the hallway while Zdenka knelt at the door to the guards' rooms, her weapon ready. A man, holding a girl in front of him like a shield, emerged from one of the rooms along the corridor and Juho could see the pistol the man held to his captive's head. "Step out, all of you," the man said. "Put your weapons on the floor and step away from them."

The American called Reynaud spoke, in Russian, "That will not happen. If you kill her, you die. Where is our friend?"

For a long moment the man in the hall paused then he laughed, a nervous, high-pitched bray. "So, he was telling the truth. He is upstairs. The next floor. You are welcome to him, if Oshevsky has not already killed him. Go ahead, go after him. Kill Oshevsky if you can, but I am leaving with the girl and if anyone tries to stop me I will kill her and as many of you as I can." He began to back toward Zdenka and Juho, pulling the girl with him.

As the man backed toward him, Juho barked the Russian word for "wait," then, as the man spun his hostage as though dancing with her, Juho snapped the rifle to his shoulder and fired a single round.

A red mist shot from the back of the man's head and Juho raced toward the still-twitching body. The hostage seemed to be trying to scream but no sound came out. Leaving her for the others, Juho looked down at the dead man's face. The corpse's left eye was still wide and staring in astonishment. His right eye had been replaced by a bullet hole.

"Zdenka, free the other prisoners," Reynaud said. "Smyth-Davis is one of us, so it's up to us to get him out."

~ * ~

Frank pressed his ear against the door at the foot of the stairway, heard nothing, and when he opened the door crack and looked out, nothing moved in the hallway.

Slipping through the door, he side-stepped to the room where he'd heard the motor. The knob turned when he twisted it and, holding his pistol close to his body, he pulled the door open. The room was empty except for a generator and several cans of fuel against the wall. Closing the door, he approached the generator and studied the wiring around it. An explosive charge had been planted between the generator and the fuel. He had to study the leads a moment before he could be sure disconnecting the charge wouldn't set it off. He also saw cables running through holes in the floor and could guess batteries on the floor below formed a back-up system.

He yanked the wires loose from the charge then, as he reached for the switch to kill the generator, he heard a shot from below. He snapped the switch and, as he turned to the door, heard running footsteps in the hallway. Keeping the pistol in his left hand, he drew his knife with his right then, in three paces and a turn, had pressed his back against the wall on the side of the doorknob, where he waited.

One set of footsteps pounded past the door but a second stopped just outside.

Frank braced himself as the door swung open then a hand, holding a pistol, was thrust into the room. Frank whipped his pistol down on the wrist and drove the knife upward, into the ribcage of the man in the doorway.

The wiry, ferret-faced man gaped in astonishment and pain.

Frank twisted the knife viciously then snatched it back, a torrent of blood following his blade out of the body. He raised his foot and kicked the body out of the way then sprang into the hallway, sweeping the corridor with his gaze and the barrel of his pistol.

A figure rushed down the stairway to his left. He snapped off two fast shots at the shape but one hit the bannister while the other whined off the steps and smacked into the wall.

Frank fought the urge to chase the man he'd shot at. The assault team had breached the building and were on their way up. With two flights of stairs on this floor, Oshevsky and his men might try to retreat here and, if they reached the generator, they'd be able to set off the explosives buried in the building.

After wiping the blade of his knife against his pants leg, he sheathed it. He'd forgotten how many rounds he'd fired, so he dropped the magazine from the pistol, cursing the Russian designer who'd put the magazine release in the butt instead of behind the trigger guard, where it belonged. He shoved in a fresh magazine then picked up the pistol of the man he'd stabbed, another suppressed Makarov, and crouched just inside the door, trying to watch both stairways.

~ * ~

As the room lights dimmed to nothing, Oshevsky flung open the heavy drapes, admitting the pale, watery light then wheeled, glaring at the Englishman, then at Jerzy. "When you brought me the battery, did you reconnect the gang relay?"

"No sir. You wanted it immediately."

"You fool," Oshevsky raged. "Reconnect them!"

As Jerzy reached for the doorknob, the Englishman suddenly shouted, in Russian, "Don't do it."

Oshevsky whipped out the pistol in his belt and shot the prisoner in the face then, as the head recoiled from the shock, he fired again, placing the bullet below and behind the ear. Almost as surprised by his action as Jerzy seemed to be, Oshevsky stared at the corpse, wondering at the expression on the Englishman's face as he died. It had almost seemed like an expression of triumph then he realized that by shooting the prisoner he'd deprived himself of a hostage.

Jerzy had stopped, his hand on the doorknob.

"Do as I told you," Oshevsky rasped, and waved the pistol at the Pole. The former ZOMO opened the door and ducked out into the hall.

Oshevsky took only a split-second to consider his next step. All the demolitions on this floor were electrically detonated and, without the generator or the battery back-up, were as lethal as so much snow. Trying to patch in the battery he'd been using for interrogation would waste precious time. If Jerzy reconnected the gang relay, he could fire the charges. The manually-operated detonators were on the first and fourth floors. With the observatory invaded, it'd be impossible to reach the bottom floor but he could still go up.

He heard a flurry of suppressed gunfire in the hallway, with a single, unsilenced weapon dominating the rest of the noises.

The first thing he needed was to get to his room. He dashed to the door connecting this photographic laboratory to the one he'd claimed for his own quarters. He'd just opened the door when a man kicked open the door from the corridor and stitched a line at him with a suppressed submachine gun. A bullet stung and burned as it hit him in the calf and another round nicked his side. Oshevsky spun and fired two quick shots at the man then ducked into his room.

Snatching up a grenade from the table, he pulled the pin, opened the door just enough for him to toss the grenade into the room he'd left then slammed the door.

Pulling a ballistic vest from the back of a chair, he flipped the back over his head and pressed the Velcro tabs to close it. The enemy had gotten further into the observatory than he'd thought possible. The blast of the grenade suggested one of them had gotten in as far as he could. The stairs were obviously held by the men in the ORMO smocks, but if he could get across the hallway he could reach the fire escape and the detonator on the floor above. Seizing the AK leaning against the wall, he snapped off the safety. If he waited any longer, then men outside would be able to storm his room.

~ * ~

Steve turned and charged up the stairs as soon as the man with the hostage shouted Smyth-Davis was being held on the floor above. As he rushed up the steps he saw a man dart out of one of the doors on the left and rush toward the stairs. Steve swung up his pistol, holding it with both hands, arms rigid, fired off a shot, and missed.

As soon as he'd recovered from the recoil he pointed the weapon at the man again, this time holding lower. As he touched off the second shot, the man fired a burst from his machine pistol. Steve heard the bullets streak overhead and slam into the wall behind him, then the man jack-knifed forward, his weapon clattering and skidding across the floor.

The wounded man fell, then propped himself up on an elbow to reach for his weapon.

Steve fired again, holding low; the bullet hit the floor then ricocheted upward into the man's face and he collapsed. More suppressed gunfire erupted along the hall and the Finn's rifle boomed again, its noise, in the closed space of the corridor, driving needles of pain into the ears of everyone on that floor.

Steve realized he'd been firing from a prone position on the floor, although he couldn't remember throwing himself forward and down. As he scrambled to his feet, Reynaud and Logan raced past him. Each of them kicked open a door, Logan to the left and Reynaud to the right.

Reynaud shouted something lost in the confused yelling and fired a burst into the room then crouched behind the door frame, tossing away an empty magazine and inserting a fresh one.

The blast of a grenade momentarily silenced the other noises and everyone in the corridor seemed frozen in place. Juho was the first to move again as he rushed at a door. Oshevsky sprang into the corridor. Juho lunged at the Russian with his bayonet and Oshevsky parried with his rifle then fired a short burst and knocked Juho down with his gun barrel. When Oshevsky swung his weapon toward the Finn, Steve pointed his pistol at the Russian's head and fired until the slide stayed back, the gun empty.

Oshevsky's face snapped toward him and everyone seemed to be firing at the Russian.

Oshevsky spun in the hallway, flinching from hits, but he sprayed the corridor with short, savage bursts that sent most of the team scrambling for cover.

~ * ~

Juho pounded up the central stairway, crouched forward, and as he cleared the top of the stairs he saw movement to both sides. A man with a pistol had come down the stairs to his right, while McCluskey was dashing up from the floor below. Juho rested the forearm of his rifle on the stairwell railing and fired a single shot at the man on the stairs, who was flung backward, his arms limp, then slid down the stairs leaving a moist, dark trail.

McCluskey had fired past him and Juho spun to the left. For a moment he thought McCluskey had shot Oshevsky then he saw the dead man's face was different, except for brutality. Another man had run out of a room and rushed to the stairs on the left but had fallen, dead, or badly wounded.

Most of the team joined the confused battle. McCluskey fired another burst at something behind Juho then a grenade exploded in one of the rooms. A door was snatched open and Juho saw Oshevsky, framed in the doorway. He swung his rifle toward the door and pulled the trigger but the weapon seemed to be jammed.

Fury swept over him and he charged Oshevsky, lunging with the bayonet. Oshevsky raised his rifle and tried to block the thrust but as his gun's barrel was shoved up Juho managed to lay Oshevsky's cheek open.

The wound wasn't a serious one and the men stood straining, both trying to force the other's gun barrel up and to the side then Oshevsky fired a burst

Juho was momentarily blinded by the flash and the concussion of the muzzle blast hit him in the face like a fist, then something smashed into the side of his head and he felt his knees fold under him.

~ * ~

Billy Joe had, like Steve, started up the stairs as soon as he'd learned Smyth-Davis was being held on the floor above. He'd charged three or four paces into the corridor when he saw a huge, bear-like man step out of a doorway. Almost certain the man was Oshevsky, he'd fired a burst from Frank's submachine gun.

The body had jerked and twitched then stumbled forward, almost performing a forward roll. A muzzle flash from the center stairwell and the roar of the rifle made him duck then he heard a body sliding down the stairs behind him.

Moving more cautiously, he advanced down the corridor. A door to his left swung open and Billy Joe fired a short burst that tossed the man at the door back into the room, then the Finn charged a door and battled, gun to gun, with Oshevsky.

Billy Joe raised his weapon but the two men were too close together to risk a shot then, as noisy as the apocalypse, came a burst from Oshevsky's AK and Juho went down and Oshevsky staggered. Seizing the chance, Billy Joe pointed his weapon at Oshevsky and held down the trigger but the gun emitted only a short belch before it was empty.

Oshevsky ducked and spun, firing bursts all around, and Billy Joe flung himself at the open door to his left. He frantically reloaded but by the time he could look out into the passage, Oshevsky had vanished and Logan was sprinting toward an open door.

~ * ~

Logan ran up the stairs with Reynaud and saw a door to his left. Kicking it open, he charged into an office, in which nothing moved. Cautiously, he prowled through the room. He'd dropped his pistol on the second floor and the MAC was ready in his hands.

The blast of a grenade made him turn and rush back toward the hallway. As he emerged from the door he saw two men struggling then a burst of gunfire and a quick, slashing movement ended the fight.

As though it were a nightmare, Logan saw everything in slow motion. The man still standing was Oshevsky. The Russian started to swing his gun barrel toward the figure on the floor then spun toward Logan, blood gushing from a slash on his cheek and left ear, and more blood ran down his left sleeve.

Another gun fired from the far end of the hallway. The Russian flinched, and a gout of blood shot from his left arm.

Only the flickering muzzle of his MAC told Logan he was firing his weapon. He was sure he'd put half a magazine into the Russian's chest but Oshevsky only turned slowly. One of his rounds hit just below the Russian's right arm, tearing into the muscle and the shoulder blade.

Oshevsky seemed willing to absorb all the damage the team could inflict then he fired, short bursts that seemed to probe for his tormentors. Logan ducked back behind the edge of the door, dropped the empty MAC, and drew one of the spare pistols he carried. When he looked out into the corridor again, Oshevsky disappeared through a door further down the hall.

Logan sprang to his feet and ran for the door. Before he reached the room he heard the sound of glass shattering and when he dived though the door he saw Oshevsky climbing the fire escape.

~ * ~

St. Jacques watched as Frank crept up on the guard and killed him. He had no more targets on the roof, so he eyed the rows of windows and the door inset on the back of the ground floor.

Perhaps a quarter of an hour after Frank disappeared from sight he heard, inside the building, a rifle shot. Less than a minute later he heard a second shot from a high-powered rifle. He continued to scan the back of the building.

Seconds later, a real firefight broke out in the building. A grenade roared then he could distinguish the characteristic sound of an AK, being fired in short bursts, mixed with the racket of a fast-firing submachine gun, probably the Ingram.

A chair smashed through a window on the third floor and a blocky man in an armored vest, splashed and smeared with blood, followed the chair out onto the fire escape.

St. Jacques peered through the telescopic sight but Oshevsky was bounding up the steps of the fire escape, not presenting a clean target. He swung the barrel up so he was aimed at the landing, where the Russian must pause for a split-second, determined to make a head shot, but as Oshevsky reached the landing the Russian whirled and tried to bring his gun to bear on the window he'd just clambered out of.

The Frenchman knew a round from his rifle could smash the bones of the Russian's upper arm and still punch through the ribs and into the chest. He centered the crosshairs on the man's shoulder and caressed the trigger.

After the long wait for action, the gunshot was almost a shock. Oshevsky jerked from the impact, slammed against the wall of the observatory hard enough to bounce, then lurched forward and out. The body rolled over the black iron railing and dropped nine meters into snow- covered shrubs.

St. Jacques slapped the bolt handle up and back almost with the shot and as the rifle recovered from recoil he'd already driven the bolt back into battery. Swinging the barrel slightly, he looked through the scope at the man who'd appeared at the open window. Logan waved at him.

St. Jacques returned to waiting and watching until the assault team filed out the back door and signaled him in.

~ * ~

Reynaud heard the rifle shot and, moments later, his expression a mixture of satisfaction and regret, Logan said, "The Frenchie got him."

Reynaud levered himself to his feet and stared down at his submachine gun. Shrapnel from the grenade had perforated the suppressor and a piece of rubble flung by the concussion had bent it badly. He tore the magazine loose and tossed the useless weapon to the floor. "Smyth-Davis is inside," he said, with a jerk of his head at the room. Logan followed him in to where the body lay, still strapped to the table.

They could hardly recognize the man they'd escaped with. The face was swollen and distorted, and nearly a quarter of the skull had been blown away by the two point-blank pistol shots. Finding a key hanging from a nail in the side of the table, Reynaud used it to unlock the manacles. Somehow, leaving Smyth-Davis's body in chains would've seemed the ultimate desecration.

Reynaud felt empty, desolate. They'd known the odds

against rescuing Smyth-Davis were steep, but the loss cut more deeply than he could've guessed. It was an ugly reminder of their common mortality.

Juho entered the room, prodding a prisoner ahead of him. The Finn still seemed a little unsteady on his feet, and the side of his head and face were beginning to swell.

Juho shoved the man again. "Villareal and McCluskey found this one in a corner. They said to turn him over to Captain Wyszynski."

The man looked like a clerk and peered near-sightedly at his captors. Reynaud stepped up to the man, standing almost nose-to-nose with him. "Do you speak English?"

"I speak a little English." He had a heavy accent but could be understood.

"Are there any more FSB on this floor?"

Before the clerk could answer, Steve ducked into the room. "This floor is cleared, and Frank's coming down." He glanced at Smyth-Davis' body and winced. "We want to go down and find Oshevsky's body. We have to know he's dead."

Frank entered the room. "I'll watch this one for you until Wiktor can get a security team here."

As they started down the stairs, the Deacon handed Reynaud an AK. "Here, you may need this."

Reynaud checked the weapon and pushed the safety up into the safe position. As they scattered out the back door, he waved for the Frenchman to come in from the field.

"Over here!" Steve shouted, a trace of awe in his voice. "Here's where he fell, but there's no body, just a blood trail leading away. What does it take to kill that bastard?"

Reynaud saw the crushed shrubbery and the imprint of a body in the snow, along with bloodstains that'd turned the churned snow to red and pink. "Anybody know if he's armed?" Everyone looked up, but if the AK Oshevsky had used was on the fire escape, it was out of sight.

"Hey, this guy isn't a cornered lion," Logan said, "he's more like a jackrabbit everybody's had their shot at." He spoke loudly enough to make Reynaud wonder who he was talking to, who he was trying to convince.

Juho had been the first to follow the blood trail, and he

shouted, "Here!"

Oshevsky had crawled under another shrub and had made his way under the greenery for almost twenty feet. The Finn bent down and broke the frozen boughs away, exposing Oshevsky, lying face-down on the black dirt.

Slowly, awkwardly, the Russian rolled onto his back and Renaud was reminded of a cornered, dying animal. Oshevsky's eyes seemed unable to focus for more than seconds at a time but they still burned with a feral hatred.

The Deacon strode to where the Russian lay. "'Ye shall reap whatsoever thou hast sown,'" he said, through clenched teeth. "Remember when you shot Lieutenant Saunders' kneecaps before Chernikov killed him? 'An eye for an eye and a tooth for a tooth.'" The Deacon drew his pistol and shot Oshevsky in the left knee.

Oshevsky had been slowly, painfully groping down the side of his vest. When McCluskey shot him the hand paused for only a moment then continued its slow progress downward.

"Don't bother," Logan snapped. "He's too far gone to even feel it." He stared down at Oshevsky. "If he was a man, I'd turn him over to the Poles and let them try him and hang him, but he's more like a Gila monster, so full of shit and venom he'll bite anything." Very deliberately, he raised the MAC and pointed it at Oshevsky's head.

The weapon yammered briefly and Oshevsky's head disappeared in a spray of red, pink, and white, and when the gun was empty, a headless body twitched in the snow.

Reynaud bent and felt along the side of the vest until he found the tiny Russian pocket pistol Oshevsky had been reaching for. "As you said, Logan, venomous to the last."

Chapter 14

Reynaud moved slowly down the corridor, careful not to spill anything on the tray he'd brought from the kitchen and his feet made almost no sound on the carpet. Logan had insisted on staying with Smyth-Davis's body, even when the others had gone to dinner. As Reynaud approached the room, he heard Logan's voice.

"Goddam hotdog. You had to go and get yourself killed, you batty limey."

Reynaud stopped outside the door, which had been left slightly ajar. He looked through the opening and saw Logan had unwrapped the bottom of the shroud and was putting the coveted socks on Smyth-Davis' bare, dead feet.

He waited until he was sure Logan had finished before he kicked the frame and pushed the door open with his foot. He carried the tray across the room and set it on the seat of a chair. "I brought you some chow."

"I'm not hungry,"

"Bullshit. Going without a meal won't do a thing for Smyth-Davis or anyone else.

"Y'know," Logan said, as he started on the dumplings. "I don't even remember his first name."

"A lot of Brits are like that. You have to know them forty years before you can call them anything but 'Mr. Smyth-Davis.'"

The rest of the group and Kommando Krakow filtered into the room and they all seemed awkward and tongue-tied; speaking little, and then only in undertones. Logan had just finished the meal Reynaud had brought when Wyszynski entered and stood behind the table on which the body lay.

"I want to thank all of you," Wyszynski said softly, "and I wish I could thank your companion. None of the FSB files were destroyed and that was the headquarters. Now we have information on all the FSB operatives and contacts in southern Poland. We also know the other regional FSB headquarters are in Lublin, Poznan, and Gdynia, with some clues where they may be found. That makes our work much easier.

"Besides our thanks, all we can offer you is a Mass with a military funeral, with full honors, for your friend."

"That's more than Teller and Schiller got," Reynaud said.

"We also have some news for you, and a request. The reconstructionist network in Texas requested you be sent there. Since you know Chernikov by sight, they reasoned you would have the best chance of finding him. Do you want me to give them your reply?"

"Damn straight," Logan said. "Tell 'em we'll be there with bells on. I want to see that bastard dead, dead, dead. We all owe him some grief."

"A submarine will be dispatched and should reach Gdynia by the fourteenth. This means you must leave Krakow no later than the tenth, and preferably by the seventh."

"What do we do in the meantime?" Steve asked.

"Rest. You've more than earned it. The Mass and funeral will be tomorrow afternoon. After that, your detached unit will be marked for rest. You can turn in your ORMO equipment just before you leave." Wyszynski rounded the table. "If you visit *Zyc, Nie Umierac!*, do not be surprised that the help has changed. The bartender was in the pay of the FSB."

"How do we get to the sub?" Reynaud asked.

"We have convoys that make the trip every few days. I can tell you in a day or two what their schedules are."

Wyszynski offered to make a truck available to take them back to their apartment but only Tadeusz, St. Jacques, whose limp had worsened from his time in the snow, and Zdenka, who seemed to take responsibility for the care of the wounded; chose to ride back. Even Juho, with his nasty bruise turning purple, preferred to walk the distance back to the place on *Batorego*.

Reynaud chose to walk because he suddenly realized he'd learned to love the city. It was more than just a place where he'd risked his life and survived. He found himself admiring the people and the culture—he'd miss the *hejnal*—and even the cold and gray beauty of the city itself; its medieval towers, its renaissance spires, and all those things that made Krakow different from all the places he'd known.

Preparing for the funeral and attending it kept the next day busy, but in the evening the mood of the group turned dour.

Some of it was grief for Smyth-Davis, which reminded them they were also mortal. Another part of the grim mood was the let-down after seeing Oshevsky dead in the snow; a mission complet-ed, which meant one reason less to continue to live. And they also faced their return to the states with some trepidation. Hunting Chernikov down and trying to kill him would probably be even more dangerous than their struggle with Oshevsky and the FSB had been.

Reynaud also had mixed feelings about seeing the US again. He was homesick for his country, but afraid to find out what it'd become after the war and the plague.

A blizzard kept them inside for the two days after the funeral and they began to get on each other's nerves. Even Juho, usually as silent and imperturbable as a paving stone, became more high-strung, so it was with a sense of relief they went to the Wawel on the third day after the storm.

They found Wyszynski in his office, poring over reports, and he also seemed relieved to see them. "A convoy leaves the city for the Baltic coast at dawn on the third—"

"You trying to get rid of us?" Logan inquired. "The sub won't be in to make the pick-up until the fourteenth. What's the rush?"

Wyszynski grinned. "No, I'm not really trying to be rid of you but the trip may take longer than you think. There are still some Russian units in Poland, and bandits, who prey on smaller convoys. It is rare but it does happen. There is also the weather. Part of your escort will be two tracked vehicles fitted with snow ploughs.

"Another problem is the distance. Krakow is about five hundred kilometers—about three hundred of your miles—from *Gdynia*, and that is in a straight line. But because you will have to detour around Warsaw, the distance is at least half again as great." He paused a moment. "You will still have to go through *Gdansk*. I have heard most of the streets have been cleared, and the radia-tion has gone down to safe levels—as long as you go through the city without stopping."

"Sounds like a real cakewalk," Logan said. "Hey, how about joining us at the bar tonight? We'll show you a good ol' American New Year's Eve."

"I have work here—"

"Aw, c'mon," Logan insisted. "Hell's bells, you look like you were born in that uniform. You gotta learn to unwind. Loosen your collar. Have a few laughs."

Wyszynski looked uncomfortable, as though his collar were indeed too tight. Finally, he grinned at them all. "I will be there at nineteen hundred."

~ * ~

Reynaud was never too sure about the events of the New Year's Eve party at *Zyc, Nie Umierac!* He remembered trying to keep pace, drink for drink, with Logan, who was apparently competing with Wyszynski. Sometime before midnight, a Pole wearing a black tanker's beret slammed his face, several times, against Logan's fists. More of them became involved and, since Logan had only two fists, consulted his friends.

The Frenchman shouted, "Airborne! To me!" in Polish, and two Poles in red berets joined them. Reynaud recalled a collison between his face and a Pole's elbow left him on the floor while the Pole, or another one, tried to present an exhibition of plain and fancy stomping. Wyszynski threw a cross-body block into the Pole and slammed him over a table, then helped Reynaud to his feet.

"I think it would be an appropriate time to leave," Wyszynski said, slowly and a bit too distinctly, especially since he was speaking through split lips.

The two of them hauled Logan out of a heap of thrashing bodies and gathered the rest of the group, along with the red-bereted Pole who was still conscious, and beat a retreat to the Wawel.

As Reynaud remembered it, they celebrated the birth of the new year by applying alcohol to each other's cuts and sleeping in the barracks in the Wawel.

~ * ~

Recon 9 was still wearing its bruises as their BTR joined the convoy. The line of vehicles formed slowly and some of the crews were standing beside their machines. Reynaud and Logan joined some of the Poles beside the road.

One of the Poles, wearing a parka, turned to face them.

Both his eyes were blackened and they noticed beneath the hood of the parka he wore a black beret. He stared intently at them then, in Polish, asked, "Where have I met you? You look very familiar."

Logan grinned at Reynaud and, in English, said, "I thought I was the one related to the Lone Ranger. What's he doing wearing the mask?"

"Cool it," Reynaud muttered. "I really don't need someone dancing on my ribs again." He smiled at the Pole and shrugged. "I don't remember your face."

The Pole frowned, obviously trying to connect memories with their faces.

Logan grinned and thrust out a hand to the man. "Now I remember you. You've got a damned nice left hook."

The Pole grinned back and shook Logan's hand. "Now I remember. You fight well. Maybe there will be bandits. We can hope."

As Logan and Reynaud returned to the personnel carrier, the Cajun shook his head. "I keep forgetting how many of you guys enjoy pain—giving or receiving."

They'd just seated themselves in the carrier when the convoy began to roar to life and, in a fog of fumes, inch forward.

Reynaud guessed the speed of the convoy never rose much above twenty miles an hour, with one of the tracked machines in the lead, clearing away snow from the road. As they rode, they often looked through the viewports and observed the area around Krakow had once been heavily settled but most of the small towns had been deserted. In the late morning they arrived in a city the man refueling the BTR identified as *Chosgow*. Two trucks left the convoy there, and another joined it.

Boredom and the ever-present cold quickly set in, and those were only slightly allievated by singing and taking turns manning the gun turret. Steve started the singing but they lost interest while there were still seventy-six bottles of beer on the wall. The country through which they now passed had fewer towns and villages, and they stopped for noon at a city named *Czestochowa*, where three more trucks and an armored vehicle, spouting black smoke, left the line and several trucks joined it. The column pressed on and by nightfall they reached *Lodz*.

The next morning they formed up under a sky leaden with the threat of more snow. The major in command of the unit conferred with the local captain, who kept shaking his head, but they continued northward.

The threat of snow became a blinding reality at noon and the convoy slowed even more as the intervals between vehicles became shorter, as each machine pulled forward to keep the truck or personnel carrier ahead in view. The trip became a nightmare then, as they pushed into the driving snow, hearing an occasional muffled crash as one or another of the trucks was rear-ended.

They proceeded, without a stop, to a city called *Torun*, where they spent two days doing little but waiting out the storm, and their bruises faded from purple to yellow. Reynaud improved enough to be able to stop wincing when he coughed.

When the convoy assembled at dawn on the third day, the line of trucks was noticeably shorter, and Reynaud saw a truck loaded with heavily dressed, unarmed men in the back. When he asked a Polish sergeant about the truck, the man explained. "Those are prisoners who will work at clearing *Gdansk*. They are black marketeers, bandits, and some deserters."

Reynaud stared at the men huddled in the back of the truck. "How can you make them work, or keep them from escaping?"

"For the first thirty days they will be chained in work gangs to keep them from escaping, and if they want to eat, they will work. After thirty days they are unchained. If they want something to eat, they will continue to work, and if they want to escape, they can either be shot or die of radiation sickness before they've been gone for more than a couple of weeks."

"Jeez," Logan said, "that's pretty stiff. What about the guards?"

"They stay well away from the center of the blast, and we rotate every guard out after two weeks."

"Draconian, but efficient," Steve observed. "It puts a whole new light—or glow—on the old bit about working freeloaders to death."

The convoy pulled out, crawling through a lake region, with lush forest growth. It wheeled into the edge of *Gdansk* in the late afternoon and perhaps half the trucks left the column and the rest continued on to *Gdynia*, which they reached just as the sun was setting.

They dismounted from the BTR onto shaky legs and presented the papers Wyszynski had given them to the aide of the colonel responsible for the district.

Their casual study of *Gdynia* didn't inspire a desire to examine it more closely. *Gydnia* was *Gdansk's* sister city, and appeared to have been damaged almost as much, although in a different way. The derelict bones of the shipyards lay rusting under a blanket of snow and ice, and ships tied at the dock lay dead in the icy water. Unlike Krakow, *Gdynia* had been an industrial city and it lacked much of the beauty of the old/new capital of Poland.

The aide assigned them an apartment and issued cots, blankets, and coal for the stove. They were also issued ration chits but decided to use some of the MREs the Krakow group had given them.

Arctic blasts pounded the city and drew another blizzard in its wake. The group drew straws and Reynaud and the Deacon, the losers, made the trek to claim the group's daily ration of coal. At the center they learned, first hand, about waiting in a long line in sub-zero cold and a wind that tore the breath from their throats and drove the snow into every opening in their clothes.

As they returned, carrying the coal, the Deacon kept turning around to study the way behind them.

"What's the matter, Deak?"

"We were being followed, I think whoever it was has given up but they may have taken cover somewhere and be watching us."

"In that case, w'd better add a few twists and turns to the route," Reynaud said. "Could you guess who it might've been?"

The Deacon's parka twisted as he shook his head. "Everyone looks the same in heavy winter clothes."

Reynaud turned the next corner and led the way over tangled tracks in the snow, kept to the same street for three blocks, then angled back sharply, keeping to well-traveled streets. By the time he'd finished laying false trails and trying to force anyone following them to expose themselves he and the Deacon were both trembling uncontrollably from the cold.

Ducking through the door of the apartment like rabbits going into their warrens, they set the buckets of coal by the stove and Reynaud turned to Logan, who'd stripped his Ingram and was cleaning it. "I'd keep that loaded. We seem to attract a lot of attention."

With an economy of motion, Logan reassembled the weapon, slapped in a magazine, and charged the gun. "Any idea who it is?' At the shake of the Deacon's head, Logan put the safety on and let the MAC dangle by its strap. "Any guesses?"

Reynaud shrugged. "The FSB? I'd say we pissed them off. Or maybe it's part of some new kind of turf war. Maybe somebody in the local army or ORMO doesn't like Wyszynski and is taking it out on us. Any other ideas?"

"No." Logan put coal in the stove and started a fire then put a kettle of water to boil. "But I don't like ducking into a hole and pulling it in after me, either. I'm not about to hole up here, or be shuttled from one place to another."

"I know," Reynaud said, grinning, "you'd rather go kill something. But whoever is after us—if anybody is—is playing hide-and-seek."

"There's got to be a way to flush that shit out," Logan grumbled.

Boredom returned, worse than ever, and set in like rigor mortis. Between the alertness for any sign of attack and the weather, they were largely confined to the apartment. They'd explored the building, partly for something to do and partly to learn all the weaknesses and any possible exits. They'd taken the front apartment on the ground floor, and the building was empty except for an engineer who occupied the third apartment. The second floor was completely empty, the ORMO having stripped the upper floors of anything of any use at all.

Their section consisted of two rooms and a tiny bathroom, and they ate and slept in the room with the kitchen stove, using the second room for storage and as a refrigerator.

The only other thing to do was to keep their weapons maintained, and Reynaud intimately learned the functioning of the old Russian Winchester '95 and the .45 service automatic he'd kept. Steve worked often on the Beretta M-9 pistol and an AK, while the Deacon had kept the AK-74 with the grenade launcher under the barrel and, like Reynaud, one of the old .45 automatics. Juho was almost inseparable from his Dragunov while Logan had limited himself to the MAC, a Makarov, one of the suppressed Makarovs, and an AKR.

They hoarded the coal and stayed inside on Sunday but on Monday Logan and Juho made the trip for coal. When they returned, Logan set down the buckets and pulled off his parka. "You guys must be getting jumpy in your old age. Juho and I kept a real sharp eye out, and we didn't see anyone watching us."

"If they were very good at it," Reynaud replied, "you wouldn't see them. Oh, well, we'll be gone sometime Friday. We only have to sweat it another four days."

On Tuesday, while they still had enough coal for another day, Logan dressed himself in his heavy gear and went for a walk but when he returned he wore a frown that looked as though it had frozen on his face.

"What's the matter, Logan," Reynaud asked, "you look like you couldn't find a dog to kick."

Logan dropped into a chair and began to wrestle his boots off. "I thought I saw Laura."

"Well, Logan," Steve chimed in, "after six months in the p-camp, you'd miss a two-by-four with a knothole. Probably just some Polish woman who looked a little like her. With your luck, she's probably married to some guy who works in a slaughter-house and likes to bring his work tools home with him. I'd say leave it alone while you've still got all your parts."

Logan shook his head. "I'd have sworn it was her. I happened to look in a shop window and there she was, talking to some clerk. I had to look to find the door and by the time I got inside—no Laura. The clerk told me he hadn't seen a blond wom-an all day, but I'd have bet the farm it was her."

Reynaud scratched the stubble on his cheek. "If it was her, I wonder what she's doing here."

Logan shrugged. "Maybe the same thing we are—getting ready to hitch a ride home. After the way we trashed their head-quarters, the CIA's probably decided to pull in their horns and call it a war."

"Maybe." Reynaud neither sounded nor felt very convinced. "Or maybe she'd like to collect our scalps for what happened in Krakow."

"That doesn't make any sense," Logan protested.

"I got the impression that good sense is the farthest thing from the alleged minds of those CIA clowns in Krakow," Steve shot back. "They were ready to murder the head of the Church in Krakow, throwing the government into a tailspin, just to give the FSB some bad press and try to shove Poland into a far-right dictatorship. What sort of sense does that make? Hell, Poland can't even be an ally anymore. What the hell could they do? Sign a pact with the rubble of New York, or maybe Lincoln, Nebraska?"

"Okay, so the spooks in Krakow were on their own trip," Logan admitted, "but that doesn't mean Luara bought into the program."

"Oh, hell, Logan," Reynaud snapped, "stop thinking with your gonads. She was willing to let a twelve-year-old kid die rather than risk blowing her cover. You forget that?" Reynaud got out his rifle and began to strip it down to give it another unnecessary cleaning and give himself a way out of a pointless argument.

~ * ~

They heard a knock at the door a little after ten the next morning. The Deacon opened the door to a young man in a battered Polish uniform with an ORMO armband. The young man looked at a piece of paper in his hands and, in Polish, asked, "Is Lieutenant Reynaud Dechaine here?"

Reynaud was perversely pleased his name gave Poles almost as much trouble as their names gave him. "I'll be right with you," he said, and added two more layers of clothes to what they wore to keep warm in the badly heated apartment. "Is there some kind of trouble?"

"No trouble, but Lieutenant Kowalski needs your report on what happened in Krakow. The report in the paper you gave our man was somewhat incomplete."

Reynaud was both annoyed and amused. The military in Poland was as tangled in red tape as the American forces had been. He turned to pick up his rifle and caught a glance at Logan, who was staring hard at the young man.

"That will not be necessary," the Pole said. "You may wear a sidearm but I am responsible for your safety." Reynaud noticed then the young man carried no weapon but a holstered pistol. "No one but the army or the ORMO carries shoulder weapons in

Gdynia, and not all of us."

Reynaud finished his preparations by pulling on the Russian fur hat. "All right, in that case, I'm ready now."

The young man glanced around the room. "If there are any other questions, I may have to come back for one or more of you for corroboration, but this officer's report will probably be sufficient."

Reynaud followed the Pole outside into a vicious wind that made it a struggle for him to catch his breath. The route they followed was full of twists and turns, and the Pole gestured down an alley. "This will save us steps, and it is out of the wind."

Reynaud hesitated but the Pole was already leading the way, his boots sinking into the snow with a scrunching sound. The buildings on either side of them were large and featureless, warehouses, he guessed. As he walked past a door set in a wall the Pole ahead of him suddenly wheeled, a pistol in his hand. "Open that door and step inside. No, don't raise your hands," the young man snapped, gesturing at the door with the pistol barrel.

Reynaud felt a sort of numbness of shock. Reaching for the door, he wrestled it open. "I take it, then, that you are not from the ORMO. Are you FSB?"

"No, he's a Polish patriot," a woman's voice said from inside the warehouse.

Reynaud was too snowblind to see clearly in the dim building but the voice was familiar. "Laura Wessel, isn't it?"

"No flies on you," she said, sarcastically.

Reynaud was afraid but also angry and disgusted, mostly with himself for falling into such a simple trap. "It wasn't too hard to figure out. You're the only American I know who confuses patriotism with some form of insanity. Do you know that makes you more like Oshevsky and Chernikov than anybody I want to know?"

Laura stepped out of the deep shadows, a suppressed Makarov in her hand. Her other hand swept forward and slapped his cheek with stinging force. "At least they're real enemies, not spineless cowards who only want to run out on their country. I have more respect for them than I do sunshine soldiers."

"That figures." Reynaud calculated his chances and found them dismal at best. The young man had come into the building and Laura, after slapping the Cajun, had stepped back out of reach. "It really figures that you'd feel kinship with them. You all play your little war games and kill a lot of people better than you'll ever be. You don't give a damn who gets killed in your 'game,' as long as you can keep the murder machine going. I do have to thank you, though."

"For what?"

"I'd had some twinges of regret about helping blow away your buddies in Krakow, but now I can really appreciate helping wipe out a nest of snakes."

"You're going to die slowly for that," Laura rasped. "It won't be the first shot that kills you, or even the second. Where did the Krakow group move to?"

Reynaud's laugh was a tight, nervous sound that made his throat hurt. Laura turned to the Pole and, in English, said, "Go get another one. Bring Steve Villareal this time." The young man stepped out the door.

"It'll be interesting to see how long Villareal can hold out when he sees you without kneecaps. I'll save the shot in the groin until I've asked him, one time, where Frank and his little band of renegades are hiding."

"Oh, I understand," Reynaud said. "You're the only one who gets special rules, who gets to hide and shoot from ambush. The rest of us are just to be your shooting gallery ducks."

Laura lowered the barrel of the pistol so it was pointed at Reynaud's left knee. "You make it so easy to enjoy doing this."

The door opened and a blocky shape slipped through and into the shadow of the wall. "Don't get too thrilled, Laura," Logan's voice said. "Drop the gun."

"Logan!"

"That's the name, and cavalry rescues are the game."

Laura slowly began edging to the left. "It looks like a standoff. I suppose you killed Stanislaw?"

"Sorry about that," Logan said, "but I was kind of in a hurry. You shouldn't have used the ribbon clerk I'd met. Recruiting down?"

"I was going to keep you alive, Logan. The two of us could go back to the states together. We can track down Chernikov as well as they could. What's this Cajun to you? Or a crazy old Bible-thumper? Or a yuppie spick?"

"Nothing to say about Juho?"

"What's to say? He barely speaks English, and if you killed him you'd hardly know he was dead. Just as you hardly know he's alive now."

"The trouble with that crap is that every one of them has stood by me. Who'd you ever stand by, Laura?"

"I stand by my country."

"Bullshit. You just want to go down on the flagpole. Now, drop that pistol and put your hands up."

"I'll drop your Cajun buddy before I drop my gun." She raised the barrel to point it at Reynaud's chest. "I'm not going to just let you blow me away."

"You drop the gun, and I'll turn you over to the Poles alive. It's their country and their laws."

"Right. And if they don't hang me, I'll be worked until the radiation kills me. Is that what you want?"

"No, but you knew the rules when you played the game. That's what justice is all about."

Reynaud dared not move quickly with Laura's pistol pointed at his chest. He had no doubt she was an expert shot and he knew she was primed for action. The delicate balance of the stalemate favored no one, and he considered springing to the side, just to end the suspense.

~ * ~

Laura also felt the strain. She knew Logan was the greater danger. If she shot the Cajun, she'd be dead before she hit the floor, while if Logan shot her, she could kill Reynaud with a convulsive jerk of the trigger. The only alternative was to chance a sudden attack on Logan but her position was bad. She'd tried to sidle to the left to put Reynaud between herself and Logan, but the Cajun had been moving with her.

What she needed was a diversion. Her only weapon, besides the pistol, was words. If she could just establish a rhythm she could choose the time to break it.

"Maybe we could just forget the whole thing, Logan. Start over with a clean slate. I could go back to the states with all of you." She continued to slowly circle left so she was almost facing

Logan, holding her gun almost across her body to keep Reynaud covered. "Do you remember the first time, in Krakow? My only regret is that we didn't have more time. There are so many ways we could—" She swept the pistol toward where Logan stood.

~ * ~

Logan had expected it. The MAC was ready in his hands and the selector was set on auto. As Laura swung the pistol, his grip tightened and the Ingram sprayed a stream of .45 slugs that chopped into her and flung her body like a rag doll in a gale, all the bullets hitting her between the throat and her lower belly. Blood splashed onto the floor around her then the body crumpled in mid-air and dropped to the floor.

~ * ~

Reynaud had been ready to drop and roll, to force the battle, when Laura had tried her move. He watched in fascinated horror as bullet after bullet ripped into her. He knew the Ingram emptied a thirty-round magazine in no more than a second and a half, but the burst seemed to go on forever, then Laura lay on the floor, a bleeding mass of blood and rags, almost sawed in two.

He didn't even draw his pistol as he walked slowly forward and leaned over the body. One arm still moved, as her muscles spasmodically tensed and relaxed, but Laura was dead, as lifeless as a stone. He glanced at Logan, who'd stepped away from the wall and was changing magazines. Logan's face was pale, and his jaw set.

"I know it was hard to do, man," Reynaud said, "but Laura's been dead for a long time. Hatred was the only thing that kept her breathing."

"I suppose so," Logan replied, "but she was an awfully good lay."

Together they found their way to the ORMO headquarters and reported the killings. The aide, a sergeant, wrote down their report then closed the book. "Wiktor—Captain Wyszynski— mentioned in his report this woman might be here. I appreciate your...resolving the matter."

He leaned back in his chair and steepled his fingers. "You seem to have many enemies, and they all seem to seek confrontation. I mean no offence, but I will feel far more comfortable when you are gone from Gdynia. Your submarine is to surface two hundred meters or so from the dock, the day after tomorrow, at fourteen hundred hours."

"How do we get from the dock to the boat?" Reynaud asked.

"We will have a fisherman take you out to it."

"It'll do," Logan said. He stood and turned to go, then faced the sergeant. "How well do you know Wyszynski?"

"I'm in the network."

"I thought so." Reynaud nodded to himself. "You might pass the word back to Kommando Krakow that Laura's gone to her reward, as the Deacon might say. I suppose that bit of news might set Frank's mind at ease."

Logan remained silent and grim on the way back to the apartment. After a single tap on the door, they strode into the room. Steve was just lowering the automatic he'd caught up, and the Finn leaned his rifle against the wall.

"Did you have any trouble with the ORMO?" Steve asked.

"Nah." Logan dropped into a chair. "I just corroborated what Rennie said. No problem. Oh, and don't worry about that tail we grew. It was just Laura, trying to get in touch with us to bury the hatchet. She decided to stay in Poland and wished us luck in bagging Chernikov."

After staring at Logan for a long moment, Steve ran his hand through his hair. "I'm glad to hear that." He seemed to be considering possible questions but apparently decided against asking them.

Reynaud watched the scene with some amusement, knowing he was learning more about Logan than he would've guessed was there. He studied the others. The Deacon and Juho seemed unconcerned, while Steve was troubled by mysteries best left unsolved.

~ * ~

They watched the surface of the Baltic Sea through binoculars from the shelter of the trawler's cabin, and most of them were a little green from sea sickness. Cold waves lapped against the sides of the vessel, and Reynaud was grateful the wind was relatively still and the sea had calmed from the storm of the day before. He looked at the ship's clock and saw it was two minutes from the last time he'd looked.

"They're late," Logan said. He apparently wanted to pace but there was room for no more than a step or two in any direction.

Reynaud bit back the impulse to point out that the statement was obvious and stupid. Their barely-stifled excitement had put them all on edge.

"Maybe they're still on Greenwich time," Steve suggested.

Suddenly a black conning tower appeared in a swath of white foam and a long, black, sharklike form broke the surface.

"Sonofabitch!" Logan crowed. "Our cab is here!"

The Polish trawler throbbed to life and chugged out toward the submarine, which had surfaced no more than three hundred yards from the dock. The wakes of the two ships angled toward each other on interception courses.

As they drew nearer the sub, Reynaud noticed signs of repaired damage aft of the conning tower, and when they approached near enough to see the few men on the tower, he pointed out to Logan the man in the Navy blue wooly-pully whose rank badges looked like afterthoughts. Under the bill of the man's cap they could see one eye was covered by a patch.

Logan groaned. "I'm not getting on that damned thing until we're sure they aren't getting ready to run up the Jolly Roger."

"Check out his legs," Steve said. "If one is wooden, I'm staying here. My mama didn't raise me to chase big, white fish."

Both boats slowed to a halt within hailing distance of each other. After several minutes of frantic labor, lines had been run from boat to boat and, as a test, their equipment was drawn across. After ascertaining the lines were firm, a bosun's chair was rigged and Reynaud permitted himself to be hauled across to the submarine.

"Welcome to the *Portland*," the one-eyed captain shouted. "Sorry we're late but the old girl's getting a bit cranky and slow since she took some battle damage."

The Deacon was the next to cross. "I'm beginning to understand how Jonah felt," he said, as he freed himself of the chair.

Steve followed McCluskey. "The captain of the trawler is going to take Juho home."

Finally, Logan crossed from the trawler to the submarine. The lines were cleared and the trawler drifted away. They saw Juho on the deck, waving to them.

"I think that's the most emotional I've seen him since we met," Logan said. They waved back then joined the sailors going below. The last of the fliers down the hatch was Logan, who paused a moment, looking up at the captain. "Home, James," he shouted, and went below.

About the Author

James K. Burk is a sometimes serious writer who enjoys a challenge. He has written five novels and many shorter works. His previous novels from WolfSinger Publications are THE TWELVE and HIGH RAGE, both fantasies. He's also written two science fiction novels: HOME IS THE HUNTER and REDEMPTION, and a weird western novella, "The Ghoul of Socorro" which is the fourth book in the Night Marshal series.

His shorter works were published in two chapbooks and several anthologies. One of his highlights was "The Trailer Park Vampire Meets the Bubba Yumbie" in THE INTERNATIONAL HOUSE OF BUBBAS.

He doesn't own any cats. His writing tends to be quirky.

Other Books by James K Burk
from WolfSinger Publications

The Twelve

Valtierra, a city-state, is governed by archetypes. Every two years they choose twelve men and women to wear the masks and to become the Wise Old Man, the Fool, the Mother, the Harlot, the Warrior, and the rest of the council. But now Valtierra faces hunger, decay, and an enemy on their border and, when the need for leadership is greatest, one mask is worn by a foreigner and one mask hides a traitor.

High Rage

Scarface, on his way back to a clan stronghold after assassinating a legate, meets and falls in love with a woman even more ruthless than he. To win her, he must reunite an empire and create a kingdom. His only allies are his wits, his sword, and the power in his scars—black marks like the taloned finger prints of a demon.

To achieve his goals, he must deal with old enemies, gods of dubious worth, and his own family—who may be the most dangerous of all.

Taking Hope

The power he once held depleted, Scarface has found contentment as Morgan. No longer seeking power or building kingdoms, he is happy with his current life.

However, when what he most loves is threatened, Morgan must again become Scarface to correct past mistakes. He must defeat a king and a god. Knowing one god can only be beaten by another, he seeks an alliance, but what price will be demanded?

With only a few allies, one of them mad with rage, and the power in his scars returned, he must confront old enemies, including one who knows his deepest secret and greatest weakness. Will he be able to lay to rest his past, defeat his enemies and return to the life he has made for himself. Or will he lose everything and everyone he has come to truly care about?

www.ingramcontent.com/pod-product-compliance
Lightning Source LLC
Chambersburg PA
CBHW071427260626
47170CB00008B/2626